Hell and High Water

Hell and High Water

P. V. LeForge & Anne Petty

Black Bay Books

Hell and High Water

Black Bay Books
1939 Sand Basin Road
Grand Ridge, FL 32442

Printed in USA
First printing in 2011

ISBN-13: 978-0-9624878-6-6

Library of Congress Control Number: 2011919215

Front cover photo: P. V. LeForge
Cover design: Anne Petty

First print edition

*Many thanks to those long-suffering editorial friends
who read early drafts of this book so many years ago,
wondering what the hell we were up to.
So. Now you know.*

Prologue

Aunt Sookie Darbyville sat in the darkened church and waited, a smile hiding among the many lines of her face. The church was dark because there was no electricity; never had been electricity out this far. And except for herself, the church was empty, the last sermon having been preached almost twenty years before. The pew she sat on—and the church—had belonged to her family for almost a hundred years, which was damned close to her own age, give or take a decade. Over the last twenty years, vandals and wild animals had gotten in the church and moved things around—benches were awry, flower pots had been broken, hymnals scattered. The wooden timbers of the walls and ceilings showed dark patches where water had oozed through.

Sookie admired a cracked stained-glass window depicting a black virgin holding the Negro Jesus, backlit by the setting sun. Her smile twitched imperceptibly; the window had been designed by her grandmother, who had been a slave, who had been many other things, too. The sun told her that it was an hour until dusk. She heard the soft whine of a car engine as the driver carefully negotiated the road ruts outside. The engine idled, then stopped. She heard the metallic thud of the car door closing, the hesitant sound of shoes climbing the worn plank steps. The creaking of the church door on its rusted hinges. Silence.

Sookie didn't turn around, but her smile broadened. "You in the right place," she said. Her voice was high, quavery.

A voice came from the doorway. "Where are you?"

The voice made Sookie stiffen. This was not who she was expecting. Not yet. She stood up and turned to face her visitor.

"You early, ain't ya?" she asked.

"What? Who? What are *you* doing here?"

"I'm the one you here t' see."

"You're kidding me!"

"Ain' kiddin," Sookie said, her voice flat. "Why you think I be kiddin? Cause I'm just an old black lady? Just a conjure lady that nobody don't pay no tention to?" Sookie stepped away from the pew and shuffled down the aisle on feeble legs, a tiny woman in a hodgepodge of fabrics, the uneven hem of her dress trailing over old, black clodhoppers. Her head was wrapped in a scarf of red and orange. But the most striking thing about her was the necklace she wore. It was an array of faces carved in stone, some black as night, others gray like dawn—bizarre, nightmarish faces with painted lips and bulging eyes that seemed to stare, to see, to understand. "You 'member the time you called the sheriff on me? That was bad manners."

"You were trespassing. You were digging in my yard."

"Wasn't *your* yard."

"Who was that messenger you sent?"

"Just somebody doin a job, deliverin a message. I see you got it."

"I think everything in that message was a lie."

"Ain' no lie." Sookie looked out the open door, listened for the sound of another car, but the road seemed deserted. She would have to press on alone, but she'd been doing all right alone for eighty years and more. "Ain' no place for you here now."

"You can't get away with this!"

"I reckon I can. You'll find somethin else, I spect."

"But why? Even if it's all true, why are you doing this?"

The speaker's voice was getting louder, echoing off the walls of the empty church. Sookie could hear desperation in the voice. She had heard that same kind of desperation in thousands of other voices over the years. From folks who were desperate to keep their husbands, desperate for riches, desperate to cause hurt. They all came to *her* to work her *ifa* magic. To grind them up some roots, to give them something to bury near their enemy's front door when they were out. To try to talk them out of whatever evil they wanted to cause in this world. Had she been able to help? Maybe. But there was still too much to do, too much to teach, and she was old.

"I asked you a question!" shouted the visitor. "Why are you doing this?"

"Cause I be tired," Sookie said.

"Tired?" The voice was shrill. "What do I care if you're tired? What you're doing is evil!"

"You stay back, heah?" There was no smile, now, only skin like wrinkled parchment.

"No. I'm not going to let you!"

Sookie tried to take a step back, but one of the pews blocked her way. She felt strong hands around her neck. The cord holding the necklace of many faces snapped and the amulet clattered across the floor. Sookie struggled to get away, to breathe. She tried to wrench herself from the interloper's grasp but the effort sent her backwards, over the pew, down in the dust of the splintered wooden floor. The last thing she saw was the face of her killer. It wasn't an evil face, the eyes didn't have death in them, the mouth was not snarling; in fact, it seemed oddly horrified.

Chapter One

Wind shrieked in Carla's ears and tore through her hair. She gripped the tiller, urging the lifeboat through the gray storm surge, the hurricane howling around her.

It was foolish to be out in swells this big in a lifeboat this small, or even out in the Gulf at all in such weather, but there she was. The circumstances of how she came to be in the lifeboat were simple: a radioed mayday in a vaguely familiar voice frantically telling her that a ship was foundering nearby. Gray and white foam crashed over her, tossing the lifeboat like an empty abalone shell, but through the mist and rain Carla saw the swaying hull of the distressed ship. From its wooden deck, howling voices streamed down the wind like drowning ghosts. The steady, whistling maelstrom obliterated the ship from sight, then hove it to again, slightly closer than before. With a shock, Carla realized these desperate voices were calling her name.

She clung to the gunnels of the lifeboat, committed now in spite of her terror of the gray shape filling her field of vision. Three towering masts creaked in the wind, their torn and shredded sails streaming behind them like banners. On deck, a line of black men and women stood chained together near the railing, hollering at her over the wind in a language Carla had never heard before. The mainmast tilted dangerously, and the men and women screamed. If it came down and swept one of them overboard, the chains would pull the others down as well, one after another, into the heaving depths.

The doomed vessel loomed over her, monumental. A

student of history, Carla knew without doubt what it was: a slave ship, circa 1800. The deck was spilling water over the sides in torrents, carrying its human cargo perilously near the edge. As the ship got closer, she searched the faces and was shocked to find a single white face among the dozens of darker ones. A stocky man in his late fifties, gray hair slicked with brine, reddish cheeks and a bushy mustache. It was the same kind of mustache...

"Daddy!" Carla cried out over the storm, and the man looked her way sadly and shook his head. The ship listed badly to starboard and the chain of people swayed forward. Then the mainmast snapped like an explosion of thunder, and the inevitable played out before her disbelieving eyes.

Thunder jackknifed Carla Clements wide awake. Saltwater poured down her face and for an instant she was unsure of where she was. A dim, stuffy room, a low ceiling, the sound of sloshing water. Sweat running into her mouth. Hell! What time was it? She pushed herself off the narrow bunk, shaking sleep out of her head, and hurried topside. Shark shit, it was daylight. The wind had picked up, and thunderheads were massing on the horizon as thick as putty. Scratch one more weather report—her own fault for relying on the TV weathercasters and for not being born with a gut-level intuition that would tell her when a storm was brewing. Her daddy had the knack; he could feel a storm coming like other people felt heat in their veins or cold in their bones. Carla stopped short, one foot on the deck, the face on the foundering slave ship suddenly vivid in her mind again. She tended to forget that about her father...that he had been a first-class shrimp boat captain before he was bitten by the political bug. Before he died and left nearly everything to Marietta. Carla blinked and wiped at her eyes. He was barely a year dead, but it seemed like he'd been gone forever.

Mist rose around the shrimper, thin and tasting of brine, as choppy Gulf water slapped at its sides. How long had she been out, having the weirdest dream of all time? Carla shook the sweat from her face, and long wisps of black hair whipped around and stuck to her cheeks and neck. Witch's hair, her father once called it, now flecked prematurely gray. She adjusted her halter top and walked aft, spotting a wrinkled brown leg on the other side of the hold.

"Comer!" she shouted. "Pick up your ass and let's get some work done before the rain catches us."

From behind the hold, another brown leg joined the first. Then a hand pulled the rest of the body to a sitting position. The glassy clunk of a bottle falling to the deck from the old man's chest told Carla how her only deckhand had been passing his time, but not how he had smuggled the bottle on board. And what the hell had happened last night? What was she doing sleeping when she should have been trying to bring in enough of a catch to pay her light bill? She recalled culling the nets last night at least ten times with little to show for it. At about 3 a.m. she'd left Comer on deck, pulled a Coke from the fridge, and gone below to rest for a few minutes. Then what? Four hours had gone by while Comer juiced himself comatose and she dreamed about her father on a slave ship.

Carla spat the taste of sleep over the side. The water was as dark as the backing on a mirror. Carla didn't like mirrors—they showed all too clearly the result of too many days and nights spent out on the water with the salt spray in your face. She also didn't like getting caught by unexpected storms. When you spent fully half your time trawling the Gulf of Mexico, you got to know the winds, the currents, and the weather patterns as well as you knew what kinds of sea creatures you were likely to bring up in your net. But sometimes the elements surprised you. The clouds were turning black and stretching themselves into thick, dark chunks along the horizon. The squall was still a ways out, but clearly gathering momentum. Carla weighed the odds. They might have enough time to make another run before turning tail for shore, might even make it to port without a soaking... if they were lucky. She watched her first mate run both hands through the few strands of hair left to him and groan as he tried to stand on unsteady legs.

Grunting, Carla set to work reeling in the anchor and hauling it over the deck, where she let it plunk down heavily on the weathered planks. "Comer! Get a move on! Let's do one more run, then hightail it back to port before we get blown all the way to Tate's Hell!"

Comer straightened and scanned the lowering sky. His grizzled face was puzzled. "Wha time is it anyways?" Before the breeze could whirl it away, he bent down and grabbed a straw hat as battered-looking as he was.

Carla reassessed the cloudbank—nimbus alligators crawling toward the mainland instead of staying out over the Gulf of Mexico where they belonged. A rumble from above sent her scurrying into the wheelhouse to start the engine.

"Lower the outriggers and get the lines out. Move it!"

Comer looked at her sideways with a lunatic's eye and spat through his teeth over the side. He jammed his hat down on his head, looked at her crabwise, and said, "Bargle."

"Don't give me that, you drunken old bunghole," Carla warned.

"Ah don't take orders from nobody ain't got no balls," the old man mumbled.

"Then you can swim back to Tate's Hammock." Carla took a few steps toward him. "You think I won't kick your ass overboard?" She thought she had put a stop to his boozing on board, even going so far as to pat him down, police style, to make sure he was clean of the mist, as he called it. On land and sober, he bore it with good humor. She knew he needed the money and—even though he had never learned to swim—would put up with whatever demands she heaped on him in order to keep his steady gig. She also knew he was scared silly of drowning—so terrified, in fact, that only a good drunk could belay that fear. It was a useful piece of knowledge, and his comment about balls convinced her that she wasn't patting him down quite thoroughly enough. She would remedy that next time. The clouds were crawling toward them in a widening arc, snapping out lightning. Thunder growled close behind.

Comer had started hauling on the lines, but slowly, and was muttering things just above his breath. Carla had good ears, and as she started the trawler in motion, she listened carefully in case he said anything else she might want to bop him for later. "Shouldn't be scarin folks like that," he was saying. "Yah daddy now, he woulda taken yah pants down an whipped yah with a cane pole. Ha! Wouldn't be able to tell yah fanny from the Red Zebra of Rangoon."

In five years of shrimping full-time with Comer, she'd heard a lot of muttering and complaining, but she'd also heard enough stories to write a book. The Red Zebra of Rangoon was a Burmese boogie monster, called upon to chastise misbehaving children. Many of his other stories took place closer to home, either in her coastal town of Tate's Hammock, or just outside, in the tangled swamps and forests of the Florida Panhandle. He told a hodgepodge of tales—Native American stories, animal legends, early settler yarns. Some were even about her father, Carl "Bull" Clements, a legend in his own right according to newspaper accounts and Florida legislative scuttlebutt. Bull Clements had owned a fleet of fishing boats, including the one she worked now, and had parlayed his knowledge of the coast into, first, enhancement of the family income and, later, a seat in the state legislature.

"You just shut up about my father, you don't know shit about him!" She still had a hard time believing the man who'd dominated her life for nearly three decades was so suddenly gone.

Behind the cabin, Comer patrolled the business end of the shrimper, making sure the nets were riding smoothly. Carla heard him mumbling again. "Yah daddy was a good ole boy, at least he was some a the time. Other times he was meaner'n a steer with a hornet on his balls. But he wan't as mean as you. Gotta be female to be as big a bitch as you are. Lookit yerself. Why, yah ain't chicken scratch. Don't have no friends except them mojo-workin people…"

"What the hell are you barking on about? If you mean Sookie and Pixie, you're sharkbait! Sookie was my nanny when I was growing up, and Pixie—"

"They gonna bring all kinda trouble down on yah—on me, too. Gonna get us sunk to the bottom, sure's mah name's Comer Whitehead an yers is—"

"Yours is mud. At least if Sookie were here she could have told us this storm was coming." Carla hadn't seen Sookie Darbyville for months. If her father had been able to predict storms with his skipper's senses, Sookie had been able to predict them with her *ifa's* intuition, inherited from her Yoruba ancestors.

"Ah could tell yah stories about that old witchy woman—" Comer began, but Carla cut him off.

"Just get the damn drum," she told him, some of her fury slacking off.

Comer shuffled over to the net winch and propped himself against the rail, waiting for her to complete the run and stop the engine so he could send the winch motor grinding into action. He aimed his steady stream of mutterings into the rising wind. "Been to college, but what good did it do yah? Yah only lasted three years. An yah still ain't got a you-know-what. Some captain you are." He hawked and spat over the side again.

Carla glared at him. On days like this she'd rather be cane-pole fishing with the worm from a bottle of premium Jose Cuervo. Sitting at the wheel with the boat in a slow cruise, she reminded herself for the millionth time why she had chosen to spend her life like this. Even with the time she'd spent in college to please her father, she didn't know how to do anything else. Shrimping had been her daddy's business and now it was hers. A lightweight—just five-three in her deck shoes—here she was trying to do a job that six-foot men often failed at. Some days it seemed the sheerest nonsense.

She had other doubts as well. Hell, she was only twenty-seven years old and already her wild hair was turning gray, as if each new spray of salted sea air left its trace in her follicles.

These days she just felt shopworn. Sunscorched on the bottom and graying on top. Green eyes faded from squinting too long into the sun. Not that anyone looked at her that closely. Her current male companionship consisted of Yancy Vause, and he was a loser from the word go. The fact that he had spent some quality time in the jungles of Vietnam only made it worse; everyone knew he was a little unstable, hell, cracked even, but at least he was interested in her. Which was a piss-poor reason for going out with him. The last time they'd gone somewhere together he'd managed to get her arrested. She ground her teeth and tried to shut out the humiliating image of her encounter with the law.

She shut off the engine and walked barefoot out to the weathered deck to help with the net, clinging to the unlikely hope that it would be full of fat shrimp. It would be nice to have more than two nickels to rub together. Her father's will had left her only a small sum of money and the few remaining boats of the fleet. She'd promptly put them all up for sale to pay off the mortgage on her little house near the docks. She had kept only one boat—a sleek, well-constructed trawler her dad had named the *Miriam C.*, after Carla's mother. It was all she needed. But running and maintaining the shrimper was an ongoing expense. Plus there were escalating car repairs she hadn't counted on. It seemed like a lot of money going out, but not all that much coming in. If things got really bad, she supposed she could move in with Marietta. It was a thought that turned her stomach sour.

She saw that Comer had winched the net up nearly even with the gunnels, so she threw a hitch knot around the top of the net and tugged it across to the deck, feeling slightly nauseated. The tang of the salty net slime and the sharp breeze whipping her hair and thin clothing didn't help. Maybe she was coming down with something. It all felt so futile. By this time of day, the shrimp had stopped feeding and gone home to deeper waters. They'd be lucky to net enough fish to supply the few eateries along Cincinnati Street, the town's main drag, much less the whole Gulf Coast.

Comer, sobering, as usual, with work, said, "Of course ya daddy liked to hoist a few now and then with the fellas. Ole Bull, if yah wanted a man who could think big and live bigger, wasn't nobody else like him…"

Thunder drowned out his words. Shivering, Carla focused on the work of getting the nets hauled up, the bad weather closing in faster than she'd anticipated. Almost directly overhead, clouds snapped and fought over the boat, and a bright tongue of lightning licked down in an instant from cloudbank to waterline.

Comer shrieked like an old woman. "Goddog, hit's somebody's hoodoo spell a-brewin—shitfuck, we all gonna die!" Shut up and help me," Carla yelled, "or I really will kick your sorry butt overboard."

As she had supposed, the net was only half full, although a few good-sized fish—including a two-foot black grouper—were mixed in with the dirt, seaweed, trash fish, shrimp, and inevitable crabs. As she waited for Comer to get clear, she reached for the drawstring that would rip open the bottom of the net like a silent zipper. Before she could give it a tug, the rain came pelting down, drenching everything at once. Carla lost her footing on the slippery deck and, as she held frantically to the rope, her weight pulled the net open, bringing the load of fish, shrimp, crabs, kelp, and sea slime down on top of her with a flatulent squelch. The grouper flew onto the deck as well, flopping on top of her and, astonishingly, clamping onto her bicep like a bulldog. It was such a shocking thing to happen that Carla could only look at the fish in amazement. The fish looked back at her. The clouds spit lightning.

Soggy, depressed, diminutive, ball-less, and old before her time, Carla Clements, a woman named after her father, lay on the deck of a boat named for her mother, and sighed. In a shaking fury, she pushed the blanket of slimy, wiggly sea crap off her head and chest and sat up, letting the rain wash over her. The fish remained clamped, and the entire

sky laughed like hell in a deep voice. Carla yelped in spite
of herself and remembered something that her automobile
mechanic was always telling her: If one thing goes wrong,
can the rest be far behind?

Carla knew that black grouper have well-developed
canine teeth and several sets of raspers—strong, slender teeth
that they use to grasp smaller fish they intend to have for
dinner—but she'd never had one try to bite her. With a thin
trail of blood oozing down her arm, rain stinging her face,
and hordes of angry crabs festering around and over her legs,
Carla lost it. She tried to pry the grouper loose with her free
hand but couldn't get enough leverage. Looking around for
Comer, she spotted him standing next to the hold, having
trouble keeping his balance and laughing his ass off at the
same time.

"Help me get this damn fish off my arm!" she shouted
above the storm.

Comer cut his laughter to a giggle, but she could see
it was not without a fight. He looked around for a weapon,
and seeing none, grabbed up his empty pint bottle of Florida
Mist that was sliding around the deck. Sloshing over to her,
he raised the bottle as if to club the grouper.

Carla flinched and jerked her arm out of the way.
"What, are you going to hammer it into my arm for good?"
she cried. "It's not a barracuda, damn it, but it's still got teeth.
Just pry the jaws open." The fish was surprisingly tenacious,
but Comer managed to extract her arm from the its jaws,
leaving an archipelago of nasty red dots. Carla got to her feet
and slogged through the wriggling and swirling mass on the
deck toward the cabin while Comer ducked in just ahead of
her, started the engine again, and put the trawler into running
speed. Energized, it bucked and sloshed in the heavy waves.
Carla sat down and pulled a first-aid kit out of a bulwark. She
dumped a quarter of a bottle of iodine on her arm, wrapped a
bandage around it, and wondered if they were going to sink.

But the clouds were dispersing as quickly as they
had appeared, and tiny patches of blue showed through

the tattered thunderheads. Summer squalls were like that—they blew up in a flash and as soon as their fury was spent, dissolved almost as quickly. Not unlike her temper, as she'd been reminded by Comer and Yancy and Marietta and her daddy and just about anybody who'd hung around her for more than a week. She stood up and went to the navigation station.

"Here, I'll take the wheel," she said. "Why don't you fillet some of those fish for us to take home, and make sure you get the one that was eating my arm! Then put the catch on ice."

Comer pulled the hatch cover over the hold to use as a cutting table. He cleaned fish as smoothly as lighting a match, and Carla watched as he grabbed the first fish at hand—a good-sized flounder—and killed it with a sharp, quick thwack against the side of the boat. He sliced and cleaned out the belly in a single motion. He was in his element, looking much more like a Japanese TV chef than a sixty-five-year-old sot. It was for times like these that Carla kept him on.

Carla reached for the pack of Winstons in her cutoffs, but they were soaked and so were her matches. Cursing, she stalked out of the cabin and threw the whole mess into a plastic trash bag she kept on deck. Fish and shrimp were flopping around her bare feet, but none seemed to want to take a bite out of her. Comer had just picked up the grouper and slit its belly when Carla heard the low sputtering of an airplane. Comer heard it too, but didn't bother to look up. They both knew who it was because it was the only local single-engine taildragger that always sounded as if it were about to crash.

"Damn boyfriend again," said Comer, looking disdainfully at Carla.

"He's not my boyfriend," said Carla wearily, preparing to duck and be scared witless if Yancy Vause buzzed the boat in his usual careless fashion. They were lucky. This time he only waved, dipped a wing, and circled.

"Wahl then, if he ain't, he should be," said Comer,

taking another tack. "Gal your age..." The old man took from his pants a baggie-wrapped pack of Camels and a box of sulphur-tipped matches. With a sly look on his face, he lit one and inhaled deeply.

She growled at him. "Gimmie."

"Give yah what?" he asked innocently.

"One of those cigarettes, damn it!"

"And what'll yah give me for one?"

"I'll give you a kick in the ass if you *don't* give me one," she retorted.

"How bout this fish?" he asked, holding up the grouper he had just disemboweled — they both knew it would fetch good money from a local restaurant.

"You got it." For a cigarette, she'd eat trash fish for a week. Overhead, Yancy Vause was circling the boat in wider spirals.

"I always wanted to taste an animal that was fattened on human flesh," said Comer. Cackling, he bent over the fish and started to clean it.

Carla touched her bandage cautiously. Her arm stung, although the bleeding had stopped. Probably be good as new in a couple of days, but better have a doctor check it when she got in. She didn't want to take a chance of getting fish rabies. That was another tall tale she'd heard somewhere as a little girl, either from her father or from one of the men who sat out on the loafer's bench in front of Crozier's Old Country Store. The Liar's Bench, as she thought of them, was populated by the town's oldest, most cantankerous, most long-winded retirees, whose overall-clad butts had worn the plank surface of the bench as smooth as if it had been sanded. Comer joined them often enough, even though by their standards he was gainfully, if not happily, employed. She'd been listening to their tall tales and old men's rants since she was old enough to climb the steps of the darkened store behind her daddy, big as a bear in his canvas pants and rubber fishing boots.

Comer's yell startled Carla back to the present, where Yancy Vause appeared to have decided the time was ripe to buzz the boat. "Here comes that bastard again! He's gonna crash land on us!"

Instead of diving flat out on the deck like Comer, Carla flipped him a bird and sat down on the gunnel. When the prop wash died away, Comer staggered to his feet, handed her a cigarette and lit it with trembling fingers. He looked around, apparently searching for his own, and discovered it in his mouth, burned down perilously close to his stubble. He threw it overboard and lit another.

"I need a drink," he said.

"You're not the only one." Carla dragged on the unfiltered Camel and squinted into the sun, watching the plane climbing out over the gray water.

Comer studied the empty bottle of Florida Mist with sadness. "Wahl," he began, "once we get in…" He broke off, wiping sweat out of his eyes as steaming sunlight baked the deck around them. "Say, where the hell did that storm go to?" He stared skyward.

Carla looked around the wide blue arc overhead, but the only thing it held was the yellow fins of Yancy Vause's taildragger flickering in the dazzling sun over the mainland.

The port in Tate's Hammock was set at the end of an inlet, curved like a jack 'o lantern's grin, and Carla kept her sailor's eye on the salt-bleached snaggle-teeth of the dock pylons as she piloted the boat toward its berth. Comer had finished culling and icing the shrimp and was busy swabbing the deck with a large squeegee, pushing anything undersized back into the bay along with the seaweed and other trash. He was tunelessly mumbling the words to a country tune, an inch of lit cigarette dangling from his lower lip. Carla stepped into her wet deck shoes and expertly guided the boat into its bay, where Stinky the Fish Man was already waiting. She cut the engine and glided the last few yards until a soft bump against the pylon tires told her they were home. Comer threw Stinky a rope and scrambled up onto the pier. Carla went below for the black waterproof bag that held her personal possessions—a book on the Galapagos Islands, some cash, and a few toilet articles—and followed suit.

Stinky the Fish Man didn't look much like a fish—at least none that Carla had ever seen—but he did smell like one, so the name was well-earned. He was a thin, gangling man somewhere in his thirties, with straw-red hair, a big grin, and elephant ears. He was wearing his usual uniform consisting of a pair of Sears khaki work pants, high-topped black basketball sneakers, and a faded T-shirt with Clem's Clams silkscreened across the front. Clem was his daddy, who not only owned the seafood restaurant in question, but the dockside fish processing plant as well. The Fish Barn was probably the most important building in town—it bought, processed, and distributed virtually every boatload of fish, shrimp, and shellfish that came into port. In Carla's opinion, Stinky's IQ was probably a long way from triple digits, but he knew enough to attach a winch to the cargo hold of incoming fishing vessels, turn on the scales, and give an accurate weight to the day's catch.

"Hi ya, Carla," he said a little too loudly. Carla suspected that, despite his large ears, Stinky was partially deaf. His loudness, like his odor, never diminished.

"What's up, Stink?" She gave him a nod and a smile.

"Oh, not a whole lot. Not a whole lot of boats come in yet. Yours is the first one."

"Well, it was a lousy night," Carla replied. Comer nodded and began helping Stinky with the winching. This part of the job—the hoisting and weighing, the transferring of the catch from the boat to the fish house, where it would later be separated and sold to restaurants, grocery stores, and street vendors around the state—took little effort, but it was boring. What Carla really wanted to do was flop down somewhere, but a job was a job, and she didn't like to leave Comer holding the bag. Somehow, she managed to reply to Stinky's aimless conversation with her attention elsewhere. "Pretty lousy all the way around."

"I don't know about that," shouted Stinky, "I've seen

a lot worse catches than this. And you weren't out that long."

"Enough to pay the light bill, maybe," she said.

"See there," he nodded.

Comer grumbled, the winching machinery creaked, the waves plashed up against the pilings, and Carla sighed. Time crawled, but eventually, with some money in their pockets, Carla and Comer headed down the dock toward Jody's Café.

Like most other North Florida fishing villages, Tate's Hammock reached inland for several miles and stretched along the coast twice as far. Yet much of the coastline on either side of the docks dissolved into swamps and marshlands, teeming havens of plant and animal life interlaced with mysterious waterways. From the bottom of Front Street, one could sight down rows of giant, twisted live oaks older than the vanished Timucuan Indians who'd first settled the area. And laced through the sea-breeze scents of fish and beach seaweed, it was possible, if one paid attention to such things, to inhale the aroma of wild honeysuckle and love-vine.

Carla was only half aware of her surroundings as she walked briskly ahead of Comer, the docks at their back and the scent of flowers in the air. It wasn't a bad place to live, but with her daddy gone, it felt empty. She had friends, of course, some of them questionable for certain, but there was a sense of aimlessness to her days and nights that hadn't been there before. What she needed was a smoke and an oversized mug of Slow Madge's black gold. Or sludge, depending on your point of view.

Another half a block and they reached the diner. Carla could've found it with her eyes shut; all she needed to do was follow the smell of burned java and over-fried pork sausage patties lingering near the entrance. Squeezing into Jody's Café with Comer close behind her and settling down on a stool at the counter, she wondered what it was, beyond the need for money, that was keeping her here.

Jody's Café was the barest of holes in the wall — a long counter with ten stools and two tables, all packed so close together it could have been patterned after a tackle box. Still, it was the first place every fisher, shrimper, and oysterman in the area went as soon as they hit port. Behind the counter, a stove grimy with grease wedged itself between the wall and a sink with three basins. Glasses, cups, and plates were stacked in rows on a sideboard next to a hulking white freezer. On the wall over the stove hung a stuffed marlin that the original owner had caught near Palm Beach in 1959. A vintage air conditioner had dripped for thirty years on the stool nearest the wall, and the wooden planks of the floor and wall were soggy and dark from its splatterings. The Café's only inhabitant now, however, was Slow Madge, the present owner, who worked the shop twenty-four hours a day. She knew the tides so thoroughly that no one could remember her not being open when she needed to be, and it was rare to see anyone else behind the counter. She was a woman who seemed always to have been fifty years old, born with a hairnet around her red-and-white streaked hair and a smudged flower-print dress swathed around the rest of her.

"Black coffee for me, Madge," Carla said. "And one of those sugar doughnuts."

"Same for me," said Comer, "but no doughnut."

Madge slid steaming coffee in front of them. "You all in after only one night?"

"One more night like that and I'll be begging you for a job," said Carla. She shivered in her soggy cutoffs. The coffee was very hot, and she used the cup to warm her hands. Comer drank his down like water, and Carla wondered whether her insides would turn to leather too when she got as old as he was.

"One of those, huh?" Madge asked, pouring herself a cup.

"Worse," Carla began, but before she could say more, the door of the Café creaked open and banged against the wall. Carla turned and saw Yancy standing and smiling in the doorway. He had put on his imitation California leisure suit, and his blow-dried hair had just the right hint of dishevelment that only an early morning bombing run in a Cessna Scout could give it. In fact, despite everything, Carla was unpleasantly attracted to that look. Also, in spite of her best attempts to ignore them, she admired his dark, long eyelashes and straight teeth. Trouble was, Yancy Vause was both a butthead and a scumbag. "Shit on parade," she said softly.

"Thought I'd find you here," he said, walking the step or two it took to bring him to the counter. He put his hand on Carla's shoulder, but she shook it off.

"Beat it, rat bait," she told him.

"Hey, you're not still sore about the other night, are you?" He batted the eyelashes.

"How could I be? I'm not in jail, am I?"

"Well now, if you're gonna be like that—"

"That's *exactly* how I'm going to be," Carla said fiercely. Then she softened. "Look. I'm not mad at you, I'm mad at myself. I knew you were an asshole, and I went out with you anyway. Well, I paid the price and now I know better. But from now on, just leave me the hell alone."

Yancy stiffened. "You seeing somebody else?"

Comer chortled and said, "She went out with *me* last night."

"I'm not talking to you, you old fuck," Yancy snapped.

"And I think Stinky down at the fish house has a crush on her," Comer added.

Yancy ignored him and turned to Carla. "You seeing somebody else?' he repeated.

Wearily, Carla looked him squarely in his blue eyes. "All you have to worry about is that I'm not seeing *you*," she told him.

"Well, fuck you, then,' Yancy said. "You're not the only fish in the Gulf."

"Better get yourself a bigger pole, then," Carla shot back, but Yancy was already gone. Carla heard the cackle of laughter from behind the counter.

"Don't pay no attention to him, Carla," Madge smiled.

"He just thinks he's a big shot because his daddy and his uncle make big money rippin people off."

"You got that right. One sells sand dunes to the condo people, and the other sells just enough car to get out of the county before it breaks down." Carla gulped coffee, feeling a masochistic satisfaction in its hot pain.

"And what's with you, just sittin there on your tiny old ass and cracking jokes?" Madge said to Comer. "Why didn't you stick up for Carla just now?"

"Hell," said Comer, his lunatic eye aimed in her direction. "I ain't defendin no criminal."

"That does it," said Carla. She could feel the fury rising up her neck and flushing her cheeks. "Next trip, you swim *out* to the boat and back too. I'm going to Hamp's for some cigarettes. You coming?" She put a dollar on the counter and stood up.

"Course." Comer grabbed up his fish, which he had wrapped in an old newspaper he found near the dock, and hurried after his employer. Carla knew that no amount of verbal abuse could keep the old sot from spending a couple of hours with his buddies on the Loafer's Bench at the country store. She sighed loudly, letting the screen door of Jody's Café slam behind her. Something had to change.

Chapter Two

Billy Joe Lord was sitting on the Loafer's Bench outside Crozier's Old Country Store. At eighty-three, his eyesight was still good, and he watched Carla and her first mate walk briskly toward him where he shared the shade with a couple of his old pals. It was her usual route: down Front Street, past the market, the tackle shop, and the taxidermist. Crozier's Old Country Store, which everybody simply called "Hamp's," was next in line. The brick outside was chipped with age, but sealed so tight with whitewash that an ant couldn't find its way in. A shallow wooden porch of graying cypress led up to two huge windows that framed both sides of an ancient screened door. Overhead, a metal awning hung off-center on its cables, but Billy Joe and the others never noticed; it remained intact after a century of hurricanes—and Billy Joe remembered most of them.

On both sides of the door sat church pews, worn smooth and shiny from the restless back scratchings and seat itchings of generations of loafers. None of the bench sitters was under sixty-five. Billy Joe was the oldest of the bunch and was the most regular of the Loafer's Bench clan. Although they were all liars and tale-tellers, it was Billy Joe's crotchety and sourdough camaraderie—his almost youthful pleasure to just sit and "conversate"—that kept the others coming back day after day. He would often jump up in great excitement, remembering a story he had heard as a child, and brandish his arms, thin in girth and thick with liver spots, in the manner of someone about to cast a spell. The others, Hamp Crozier, in his late sixties, owner of the store and never seen without his apron; Clarence Revell, a golf-hatted seventy-year-old farmer; and Comer Whitehead, deckhand and sot, were usually content to sit and listen to The Old Man rant and lie about things he swore he had personally witnessed or that had been told to him by truthful people. Billy Joe, Hamp, Clarence, Comer: they all had stories to tell. But Billy Joe had the most.

Billy Joe remembered that Carla, as a young girl, used to sit with her back against a worm-eaten wooden post in front of the store with her daddy, listening to their tales. Bull never believed half of what they said but Carla seemed to take in every word as if it were scripture. Funny how things turn out sometimes. Of all the kids in Tate's Hammock, Carla had been his favorite, and he knew that the others felt the same way. She was respectful and listened hard. She learned. And they were all so proud when she got in college. They knew she would make something of herself in the state capital, maybe get to be a teacher. And the fact that history had been her subject had made every loafer and storyteller at Hamp's feel like they had contributed something good to the world. Then, one day, Carla had just showed back up. No degree, no husband, no explanation. And she had changed; she had become more like her daddy. Harder. Quicker to criticize and less likely to smile. These days, she'd jump on yah for battin an eye. Bull had been okay before he got into politics, but after... Billy Joe shook his head.

"Tiny-mite seems a bit out of sorts, don't she?" asked Clarence, making no effort to keep the approaching Carla from hearing him.

"Wouldn't be her if she wasn't," answered Billy Joe, with the same disregard for Carla's ears.

"What are you all yammering about?" Carla asked as she slogged up to the porch in her soaked deck shoes, Comer in her wake.

"What the hell happened to you all?" asked Billy Joe. "You fall overboard?"

"Not quite," said Carla. "Where's Hamp?"

"Inside," answered Clarence. "Doin some business with Daddy Blue. Whatcha got there, Comer?" he asked, nodding at the package Comer had under his arm.

"What do you think it is, it's a fish," said Comer, elbowing his way onto the bench despite his still-damp clothes. As always, he took off his straw hat and stowed it out of the way under the pew.

"What kind of fish?" said Billy Joe.

"Black grouper. Big one, too!" He held up the fish wrapped in newspaper. "Pulled it in just before that storm come up."

"What storm was that?" asked Clarence.

"That dagblasted storm that looked like it was going to blow us from here to Wewahitchka."

"Hell, we didn't see no storm," said Billy Joe.

"Only reason you didn't see no storm was because it got so dark you thought it was night and went to sleep."

"You all see any sign of rain on that street in front of you?" asked Billy Joe.

"Hell," chipped in Clarence, "you probly got drunk, fell overboard, then bought that fish from Stinky. And what's the matter with ya arm?"

"That fish bit it," Carla said.

"Yeah, well, you'll probly get fish rabies," he said and yawned.

"I knew a man who had fish rabies, once," said Billy Joe excitedly. "It happened on the river, though, not in the Gulf. Forget the man's name but he had on his waders and was fishin with one of them fly rods. Man had a nose on him like a banana and damned if a bass didn't jump right out of the water and clamp onta it like a dog. He got him a fish all right, but in all the excitement, he dropped that expensive rod. Ha!"

"I was there too," said Clarence, "and he didn't get no fish rabies."

"Wahl, that's only because you can't get fish rabies from bass. It's gotta be—" Billy Joe's attention was grabbed away by Daddy Blue, who had poked his head through the screen door and was staring at him like he was the Green Ghost of Gretna. "What you lookin at, you old fart ya?" he asked, but Daddy Blue, instead of answering, stepped quickly off the porch and half ran down the street, clutching his bag to his chest like he was afraid it might fly out of his hand.

"Gwan, then. Boo!" Clarence shouted after him. Then, in a lower voice, said, "Weird old spook, ain't he?"

"He's not old," Carla answered. "And he probably doesn't believe in fish rabies. He's got enough to worry about with Aunt Sookie always trying to make his daughter into a root doctor."

"Don't matter," said Clarence. "He's still a weird old fart."

"He's got swamp fever," said Hamp, who had followed Daddy Blue out of the shop. "If you live out near the edge of the swamp and drink enough whisky, lots of things'll start ta spook ya."

"But yah know," mused Billy Joe, his voice dropping to a whisper, "that feller ain't the only spook out there in that swamp." He took out a canister of snuff and opened it, only to find it was empty.

"Well, I'll tell you what, Billy Joe," said Hamp, leaning in the doorway. "I'm too old to be traipsin in there to find out about no damn spooks."

"Then I'm the one to tell you about em," stated Billy Joe.

"Doubt if you've ever been in that swamp," said Comer. "Now me, I—"

"Hold it a minute," said Carla. "Is this a story? Let me get some cigarettes first." She took a dollar out of her black bag. "And Daddy Blue lives in Blanchard's Bluff, not the swamp," she added.

"Thirteen of one and a baker's dozen of t'other," muttered Billy Joe. Used to be a time when he could tell a story from start to finish without being interrupted.

Hamp and Carla went through the screen door and

Billy Joe shuffled after them. The dark room was permeated with the smells of oak barrels and flour sacks piled in corners. Shelves behind the counter reached the ceiling and contained things that most people'd never even heard of, like snake oil and Doctor Bodine's Feel-Good Anodyne. The walls and ceiling beams were of heavy oak, dusty with the years but as sound as the day Hamp's granddaddy had fitted and hammered them together. Billy Joe knew; he hadn't actually been around to see it built, but he knew all about how the store had come to be, like everything else in the town.

Most of the front counter was glass-topped and crammed from right to left across its scratched surface with candies and chewing tobaccos and boxes of cigars and bubble packs of fishing lures, red-topped glass canisters containing licorice and chewing gum and chocolate kisses. Billy Joe remembered the taste of most of these from his boyhood. His taste buds had dulled with age, though, and just about all he enjoyed any more was snuff—the stronger the better.

The space inside the glass counter was reserved for Hamp's artifacts. A pipe carved from a whale's tooth, an old sextant, a fifty-cent coin from the Kingdom of Hawaii dated 1883, and other objects Hamp had gathered. Billy Joe noticed a rounded, gray shape he hadn't seen before, and bent down to investigate.

"Got something new, eh?" he asked. "What is it, a rock?"

"It's a tomahawk," said Hamp proudly. "See the markings on the side? Might be Timucuan."

"I used to be married to a Timucuan woman…" Billy Joe began, reaching for a can of Kodiak snuff near the cigar displays. He handed Hamp some money and listened to the familiar clanging of what was perhaps the only nineteenth-century cash register in America still in continuous use. The numbers on the keys had worn so dim that Hamp must have been punching them from memory for years.

"Hold on, Billy Joe," said Carla. "No stories until we get back outside. Anyway, you know you weren't…oh, never mind. Hamp, let me have a pack of kitchen matches and a bag of Cat Chow." Billy Joe watched as she fished two more dollars from her bag and handed them to Hamp, then ripped the cellophane from the pack.

"That cellophane helps to keep em fresh," admonished Billy Joe.

"I'm not going to give them a chance to get stale," Carla said, sticking a cigarette in her mouth and lighting it with a flame so long that it nearly lit her hair as well. Billy Joe watched in alarm as she inhaled deeply and tucked the pack and the matches in her bag. "Now I'm ready for some conversating," she said.

Billy Joe followed Carla and Hamp back across the worn wooden floor to the door and found that Comer was telling Clarence his own story of the morning's events, probably embellishing it for all he was worth. Billy Joe and Hamp took their seats on the bench on either side of Comer and Clarence; Carla sat on the porch, her back against the old wooden post.

"The damn rain was coming down so fast that the scuppers couldn't handle it. And then this yard-long black grouper hops on board!" Comer had opened his parcel and was showing off his dinner. Billy Joe sniffed. He'd better eat the damn thing soon.

The others mumbled and nodded for a while, touching the package as if for good luck. Clarence and Hamp took out plugs of tobacco from their overalls and packed their cheeks. Billy Joe took out his new box of Kodiak and pinched some under his lip. When he was sure he had their full attention, he let the story flow out.

"There was rain in that swamp some sixty years ago when I saw that eight-foot hog bear."

"Hell," said Comer. "Yah didn't see no eight-foot hog bear."

"Well, maybe I did and maybe I didn't," he said. "Me and Pap had been huntin coon down off of Blanchard's Bluff."

"Ain't no coon down there," said Comer.

"Was then," said Billy Joe. "Probly still is if you know how to find em. We had some prize blue-tick hounds that year and towards daybreak one of em—we called im Birdshot—caught onto a scent and went flyin off, barkin like a son of a gun. Now we had been headin due south for a couple hours and we figgered we was purt near Sookie's mama's property. The trees was wetter and darker and the Spanish moss used to grow a lot thicker down there. It started to drizzle, which was somethin we didn't care for. We also wasn't too happy about the ground, which was tryin to eat our boots so that every time we'd take a step it would make a slurping noise like Pap would make when he'd suck his teeth."

Billy Joe paused, spat into an old Prince Albert can he kept stashed under the bench, and stuffed his gums with more Kodiak. "Now you young men don't remember this, but Sookie wasn't no old witch back then—but her mama was. I know stories about ole Freeda that would make you people age so fast you'd think I was a teenager, but I'll leave those for another time.

"You all never knew Pap too well neither, but he didn't like no black folk and he specially didn't like nobody that worked roots, probly because Freeda put a curse on his hens once that caused them to stop layin for sixty days so he didn't have no egg money to buy sour mash from Buckeye Henty over in Panacea. But we didn't want to lose Birdshot, so we rounded up the other two dogs and pointed ourselves in the direction he'd lit off in. Sides, we was kinda interested in what coulda made that dog take on so. Pap held his gun at the ready in case he saw old Freeda. Told me he'd like to send a bullet so close to her nose that she'd smell it as it was goin by. But we walked on and on and no Freeda; no dog neither. Pap looked at his watch but it was stopped and so he looked up at the sky, but the trees was so thick that it coulda been midnight. The brambles was thick thereabouts too, and I kept getting caught no matter which way I turned. I could swear that I saw one long skinny thorn vine reachin out in my direction. Hell, I didn't believe in no haunted plants or stuff, but damned if I didn't have to take out my huntin knife and chop that sucker off my leg. That's when we heard the dog again. Fact is, the other dogs commenced to gettin restless too and didn't want to come when Pap whistled. But then we heard a cracklin and a thrashin in the underbrush and out comes Birdshot at full speed, looking like he was trying to keep up with his eyes, which were just a mite ahead of the rest of im. Well hell, that hound didn't slow down when he saw us, and them two other dogs weren't agoin to wait around to find out what Birdshot'd seen, so they near bout ran over us scamperin out of there. I wanted to go too, but Pap said no. He thought that the only thing coulda scared that dog so bad was a hog bear, and Pap had always wanted to kill a hog bear. So we went ahead, careful as could be, tryin not to crack any twigs, which wasn't too easy considerin that it was hard to see the ground, and which didn't make any difference anyway bein as that same ground was filled with that sucking mud that complained every time you stepped in it. I had on high-top boots to keep out the snakes and the leeches, but I was a mite afraid of gators. We didn't have to go far, though, because just then we came to a clearin. The moon was still out and shone like a police spotlight on a patch of ground about the size a somebody's back yard. Seems like we must've been walking zig zag cause we'd come to the Old Pisgah Church. But I didn't have no time to think about it very long cause Pap shushed me and put a hard grip on my shoulder. Then he pointed to the corner of the clearing, which was what people used to use for a parking lot. At first I didn't see nothin, but then I saw a shadow. The shadow moved, and then turned into two shadows, then three. The first shadow moved into the clearin, followed by the other two. And Pap was right. They was hog bears, a mama and two younguns, although the younguns were still bigger'n I was, and I was about twenty years old at the time and bigger'n I am now. The mama was a good two foot taller. They was walkin on two legs, not lookin around em much like bears usually do, but travelin purposeful like towards the church, like they had to be at a hog bear convention at a certain time. Well Pap raised his gun to shoot, but the barrel hit against a tree branch and made a noise. By the time he could fire, the bears had dropped down on all fours and scampered off through the brush. Pap started hollerin and runnin after em, so I did the same. Hell, I figgered that hollerin might scare off any snakes or gators that might be layin around dreaming about me, and if I ran fast enough they might not be able to catch me noways.

"Wahl, we pushed on more'n half a mile maybe, until we pushed through some cypress trees and found ourselves on the bank of the river. I was thinkin the same thing Pap was thinkin, namely that the hog bears had nowhere to go, but when we got to the edge of the river the bears was gone. It was the damndest thing though, just as we got there we saw three gators slither into the water. One was a huge monster, the other two was smaller. Pap and I took a couple of shots at em, but I guess they didn't like our way of sayin howdy and they didn't stop."

Billy Joe walked over to the curb and spat in the gutter. "Funny thing about that," he said. "The two dogs we'd kept with us turned into even better huntin dogs than they was before. But Birdshot never hunted again; when we found him the next day, he was purt near blind."

His tale told, Billy Joe flopped back onto the bench to catch his breath and waited to see its effect on his listeners. Clarence took the Prince Albert can from him and spat tobacco juice into it. Then he handed it to Hamp who followed suit. "What are you tryin to tell us, Billy Joe?" Clarence asked. "That those hog bears turned themselves into gators?"

"Or that they maybe weren't hog bears in the first place?" Carla added.

"And what did that old church have to do with anything?" asked Comer. "You know we don't believe in any of that supernatural shit. Cept, you know, for stuff that we really seen."

"Supernatural shit goin on in my cow pasture every

spring," said Clarence, looking sideways at Carla. "Soon as any mushrooms grow, naked hippies start springing up in the moonlight like magic. Sometimes," he cackled, "I don't run em off."

The other men cackled along with Clarence. Carla stood up, stretching. "Gotta run, fellas,' she said.

"Goin back out tonight?" asked Comer.

"Let's give it a rest for a day," she responded. "We'll try tomorrow."

Billy Joe Lord watched Carla pick up her cat chow and adjust her purse on her arm. Out of the corner of his eye, he spotted a sheriff's cruiser as it turned onto Front Street. He had heard something about a row between Carla and the sheriff a few days back and thought maybe if he kept her on the porch, talking, the sheriff wouldn't see her and just drive on by. "Sure you don't want to hear about the time I was married to a squaw?" he asked.

"Next time," she replied.

Billy Joe spat into the can and smiled. That was a story he'd like to hear himself.

Chapter Three

Roach, thought Carla, as the brown and beige patrol car crawled up behind her while she was waving goodbye. There were not many things Carla hated more than roaches, but as she stood on the curb and waited for the car to inch by, she wasn't sure that the sheriff might not be one of them. She glared at the tinted passenger-side window as the car came to a halt beside her. The door opened and Sheriff James Dickey stepped out, looking like a stockbroker in a Stetson hat and snakeskin boots. Despite her very real dislike of the man, Carla was always impressed by the cut of his uniform, its starched perfection, its absence of stains or wrinkles. The clothes, including the dark brown boots and off-white Stetson, seemed to be daring someone to wear them. And the sheriff wasn't a man to back down. Dickey was in his mid-forties, slim and tight, looking more like a New York businessman than a small-town sheriff. His silver-gray hair was cut short but fashionably, and his eyes flashed a steely gray. The only physical flaw Carla couldn't ignore was that his teeth were stained, uneven, and too short. His smile, which occurred way too often, revealed brownish gums, the result of constantly chewing, smoking, or simply biting on a thin, twisty cigar called a Coban Crook. Dickey adjusted his gun belt and walked around the car, stopping so close he was almost brushing against her. He scratched his head just below his hat and said, "Hey ya, Carla." He was all ten shades of suave, but all Carla could focus on were his noxious teeth and gums. "Whatcha doin?"

Carla had never used the word unctuous before, but

she was tempted now. The only thing is, she knew it would sail right over his hat. She also didn't want to get into any arguments in front of the old men, who generally thought of the home-grown sheriff as a good old boy. They also licked his boots a little too much for her liking.

"I'm just looking for someplace to walk my cats," she said.

"Har har," said the sheriff in a tone dry as dust, at odds with his smiling face. "Did you hear that, boys?" he asked the clan on the bench. But Hamp had gone inside and the other three old men just smiled.

"You say somethin, Sheriff?" asked Billy Joe Lord finally. "You know us old fellers is mostly hard of hearing."

"You fellers is mostly vagrants," said the sheriff, still smiling. He took the crook out of his mouth, looked around, replaced the crook, scratched his head under his hat, looked back at the three men on the bench, and said, "I ought to have Oskie arrest the whole bunch of ya."

The dark screen door with its faded Sun Drop Cola sign in the center banged open and Hamp Crozier walked out. "A brave man'd do his dirty work hisself," he said.

"Hell, I ain't tackling you four old buzzards," said Dickey. "But at least I got you trained." He shifted the crook in his mouth and winked at the old men. "It's this little canary here that gets flighty sometimes." Looking at Carla, he lost part of his smile and added, "Good thing her daddy ain't around to see her turn into a jailbird."

"I'm not a jailbird," Carla said, hot anger flushing across her cheeks.

"Hell, Jim," Clarence Revell said. "Carla ain't done five things wrong in her life."

"One's enough," Dickey said. He was eyeing Carla's water-shrunken cutoffs with the thoughtful expression of a man in a tomato-squeezing mood. Carla stared him off as her friends tried to balance their loyalty to old Bull's only daughter and the town's only voice of authority. They shifted looks unhappily from one to the other.

"Why don't you go catch some criminals or something," she said, "and leave me alone?"

"Hey, yah know, that's a damn good idea," he answered. "Why, I caught one just the other night out at Clem's. Hell, she looked a lot like you." This time his har hars were real, and the sheriff was shaking with them as he got back in his brown patrol car and drove off as slowly as was humanly and mechanically possible.

"You've heard of a sheephead, ain't ya?" Billy Joe asked. "Well, that man there's a fuckhead. A good ole boy, but still a fuckhead." The other three men cackled.

"You all take it easy," Carla told them. "If he comes back, just shoot him." And so saying, she crossed Front Street onto Cincinnati, a street whose name, she was sure, had been chosen by some homesick carpetbagger. Ambling along the sidewalk, she tuned out the Monday morning traffic and focused on the gulls calling and wheeling overhead in the cloudless sky with its bright shimmery blue haze so typical of late summer. The streets in town were bone-dry, and the gulls circled closer to the fish-processing plant hoping for scraps.

Not that there were many scraps to spare these dry days. The fact was, commercial fishing was getting pretty thin in the area. Shrimping was a little better, but not much. And what *did* come in was quickly shipped out, not only to restaurants and supermarkets, but to fertilizer manufacturers and cat food makers. Carla had often wondered whether the little fish-shaped pellets of dried soy that she shook into her cats' dishes every evening had anything of Tate's Hammock in them. The distilled essence of mackerel, or maybe a whiff of whitefish. Overhead, three gulls were fighting over a tidbit they'd scrounged from somewhere. As they flew closer, one of the birds tore what looked like a fish skeleton loose from the other's beak. While they squawked at each other, the skeleton began falling toward Carla. She skipped lightly aside so she wouldn't be hit, but as she did, the third gull dived bombed the skeleton and plucked it out of the air only a few feet from Carla's face. Carla shrieked and ducked, misstepping off the curb. She put her hands out for balance and the bag of cat food flew onto the asphalt and burst open. "Shit!" Carla sat down on the curb to scoop the spilled niblets back into the bag. "Fucking gulls." She hoped the gull would swallow the bones and choke. Fat chance, though. They *liked* bones!

The shrill blaaaaat! of someone leaning on a horn and stomping a brake pedal sent Carla scrambling back onto the sidewalk on her hands and knees. She looked up, panting, at the grinning face of Yancy Vause. Her eyes narrowed into slits.

"You stupid sh—" she started to shout, but Yancy aimed a smooch in her direction and scratched off across the intersection. "Drop dead!" she yelled at his smoking exhaust.

Quickly crossing the street, Carla cut through the First Baptist Church grounds, where a "God Gave Me A Vision" banner announced special services by a visiting evangelist. Her tolerance for religious ecstasy had waned with the years, and she much preferred a Loafer's Bench tale to a Sunday sermon. She kicked through the weeds and sandspurs at the back of the lot and stepped out onto Second Street, a frequently traveled, straight road which ran for another two blocks down to the seawall. It was a quiet neighborhood of small, unpretentious houses built with little imagination and much expediency right after World War II. Now it housed mostly older couples whose children had grown and moved on, and a few single people like Carla. Not many children played along its unsidewalked streets anymore.

Her house was situated on the corner of Second and Lake Avenue, with a shallow front yard and deep back yard. Of simple concrete block construction, whitewashed, with green fungus stains creeping upward from the foundation, the bungalow squatted comfortably between two immense white oaks that trailed mossy tresses over the roof. Their shade made it possible for Carla to go well into June without turning on the air conditioning. A large screened porch in back served as both greenhouse and breakfast nook. Carla knew a lot about herbs, not just the fragrant ones like sweet basil and lemon verbena, but other, more exotic plants and roots such as monkshood, pennyroyal, and woodbine, that the old folks used for medicine. The porch faced south toward the seawall another block away, and although she couldn't see the Gulf from her house, she felt its presence in the sea breeze that breathed across the neighborhood. Carla often sat on the porch listening to the gulls crying and dogs barking down by the shoreline.

She quickened her steps and crossed Second, heading toward the house. Her ten-year-old Honda Civic sat in the front yard in a space worn bare of grass and partially filled in with gravel and oyster shells. For the third time this month the car hadn't started, and she'd been forced to walk all the way down to the dock and back. What she really needed was a pickup. A Ford, maybe. Something big enough to carry fishing supplies and—Carla stopped short in the middle of the road. Someone had broken into her car. The door on the driver's side was open and a set of spindly legs was folded over the steering wheel.

She wasn't frightened, just cautious, and stepped quickly behind her neighbor's box hedge. The Honda contained nothing of any value; in fact it reeked with shrimp slime and had a quarter of an inch of mud on the floorboards where the mats used to be. She looked over the hedge, then moved cautiously to the edge of her lawn, trying to see inside the car. It couldn't be Yancy, or his own car would be nearby. Besides, the legs were much too thin and dark. The brown legs ended in filthy sneakers that pushed against the windshield. She could also make out the rest of a female figure scrunched uncomfortably in the driver's seat, her gangly arms crossed over her face. As Carla crept closer, her shoes made a scuffling sound on the driveway gravel that brought a stirring from the figure in the car. The arms and legs languidly uncoiled to reveal a skinny tatterdemalion in cutoffs and a torn T-shirt with No Nukes Y'All silkscreened on the front. Loose corn rows crowned the head.

Pixie. She should have known.

A black girl in her early teens twisted herself up out of the driver's seat, yawned, and pushed the door shut. Carla had known Pixie Blue ever since Pixie was born. Their meetings were sporadic but frequent, and Pixie was one of the few people in town Carla never minded seeing. At fourteen, Pixie was already several inches taller than Carla. Thin and springy, like a sapling. But Pixie was both a mimic and a changeling, and Carla never knew in what form she would appear. Today must be ragamuffin day. "What's up, Pix?" she asked.

"Just nappin. You been out on the boat?"

"How did you know? Do I smell?"

"A little." Pixie paused. "Well, more than a little."

"I'm not having a good day," said Carla. "Come on in and tell me why you're sleeping in my car instead of your own bed."

Pixie followed Carla across the lawn. "I'm here cuz Aunt Sookie say she wants to see you."

Carla looked at Pixie with interest. "Funny, I thought about Sookie today," she said. She unlocked the front door and motioned Pixie inside. Cats meowed as she placed the damaged cat food bag on the dinette table and headed for the kitchen. Pixie flopped down on the couch and splayed out her long legs.

"What does she want, do you know?"

Pixie was in the middle of opening a package of Carefree Sugarless Gum.

"She's not sick, is she?" Carla asked, concerned.

Pixie laughed, showing a mouthful of teeth Carla envied. "You know Auntie don't never be sick."

"Sure," said Carla. "Tell her to come on over. You'll have to give her directions, though. I don't think—"

Pixie's smile faded, a look of concern taking its place. "Naw, Carla," she broke in. "She want *you* to come see *her*." Pixie folded two sticks of gum into her mouth. "But I be worried."

"Worried about what?" Carla asked, "and where does

she want me to meet her?" She had known Aunt Sookie all her life but had never been to her house. She didn't even know where it was except through the stories of the old men— somewhere inside a heavily overgrown swampland some ten miles west of town.

"That's just it. She wanted you to come to the church."

"What church?"

"Aunt Sookie church."

"The Old Pisgah?"

"Umm hmm."

"Why would she go there? It's been closed for years."

Pixie shrugged. "She go there sometimes for grave dirt. But she probly just making it easier for you to find her. But that's not what—"

"Okay, I suppose," Carla said, although she hadn't been near the old church in over fifteen years. "When?"

"I been tryin to tell you! She wanted to see you last night."

"Last night?"

"She told me to get you there by six sharp."

"But how could you? I was on the boat."

"I be knowin that now. But when I went to her house to tell her, she was gone."

"And you're worried about her?"

"She be old. And she be actin kind of sneaky."

"Sneaky?" Carla asked. "Like how?"

"Like maybe a cat who's got a mouse hid somewhere and don't want the other cats to know."

"When did you see her last?"

"I donno. Maybe about four yesterday afternoon. I got back to her house about eight and she wasn't there. I waited there all night."

"You didn't go back to your own house?"

"Naw. You know, Daddy be actin kind of crazy. Got him a new suit; says we movin to Tallahassee. Had some whisky, too, so I snuck out."

"Did you go to the church to look for her?" Carla

asked.

"Naw, I be scared. I wanted to wait for you."

"All right. Let me feed the cats and take a quick shower and I'll go look for her." In the kitchen her three cats roiled around her ankles, yowling as if from utter starvation and neglect. She dumped some loose crunchies into an empty yellow plastic bowl on the floor by the refrigerator, then realized that she had forgotten to get milk.

"That'll have to do, boys. Milk when I get back." She tried to ignore the cats because she knew they'd be looking at her in a way she didn't want to be looked at. Fang meowed. "Life's tough, cats," she responded, and hurried out of the kitchen and into the bathroom. Dropping her clothes in a trail across the floor, she stepped into the tub and luxuriated in the feel of warm, *clean* water. She soaped quickly, letting the Water Pik Shower Massager spray alternating bursts of water through her hair. But Aunt Sookie's unusual request gave her a feeling of urgency and she reluctantly turned off the taps.

She didn't expect Sookie to still *be* at the old church— not after eighteen hours or so—but the old lady had done stranger things. And if she wasn't there, maybe she had left Carla a message. As she threw on a light white blouse and stepped into a clean pair of jeans, Carla realized that, bad day or not, she was looking forward to seeing the old woman again. She remembered, for a brief moment, being at the Old Pisgah with Sookie in younger, happier times. Sadly, those days were gone, and this was now. Walking into the living room carrying a pair of old running shoes, she was surprised to see Pixie sitting in a lotus position on the couch, totally immersed in *Far Tortuga*.

Carla sat down and slipped the shoes on over a pair of detergent-grayed socks. "Ready, Pixie?"

Pixie looked up from the book. "Do folk in the Tortugas really talk like this?"

"For shore de *do*, mon," Carla said. "Now let's go."

Carla patted her jeans for cigarettes, grabbed her keys, and went out the door after Pixie. That's when she remembered that her car was a piece of shit. Well, at least if it didn't start she wouldn't have to make the long drive out to Blanchard's Bluff.

"You can just let me out by my street," Pixie said, jackknifing her legs into the narrow passenger seat.

"I thought you wanted to go to the church with me," Carla said.

"Well, um. You know. Daddy might be needin me for something."

So the girl was still scared. Carla didn't blame her, really. Aunt Sookie had always been too steeped in superstition for anyone to be comfortable around her. It was no wonder Pixie's father wanted to take her away to the capital.

"Yeh," Carla said, putting her key in the ignition. "I saw him this morning at Hamp's, and he was acting a little strange."

"He drunk?" Pixie asked.

"I don't know. I don't think so."

Carla went through her car-starting ritual. Turn the key to "on," wait for the automatic choke to engage, put the gearshift in neutral, pump the accelerator at least three times, turn the key to ignition, and pray. Amazingly, the engine responded on the first try.

"Why didn't you do that yesterday?" she growled, backing out into the street.

"You oughta get a new car," said Pixie. "Old cars be like old people—most of the time they just be wantin to sit around and smoke."

"Damn straight," agreed Carla. Sell the boat and buy that pickup. Some days it was tempting. Or sell the house and sail down to the Keys or the Bahamas.

They headed west down Cincinnati, toward the outskirts of town. Once the Honda was underway, its zippy little aluminum engine easily cruised at seventy-five. Carla eased her foot back off the pedal as groves of pecan trees dotted by drab, weathered homesteads flew by. Cincinnati turned into State Road 165 and soon ran through a corridor of tall oaks, beeches, and magnolias.

"Are you sure you don't know what Sookie wants to see me about?"

"Naw. I think she was gonna tell me later, though." Pixie stared out the window and chewed gum at the passing trees. "Only thing she *did* tell me was that you got taken down by the Man the other night."

"Shit, does *everybody* know?" Carla asked.

"She was out prowlin the other night down around Clem's Clams. Said she saw Dandy Jim cart you away and leave that fancy man of yours standing around lookin like an ape."

"He's not my fancy man."

"No?" Pixie asked. "And I spose I ain't seen his car parked outside your house at night?"

Carla almost choked. "You've been *spying* on me?"

"Naw, just visitin, but didn't want to interrupt."

"Nothing to interrupt," Carla lied. At least, there would be nothing to interrupt in the future. "Did Aunt Sookie tell you what happened at Clem's?"

"She be too far away to hear anything."

"She was lucky, then," began Carla. "I mean, Yancy's just a little too freaky for me." The sun was bright overhead and felt good on her bandaged arm. She squinted as light periodically splashed through the branches of the trees in blinding stabs that left red and green spots floating in front of her eyes.

"You hang out around my daddy and Aunt Sookie for fourteen years and then tell me what freaky is," said Pixie.

"No arguments there," she answered.

"What'd Yancy do?"

Carla took a deep breath. "He came over Saturday night and he was already a little drunk. That's all right, you know, because sometimes he's funny when he's a little high. We drove out to Clem's and had a pretty good meal and a couple bottles of wine. The second bottle was a mistake, because he started telling me secrets about how it was in

Vietnam."

"I thought you liked history stuff," Pixie said.

"I do. In fact, I'd tried to get him to tell me about Vietnam before but he always clammed up. What happened on Saturday, though, is that he started assuming that everybody in the place wanted to know about it, too. I mean, there are a few things people in a restaurant don't want to hear."

"Bout blood and stuff?" Pixie asked.

"Right, about blood and stuff. But when some woman tried to shush him he pulled a pistol out of his jacket and put it down in the middle of his plate. Broke the plate into sixteen pieces. One guy came over and told him to cool it, but Yancy really didn't feel like being his cool self right then, so he invited the guy outside."

Carla swerved to avoid a dead possum, then smoothed the car back into her lane.

"So what happened?" Pixie asked, popping gum on her back teeth. "Auntie ain't say nothing bout nobody getting shot."

"Luckily, nobody did," Carla continued, "I was trying to get us out of there as fast as I could, so I threw a twenty on the table and asked the other guy, who was about six ten and two fifty, to let me handle it. I did manage to get Yance to the car, but then he started shouting and even aimed a couple of shots at a streetlight about a block away. He hit the damn thing, too. I don't know what would have happened if the sheriff hadn't come up just then. The flashing lights must have sobered Yancy up because he got real polite real quick. He got in his car and started it. I got in too, and hoped that would be the end of it, but Sheriff Dickey came over, reached in, and turned off the ignition. He made Yancy get out and, you know, assume the position. But when he patted him down, he didn't find anything. So then Dickey orders *me* out of the car too and makes *me* assume the position, and let me tell you, I've been to bed with guys that didn't feel me up as much."

Carla heard a shriek and looked over to see Pixie

shake-laughing so hard she'd dropped her gum onto her lap. Carla allowed herself half a smile.

"He finally stopped and reached in the car for my purse, and what do you think he found inside?"

"Drugs?"

"No, silly. The gun. Yancy must have put it there when he saw the police car lights flashing."

"You told him it wasn't yours?"

"Of course. All the rubberneckers in the restaurant backed me up, but it was me he took down to the station for carrying a concealed weapon."

"You went to jail?" Pixie asked, her eyes wide.

"*To* jail, but I didn't have to go *in* the jail. I told Yancy to call Ronnie Wyche—he used to be Mama's lawyer—and he met me at the police station. If he hadn't been there I don't know what would've happened."

"They fingerprint you?" asked Pixie.

"Right. The works. But at least I didn't have to go into a cell. Ronnie Wyche paid my bail. I don't know when I'll be able to pay him back."

"You know," said Pixie. "I think *you* the freaky one. You probly even worse than me."

"Why?" Carla laughed.

"You go out with crazies," Pixie replied.

"Well, *somebody's* got to do it," Carla said. As she drove, Carla remembered another "freaky" thing that had happened. After the lawyer had posted bail for her, she tapped a cigarette out of her pack that turned out to be a joint. Yancy must have stashed that, too. But why? Pixie was right; she went out with idiots. No matter how careful she tried to be, it seemed like she always—

"Whoops," said Pixie. "Here comes the street. Down there on the left across from Blanchard's." She indicated a dirt road marked by a tin sign peppered with buckshot holes. Across the highway was a sign with faded red and blue lettering:

BLANCHARD'S PIT STOP
Bait—Tackle—Oyster Bar

"I remember," answered Carla, easing the Honda across the highway and onto the sandy margin of the intersection.

"Better watch it," said Pixie. "The city don't fix our roads."

"Don't worry,' said Carla. "I've dated guys with faces worse than this."

Pixie made numerous high-pitched noises, but this time held her gum in her mouth. "You a mad woman," she said.

When Carla had driven another quarter mile at a top speed of about twenty miles per hour, they came to another dirt road.

"I'll get off here," said Pixie.

"You sure you don't want to go with me?" Carla asked, a little hopeful for some company. She couldn't blame Pixie for being nervous. She had never liked to drive around these back roads by herself, and she especially didn't like the possibility of encountering anyone other than Sookie at the Old Pisgah Church.

"Nope. I'll just, you know, go on home for a while."

Carla stopped the car and Pixie got out. "You be all right," the girl added, shutting the door and backing away. "Ain't nobody used that church for years cept Aunt Sookie." Carla watched her for a moment as the girl hurried down to a smaller, one-lane dirt road leading off into the trees. Then, letting her breath out with the clutch, she headed forward again in search of the Old Pisgah, which she knew was somewhere further down the moss-draped canopy road.

The ruts slowed her down to a crawl while mosquitoes flew in her window as if for lunch at a drive-in. Carla smacked her neck and shoulders as she guided the car carefully over ridges and around potholes. The heat was bringing out a new layer of perspiration on her recently washed skin, and her cotton shirt clung damply to her torso. At least Yancy hadn't minded the smells. They even turned him on. Anyway, screw Yancy. She should never have bothered with him in the first place; shouldn't have wasted her time with *any* of the guys she had dated.

She fumbled around for the fan switch to get some air stirring, taking her eyes off the road for a few jolty seconds. If she ever got her new pickup it would have a working air conditioner and a good one. The car lurched down suddenly, then back up like a slingshot propelled and released—that crater of a pothole had looked just like a shadow across the road. The sunlight filtered though the increasingly thick canopy of trees, dappling the road's dusty surface and tricking her eyes. Better pay better attention, she decided. She began to scan the sides of the roadway for the church, impatient to get there, see if she could find Sookie, then get back home to her cats.

Freaky was not the word for Aunt Sookie. Carla assumed the woman must be in her eighties by now, which only added to her mystique. Sookie usually wore a dark, drag-in-the-dust dress of light muslin with multicolored scarves set in different places around her neck, arms, and forehead. She often wore cloves of garlic around her neck as well, along with a leather bag containing some secret mixture or other to ward off evil. What kind of evil, Carla never knew, because, she supposed, the charm kept it away. Aunt Sookie had been her nanny and helped Carla's mother bring her up, despite the fact that her daddy had not liked the old black woman. But when Carla's mother died in an influenza epidemic, Aunt Sookie had been let go. Losing them both had been the greatest blow Carla had ever suffered, but through the years, Sookie had kept in touch by one means or another, without Bull Clements knowing. Carla was accustomed to her whims and secrecies, but why did the old witchy woman want to meet her at an abandoned church of all places? Most people would have called, but of course Sookie was not like most people. For one thing, she was possibly the only person in Blanchard's Bluff who didn't have a phone. For another, she could never resist putting a touch of secrecy or mystery into whatever she did. But deep in Carla's mind was the thought that maybe Sookie had a good reason for seeing her alone. Maybe Sookie was in some kind of trouble.

Carla blew a mosquito away from her face, her thoughts drifting back to Yancy Vause and more ominous impressions involving the county courthouse and Sheriff James Dickey. She swallowed dryly and wiped sweating palms on her thighs as she remembered Dickey's face the night she had been arrested. Those piercing gray eyes, that's what she remembered most—those eyes and his obsequious smile that revealed Coban Crook-stained teeth. She blew at another mosquito, as if to shoo away the unwanted image.

A stiff breeze was rising, rummaging through the branches overhead and stirring the heat with its attendant cloud of mosquitoes. Then a whirlwind of leaves and dust went scudding across the hood of her car and Carla was snapped out of her daydream. There was the church, right alongside her car; in another moment, she would have driven past it. She hit the brake pedal, sending the car to a scrunching halt just past the weathered clapboard church. It sat forlornly on its plot of sand and palmettos, nearly swallowed by the encroaching woods. The sun faded momentarily as the wind picked up and clouds appeared over the semi-clearing in dark pillows heavy with rain. She sat in front of the church for a while, listening to branches creaking in the wind and distant thunder, counterpointed by the quiet interior pinging of the Honda's engine as it cooled. She didn't really want to go into the dilapidated old building, not because she was scared but because it held such conflicting memories for her. The last time she had been here it was a happy, exciting time for her. She'd been just a kid, maybe six or so, but she remembered quite well Aunt Sookie dressing her up all in white and taking her to the service one Sunday morning. On that day, the weeds were a closely cropped lawn and the faint path she saw now was a cobbled walkway. The stained-glass windows were so clean they shone like colored lights, and the old boards were freshly painted. The bell rang out sharply from the bell tower under the steeple in front. There were dozens of people dressed in light colors carrying bibles and handkerchiefs, for it was a hot morning. Hers had been the only white face in the crowd, but no one seemed to mind. In fact, it was almost as if Aunt Sookie were showing her off. She'd been fascinated by the sound of the preacher's voice as he delivered the sermon with more passion and fire than she'd ever experienced before, and the singing that echoed from the high rafters made her want to join in, even if she didn't know any of the words. It was spontaneous, joyous singing, and was like nothing she had ever heard before or since. They had even let her ring the bell at the end of the service.

When Carla breathlessly told her father about her trip, he yelled at Aunt Sookie and forbade Carla to ever go there, or anywhere, with the old woman again. Sitting in the car watching the clouds building overhead, Carla realized that was the point, twenty years ago, at which she and Sookie had begun to lose their devotion to each other.

What the hell, she decided. She switched on the ignition key long enough to punch in the dash lighter. When it popped back out, its rays seemed to replace the fading light, as if the entire sun had retreated into that glowing red circle. What the hell indeed—she was starting to spook herself. Armed with a cigarette, she rolled up the windows and got out. The temperature was dropping quickly and Carla checked the sky. Then, a large raindrop hit the roof of the car with a flat splat. Frowning, Carla walked around the front of the car toward the church, cigarette in one hand and car keys in the other. Two rotting plank steps led up to a wooden threshold. The heavy wooden door on its rusted hinges stood wide open. The interior of the church was dark.

"Aunt Sookie," she called. Her voice loudly violated the silence. At that moment, the storm descended in a torrent, drenching Carla and dousing her Winston. She gasped and fled up the crumbling steps and into the shelter of the church. To be caught in two gullywashers in one day was more than her limited patience could stand. Damn the old woman anyway.

She shook out her hair and let her eyes get accustomed to the dark. "Aunt Sookie? Are you here?"

Although still mid-afternoon, the cobweb-feathered and grime-encrusted church windows admitted practically no light. Aromas of rotting wood, mildew, and rat droppings made her sneeze. On cue, a dozen wings erupted from the rafters in a fluttering, flapping deluge. Holy shit, real bats, she thought, scrambling out of their way and nearly tripping over a pew in the process. The blood pulsed in her temples. The dislodged bats swarmed the vaulted ceiling and some managed to duck through a gap in the wall and into the belfry. Carla sat down on the dusty pew, placing her keys beside her and wondering what to do next.

Irritated, she got up and walked back to the entrance. Out in the churchyard, rain pummeled the car and washed down the road. A small estuary was forming in its ruts and crevices, the water curling and eddying around tree roots reaching out into the sandy soil. The storm showed no sign of letting up, so she turned back into the church to wait it out. Craving another cigarette, Carla walked between the rows of decaying pews and benches, some toppled into each other like dominoes. Her footsteps echoed with muffled thumps along the dusty tongue-in-groove flooring. Years of drying had split the seams in places, and she could see faint patches of outside light coming from beneath the church. She walked all the way down to the shallow dais where the Reverend Isaiah Brownlow had once expounded from his pulpit and where the maroon-robed choir had crowded its benches. The upright piano was long gone, as were the benches and pulpit. Carla sat down on the edge of the platform, looking back at the doorway, a bright rectangle in the encircling gloom. She could appreciate the high-ceilinged roominess of the building and imagined it even earlier than she had seen it last—filled a century ago with ex-slaves and their descendants, the walls reverberating with the responses of the congregation that supported the rising and falling cadence of the preaching—probably the exact swelling and humming that Carla had heard eighty years later. But two world wars and the thing called progress had moved the black community inward toward the town. The church was a discarded old shell now.

Time to go. If Sookie had left a message, she had seen no sign of it. Thunder boomed loudly, followed instantly by the white flash of cosmic electricity. Jesus, she thought, she'd need to be a fish to get home in this. If the puddles got too deep her silly toy car would drown out. Better try now, though, before things got worse.

She walked quickly down the aisle between the cockeyed pews and hesitated a moment on the threshold. Here we go again, she thought. Holding her breath, she made a mad dash through the sheets of rain and wrenched the car door open. Dropping into the driver's seat, she hauled the door shut and wiped rivulets of water from her eyebrows. Her hair was plastered to her neck and face like seaweed. She wiped it out of the way and reached into her shirt pocket for the keys, then patted the empty pocket in disbelief. This was really enough. Where were the fucking keys? A controlled search of the car and her person disclosed nothing. She must have left them in the church. Well, nothing for it but to go back and find them.

Resigned, Carla got out of the car again, not bothering to run, but instead stomping through puddles inches deep. Why should she run when it was so much fun to be cold and wet? She climbed the steps, one of which promptly gave way, sending her leg down through the wood and sprawling her across the threshold. She managed to catch herself enough to keep her leg from breaking, but she had taken the brunt of her fall on her bandaged arm. Gingerly she raised herself and pulled her leg up through the step. Her shoe had come off and there was a jagged scratch down her calf—her only good feature, she thought wryly, marred by the storm. Lying across the threshold, Carla reached down through the hole for her shoe, certain she would grab onto a snake instead. No, the shoe was there, and now for the keys. She'd give Aunt Sookie shit for this the next time she saw her.

She stood dripping in the doorway, trying to mentally retrace her steps. First, she'd come in and shaken the rain out of her hair. Then the bats came, and…then what? Had she put them in her pocket? She couldn't remember. No, she had sat down on one of the pews. Oh, hell, yes. She had laid the keys beside her on the seat.

Carla hurried to the pew that was dusted clean by her jeans, and there they were: silver car key, red house key, brass trunk key. Grabbing them up, she turned to leave, when her foot came in contact with something on the wooden floor; something that clattered. Carla bent down and could see just enough to tell that the object was some kind of toy instead of a dead rat or beetle. She reached down and her fingers touched what felt like a smooth stone. She closed her fist around it and found that it was fastened to an old piece of twine. In fact, there seemed to be several stones beaded to the string, some smooth and some rough. She lifted it and peered closely in the gloom. At that moment a flash of lightning made Carla scream for one of the first times in her life, for she could see the object closely now. It was a necklace of some sort, a dozen stones the size of robins' eggs carved with bizarre African faces—eyes bulging and teeth shining. With the lightning came a crashing gust of wind that blew in through the belfry, sending its door flying open against the far wall.

Panting, Carla tried to think. Her heart was pounding, but she told herself she had nothing to fear. The necklace was probably Sookie's; she had dropped it by mistake. The faces even seemed familiar, somehow, as if she had seen the necklace before. Yet the only necklace Sookie ever wore consisted of an old brown bag of herbs on a leather strap. Maybe Carla had seen the faces in a painting, or maybe Hamp had something like it in his glass case of oddities. Holding the amulet in one hand, her keys in the other, she walked toward the door again, passing near the small room at the base of the bell tower. She remembered the one time she had been inside, the clarity of the bell, the firmness of the rope she had pulled with such effort, hauling on it two decades ago. She stopped at the door and looked in, but it was too dark to see anything. She put one foot in but there was some kind of debris on the floor and she was afraid she would trip if she went in any further. She leaned forward and felt around for where she imagined the bell rope should be. She was peering hard into the darkness when a laser shot of lightning revealed not only the rope, but the obstruction at her feet, a sight that nailed Carla fast to the wooden floor, and caused her to drop the necklace in the doorway. It was Aunt Sookie, looking like an old rag doll that someone had tossed into a corner, her neck angled sharply to one side and her lips drawn back over her teeth in the grin of death.

Chapter Four

The patrol car hugged the highway curves, its powerful engine sucking gas with every punch of the pedal. It was cruising over the speed limit, but High Sheriff James Beauregard Dickey had little fear of being stopped. His tan Impala owned the highways.

He pressed the accelerator into a sharp turn on the two-lane county road heading toward Blanchard's Bluff, his mind in overdrive. There weren't many homicides in Wakulla County and even this one, from the sound of it, probably wasn't worth his time. He would have sent Oskie, except for one thing: it had been called in by the Miss High and Mighty Clements herself. Dickey had nearly laughed out loud when he'd heard her voice on the phone in the sheriff's office. Fear, anger, grief...all those emotions spilling out of the receiver into his ear. Dickey licked his lips. He hadn't understand half of what she was babbling, but he had finally understood that the old witch, Sookie Darbyville, had been murdered out in the swamp somewhere.

"Where are you now?" he asked

"I'm at Johnny's. Johnny Blanchard's."

"The Pit Stop?"

"Yeh."

"I'll be there as soon as I can."

Dickey smiled as he piloted the cruiser around the twists and turns of the rural highway, his left hand on the wheel and his right resting on a box of evidence he'd taken possession of during the recent arrest of a local high-school teacher. Like his name, Sheriff Dickey was a man divided—

his origins were as small-town plain as his first name, but he enjoyed the grandiose weight and feel of the middle name he'd inherited from his Baton Rouge grandfather; it was a name deemed pretentious by some, but he embraced it. He'd graduated from high school, the same one where the careless schoolteacher had been busted a few weeks ago, with a conflicted desire to leave his home town of Tate's Hammock for the big city—New Orleans, he'd imagined—or stay where he was known and make a name for himself in local law enforcement. He'd chosen the latter, mostly because the image of himself—in a crisp uniform complete with a leather gun belt rugged enough to hold a .45 automatic—was irresistible.

Dickey's fingers caressed the cover of the box in the passenger seat. He'd sworn to uphold the law and protect the innocent and all that, but as a man of the world, he had certain vices he felt entitled to enjoy, one of which was savoring evidence of this type. His crotch twitched at the thought of Mistress Mindy, whose whip-wielding, leather-clad body appeared in most of the 8x10 color glossies in the box. Her autograph, scrawled in big, loopy letters, appeared on one of them. Her client, wearing only a hood and a stiff pecker, writhed beneath her stiletto-heeled boot. Tiny trails of blood decorated the man's chest, as the Mistress licked what Dickey assumed was that same blood off her whip and fingertips.

Dickey wouldn't have minded participating in sexual bloodsports himself, but a little harmless voyeurism was as far as he'd pursued that itching desire, unlike the careless schoolteacher. As far as he was concerned, the man could get whipped by a dozen women; it was fine by him. But as an employee of the county educational system, for the man to sneak pictures like this into the school and share them with a couple of his "pets" after class—one of whom ratted on him— Dickey had busted his ass good, and it was an ass-whipping that the schoolteacher definitely had *not* enjoyed. His crotch gave another twitch, threatening a growing enthusiasm for Mistress Mindy, but he willed it away. Wouldn't do to go investigate a homicide with a hard-on.

The schoolteacher claimed no personal knowledge of Mistress Mindy or her place of employment, the Devil's Den, a lounge/strip club in a larger town up the highway, but evidence to the contrary indicated he was a frequent flyer. Dickey looked forward to studying the box of evidence at his leisure, with the excuse that he intended to infiltrate the club, pose as a client, and bust the lot of them. He'd enjoy that—dominating the dominatrix—even more than the sight of her enormous cleavage and wasp waist. Power was, and always had been, his drug of choice.

Dickey eased off the accelerator and watched the speedometer drop to 70. He knew all about power and how you acquired it. You watched people, you listened, you got things on them. He was good at reading people; he'd been doing it, watching body language and paying attention to shifts in pitch or tone of voice, for the past thirty-odd years. His turd of a brother, his parents, his wife, his own kid... he'd watched them all, not to mention the parade of felons, vagrants, hookers, lowlifes, highrollers, Vietnam vets, and shrimp-boat captains that came with his job. Give him a couple of minutes one-on-one, and he had them nailed.

So, in a decision that made his parents and fiancée happy, he'd decided to stay in the Tate's Hammock area where he'd grown up. True, it was a rural county with few towns large enough to have their own municipal police force, but that had made it more likely that he would eventually work his way to the top. It might not be the biggest pond around, but in this county of minnows and mullets, he was the great white shark.

A Jeep Cherokee came around a curve too fast, cutting the corner and nearly running the Impala off the road. Dickey was on his CB radio in seconds.

"Oskie! Get somebody out to the intersection of Highway 267 and Blanchard's Bluff Road ASAP! Bastard in a black Jeep Cherokee, tan top, university sticker on the back, nearly ran me off the road! Vehicle's headed south on State

Road 165—get a squad car out there now and intercept him."
Ordinarily, he would have wheeled the patrol car around and
given pursuit, lights flashing and siren blaring, but not today.
He had a date with Ms. Carla Clements, and that trumped
speeders.

"When you stop him, I want that driver out of the
car and searched for drugs, booze, anything you can find—I
want to see his ass in a jail cell when I get back! Over and
out." That was power.

Dickey settled back against the padded seat and
pressed the gas pedal. A bullet-riddled sign stating that
Blanchard's Bluff was a mere four miles up the road flew by
on his right. His thoughts returned to Mistress Mindy, who
looked somewhat like a lady friend Bull had once introduced
him to, somebody the senator's uppity second wife and ill-
tempered daughter wouldn't like to meet. Dickey stuck an
unlit Coban Crook between his teeth. He was going to miss
old Bull. There was a man who understood power. Once he'd
made it all the way to the state legislature—with no small help
from Dickey—good ole boys rallied round him like fruit flies
to a rotten persimmon. Too bad he had to go and die under
the surgeon's knife like that. When he had read the newspaper
headline: "Prominent Lawmaker Dies during Heart Bypass,"
Dickey had felt both surprise and disappointment. Bull had
still owed him a favor or two.

Dickey thought of the bereaved. He'd suggested to the
new widow that she might want to look into a malpractice
suit…wear a black veil to the hearing and it was a slam
dunk. He'd also offered to recommend a lawyer, if she felt
so inclined. He'd offered to help her in other ways as well
and felt certain she wasn't as offended as she appeared to be.
In spite of those tears of shock and grief wiped away with
a gardenia-scented handkerchief, she'd neglected to tell him
no.

Approaching another bend in the road, Dickey
slowed the cruiser and turned into the gravel driveway to
Blanchard's Pit Stop, a combination garage, oyster bar, pool

hall, and gas station seated on a quarter acre of land scraped bare of all vegetation—a county landmark and hangout for as long as he could remember. Built as a feed store and wayside horse watering stop by the Blanchard family several generations ago, its present incarnation served the modern population who rode the steel horse instead of the flesh and blood variety, and gave Dickey and Deputy Sheriff Holt occasional business on weekends when the pool hall got too rowdy even for locals.

And there in the parking lot was the ugly gray Honda that belonged to his business for the afternoon. He pulled the patrol car up beside it and got out. Dickey raked the Honda with his eyes, swiftly noting the ghost of dirty shoeprints on the dash; he sniffed and took in the scent of the docks drifting up from the worn upholstery, mixed with the slightly burned smell of leaking oil. Settling his sheriff's hat at a comfortable angle, he pushed open the screened door to the oyster bar and stepped inside, his eyes taking a moment to adjust to the dim interior. Three ceiling fans kept the tepid air swirling around the cavernous room that held a counter with stools and two floor-to-ceiling refrigerated cases stocked with milk, soda, bottled water, half a dozen brands of beer, frozen TV dinners, and rainbow-colored popsicles. Through an open doorway beyond the counter was another room just as large, stabling three pool tables, currently unoccupied.

He spotted her on the farthest stool, hunched over, elbows on the counter, feet wrapped around the stool shaft, head down. Abject misery if he'd ever seen it. He wouldn't know if this was an act for his benefit until he got a good look at her face—then he'd see what this was all about.

"Hey Carla, he's here!" Johnny Blanchard's voice came from the poolroom doorway. "Glad to see you, sir… she's been in a right state, ever since she got here."

"And how long ago was that?" Dickey looked Johnny Blanchard over. Wormy little guy, dough-faced and solicitous, older looking than Carla, although he knew they were close to the same age. With his thinning straw hair, blue work shirt with oily stripes across the sleeve where he wiped dipsticks when he was in a hurry, and deep blue eyes, Johnny Blanchard was the spitting image of his pa, a man Dickey remembered fondly for his willingness to stock Coban Crooks on the rack of cigarette cartons and tins of snuff. Johnny blinked under the sheriff's scrutiny.

"Bout thirty minutes ago. Hell, I don't mind her cryin and yellin, but she tore three pages out of my phone book lookin for the sheriff's department. What the hell happened out there?" Johnny looked at Carla, and the sheriff did likewise.

"Well, Miz Clements, what's your story?" He came up behind her, close enough to invade her space and make her twitch. He could sense the tension across her shoulder blades by the way a vein pulsed in her bare neck. She'd pulled her long hair up and pinned it on top of her head, which forced Dickey to admire the curve of her shoulders.

Carla put down the Styrofoam cup of a foul-smelling drek Dickey assumed was Johnny's attempt at brewing coffee. He studied her profile as she looked over her shoulder. "It took you long enough." Her tough-girl attempt almost made Dickey laugh out loud, but he kept his cool.

"And I can just leave again unless you tell me what you dragged me out here for," he said evenly, waiting for her response. He saw the vein pulse and the shoulders hunch tighter. "Somebody murdered Aunt Sookie," she said, turning the stool around to face them.

Johnny's blue eyes registered shock. "Hell," he said.

"Up at the old church," she went on, cutting her eyes toward Dickey.

He took the Crook out of his mouth. "Now who would want to do such a thing?"

"I have no idea," she said. "But I want to find out."

"Hell," said Johnny. "To a lotta folks she was a saint, but the rest were scared silly of her. He shrugged, apparently not sure which of his two visitors he should please. Dickey readjusted the .45 at his hip and gave him a reassuring smile, then turned to Carla.

"That's true," Dickey agreed. "I heard plenty about some of the tricks that old woman pulled on people. Givin people hives or making em hear voices."

"I don't believe any of those stories," Carla said, "and we're wasting time."

"So where's the body?" Dickey shifted his weight. He was starting to enjoy this and leaned in closer. Crowd the bitch, he thought. See if she squirms. He cared little about the murder of some ancient black woman nobody liked anyway, but the chance to intimidate old Bull's spitfire daughter was a tasty thing. The fact that she'd called him out there because she needed his help made it doubly so.

"The Old Pisgah church—I'll show you."

Dickey stepped aside. "After you," he said, gesturing toward the door.

She slipped off the stool and quick as a cat sidled around him. He hitched up his belt, stuck the Crook back between his teeth, adjusted his hat, nodded to Johnny, and followed her okay butt out into the parking lot. She turned toward Johnny.

"We'll go in the sheriff's car. Keep a watch on this piece of junk and don't let anybody steal it while we're gone," she said, rolling up the windows and locking the door to her car. "We won't be long."

"Sure, Carla." Johnny stood with the screen door held open, scratching his sandy thatch. Head lice, thought Dickey. "I hope you catch whoever did it," he added.

Watching Carla stuff her keys into her pants pocket, the High Sheriff wondered why she'd decided to ride with him instead of following in her own car out to the church, knowing that he wasn't her favorite person in the world right now. He thought about that for a minute, watching her, and then he began to smile. By leaving her car here, he'd have to bring her back. That way, Johnny would know how long she'd been away in Dickey's company and he'd have to return her unmolested. Clever, like her daddy.

He walked around to the passenger side of the patrol car and opened the door. "You get to ride in the front seat, this time, Miz Clements." The look she gave him was worth the entire trip out there—fury smoldered in her green cat's eyes. But there was something else there, too, something below the surface. He stopped for a moment and gave her a leisurely look up and down. She was a tidy little package, but mean as a snake. No wonder she was still unmarried.

He went around to the driver's side and got in, then looked at the passenger seat with smothered amusement.

"You need to move this crap," Carla said, looking at the box of evidence.

"No problem. Just hold it on your lap till we get where we're going."

Carla gave him another one of those looks, but got in and balanced the box on her knees, oblivious of its contents. Dickey ran his tongue over his lips; this was better than he could have hoped for. He breathed in her scent—bath soap (nothing fancy), clean hair smell, and a pungent sweat tang he recognized immediately. People sweated like that from fear.

Carla sneezed and looked at him. "What's that smell?" she said, wrinkling her nose.

"You mean my aftershave?" he asked.

"I guess you're not an Old Spice man."

Dickey cranked the Impala and drove away from Blanchard's Pit Stop, headed east on the county road. "Drakkar Noir," he said. "Black Dragon, you like it?"

Carla sneezed again. "Not overly," she said, rolling down her window.

Dickey's eyes narrowed. "I reckon you can't appreciate a first-class cologne because you prefer the stink of unwashed used-car salesmen." The glare she shot him could have killed puppies.

"You make it real hard to be sociable," he said, watching her hands cradling the box of Mistress Mindy and her clients.

"This isn't a date!" She turned her face away from him and stared out at the passing trees and pastures. "And you need to turn right here on this dirt road."

Dickey settled back in his seat, clamped the Coban firmly between his teeth, and turned where she indicted. It was a dirt road so small and unused that he wasn't sure he had ever seen it before, muddy and so full of ruts that the box of evidence bounced up and down on Carla's lap.

"Better not go any faster unless you want to break an axle."

Another reason to take his car and not hers. He was about to respond when Oskie's voice crackled over the CB radio.

"Chief? Got yer man in the Jeep."

"Dickey here. Good work."

"Busted him for speeding and carrying an unpermitted firearm, which we confiscated."

"Impound the vehicle while you're at it. I'm headed out to the church with our favorite jailbird. If there's anything to see, I'll call you back. Over and out."

He could tell from Carla's clenched fists that she was flaming mad, but she held her tongue and continued to stare out the window.

He had a thought. "You seen any of the old gang?" he asked her.

"What old gang?"

"Oh, you know, people you went to high school with."

"Why would you ask me something like that? Most everybody I went to school with are still here—I see them every day."

Dickey shifted the cigar from one side of his mouth to the other. "Funny thing," he said. "I saw a guy in town the other day that I thought was gone for good. Basketball player named Buddy Love. He was a year or two ahead of you, I think, back when—"

"I'm not interested," she told him.

"No? I thought you two used to be—"

"Drop it, please."

"All right, all right," he grinned as Carla made it a point to look out the window.

Exactly twelve minutes later, by the dashboard clock—all of it conducted in prickly silence—Dickey pulled off the road and into the weedy patch in front of the old church. Carla was out of the cruiser almost before it rolled to a stop.

Dickey pulled himself out of the car, settled his hat on his head, reached into his shirt pocket for a match, lit the Coban Crook, looked at her with a mixture of scorn and suspicion, and said, "So there really is somebody dead in there?"

"Yes, of course," Carla snapped back. "I told you that a hundred times. Can we go in now?"

"If the killer's still around, it wouldn't be smart to go rushin right in, now would it?" That stopped the bitch in her tracks. He could see her fury and bravado evaporating away and he liked it.

She faced him and nodded. "Okay, what do you want to do?"

"I want you to tell me exactly what you discovered and when."

Carla took a deep breath and began. "Okay. I got a message from Aunt Sookie that she wanted to see me at the church so I drove out here. I waited for a few minutes in my car, then went in. But that storm that blew over made everything so dark that I couldn't see where I was going and...and that's when I found her. On the floor of the belfry." Carla shut her eyes. Dickey waited. "It was horrible."

"I'm sure." He reached out to put a hand on her shoulder, but she shrugged him away. He let smoke seep out from his half-closed lips, and then turned toward the church. "All right, why don't you show me where the body is."

Carla walked past him, fists clenched. The door of the church was hanging open, and, despite the bright afternoon sun, he could see that the church was dark inside. He watched her go up the plank steps, avoiding a broken board and stepping over the threshold. Dickey stepped into the gloom right behind her. The door to the belfry was just ahead on their left, closed. Carla stumbled, nearly tripped over a toppled pew, and pointed. "In there," she said.

Dickey drew his pistol and motioned her back further, then pulled the door quickly open and crouched. Nothing happened. Carefully, he pulled a flashlight out of his belt and shone its steady beam inside the small room, painting each wall momentarily in white light. He walked into the tiny room and looked up. There was nothing to see but the bell rope hanging down from the belfry. He stood still for a minute or two, just listening. A crow cawed somewhere in the distance, but beyond that, there was no sound at all. The church was empty, as far as he could tell. He turned around once more, shining the light, but there was not even a roach to be seen. Satisfied, he put the pistol back in its holster and went after the bitch where she was cowering in the shadows.

"What kind of shit you trying to pull here?"

She appeared surprised. "I don't know what you mean."

"Point the body out to me, if you'd be so kind." He watched with growing irritation, beginning to wonder if he might be the butt of someone's joke.

The girl stopped short at the belfry door, then turned toward him, a stupid look on her face. "She's gone," she said simply.

"Tell me about it," he responded. "And while you're at it, tell me where it walked off to."

He watched as Carla poked her head into the belfry and looked up. Through the dimness, the end of the bell rope hung about six or seven feet above the floor. He watched, arms folded over his belly, as she searched for traces of a body that wasn't there, biding his time. If she intended to make a fool of him, she'd be very sorry. Maybe that fool Yancy had put her up to it. If that was the case, he was going to have to have some well-chosen words with that young man.

The bitch was walking toward him, looking helpless.

"Look, Sheriff, you know I didn't call you out here just for the hell of it."

He kept the smile off his face. "Yes. I do know that. But I been wonderin just what you *did* get me out here for."

"What are you talking about?" she said. "I saw Aunt Sookie's body here not an hour ago. If someone had time to move her body, they must've been here all the time. They might have even been watching me!"

"Or maybe you got scared of the dark and had a hallucination. Better yet, maybe Aunt Sookie rose from the dead and walked away. Maybe she's going after her killer right now—save us all the trouble of looking for him."

"She was just an old woman, and somebody killed her. There's no need to treat her like—"

"Cut the shit." Dickey took her by the shoulder and held her firmly. "It couldn't be that the mighty Miz Clements called me out here so she could pay her debt to society, could it?" He took a few strands of her hair in his fingers.

She fought his grip, but he held onto her shoulder, which felt surprisingly firm. Still, she couldn't weigh more than a hundred and twenty pounds. Easy to shove around for a man his size.

"What are you talking about!" she was yelping at him.

"I'm thinkin you were tryin to come up with a way to make me tear up those charges against you."

"Oh, hell," Carla said, staring up at him. "This isn't more of your usual shit, is it?"

She reached out to push him away, but he grabbed her wrist and tightened his grip on her shoulder. "This is a good place you picked. Nobody been around here for years." He reached out and cupped one of her breasts. Nice and taut, like her butt.

Carla kicked at him and hissed, "Touch me again and I'll kick your balls so hard they'll knock your eyes out."

Dickey considered that. Knowing her, it wasn't an empty threat. "Don't try it. I'm a trained survivalist. I could cut you to little pieces without breaking a sweat."

In a heartbeat he pulled her against him. Holding her arms pinned, he spat the Crook out of his mouth and tried to press his lips against hers. She twisted her body, giving him an elbow sharply in the ribs. He grunted and loosened his grip just enough for her to squirm free. She retreated and ran toward the back of the church, then bumped into a pew and nearly went down. Dickey followed, his blood up. There was probably a back door behind the platform where the preacher's podium used to stand, but he'd catch her before she could find it.

Instead, Carla stopped short, standing in a beam of light that angled down through a window with a Negro Jesus in it, revealing a bunch of rags on the dais. She appeared frozen and entirely unconcerned about Dickey's approach. Closing in on her, he saw why. Those weren't just rags. At the end of the beam of light lay an old black woman. Her feet were together, her gown smoothed demurely down her legs, and her arms held out at right angles to her body.

"A damned black crucifix," he said.

Carla stifled a sob and sank to her knees. Ignoring her, Dickey leaned in with his flashlight for a better look. Sookie Darbyville's right hand was gripping a knife and fork and the fingers of her left hand were coiled around a stick. Draped across her neck, but not fastened, was a necklace of heathen faces glaring up at him, their blind eyes bulging and teeth bared, as if in frustration that their magic had not been enough to prevent the death of their owner.

Chapter Five

Carla zombied her way through the next day and a half. She and Comer managed to make a shrimping run on Wednesday night, but she didn't remember much of it. Her first mate had heard about Sookie's death and left her alone, foregoing his usual grumbling and provocation. She appreciated his distance, but there was still no way she could concentrate on business. Conflicted over what to do about Aunt Sookie's death, or whether to do nothing, she spent most of the night worrying and reliving the horror of finding the old woman's body in the bell tower. Their catch was only fair, and Carla let Comer take care of things at the dock while she went home to crash.

The first thing Carla did the next morning was call the sheriff's office for information about the murder. Deputy Sheriff Oskie Holt answered the phone and shocked her by saying, "Sorry, we don't give information to suspects."

"Are you calling me a suspect?"

"You're a suspect until the sheriff says you're not."

"Let me talk to him," she demanded.

"The sheriff is unavailable," he told her, and hung up.

Carla suspected that the bastard was probably "unavailable" with good reason after their little confrontation at the church. Dickey had tied Oskie's tongue tighter than a hangman's noose until such time as he decided to free it.

But did the sheriff—or even Oskie—actually consider her a suspect? The ridiculousness of such an idea wound her guts tighter than an anchor cable.

Still in her robe and slippers, Carla fed the cats, then went out and got the newspaper. Over coffee, the headline of a short column on the bottom of page two caught her eye: "Woman Dies in Church." She read it warily.

> Sookie Darbyville, 81, a long-time resident of the Blanchard's Bluff community, passed away on Sunday, August 18.
>
> Called "Aunt Sookie" by her friends, Miss Darbyville had achieved some reputation as an herbalist for many years. Cause of death is undetermined at this time. She is survived by her great-niece, Pixie Blue.
>
> The funeral is scheduled for this afternoon at 1:00 p.m. at the Old Pisgah Church in the Blanchard's Bluff community.

Carla stared at the newsprint. The Old Pisgah Church? That was the same church where Sookie had died. Who in the hell decided that? The place was an abandoned wreck! No way anyone was going all the way out there for a funeral. And there was certainly no way *she* was setting foot in that place again.

When the telephone suddenly squealed at her elbow, she jumped, and then pushed aside the newspaper. Snatching up the receiver, she barked a hello.

"Carla?" The voice was soft, barely audible.

"Pixie? Is that you? Speak up, I can't hear you." Carla suddenly felt super guilty; she should have tried to call the girl earlier, to go see her. Her mind must have gone on vacation.

"It's me, Carla."

"Pixie, how are you? How are you holding up?"

"All right, I guess. Are you comin to Auntie's sendoff?"

"What, you mean the funeral? I was just reading about it in the paper. Is the service really going to be at that old church?"

"She wanted it there. She told me."

"Pixie, I want to, I just can't. I don't think I could stand going in there again. You don't know how freaked I was." She was thinking not only of finding Sookie's body, but of her struggle with the sheriff. It had been a bad, bad afternoon.

"Auntie would want you there, I think," said Pixie.

"I'm sorry, Pixie, it's out of the question. I'll come by your place later, though, okay?"

"Okay, I guess." But the voice, still soft, sounded sad. Batshit! Now she felt *really* guilty.

When Carla drove up to the church several hours later, she almost had to rub her eyes to believe what she was seeing. The church had been repainted, the rotten stairs replaced, and the windows cleaned and polished. The weedy lot next to the cemetery had been mowed and trimmed and was now filled with dozens of cars and trucks of all makes and colors. Even the dirt road leading up to the church had been scraped and its potholes filled. All in less than three days!

It was another hot afternoon, with only a few wispy clouds softening the fierce blue of the sky. Carla found a space for her Honda and got out. She was half an hour late and the service was in full swing—she heard singing and piano music coming from inside the building. Just to the side, Carla saw rows of tables with white tablecloths and stacks of paper plates. A cylindrical black barbecue smoker that looked big enough to hold an entire hog gave off the smoky odor of ribs and chicken. Carla noticed that the man who was tending the grill—a pot-bellied black man wearing a white apron— was looking her over like she was a side of beef. A couple of children left outside to run wild while their parents paid their respects to the departed also gave her the once-over, but more shyly.

But if Carla thought she was going to be the only white person at the service—as she had been almost twenty years before—she was in for still another surprise. At the door stood Deputy Sheriff Oskie Holt, in uniform and carrying a small notebook. She purposefully walked past him without nodding, but couldn't help suspecting that he was writing her name down as she sat in the last pew and looked around.

It was amazing. Although the walls had not been replastered, they had been spruced up enough to look presentable. Likewise the rafters and the door to the belfry. The pews had been picked up, arranged, and polished until they shone. It was hot in the church, but the audience waved their cardboard fans without concern and sweated into their finest clothes. On the dais, a preacher was trumpeting Sookie's praises along with choice bits of scripture. His deep voice had a soothing cadence that filled the rafters as he addressed the gathering. "And now we are SENDING OFF this good woman, our sister who EVERYBODY HERE KNOWS and who was a friend to EVERYBODY IN THIS ROOM. Yes, yes, yes, a beloved sister WE ALL learned from and a woman who WE ALL gonna SING about."

And the pianist—where had the piano come from?— struck up a melody, and the fifty or more people in the church, by Carla's estimate, broke into song, clapping and swaying in a way that reminded Carla of a wave in an athletic stadium. Carla didn't know the words, so she scanned the audience. Men wearing suits and fedoras, women decked out in flowery dresses and all manner of wonderful hats, mostly older people but some young ones, too. Holy shit, two rows in front of her, all four of the Loafer's Bench regulars sat swaying with the rest. Up front, she spotted Pixie. Her daddy, wearing a blue suit, sat on her right, while a white man sat on her left. Who the hell? Then she recognized him: it was Ronnie Wyche.

Wyche had been her mother's lawyer and an on-and-off-again political supporter of her father, and Carla knew him well despite the difference in their ages. But since Bull Clements' death she hadn't seen much of him. She remembered with another stab of guilt that it had been Wyche who'd helped her stepmother arrange her father's funeral when Carla had not been able to manage. Had he for some reason arranged Aunt Sookie's as well? She recalled her father's funeral as a bland, emotionless ritual. A lot of people had attended, of that she was sure, but what had been said at the service, how the casket had been lowered, and how she'd behaved when the fill dirt was shoveled in was a gray blur. Sookie's funeral could hardly be more different. The colors, the music, the hats, the feeling, the whole body language bespoke joy, not sadness, and Carla was glad about that.

Ronnie Wyche had been on the dais for her father's funeral in the town's big Methodist church, sitting near the lectern with a few other dignitaries. He had been wearing a conservative dark suit—possibly the same one he wore now—but his expression had been somber. Carla had not seen Ronnie again until the night at Clem's Clams when he witnessed the incident with Yancy's gun and went bail for her at the sheriff's office. He was absolutely the last person that she would have expected to see at Sookie's funeral. As she stared in his direction, she saw Pixie turn around in her pew and look back toward the entrance. With teary eyes she scanned the crowd, then her gaze settled on Carla and she blinked, then flashed a smile.

When the singing stopped and the preacher was finished with his eulogy, people in the congregation stood up to testify about memories they had of Sookie Darbyville. A very thin ebony-colored woman in a long dress even blacker than her complexion and a hat looking like a giant pine cone with feathers, stood up and told how Sookie had made her young daughter well by sprinkling brown powder around her bed; a plump woman in a red suit and orange hat that looked to Carla like a round, stiff rug with tassels swore that Sookie had put a love potion in her man's drink and he had turned out to be a good husband for thirty years; an elderly man in a gray suit and green tie said that if it weren't for Auntie, he'd still be a drunk and a gambler. But Carla couldn't help noticing there were some frowning faces in the room as well, possibly those who'd been on the other end of Sookie's spell-casting. Pixie's Daddy, for instance, sat grim-faced and stiff as a rail, as if he was there against his better judgment. A big woman that Carla vaguely remembered seeing somewhere before sat alongside Daddy Blue. Her alarming choice of hats resembled something Carla could only describe as a furry porcupine. She nudged him occasionally, whispering in his ear. And there were others that looked to be no great fans of the old conjure woman. Was Sookie's killer in the room? Was that why Oskie Holt was there—to list the suspects or keep some kind of violence from taking place?

When the service was over, Carla walked outside to the barbecue tables where Comer, Hamp, Clarence, and Billy Joe had settled down with full plates, licking their fingers.

"We didn't really like the old bat," said Clarence, nodding in her direction. "We came for the food."

"You're a liar and a half," Hamp told him. "I remember the time when that old witch told you how to get all them weevils out of your corn."

"Yeah, wahl, if I'd been able to get her recipe for that stuff, I wouldn't have to be sittin here with you old farts. I'd be livin it up in New Yawk."

"I just wanted to see this old church again," said Comer. "Ain't been out here in almost fifty years. It ain't changed much." He pointed a crooked finger out beyond the parked cars. "Less than half a mile in that direction is pure swampland. Hog bear country, ain't it, Billy Joe?"

Carla looked at Billy Joe, who had been strangely silent. "I donno," he finally said. "I was just wonderin if she's a-meetin up with the rest of her clan. She was the last of them witchy-women, yah know? Makes yah feel kind of mortal, goin to funerals. Seems like when one of us dies, ain't that many of us left."

"You got that right, Billy Joe," Carla replied. "Well, fellas, I'd like to stay here and chat, but I gotta catch Pixie before she gets away."

But before she could turn around, she felt a hand on her shoulder and the soft, easy drawl of Ronnie Wyche's voice at her ear. "Hey ya, Carla darlin. I was hopin you'd be here."

She turned to face him. Wyche was a bulky man without the height to carry it well, but he made up for it by dressing in handsomely tailored suits and wearing his salt-and-pepper hair raffishly long. He wasn't a pretty man, but he had style. "Ronnie," she said. "I saw you sitting up front, but what are you doing here? I didn't know—"

"I'm Sookie's lawyer, Carla."

"What?" Carla wondered if she'd heard that right. What on earth would Aunt Sookie need with a lawyer?

"I've been her lawyer ever since I put out my shingle. Listen, Carla darlin, I may have some good news for you. You're involved in the will."

"What will?"

"Whose funeral are we attendin? Sookie's will, of course."

"What would she have made a will for?" Carla asked. "As far as I know, she didn't own anything except some old shack in the swamp."

"Well, she owned a bit more than that," Wyche smiled. "Do you think you can come down to the office sometime; that's where I have all the paperwork."

"Well, yeh, I can come right now, if you want me to."

"Why don't you do that. I'll have to tell Sheriff Dickey to meet us there, since her demise is a possible homicide. There are motives to be considered, etcetera."

"Do you have to?" Carla asked, remembering their last encounter; she wouldn't forget his clutching hands and his cigar breath even if she lived to be as old as Sookie.

"I'll make sure he doesn't bite," Wyche chuckled.

"All right, then, I'll meet you there in an hour." Carla

stood quietly for a moment, her thoughts racing. Wyche's little laugh had rubbed her the wrong way. Ronnie Wyche was charming and intelligent, but he was also plugged into the good-old-boy network and could share a dirty joke with the best of them. She hoped the sheriff wouldn't give her any more trouble, but if she had to endure his Drakkar-drenched force field again to get to the bottom of this Aunt Sookie business, she was willing.

Before she left, though, she had to see Pixie. Looking around, she spotted her just about to get in a white Lincoln four-door Town Car with her father, the large woman she had seen earlier, and a younger man in his twenties. "Pixie!" she called as the car door slammed shut.

Pixie stuck her head out the window and looked around. Seeing Carla, she waved frantically. Carla ran to catch the Town Car as it began rolling down the driveway.

"Pix—"

"I gotta go with Daddy and Mae, but I'ma see you soon, okay?" Her eyes were wide and dark, but the tears were gone.

"We need to talk!"

"I know. Soon, okay? Sookie glad you came. Me, too."

The car rumbled away, leaving Carla and the rest of the mourners to finish off the feast and close the church up. She took one last whiff of the tempting roasted meat smell, and trudged back to her car. She had a date with a lawyer.

Just under an hour later, Carla pulled the Honda up in front of the boxlike two-story building that housed not only the lawyer's office, but the town's Republican Party headquarters. It was also the address of the only local bail bonding agency. She pushed open the office door and shut it carefully behind her, the rattling of window blinds announcing her entry. The receptionist was not at her desk, but the door to Wyche's office was open, so Carla approached, wishing she could be invisible. Ronald Wyche sat on the edge of his large mahogany desk holding a battered Hav-A-Tampa cigar box in one hand. Against the wall lounged Sheriff James Dickey, laughing at something the lawyer had just said. He stopped laughing abruptly when he saw Carla.

"Well, well, the subject arrives," he said, his eyes sliding over her. But they weren't the slinky, assured eyes she'd seen when he was trying to assault her. And his mouth actually looked serious—the half-sneer, half-leer was missing.

Carla ignored him and shook hands with the lawyer. His suit showed signs of perspiration, but his hair still held its part.

"I think this is yours now," he said in his slow drawl, and held out the cigar box.

Carla took the box, which might have been one of the first cigar boxes ever made by the look of it, and sat down on the edge of a leather-upholstered chair that felt every bit as stiff and official as it looked. "What is this?" she asked.

"Sookie left it with me for safe-keeping," answered the lawyer.

Carla turned to Dickey for the first time. "You find the murderer yet?" she asked.

Dickey lit a twisted cigar and the smirk was back. "Saw that basketball player again," he said. "What's his name?"

Carla flushed, thinking murderous thoughts. She turned back to Wyche. "You said that I'm involved," she began. "Involved how?" She fingered the cigar box without opening it, remembering that Dickey considered her a suspect—probably his way of keeping her mouth shut about his clumsy attempt at what sure as hell would have qualified as sexual battery.

"I told you at the church that Sookie made a will, but I didn't tell you that she made you executor."

"Me?" Carla was dumbfounded. "I don't know anything about how to…"

"Don't worry about that, I'll help you. But first I want you to take that box home and look through it. You *will* have questions, so you might want to write them down and we can go over them all when you've had a chance to get familiar with the papers. What you've got there is a legally drawn will, two deeds to some land, and some other personal effects." He half smiled and cut his eyes to the sheriff, then back at her. "You take this stuff home and read through it, then get back to me, okay?"

Not sure what to say, Carla nodded. "Sure, and...I appreciate your help. Not just about this."

"I know. Your daddy was a special person. So was your mama."

Carla had a sudden thought. "You're the one who set up Sookie's funeral, aren't you? The one who had the lot mowed, the church painted, the road fixed up, the..." She ran out of breath.

"I had some help. Lot of people liked the old woman."

"And there were some that didn't," Dickey offered.

Carla ignored him. "It was nice of you," she told the lawyer. "It wouldn't have been right to have buried her in the new cemetery. She's near her mama now, and I guess all the rest of her family too."

"You give me a holler when you've gone through those papers." He patted her on the arm next to the fish wound. "You take care of that."

"No problem, it's nearly gone. I—"

The sheriff's voice cut in. "I want you to understand that the facts of this case still ain't public. Don't go blabbing your mouth all over town while I'm trying to investigate. You can read those papers or whatever, but I'm thinkin of impoundin them for evidence, so don't lose any of it. And don't go leavin town with it." Dickey stood rigid against the wall, his arms folded over his chest.

"I don't think you need to worry, Jim," answered the lawyer. "She's not going to be careless with these effects. And it's her legal duty to know what's in there." Carla had the door open and was slowly backing out.

"I'll be very careful. On all counts." She hugged the box to her chest.

"Let me walk you to your car," the lawyer said, and pulled the door firmly shut behind them.

"Don't mind Jim," he told her. "He's not somebody you'd want to bring home to meet mother, but he's not a bad police officer."

"You got the first part right," she said. "Is he really investigating Aunt Sookie's murder?"

"I think he is, but I don't know what he's got so far."

"What do *you* think about it?"

"Me? Well, I don't know. He told me what you all found and what you told him. Was that all true? You found her inside the belfry?"

"Yeh."

"And she couldn't have just...had an accident?"

"What do you mean?" Carla asked.

"Well," began the lawyer, "what if she had a heart attack or a stroke?"

Carla was shaking her head. "I don't think so," she said, "For one thing, why would she have gone in the belfry? The whole scene just looked too violent. The way she was lying when I first found her, and her necklace..." Carla remembered now the way it had seemed flung across the floor, only to have been carefully draped over the old woman's throat when Carla returned to the church with Dickey.

"Okay, we'll see what develops. Try to forget about it for a while and just study those papers, will you?"

"Okay, I will. Oh, and wait a minute. Does the sheriff really think I'm a suspect?"

"The lawyer looked up sharply and said, "Where did you get that idea?"

"Oskie Holt told me."

"Oskie's idea of a joke, maybe. I'm sure Jim doesn't have any such suspicions."

"And what about that gun charge the sheriff got me for the other night?"

Wyche laughed softly, his bulk shaking. "Oh, that's just horse manure. He's not going to pursue that. If he arrested everybody in town that carried a gun, he'd have to build a dozen more jails. If I hear anything more about Sookie, I'll give you a call. Okay?"

"Okay. Thanks."

Once in the car and headed home, Carla tried to relax. But her jaw clenched just remembering the controlled tension in the sheriff's face. She was fed up with his smug enjoyment of making her think she was a fish he could reel in at any time. She was still furious at the thought of his hands on her body; the man was utter dogshit, but it was clear she'd have to be careful. She could see the way he maneuvered people, and she hated being one of them. The car balked at a stoplight and threatened to die, but she cursed and coaxed it back to life, willing it to keep running for the remaining few blocks to her house.

She pushed open the front door with her foot and kicked it shut as she passed through, narrowly missing a cat that slithered through the opening. Switching on the lamp beside the couch, she collapsed onto the cushions. The cigar box was tied with heavy twine and she fumbled at the knot with nervous fingers. Opening the lid, she lifted out a packet of folded legal-sized papers bound in a blue cover. Under the papers was a daguerreotype of a white gentleman in a frock coat, starched collar, and what must have been a short powdered wig. Carla picked it up with the care of an archeologist and turned it over. No inscription. She turned it back over carefully, avoiding its thick crumbling edges, and stared into the patrician face. What an odd thing for Aunt Sookie to have in her possession.

Carla badly needed a smoke and searched through her purse for a cigarette. She found a crumpled pack and brought it out. It was the pack that Yancy had slipped the joint into outside Clem's. She remembered now leaving the joint for another time after the cigarettes were gone. Maybe now was that time. She pulled the joint out, straightened it, then sighed and put it back. No, she needed a clear head.

She sank back into the couch cushions and placed the

open box in her lap. She unfolded the blue-bound packet of deeds and glanced over them. Not yet—save the heavy stuff for later. Putting them aside, she picked up the gentleman's faded likeness again. She was wondering if the white wig could possibly be real hair when she noticed there were two other photographs in the box.

She studied them in bewilderment. One was of a middle-aged black woman dressed in a variety of checks, plaids, and stripes. Her headdress of wound and tied cloth framed her face in African style, and her eyes were riveted straight into the camera—a solid, no-nonsense expression in sepia tones. A spidery inscription on the back stated simply, "1889." The other photograph was larger and slightly more recent, a full-length portrait of a well-to-do white couple. The gentleman wore golfing knickers and white walking shoes, and sported a straw hat, an odd contrast to his stolid, serious face. The lady smiled graciously beside him, her large flowered hat in hand beside the long skirt of her silk dress. The back of the photo was stamped FLAGLER HOTEL 1900.

Who were these people and what were they doing in a box with Aunt Sookie's effects? And what was she supposed to do with all this? So many questions. No clues. What had these members of the gentry been to Aunt Sookie? Past employers? And what about the dignified, forthright portrait of the black woman? Was she a relative? Carla gave it up and looked to see what else was in the box.

She lifted out a folded, yellowing document that turned out to be a heavily creased map on parchment. Not done by a mapmaker, either. Clearly, it showed a body of water and a detailed rendering of a coastline, with little bays and landmarks. Toward the center of the land mass was a settlement marked "D'Arbanville." Carla caught her breath. Sookie's name had been Darbyville; the spelling was close enough. Carla felt her historian's instincts beginning to itch. With a little local research, she might start finding some answers.

Carla yawned. She was dog-tired, and hadn't even

smoked the weed. She held the box in her lap and closed her eyes…there was just so much to take in and to sift through. Who had killed Aunt Sookie? And her funeral, held in the same church, was starting to seem surreal, like an acid trip. Why had the old woman made her executor? And executor of what?

There was something else, too. The sheriff had mentioned the basketball player Buddy Love, who had attended Tate's Hammock High a few years before Carla. The sheriff wasn't an idiot; he knew that Buddy had been more than a basketball hero to her. Why was he poking his nose into her personal affairs? Her brain felt overloaded. Yawning again, she closed the box. It could all wait. Her eyes closed, her chin dropped to her chest, and the house went blissfully quiet.

Chapter Six

Yancy Vause stepped out of Rex's Clip Joint and brushed the stray hairs from the shoulders of his new shirt. In the parking lot was a spiffy, five-year-old blue Corvette. Yancy's father had purchased the vehicle at a repossession sale a few days earlier and Yancy had taken a shine to it. The thing about having your own used car business was that you got to tool around in any car on the lot. He unlocked the car, got in, and cranked the engine. It would have been better, he thought, if his father had gotten a convertible; it was a good day to drive through town with the top down, feeling the breeze sifting through his newly clipped hair. Yancy liked to be seen, and the cars he drove usually had his signature flare, so that just by looking at the car most denizens of Tate's Hammock would know that he was inside. Since his family had moved to Tate's Hammock from Panama City three years before, Yancy had been aware of the need to make contacts. It was an insulated town, with that semi-incestuous feel of backwoods, rural communities; but if you were a salesman, you had to know people and they had to know you.

He turned the corner onto First Street and drove slowly past the sheriff's office just as two figures walked out the door. He knew them. It was Daddy Blue, solemn-faced and upright, and his daughter Pixie—almost as tall as her daddy—who was crying. The two seemed close: he had his arm around girl's shoulders. Yancy had once sold Daddy Blue a 1974 Dodge D200 pickup. Rusty red. It had lasted almost a year before it had to be junked, but what did the bastard expect living out on those old dirt roads? He had met Pixie at Carla's once. Something odd about that. He knew that Pixie was very close to Carla, almost like a little sister. Carla mentioned her every time they had gone out—how she was growing, how her schoolwork was coming, whether she was eating enough. Stuff like that. He often wondered how a senator's daughter had become so attached to a young black girl from the other side of town, but asking Carla too many questions always got him in trouble and invited a temper tantrum he would rather avoid.

Daddy and Pixie had disappeared around a corner. He wondered what they were doing at the sheriff's. Wait, he remembered now. That old woman who was found dead. Who was some relation. It was good riddance as far as Yancy was concerned. There was enough weirdness in town without having some old black bat going around putting hexes on people. Better keep that to himself, though, around Carla. Shit, the old woman had once been Carla's nurse or something— god knows why her parents had allowed it. Yancy shook his head and turned down Cincinnati, then made another turn onto Front Street toward Crozier's Old Country Store. He needed to buy something for Carla, nothing expensive, just something to please her—a peace offering of sorts. The benches in front of the store were empty—the old fogeys must be home taking a nap or something. The owner—Hamp— would probably be inside, though. Maybe he could suggest something; he knew Carla as well as anyone.

Yancy was pulling to the side of the road when the screen door opened and the fat, bloated form of Oskie Holt shuffled out. Yancy straightened the car carefully and drove by without looking at the deputy. The two were not close, and Oskie had once run him in for going 37 in a 35 zone. Yancy wasn't sure how the fat fuck had gotten to be a deputy anyway. He was short, freckled, bushyheaded, a hundred pounds overweight, and slovenly—everything that the sheriff wasn't, yet it seemed that the two got along well together. And he was even married, for godsakes, although his wife was a shrew and a half.

Yancy drove around the block slowly and came back up Front Street from the other direction. He could see Holt waddling off toward the station so he parked outside Hamp's and went in.

Hamp was behind the counter using a feather duster on the glass case containing his collection of treasures and oddities, his conversation pieces, as he called them. And Yancy knew not to ask him about any of the stuff jumbled together under the glass unless he wanted to be stuck there listening to the old fart for the next hour. Last year, Yancy had sold Hamp a nearly new Toyota Camry. Four-door, white. He had made a good commission off that one, so he felt a little guilty running the old man down for his weirdness fetish. Each to his own, he supposed. Hamp looked up.

"What can I do for you, Mr. Vause?" he asked.

"Call me Yancy," said Yancy, with his best smile. "Whenever I hear anyone say Mr. Vause I always have to look over my shoulder to see if my dad's standing behind me."

"Don't believe I've had the pleasure of meetin yer dad," said Hamp.

"Well, you know how it is," said Yancy. "He doesn't come in this direction too much. Does most of his business in the capital." He decided to come to the point. "Look, Hamp," he began. "Mr. Crozier. You know Carla, right? I mean, of course you do, she comes in here every day."

"What's on your mind, fella?" said the old man.

"Carla and me, we've been seein each other some over the last couple of months, but I've managed to put my foot in my mouth too many times."

"You managed to put your pistol in it, too, hah?" the old man asked, looking at him squarely.

Yancy managed a squirm. "Yeah, that's one time. It was a stupid thing for me to do, but—" Yancy stopped. "Who told you about that? Was that bastard Holt telling you my business?"

"Oskie just came in for some gum," said Hamp. "I heerd about it from the sheriff and from Carla."

"Oh. Sorry. I didn't mean..." Things weren't going the way Yancy had planned. He started again. "Anyway, I want to try to make it up to Carla. I thought maybe you could let me know something she likes, a favorite candy or one of those bandanas or something."

Hamp shrugged. "She'd probly preciate a carton of Winstons," he said. "Although it'd mor'n likely just kill her sooner. Maybe a new pickup."

Was the old man putting him on? "Yeah, well, I—"

"Look, son. I caint help you run yer affairs. I kin tell you that Carla likes that boat of hers and her cats, and that she dotes on that little black girl. She loves a good story, too." Hamp looked directly at him again and finished, "An she's never played a dirty trick on anybody in her life."

"I know that. Right. Just let me have a bag of whatever cat food Carla usually buys."

Hamp went over to a shelf and pulled down a yellow bag. "Milk, too?" he asked.

"Do Carla's cats drink milk?" he asked. "Sure, then, let me have a carton of half and half." If he was going to treat her cats to get back in her good graces, might as well get the cream.

Yancy thanked Hamp, paid for the purchases, and got back in the Corvette. It had been awkward, but he thought he had gotten what he wanted. He drove the few blocks to Carla's house deep in thought, and when he pulled into her yard it was without the usual horn-blasting announcement of his arrival. He got out of the car, consciously paying attention to his body language. Instead of his usual swinging, nonchalant gait (Carla called it "swaggering"), he tried to walk with a kind of shyboy shuffle.

When he reached the screen door, he looked in and saw Carla staring at him sleepy-eyed from the couch. The face he pressed against the screen was supposed to look hangdog.

"Hey, Carla," he began. He set the package of cat food

and cream on the grass near the step.

Carla made no attempt to get up from the couch, and he noticed that she was holding a small box on her lap. "I thought I gave you directions the other day," she told him.

Yancy put on a puzzled expression. "What directions?"

"Go out and get flattened somewhere."

"You didn't tell me that."

"Well, then, I should have." Carla yawned, but Yancy suspected she was putting on an act. She put the box next to her on the couch, but still didn't get up. Yancy saw the name Dutch Masters on the box.

"You switched to cigars now?" he smiled, but Carla cut him off.

"Look Yancy, I'm really pretty busy. If you have anything to say, say it."

"Well...I want to apologize." He really did feel uncomfortable—not only because of Carla's attitude but because it was hot and he was wearing a new white shirt that still had the store folds down the sides. His neck was itching from a few hair clippings that had escaped Rex's bib.

"Apologizing is one thing and changing is another," she said. "And you can't apologize for what you are."

"You don't think people can change?" he asked.

Carla seemed to think for a moment. "I don't know," she replied. "Probably not."

"Are you going to let me come in?" he asked.

"The door's open."

Yancy walked in, still shuffling a little. He chose the overstuffed chair, but sat stiffly on the edge. Without a screen between them, Carla really did look tired, almost as if she were hung over.

"I wanted to explain about the gun."

"What about it?" The coolness of her tone made him squirm. Hamp had made him feel the same, and it was not a reaction he was used to or comfortable with.

"I'm not supposed to own one," he told her.

"Well, thanks loads for hiding it in my purse. Why

aren't you supposed to have one?"

"You really want to know?"

"I'd like to know if I've been dating a criminal, yeh," she said.

"Well then, it's like this. I've got a problem," he began. He was starting to sweat like a man in court. "I like guns too much. I never had one until I was in the army, but then I had a lot of them. I'm good with guns; I can hit whatever I shoot at." He hoped his eyes appealed to her for understanding, but Carla's expression remained icy. "But, you know," he continued, "there's only one thing a gun's good for and that's to kill things. That was okay in Vietnam because we were supposed to kill things there. But in this country killing some things is against the law." Yancy stopped. Sweat dripped off his nose and chin. Then he added, "Like people things."

"You shot someone?" The look on her face shifted to disbelief.

"Well don't look at me like I was a mass murderer," he said, his voice rising. "I got ten years probation and I can't own a gun—not supposed to even be around them. When I saw that police car the other night, I panicked. I didn't know if it was Oskie or the sheriff, and I didn't have time to find out. So I stashed the gun in your purse. It was a stupid, drunk thing to do...and I'm sorry."

"You're a murderer?" Carla asked. She seemed to be staring holes in his face. He quelled the urge to squirm.

"Dammit, Carla, I'm trying to be honest with you and you're making it damn hard. I shot one guy, it was self-defense and I don't want to talk about it."

"Yancy, if you aren't supposed to be carrying a gun, what were you doing *carrying* one?"

"I was using it earlier. I went shooting with some of the guys—" He stopped abruptly, then decided to continue. "We meet in the woods sometimes to train."

"Train for what?" Carla asked.

"Just to keep in practice in case we ever want to go back in the military. I'd just forked over a month's pay for that

Walther." A bead of sweat found its way down into the new shirt collar. "It's, I don't know, it's a beautiful gun. All you have to do is breathe on the trigger and—"

"I don't want to hear about the fucking gun, Yancy! But I'm not sure I understand what you're getting at. You said you didn't know if it was the sheriff or Oskie the other night. What difference did it make?"

"I'd rather not say."

"For someone who's trying to be honest, there's a *lot* you'd rather not say. In fact, all you've told me is that you're a gun nut who just happens to be a convicted killer. What, is that supposed to make me fall in love with you?"

"I don't think this is coming out right."

"And what's going to happen to me when I have to go to court for carrying a concealed weapon?"

Yancy looked at her directly for the first time in minutes. He smiled slightly and shook his head. "Don't worry about that," he told her. "Dickey's not going to court. I don't think he even wrote out any charges, and if he did, he tore them up." Carla's tomcat Fang had wandered in from outside and now jumped up on Yancy's lap. Carla had told him on a similar occasion that the cat had bad taste in men. Yancy stroked it mechanically.

"Anyway, my lawyer already told me that Dickey's not going to file any charges. What I want to know is how *you* know."

"Sheriff came out to the lot yesterday. Might want to buy that little Corvette I have outside. And he owes me a favor or two besides. If he's still messing with you about the other night, I'll get him to stop."

"I don't need help from a convicted murderer, thanks, and please leave Fang alone."

"I'm not a murderer," he said softly, continuing to stroke the cat.

"Or a pusher," she said.

"A pu— oh, you mean the joint I stashed in your pack of cigarettes?" Yancy smiled faintly. He'd forgotten about that.

"That's right."

"Well, look, I couldn't very well get caught for possession, could I? Besides, I brought it for you anyway. Did you smoke it?"

"No way," she said hotly. "If you think I'm going to legitimize your... Look, I have a lot of shit on my mind these days. And one thing I don't need is any more—"

"Sookie Darbyville?" he interrupted.

Carla looked confused. "What?"

"Are you worried about that old black woman dying?"

"Yes, of course. She worked for my family for years. She pretty much brought me up."

"It was a minority murder," he said.

"You're as racist as the sheriff," she said. The chill had slipped back into her voice.

"Depends on what you call racist, but that's not the point. I'm just saying that it was a killing inside the black community."

"What do you know about it?" she asked.

"What else could it be?" Yancy put his finger between his neck and his collar, thought about loosening his tie, but didn't. His face was sweating again, and he could feel perspiration from his armpits soaking into his new shirt. He nudged the cat down onto the floor. "Dickey thinks it has to do with Aunt Sookie's conjure. Somebody just got tired of having spells put on them and wasted her. And everybody knows that Aunt Sookie mostly worked her roots on black people."

"That makes sense, I guess" Carla said. "Did he tell you about the knife and fork?"

"Yeah, something to do with hexes, right?"

"Maybe. Or maybe they were planted to throw suspicion away from the real killer."

"Look," he said patiently. "What white person in town would want that old woman dead? She didn't mess with them. She was crazy, but people seemed to get along with her okay. I'm sure that's what Pixie told the sheriff this morning when—"

"What's that about Pixie?"

"I was just telling you. I saw her coming out of the sheriff's office earlier and—"

"The sheriff's office? What was she doing there?"

"I don't know, but isn't she the last one who saw Sookie alive? I mean, the next to last? Maybe Dickey figures she can give him some answers."

A cat jumped up on Carla's lap, but Carla pushed it away without even looking to see who it was. "Damn!" she exclaimed.

"What's the matter now?" he asked, concerned.

To Yancy's surprise, Carla jumped up from the couch. "I was supposed to call Pixie," she said.

"Why?" asked Yancy, standing up as well.

"I saw her at the funeral but I didn't get a chance to talk to her—"

"You went to the funeral?"

"Yeh. Any problem with that?" She had that look he was hoping to avoid.

"Well, no, but..." Yancy wasn't sure what he could say that wouldn't tick her off again.

"Then maybe you'll understand that I have important things to do right now."

"I understand." Yancy realized the hangdog feeling was starting to feel genuine, and he didn't like it for shit.

"Pixie needs somebody with her, and I don't like the idea of her being in an office alone with Dickey or Oskie Holt."

"She's gone by now," said Yancy. "Besides, her daddy was with her."

Carla stopped. "Oh."

"Listen, sit down again for a minute," Yancy said. "While I was driving over here I had an idea I wanted to run by you."

"Make it short," she said, sitting back down on the edge of the couch. Yancy remained standing.

"I was thinking that maybe I had a job for Pixie,"

"A job? What, selling cars? Washing them?"

"Writing postcards. See, I keep records of every car we've ever sold at Vause Motors. I know every customer and every car—model and make—and I know what their trade-in value is. The postcard would say something like Dear Blank, Vause Motors would be glad to give you X number of dollars in trade for your 1980 Ford Fairlane or whatever. Pixie could address the cards, and I'd fill in the details. Then she could put the stamps on and take them to the post office. I'd give her a dime apiece."

"That's...that's really nice of you, Yancy," Carla said, and Yancy knew he had scored. The hung dog vanished. "I'll mention it to her when I find her. Thanks for coming over."

"I guess it didn't do any good, did it?"

"I don't know," she said, looking decidedly undecided. "Maybe."

"Well...can I see you again?"

"I don't know."

"How about if I call you later tonight, after you're through with whatever you're doing?"

"Later this month, maybe,"

"This month? But—"

"Yancy," she began. She looked exasperated, but he was pretty sure now it was just an act and he smiled inwardly, not wanting to give away his triumph. "Just go. I'll call *you* if I want to see you."

"Okay, babe," he said. "Try not to be too mad at me." He waved and walked out to his car. He consciously managed to drive off without squealing the tires of the Corvette. Only when he had gotten a block away did his smile come to the surface. And it was only then that he remembered the bag of cat food and milk he'd left on Carla's front step, a feast for the ants.

Chapter Seven

It was hard to concentrate after the interruption, but Carla gave it her best shot. She studied the photos again but still couldn't identify the subjects. The two men were complete strangers, but the woman with the parasol looked vaguely familiar. Carla shook her head; there's no way she could have met someone whose picture was taken in 1900. The black woman was even more of a puzzle. Although her picture was in Sookie's effects, she looked nothing like the old root doctor. She was tall, her face smooth and coffee-dark while her old nanny was almost tiny, with skin the color of freshly made tea. The only resemblance was the layers of clothing she wore wrapped around her.

The sound of a car door slamming snapped her head up. Not Yancy again! What was his problem, anyway? When she told him she'd call him next month, she didn't mean that he could come back in an hour. What kind of a bozo needed a neon sign flashed in his face before he got the message? She had been ready to forgive and forget; now Yancy could fuck himself. If she really wanted to keep Yancy out of her bed, she was going to have to say so in terms he could understand. Quickly she went down the hall to her bedroom and fished around in the top drawer of her dresser for the cold steel hidden under the socks. Her fingers found the checkered handle of her nickel-plated Smith & Wesson .38 Special Royal Canadian Mounted Police Combat Masterpiece. A hefty handgun by anybody's standards, her daddy used to say. He ought to know—he'd bought it for her when she'd come back from college, for protection, he said. It wasn't loaded, but Yancy didn't have to know that.

She ran back through the hallway and jerked open the front door. "You're not the only one who likes to play with guns!" she shouted at the figure coming up the steps. "When I said—" Carla stopped, goggle-eyed, as she recognized Buddy Love backing away from her, stumbling off the doorstep.

"Buddy!"

"Jesus, Carla," he said, staring in disbelief down the nickel-plated barrel of the Smith & Wesson. "I know we didn't part on the best of terms, but I didn't think you wanted to shoot me."

"Buddy," she said again, numbly. "My God, I'm sorry. I thought you were somebody else." Buddy moved gingerly past her and across the threshold. His eyes were pale blue wells, the pupils dilated in surprise. She set her own expression into what she hoped was a steely glare. "What are you doing here and where's your wife?"

"Gosh, Carla—I'd forgotten how you love small talk. Can I come in?"

"You are in."

"Then can I sit down?"

She waved the pistol in the direction of the couch. "Don't get too comfortable," she told him. "How did you find me?"

"I, uh, stopped by Chez Marais and saw your stepmother. She told me you'd moved out and gave me this address. I'm glad I caught you at home."

"Why?"

"I don't know... I don't come through Tate's Hammock much anymore, and I just wondered how you were doing." He idly picked up a piece of paper from the stack on the coffee table. "Going into real estate?" he asked.

"None of your business."

Buddy dropped the paper and picked up the photo of the couple at the Flagler Hotel. "Nice-looking pair. Somebody you know?" he asked.

Carla ignored the question. Buddy Love was the last person she would have expected to find on her doorstep, and because of the way their relationship had ended, the last person she wanted to see. Even Yancy would be preferable. And Buddy was acting as if he had just dropped over for a weekly chat, treating Aunt Sookie's papers as if they were snapshots of her summer vacation.

She looked him over carefully, as he did her. He was basically as she remembered him, ice-blue eyes peering intently out over hawk nose, and thick, slightly wiry hair with an auburn tinge. He was wearing it longer now than in school. She couldn't really tell, but his basketball player's frame still seemed in pretty good shape. He could easily add a few pounds and not show it. And of more interest to her at the moment, Buddy was a lawyer.

"You know, an old cigar box is not the best place to keep your papers," Buddy observed. "You should get a file, maybe something metal. I bought a safe from one of those security companies. Fireproof."

She tried to think of some smart remark to shut him up, but instead the events of the last few days suddenly came crashing down. She'd been holding the stress at bay, but the sudden entrance of her old lover was just too much. Carla scratched her head with the pistol barrel and started laughing. It was a shaking laughter that could as easily have turned into a fit of tears. She hugged herself and hastily sat down across from him.

"What are you laughing at?" Buddy asked.

"Everything," she replied. It was strange. Buddy had never been in this house before, yet he made the couch look like it belonged to him. The whole room, in fact. "You, the murder, the funeral, that stuff piled in front of you…"

"What murder?" Buddy asked, staring at the gun apprehensively. "Are you in some kind of trouble?"

"Maybe," she said, making a decision. She had intended to study Sookie's papers for a few days, then go back to Ronnie Wyche's office and discuss them. But Buddy was here right now and… She looked at the cat-clock on the wall, its tail switching off the seconds. "Look, it's just after five," she said. "Remember that, because I expect you to charge me the going rate."

"What are you—?"

"Hush," said Carla. She took a deep breath, wondering where to start. Probably at the beginning. So she went back to the afternoon at the church and told him everything that had happened from that moment until this, easily losing herself in her story and almost, but not quite, blocking out the fact that this was Buddy Love she was telling it to. But he listened carefully, and when she finished, he leaned back on the couch, raised his eyebrows, and said, "Jeez, Carla…it's not bad enough finding Miz Sookie dead—you get fucking Dickhead trying to get in your pants."

"Tell me about it," Carla said, trying to think of a not-too-obvious way to escape for a few minutes to compose herself. "Listen, I'd better put this gun away. And I need some coffee, bad. You want some?"

"Some bad coffee? Sure."

"Could you just look over those deeds and tell me what you think."

Carla tried to ignore his smile as she hurried down the hall, threw the gun back underneath the socks, and went into the kitchen, where she splashed water into the pot and on her face. Cold enough to chase away any illusions. She peeked back into the room, but Buddy was still there. She no longer had any idea whether that was bad or good. He looked up at her over the papers, over a pair of glasses he had never had to wear before. The effect gave him an air of studied intellectuality, and it worked so well that, had she not known Buddy so intimately, it would've seemed calculated to make him attractive not only to her, but to everyone on earth.

Too bad she hadn't aged as nicely. Her hair looked like seaweed, and her years on the boat had tanned her skin dark as cork. Still, although she was two heads shorter than Buddy, her arms were strong and well-toned from the nets, and the hard work had given her confidence. She was certainly smarter than she had been when she and Buddy were an item in college.

"You running some of the boats now?" he asked.

"Just one, the newer one."

"That's a tough job," he said.

"I don't know," Carla said. "I've been thinking about it lately. There's no money in it, that's for sure. Sometimes I think I must be crazy. Like when we bring up an old outboard motor in the net that frays the lines and gouges up the deck, or the net slips out of my grip in the rain and burns the shit out of my hands." She stuffed her hands in her pockets.

"Who's working the boat with you?"

"Comer Whitehead. He's a lot of help when he's sober. If he's not available, I just hire one of the guys down at the marina." Carla felt as if a part of her watched from a distance, amused and detached, as she babbled on, filling the space between them with words. She stood in the doorway, waiting on the coffee, and watched him read through one of the deeds. When he'd finished, he took off the glasses and chewed on the ends for a few seconds.

"This goes back a pretty good ways. You said that Ronnie Wyche was holding them for Miz Darbyville, and then passed them on to you?"

"Yeh."

"Do you understand what this is?" He held up the first document.

Carla kept her hands in her pockets to keep from twitching. "I really haven't had a chance to look at it yet. Hold on a minute and you can go through it with me." She ducked back into the kitchen and returned with two cups and a pack of cigarettes she found in the cupboard.

"Black, one sugar," she said.

"Good memory," he said, taking a cup. Carla sat down next to him on the couch, being careful to keep two feet of distance between them. She cleared a place for her cup and the cigarettes on the coffee table as he put his glasses on again and riffled through the papers.

"Okay," he began, not looking at her, "this is her will, drawn up by Ronald Wyche. Wasn't he your family lawyer?"

"Um, my mother's lawyer. Daddy used some guy in Tallahassee."

"The will is pretty simple. It leaves everything she owned to Pixie Blue, but it also makes you the executor of the estate." Now he looked at her, but questioningly.

"Exactly what does that mean?" Carla asked.

"It means that you're in charge of carrying out the terms of the will. And the terms of the will state that Sookie wants you to administer the estate until Pixie is twenty-one. If there's money, you dole it out to her as you see fit. If there's property, it can't be sold unless you approve it."

"And what does the estate consist of?" Carla asked, her throat dry.

"I can't be sure until I see the bank records, although I don't see how there could be much money involved. Other than that, there's her house and its contents, a few miscellaneous items, and these." He unfolded the two deeds. "There are deeds to two parcels of land. Metes and bounds isn't my specialty, but this one looks like it borders on the river out by Blanchard's Bluff. Pretty big, too. Let's see… Wow! Unless I'm stupider than I think, this damn thing's huge! The other one is smaller and seems to be inside the town limits, probably a homestead. I'd have to have a county grid map to tell right where it is."

Carla slumped into the cushions.

"Do you have any idea where the hell Sookie got all that property?" Buddy took off his glasses, wiped them on his sleeve, and then replaced them. He drank the last of his coffee and looked at her with those pale blue lasers Carla remembered so well. "Or why she made *you* her executor?"

Carla shrugged. "No idea," she said. "I mean, she used to be my nurse and all, but I would have thought that she'd give the job to Daddy Blue. He's her nearest relative; well, by marriage, anyway."

"Maybe she didn't choose him for the same reason she didn't leave him anything in her will," Buddy suggested. "But isn't there anybody else? I thought she had dozens of relatives around Blanchard's Bluff."

"I don't know," Carla admitted. "It's been such a long time since we said anything but hello to each other. And except for Pixie, she never really talked about her family."

"Well, you might find something out if you could examine the personal possessions in her house or see her bank account statements, assuming she has an account. In the meantime," he said, holding out his coffee cup, "could I have a refill?"

Carla stood up quickly. "Oh, sure. Me, too." But a glance at her own untouched cup made her feel silly. She picked it up anyway, then took a step toward Buddy, reaching for his cup. Her foot came down on something furry, and thorny. Mittens squealed, yanking her paw away as Carla struggled for balance. Her cup flew out of her hand, and coffee splashed all over Buddy's tri-blend suit pants. He jumped up like he'd just discovered he'd been sitting on a fire ant bed.

"God, Buddy, I'm sorry!" she said frantically, making an effort to wipe the liquid off his legs before it scalded him.

"Don't worry," he said. "It's not that hot." His hand on her shoulder and that funny way his head tilted to the side when he was about to say something she might object to brought the past back as if it had never been left behind. He pulled her to him and she didn't resist, even when she felt the wetness of his trousers against her bare legs.

The comfortable fit of his encircling hug was the same. She turned her face up to receive his kiss, lips apart, as if no time had intervened and separated their lives.

But time *had* separated them; time and anger and frustration. What the hell was she doing! She pushed free and took a step back,

Buddy creased his eyebrows into a frown. "Come on, Carla..."

"What the fuck, Buddy?" she said, backing away and lighting a cigarette from the pack on the table. "I haven't seen you for six years and you think you can come in here and assume that everything will be the same between us?"

"I'm sorry, Carla. It just happened. I didn't mean—"

"What are you doing here anyway?" she demanded.

"I have a client. I drove in the other day to get his signature and again today to deliver some documents."

"I've never heard of a lawyer that makes house calls," Carla said suspiciously.

"My client's in a wheelchair," he said.

"Oh, sorry."

"And I just decided to drop in on you; see how you're doing."

Carla didn't know what to say. She went to the kitchen for a dish towel and brought it back. "Here," she said, handing it to him.

He dabbed it at the damp spot on his thigh, giving her a half smile. Handing it back, he took the map from the cigar box and opened it carefully. "What's this?"

Carla sat down, the box between them. "Obviously it's a map. Dunno to where."

Buddy refolded the map, picked up the photos, and looked at her questioningly.

"No idea," she said. "I think that the black woman might be Sookie's mama or even grandmama. The old men at Hamp's might know. They might know who the white people are, too."

"They look well to do," Buddy observed. "Maybe Sookie or her mama used to work for them. But why would she keep their pictures…

"Wait, wait!" Carla cried, taking the picture of the single woman. She held the photo up under the lamp light for a closer look and caught her breath. She couldn't be certain, but peeking out from the swathes of scarves was what looked like the large bead of a necklace. A frisson passed through her—it looked a hell of a lot like the string of beads she had found with Sookie at the church. Could this woman be wearing the same necklace? She pointed to the photo. "See that bead?" she asked him. "It's just like the ones I saw in the church."

"I'm not sure I can see..." Buddy leaned over the picture and adjusted his glasses.

Carla bent down too, until their heads were touching. "It's there," she said. "It's hard to see..." She stopped talking because Buddy had turned his head toward her again. And somehow, their lips were together again, and this time it felt right; not *exactly* right, but right enough. Buddy moved the box and leaned in close, but Carla stood up.

"What's wrong now?" he asked.

"Your glasses," she said. "I'm not used to them yet. No, that's not it. I can't get my breath. This sounds stupid, but I feel a little dizzy."

"Better sit down again, then."

"Yeh. Boy, I can't believe this. Where've I been all your life?"

"Same old Carla. I never know when you're serious."

"Shhh. Don't ruin it. I'll just get pissed off and you'll get defensive and it'll all go to hell again. So just shut up."

"Kiss me again and I will," he said.

Carla hugged his neck fiercely, finding his mouth again. The course of the evening seemed a sure bet, so she didn't begrudge him a limping cat or a coffee stain on her rug. Settling into the hollow of Buddy's arm, she allowed herself to enjoy the pressure of his leg against hers. It was like old times, and yet not. There was this small problem of a wife at home somewhere. She sneaked a look and caught him smiling at her.

"You'd better get out of those wet pants," she told him. "And take those glasses off while you're at it."

Carla drifted up through layers of sleep fog and fading images of treading deep water, waiting for a lifeboat that never appeared. The sheet was damp beneath her and her hair clung humidly to her neck. The night air was stifling, and bright moonlight spilled through the window. She could make out her and Buddy's clothes abandoned in a pile at the foot of the bed. She rolled over and felt for him in the empty space beside her. Where was he? She half sat up, propped on her elbows, eyes wide, and then saw him standing by the open window, smoking a cigarette. She held still, breathing quietly, lips pressed together. Her eyes followed the outline of his profile, shoulders and chest, as he stood highlighted, burning his shape into her memory for good in case this turned out to be a one-night stand.

"Could I have a drag, too?"

Buddy started at her voice, then turned and walked back to the bed. "You want this one? I'll light another," he said, handing it to her.

Carla gratefully accepted the half-smoked Camel. How could he still be smoking these things without rampant emphysema? Surprisingly, Buddy Love seemed in better condition now than she remembered. She hooked an arm through his as he lit up and inhaled deeply.

"So what do you do in your spare time, besides seducing old girlfriends?"

"Girl *friend*," he corrected.

"You don't have much spare time, then."

"I don't, really," he said, getting back into bed so that his skin rested lightly against hers. "My practice is doing well, finally. I had a house built out in Killearn Lakes a while back."

"Fancy," Carla said. "But I'm surprised at you putting down roots like that. You used to talk about Tate's Hammock and Tallahassee like they were leper colonies."

"Yeah, well." Buddy shrugged and dragged a hit on his cigarette, then balanced it on the lip of the nightstand ash tray.

"Bullshit, you can't just shrug that off. Six years ago you were gung ho to pack up all our shit—including me— and move to Indiana."

"Things happen," he said.

"Sorry, Bub," she pressed, "but I need more than that. This is something that affected my life. You were pressuring the *shit* out of me back then. I even applied for umpteen *jobs* in about every high school in Indianapolis. And you said that as soon as you passed the bar, you'd—"

"I flunked the bar, Carla."

"—you'd try to hook on with the legal staff of the Pacers and—"

"I *flunked* the fucking *bar*, Carla!"

Carla closed her mouth and looked at him through the semidarkness. "What are you talking about?" She couldn't believe she'd heard that right.

"Twice. It took me another year and a half of hanging around, doing paralegal work for dickheads in the DA's office, before I finally passed. It took me another year before I felt that I had my head on straight legally. Melanie was pretty patient with me…"

"That's the woman you dumped me for?" Carla asked. Precision, that's what was called for now. Keep sharp or she was going to sink into that deep dark water of the past and never come up.

"Carla, I didn't dump you. If anything, it was the other way around. You got cold feet and Melanie was just there."

"And she made you decide to stay in the South," Carla finished.

Buddy laughed. "Just the opposite. Melanie's from Boston. Two words out of her mouth and you know. At first I thought we might go up north together. Her mother still lives there."

"What happened?" Carla asked.

"Her plans changed a couple of years ago. Her father was born in France, but lives in Pensacola; has some kind of a seafood business. Her mother divorced him before Melanie was born, and now she wants to get to know him better. In fact, she majored in French."

"But you said she was a librarian," Carla said.

"She went to graduate school. Something to pay the bills," he told her.

"So you and what's-her-name are still together?" She was more curious than hopeful.

"Yeah, for what it's worth."

"What does that mean?"

"I don't know," he admitted.

"It's not working out the way you thought it would?"

"No. I mean yes. Except for the location, it's working out exactly as I thought it would. Maybe that's the problem."

Carla perked up her ears. "Problem?" she asked.

"Nothing's a surprise anymore. We have lunch Wednesdays at Maxim's and dinner on Friday nights at the Silver Slipper. We go to one party a month, take a three-week vacation every July, and fuck one point five times a week."

"Is that all?" Carla asked.

"No," said Buddy, "It's just that she doesn't have much drive. She works in a library all day and reads philosophy in the evening, if you can believe it."

"Philosophy?"

"Remember the time I made that thirty-footer in overtime to win against Duke?"

Carla smiled as she remembered. "The crowd went bananas," she said. "So did I."

"Well, that's what Melanie is like when she discovers a new philosopher. Some German named Wittgenstein is her latest. I mean, I like having an intelligent wife, but *tractatuses* or whatever are not what I want to talk about before I go to bed at night."

Carla stubbed out her cigarette, remembering some of her nights with Yancy. "There are worse things."

"I suppose," he said, twining his fingers in her hair. Carla shivered, old memories sliding over her skin. And, oddly, talking about his wife wasn't as disturbing as she would have thought.

"Anyway," she said. "You have a house in a ritzy neighborhood and don't have to buy your clothes at

Goodwill."

"The trouble is, Carla, I like this life I've built. I've got a circle of friends, I play in a city basketball league, and practice in a profession I've always wanted to be in."

"That doesn't sound like trouble to me."

"It would be tough for me to pick up and leave here now," he said softly.

"I know," Carla said.

"*You* know? Shit, I was sure *you'd* still be here. Where would you go?"

"I've been thinking about going down to Belize or to the Tortugas."

"Doing what, winter shrimping?" he asked.

"I could make it a year-round job," she answered.

"Yeah, you probably could." He was silent for a moment. "I've been thinking a lot about this place lately." He took a drag on his cigarette, as if sucking in memories. "You know, I won an award once—in Boy Scouts. I—"

Carla began giggling. "*You* were in the Boy Scouts?"

Buddy smiled. "Hey, I was an *Eagle* Scout—maybe the only one ever awarded in Tate's Hammock. I don't know, scouting was something all the kids were doing back in Indiana in the fifties and early sixties. I just stuck with it when we moved here. Give me a compass and I could find my way in or out of any forest or swamp for fifty miles around. Good thing I didn't know you then."

"Why?"

"I probably would've spent all my time with you instead of doing any of that stuff, like hiking or sleeping out in the woods. I used to read these old books by Joseph A. Altsheler about boys in the early West, fighting the Indians. Dreamed of being like that. I got so I could tell almost any snake from its shed skin or the way its track moved across the sand. Learned to shoot my father's rifle so well I could knock pine cones off the treetops. I even tracked a hog bear once— kept her in sight for over an hour without her knowing I was even there." He crushed out his cigarette. "That was a long time ago. I guess you only realize the things you miss when you can't do them any more."

The silence that followed lasted so long Carla thought Buddy might have dozed off. "Got any kids?" she asked quietly.

Buddy turned over and pulled her close. "Not yet. Nosey." He kissed her cheek, breathing into her ear. Carla shivered again. "What's-her-name's not the motherly type," he finished.

Carla wasn't either, but occasionally she tried to imagine what it might be like to share life with children and a husband. Sometimes she cast Buddy in that fantasy, sometimes not. Yancy? Never. She studied Buddy's face and saw lines around his mouth that hadn't existed before. Stifling a nervous laugh, she bit him on the shoulder.

"You want to screw or shoot hoops?" she asked. An old challenge.

"Trash mouth. Sixty-eight okay with you?"

Carla looked at him suspiciously. "Sixty-eight?"

"You do me and I'll owe you one." Carla tried not to laugh but something slipped out the side of her mouth.

"Yuk yuk," Buddy said.

"Yuck," said Carla.

She felt his arms around her, crushing her ribs. Carla squeaked and looked across his broad shoulders, noting the numbers on the clock radio, luminous and green: 2:45. There was plenty of time yet. She shoved Buddy's wife, the Tortugas, kids, Aunt Sookie, the will, the detestable sheriff, and everything else into a place in her brain as dark and distant as the hold of *The Miriam C.* and shifted her concentration to the matter in hand. It was going to be a long night, if she had anything to do with it.

Chapter Eight

It was a dingy little bar, dark and grimy. People said it stunk, too, but Daddy Blue's sense of smell had been wrecked by years of scaling and cleaning fish at The Fish Barn. The owner of the bar was surly and the glasses weren't always as clean as they should be, but drinks were cheap and there was no jukebox and no TV. It was a place a man could sit and toss down a few hard ones, smoke a few cigarettes, and maybe do some communing with himself. And that's what Daddy Blue was doing—communing. He'd just finished the late shift and, although he had washed abundantly with the harsh soap the plant provided, he still felt slimy and scaly. He was sick to his soul of fish guts, sick of having to work such a shit-eating job, and sick of living among people who looked at him—who'd been in the Army and had a Bronze Arrowhead medal for parachutin into combat in Vietnam—like he was just another stupid black man. Well, maybe all that was finta change, um hmm. Maybe he—

"Hiram!"

Daddy Blue turned around to see who it was was calling him Hiram. The cigarette he held in his mouth dropped ash. He squinted through the smoke and frowned at the big dark-faced woman in the flower-print dress who had approached his solitary table and now stood over him.

"What you want, Mae?" he asked. "I ain't got no time for you."

"And maybe I ain't got no time to babysit that little witch of yours neither," Mae answered.

"Don't be callin my little girl a witch," he told her, pointing a finger at her face. Then he lowered it and said more softly, "You need money for her food or something?"

He took the cigarette out of his mouth and put it in an ashtray that already had half a dozen butts.

"I need you to go home sometime, Hiram. That girl need a father."

"I am home most of the time," he said, tossing down the whisky in his glass and setting it down on the table. "And I try to be a father, all right. But…" He lifted the glass and looked through it in the dim light. "I just don't, you know, I just don't like her to see me when I'm drinking."

"Which is every night."

"Naw—only once or twice a week. Anyway, things are changed now."

"Changed how?"

"I need another drink."

"That ain't no change," she told him. "An ain't you gonna ask me to sit down and join you?"

"Can't stop you from sittin, but you need to buy your own, um hmm."

"You're a hard man," said Mae. She rustled through her large purse and came up with a five-dollar bill. She planted her bulk down across from him on a chair that shouldered her weight with a creak and a groan, and handed him the money. "Same as you," she said. "And I want change, Hiram."

"Yeah, me too," he said.

Daddy didn't like to be called Hiram. Didn't much like the name Daddy neither, although his wife used to call him Big Daddy sometimes. That was good. But Lizzy was dead, had been dead for too long. Maybe that's why he didn't tell Mae Barnes to leave; she had been Lizzy's friend, had taken care of her in her illness while he was in Vietnam. And he did appreciate the times she took in Pixie when he had a few too many. A daughter should never see her father drunk.

The bar was pretty quiet. A couple sat at a table on the other side of the room from him and Mae, and there were three young bucks sitting on raggedy stools at the bar, nursing bottles of beer. One of them looked at him as he paid for the drinks, then turned back to his buddies. The bartender took his green in fists like two lumps of dough with digits and set two glasses down on the bar. Behind him was a mirror and two long shelves of liquor. The three at the bar had their heads close together, whispering something.

As he brought the drinks back to the table, he looked at the woman sitting there. Not tall, but with a big bunch of bushy hair. Good hair, healthy, but with a mind of its own. A passionate woman, he had cause to know, more lively than Lizzy had been, but he just didn't like fat women. Real dark-faced women either. Lizzy was slim and light, and Pixie had inherited those traits. He set the drinks down and pushed one over to her side of the table, along with the five-dollar bill she had given him. Then he opened a new pack of Camels and lit one.

"Heard you got you a new suit," Mae said, raising her glass.

"Ain't none of your business," he said.

Mae picked up the five from the table and stuffed it back in her purse. "And you got some money, too," she said.

"Who says I got money?" he asked.

"First time you ever paid for my whisky," she laughed. It was a raucous laugh—too much laugh for the humor. She sipped at her drink, then got serious. "Pixie tole me that you all finta move to Tallahassee."

"That was before," Daddy answered.

"Before...?"

"Ain't none of your—"

"Before Sookie died. That's it, ain't it?"

"That old woman been houndin me and my family ever since I got married."

"There was somethin strange about Lizzy and Sookie, wasn't there?" Mae asked.

"You ain't know?" Daddy sucked at his whisky.

"Lizzy didn't talk about her auntie much, and those two had too many secrets. It was like Lizzy was fun when she was alone or with the baby or even out drinkin, but when Sookie was around it was a different story."

"Sookie was training her," Daddy said simply.

"Trainin for what?"

"To be the next *ifa*."

Mae reached into her purse and extracted a cigarette and lit it. "All that conjure. Lizzy was learnin all that stuff from Sookie since she was born."

"That woman knew every plant in the woods and swamps—which'd kill you and which'd make things nice," Daddy replied, lighting his own cigarette. "She knew most of the stories, too."

"Jesus, yes." Mae breathed out smoke. "Those stories. Some of em would stand your hair on end."

Daddy nodded. "Stories about slavery times, about that old witch Freeda who built that house in the swamp— that church, too. Same one Sookie got killed in. Lizzy even knew stories from Africa, about the Yoruba people her family came from."

"You know them stories, Hiram?"

"Naw, Mae. I wanted Lizzy and me to live in the here and now."

Daddy saw a frown appear on Mae's moonface. "But Lizzy died..." she began, then stopped.

"Now you gettin it," said Daddy. "Lizzy died. So Sookie needed somebody else to teach."

"Pixie," said Mae. "But she never let on—"

"All that mumbo jumbo be secret between the *ifa* and her student, um hmm. Now you see why I couldn't stand the woman? I'm glad she's dead, and you right—I was meanin to take Pixie to some other place just to get her away from that old bat-worshiper."

"You ain't kill her, did you?" Mae asked, wide-eyed in the semidarkness. She tossed down the rest of the whisky in a single gulp.

"Maybe I did," he said. "And if I didn't, maybe I *know* who did."

"Yeah?" said Mae. "Maybe it was me."

"You drunk," he said.

Mae sat up straight in her rickety chair and put both hands on the table. "What makes you think you the only one who wanted to see her dead? Probly half the folks in Blanchard's Bluff been hexed by her one time or another."

"I don't believe in no damn hexes, Mae! And I don't want Pixie to believe in them neither. If that old woman had her way, Pixie'd be dressed in those Gypsy's rags, barefoot, and tellin stories about people that even Methuselah'd be too young to remember. Grinding up roots, doing stuff with chicken feet. We don't live in the Darky Ages."

Mae laughed, softer this time. "You sound like you had enough. Why don't you let me take you home."

"I can get home by myself," he told her harshly. Sometimes that Mae Barnes was hard to get rid of. "Got some more thinking to do. If you goin by the trailer, though, check on Pixie?"

"I guess I can do that," Mae sighed. She got up, patted Daddy on the shoulder in a kind of half caress "You be safe, Hiram," she said, and left the bar.

With Mae gone, Daddy tried to get his thoughts back, but they just wouldn't come. He got himself another drink, then another. Something was nagging at him, something he had to figure out.

The walls of the bar were made of the planks of an old tobacco barn. They were rough to the touch. They let in cold air in winter and hot in summer. A few faded tin beer and cola signs were nailed here and there. Daddy was staring hard at a Pabst sign when he felt a hand on his shoulder. Mae again. No, that wasn't Mae's touch. He pushed back his chair and whirled around, his hand gripping a razor-sharp fish knife that he had pulled from a sheath at his belt.

"Whoa, man!" The voice was unfamiliar and Daddy peered at a young man who was backing up, his hands held out in front of him.

"Why you putting your hands on me?" Daddy asked.

"Didn't mean nothing by it," said the man, a gold tooth glinting in the dim light. "Just thought me and my friends might help you celebrate."

"I ain't celebratin," said Daddy, noticing the figures of two other young men approaching him from each side. Stealthy-like. But Daddy knew stealthy and they weren't it. Just ruffians, thieves, most likely, saw him flashing his tiny roll and wanted some of it. All of it. "And I need all of you to get out of my face."

A glance out of the corner of his right eye caught a quick movement and he heard the sharp tinkle of a bottle being broken on the edge of a table. A young man with an earring stud came at him with the jagged bottle raised toward Daddy's face. Instead of attacking, Daddy feinted with his knife and darted to his left so quickly that he was behind the gold-toothed man before the fellow knew it. One hand gripped the man's hair in a death grip, pulling the head back sharply; the other hand held the fish knife against his throat.

"I'd drop that bottle if I was you," Daddy said through clenched teeth.

The gold-toothed man was gasping and gagging. "Do it, man!" he whispered. A thin trickle of blood was already running down his neck.

The bottle hit the ground with the sound of more breaking glass. Then Daddy heard a different sound: the cocking of both barrels of a shotgun. A voice behind the bar said, "Nuff a that shit. Blue, put that goddam knife away. Rest of you, get out!" The shotgun was pointed at the ceiling as the bartender came out from behind the bar.

Daddy thrust the gold-toothed man away fiercely, causing the man to stumble against a table. He coughed and put his hand to his neck. He gave Daddy a look that was half hate, half fear. "You—" he began, but the bartender stuck the barrel of the shotgun against his face and motioned toward the door. "All right, we're goin." Daddy watched them as they walked out. These were strange days; instead of slinking out like the beaten and kicked mongrels they were, the three young men swaggered out the door like they had just bested Muhammad Ali in a fist fight.

The bartender carefully put the hammers back down on the shotgun and placed it behind the bar. "Those three been hangin around most of the day," he said. "I think they in from Mississippi somewhere. Hope they don't stop here."

"I can fight my own fights," said Daddy.

"Shore you can, Blue, shore you can."

Daddy looked more closely at the man. Dumpy little guy, stubble-faced, badly dressed. What's his name, Alfie something. Although Daddy had been coming into the bar for years, he and Alfie had never had a real conversation. In fact, it was something that Daddy appreciated. He mostly liked to be left alone to drink his drinks and think his thinks. "That shotgun," he said.

"Yeah?" said Alfie.

"Nice touch, um hmm. You know; it was a nice touch."

"Yeah, well. I wasn't spectin a drunk like you to be able to move so fast."

The two gave each other dap—slapping their palms together lightly—and Daddy went back to his table to gather up his cigarettes. The bar was empty; it was time to go.

"I called the cab," said Alfie.

"I ain't need no—" Daddy began, but there was no reason to be stupid. Not only was it a long way home, but the three toughs might be waiting for him outside, with who knows what kind of weapon. And he was a little more pickled than usual. "Yeah, okay, man, thanks."

Daddy sat at the bar a while, watching Alfie dunking glasses in a sink and putting them up on shelves in no particular arrangement. It made him want to go and straighten them. Couldn't happen in his place. Everything in the trailer was where it should be, and if something didn't have a place, it got thrown out. It was what he tried to teach Pixie when she left her shoes or her books lying anywhich place. It pained him to have to live in a trailer, to have to bring up a teenage daughter in a trailer, although at least it was on his own land and not in a trailer park. That was something.

And maybe—soon—they wouldn't have to live in a trailer no more.

Two pair of headlights turned into the parking lot and Daddy got up and moved toward the door. The first set of lights belonged to a police cruiser and he watched, just inside the door, as Officer Oskie Holt got out and closed the cruiser door, one hand holding a flashlight, the other resting on the butt of his police-issue handgun. He started having words with someone just out of Daddy's range of vision, but he suspected that there were three of them. Daddy opened the door and got into the second car, Handsome Harry's Hansom Cab, not even glancing at Holt or the three young men who were just about to learn that life was exactly as hard as they always thought it was. He closed the door of the cab and said to the driver, "Home."

"What's Oskie doin with those punks, huh?" the cabbie said as he pulled slowly from the parking lot.

Handsome Harry owned the only cab in Tate's Hammock and seemed to know where just about everyone in town lived. Unlike Alfie the bartender, Harry liked to talk; he liked to talk more than most people, would jabber like a monkey if you would let him, but Daddy had always made it a point to discourage this. So when Harry asked about Oskie, Daddy just took out his fish knife and contemplated it, knowing that Harry was watching him in the mirror.

So it turned out to be a quiet drive, and a drive in which Daddy started to get in touch with his thoughts again. Just looking at the knife told him that this kind of life was not what he wanted. He didn't want to cut up fish for the rest of his life, and he didn't want to be around people who made him want to cut their hearts out.

Daddy hadn't cut out any hearts or livers or anything else when he was in Vietnam, although he thought that Oskie Holt might have. All he'd done was slog through swamps and get shot through the shoulder by someone in a tree who didn't want to mess with him face to face. So he'd had to come home and try to support his baby girl on almost nothing.

But now he had a chance to change all that, because he knew who had killed Aunt Sookie.

He had no proof, but he knew, and he knew that that kind of knowledge was worth money. But could he do it? Ask somebody to pay him just for keeping his mouth closed? That was the question, um hmm. But there was a price for everything, even silence. Who would it hurt?

And with the killer right here in Tate's Hammock, he didn't see any reason for moving with Pixie to Tallahassee. Maybe he could build a little house for the two of them to live in—the old witchy woman was dead and they could live there in peace. He might even be able to get Pixie to go to college someday, no reason why not. In a couple of years he could buy her a little car.

"Umm hmmmph!"

Daddy looked up from his reverie and saw that the cab was stopped outside his trailer and Harry was waiting for him to pay. Five bucks was the set fee; Daddy gave him ten and said, "Buy yourself a drink."

Daddy opened the front door of his dark trailer and went inside. Pixie was either asleep or gone with Mae, so he walked quietly into his bedroom and got into his sleeping clothes. He hung up his street clothes neatly in the closet and placed his shoes together, toes just under the bed. He poured out a healthy hit of Johnny Walker Red from a bottle he kept in his nightstand, lit a cigarette and got into bed. He lay there, propped up on his pillow, and made his plans. Should he confront the killer face to face or do it in some kind of anonymous letter? And how much should he ask for? A lump sum or a certain amount each month? Those were all questions he had to settle. He finished the glass of whisky, but continued to lie there, smoking and making plans for his future. And when he passed out, the cigarette dropped a long string of ash.

Chapter Nine

Late morning sun flooded Carla's bedroom and she buried her head under her pillow. The insistent, relentless ringing of the phone bored its way into her left ear, through her brain, and out the other side.

"Shove it," she yelled, her voice muffled in the pillowcase. She thought of asking Buddy to answer it, but that wouldn't have done at all. When it continued to ring without relief, she forced herself to sit up and bare her eyes to the daylight. The other side of her bed was empty except for Mittens, who lay sleeping with her head on the pillow and the rest of her furry body under the sheet. Buddy had left, this time for real—his clothes were gone.

Carla stumbled down the hall and into the living room, dropped heavily into the overstuffed chair beside the telephone table, and snatched the receiver off the hook. She was ready to chew somebody's ass off, but then put a lid on it when she heard sobbing.

They were steady, wracking sobs, as if the person crying had been flung into despair so abruptly that her breath had been left behind.

"Who is this?" asked Carla. It was certainly a female, but the only person Carla knew that was given to crying jags was her stepmother, and then only when she was drunk. "Marietta?" she asked. But it was mid-morning, and Marietta never got going until noon. The voice tried to make a sound, but was taken over by sobs again. Carla was suddenly very nervous. Could Buddy's wife have found out where he spent the night? Did he mean so much to her that she would break down in tears when confronting the enemy? If so, she was pitiful. They deserved each other. Ten more seconds passed, during which Carla cursed Buddy in her mind. Then the crying eased up and the caller found her voice.

"Car—Carla?"

"Pixie! What's wrong?" Carla was relieved for only an instant. She had never heard Pixie lose her equanimity.

"D—d—dead," said Pixie.

Carla was stung by guilt, suddenly and completely. She had forgotten all about Pixie. Here she had been screwing around with losers while the old woman who had brought up both her and Pixie was dead and in the ground. "I know, Pix. I meant to call you after Aunt Sookie's funeral, but some people—"

"Not just Aunt Sookie," cried Pixie softly. "Daddy's dead, too."

"What! What are you talking about? How?"

"He got burnt up in the fire."

"What fire?"

"The one that burnt down the trailer."

Daddy Blue dead? Carla had never known Pixie's father very well, but the news of his death was nearly as shocking as the sight of Aunt Sookie lying on the floor of the belfry in the old church. Pixie snuffled and took several deep breaths. Carla realized the girl must be making a great effort at self-control; even though she could hardly breathe without bawling, her diction was nearly perfect. Carla pulled the phone into the bedroom, hoping the extra-long cord really was, and found her cigarettes. She sat on the bed and lit one.

"When was the fire?"

"Last night."

"You didn't get burned?"

"I wasn't there. I was at Aunt Sookie's."

"Listen, where are you now?"

"Will I have to go to jail?"

"What for? Of course not."

"I killed him."

"You killed who?" Carla asked.

"My daddy."

"But you told me you weren't even there."

"I killed him just the same."

Carla crushed out her cigarette in the ashtray and said, "Pixie, where are you calling from? Are you in town? Come over here as soon as you can, and don't talk to anyone else."

"I've got something I have to do first."

"Where are you? I'll come get you and take you wherever you need to go." But Pixie had already hung up.

Carla threw on her Ron Rico Rum T-shirt, painter's pants, and sandals. She nearly gagged when she looked in the mirror, but there was no time to shower. She banded her hair into a tight ponytail and covered it with a CAT equipment cap. She was halfway out the door before she realized that she had no idea where Pixie was. Where would she have called from, and would she go back to Aunt Sookie's house? If so, Carla was out of luck—she had never been to Sookie's house and had only a vague idea of where it was. She thought harder. The map in Sookie's cigar box possibly showed the location, but she hadn't been able to make heads or tails of it when she had looked at it with Buddy the night before. Wait—the deeds would show her where Sookie's property was. All she had to do was take them down to City Hall and look up the boundaries on the county plat map. If she could find the property, maybe she could find the house, too.

She grabbed the box and was heading for the door when the phone started ringing. She ran back to catch it.

"Pixie?" she asked hopefully.

"Who's Pixie?" asked the refined and very feminine voice at the other end. This time it *was* her stepmother. Was she psychic or what?

"Listen, Marietta, let me call you back. I've got some pretty important things to do right now."

"I know."

"What does that mean?"

"Mr. Wyche told me."

"Told you what?"

"He said you'd be needing to talk to me."

"About what?"

"He didn't elaborate."

Carla heard a sharp hiss of breath and knew that Marietta was smoking a cigarette. Carla, who was about to light one, too, didn't. "Look, Marietta, I've got to find Pixie. I'll come over later."

"Who's Pixie?"

Carla hung up without answering. She jumped in the car, gunned it around the U-shaped driveway, and headed toward City Hall. It was only when she was halfway there that she began to wonder what Marietta had been talking about. If Ronnie had told her anything, it had to be about the papers in the cigar box, but what interest could Aunt Sookie's death have for Marietta, who had been in Tate's Hammock less than ten years and who had made almost no friends in that time? Fuck Marietta; she was probably just starting to drink earlier now.

When she was six blocks from her destination, the Honda stalled at a light and no amount of coaxing or cursing could start it up again.

She spent the next hour trying to get the car off the road, searching for a telephone, and inveigling Jake Munroe, her mechanic, to come tow the car in one last time. She finally succeeded in all three, and was standing in Munroe's service station drinking vile-tasting vending machine coffee while Jake probed around in the engine.

"See," he said, looking up from under the hood, "there's these little brushes in the electric starter that's worn out. I'll hafta replace the whole thing... run you about eighty-five, maybe less if it don't take me too long."

Carla listened to him with dread. He always seemed to know what he was talking about, but his knowledge always cost her money. Where the hell was she going to get it this time? It was a horrible cliché, but all she could think of was a flock of dollar bills flying away on tiny wings. Her finances were as bad as her love life.

"Yah know," Jake said, burrowing again, "if one thing goes wrong..."

"I know, I know," Carla answered wearily. "The rest can't be far behind. But if I had money to buy a new car, I'd buy one." She threw her empty Styrofoam cup at a receptacle and missed. "If you fix the starter, will the damn thing run?"

"Should."

"Should?"

"Unless the Bendix gives out or the alternator dies. You probably oughta know that left front axle's gettin worn. Hear any bumpin or tickin noises when you turn sharp to the right?" Recognition flashed in Carla's mind. "Well, you can just let it go unless it gets louder," he said noncommittally.

"Just do what you have to about the starter," she answered, resigned. She went back to the car and took the cigar box from the seat. She could walk the rest of the way to City Hall while Jake was working on her starter.

"Check back in an hour or two," came the mechanic's voice from under the hood.

"Okay, I will. Thanks, Jake." For nothing, she added to herself, frowning. Shit on toast.

She crossed the shop parking lot and headed for City Hall. Except for the heat—already into the nineties, by the thermometer on Jake's garage wall—the day was gorgeous. Only an occasional cloud like a soft puff of cotton drifted by on the balmy Gulf breeze. Carla deliberately ignored it, determined to suck up her current state of misery to its dregs. Tears formed at the corners of her eyelids and she willed them away. Save them for later. When she got the bill.

That reminded her. She figured that she owed that adultering and deserting bastard Buddy Love for about twelve hours of services rendered. And she was determined to pay every penny even if she had to take out a loan. The problem was, she didn't know what lawyers or gigolos made these days.

Taking her time, she walked down the nearly deserted streets. At this time of day the place was a ghost town. Why did people stay here if it was such an economical disaster area? Several theories presented themselves, but she knew what it really was. It was the place the dousing rod pointed, as if the town bred something into your blood that just naturally turned you around and drew you magnetically home, no matter how hard you tried to deny it with education, travel, or whatever. Even cosmopolitan latecomer Buddy Love, who had held onto his looks, his charm, and his youth far more tenaciously than she, couldn't resist the ties his adopted hometown had on him.

She stopped in a vacant lot and listened. Mockingbirds shrilled at one another in a tall magnolia nearby, and a light breeze sighed through its upper branches. She closed her eyes and imagined the crystalline waters of the Bahamas lapping the sides of her boat. A soft voice whispered in her ear and someone's caress brushed the nape of her neck. Yeh, mon... Carla inhaled pollen and sneezed violently, nearly biting her tongue. What the hell had she been thinking, daydreaming like that? She needed to get moving if she expected to find Pixie before dark. In this heat she'd be dripping with sweat before she even got to City Hall.

She picked up her pace, her sandals flapping with each step. Soon, the familiar row of buildings on Main Street hove into sight and she slowed up, crossing the remaining yards to the parking lot. Then she stopped, realizing that she could kill two birds with one stone. Ronnie Wyche's office was in the next building. Carla wiped her brow with her cap, then ducked into the lawyer's office. The front room was empty, but a woman came out of another door holding a file folder. She was fiftyish, with slightly too much bulk and far too much hairspray. "Can I help you?" asked the woman.

"I'm looking for Ronnie Wyche."

"He's at court today. Is there something I can help you with?"

"Are you Ronnie's sec—"

"I'm the junior partner," the woman interrupted. "Moira Watson."

And I'm an idiot, Carla thought. "Um, well, I just wanted to find out about a fire."

"You mean the one that killed old Mr. Blue?" Moira Watson shuffled through a file drawer and extracted another folder.

So it was true. "Yeh."

"I heard the fire engine go past my house last night just after midnight. I guess Mr. Blue should have paid more attention to the warning message on the cigarette package."

"Why's that?" Carla asked, confused.

"He fell asleep with a cigarette in his hand. That's what started the fire."

"How do you know that?" Carla asked.

"Sheriff was here early to see Mr. Wyche about something. He told us that's what happened. The trailer was totaled, but the fire didn't spread to anybody else's property." The woman closed the filing cabinet. "Do you want to leave Mr. Wyche a message?"

"Um, no, I'll call him later, thanks."

Carla was thinking furiously as she walked out of the office and headed to City Hall. If Daddy Blue had fallen asleep with a cigarette in his hand, then what was Pixie talking about when she said she had killed him? Besides, Carla knew that Pixie was very fond of her father. She would just have to wait until she could question Pixie in person. If she was lucky, her next stop would help make that possible.

The land clerk's office was a small, cramped room cut in two by a counter. Carla entered quietly. Behind the counter sat a man and a woman, both working with concentration at separate desks. She had a nodding acquaintance with the man, although his name escaped her, but she had never seen the woman before. On Carla's side of the counter was a library table piled high with gigantic books, red-leather bound and gold-stamped. The wall by the door was decorated with old fashioned maps, all attractively framed and mounted. In fact, except for the table, the room was tidy and efficient. It smelled of varnish and buckram. As Carla approached, the woman, whose desk was closer to the counter, looked up through designer glasses. "Can we help you with something?" she asked.

"Yeh," said Carla, placing her box on the counter and taking out the deeds. "I have deeds to some property here, but I don't know where it's located."

"Umm." The woman got up and walked to the counter. "Let me see."

Carla took the deeds out of the cigar box and handed them over. The woman scanned them intently through her glasses. After only a few seconds, she turned and told her colleague, "Sookie Darbyville's land."

The man looked up from his work, adjusted his own designer spectacles with a middle finger, and said offhandedly, "Blanchard's Bluff."

Carla vowed that if her sight ever went bad, she would ask these people the name of their optometrist. "How did you know that?" she asked.

"It's our job to know," said the woman simply. Her tone sounded so professional that Carla wondered for an instant whether they gave degrees in clerking.

"Exactly what did Sookie own in Blanchard's Bluff?" Carla asked.

"What do you mean?" asked the woman.

"I mean, where in Blanchard's Bluff is her property?"

The clerk pointed to the library table. "Bring Volume Six up to the desk; the second one from the top, that's it." When Carla plopped the book on the counter, the woman found the exact page almost at once and pointed a manicured finger directly at the center of the page. "That's Blanchard's Bluff," she told her. The woman used the same finger to outline the borders.

"I can see that," said Carla, getting exasperated, "but where's Sookie's property?'

"That's it."

"That's... You mean...?"

"Sookie Darbyville owned Blanchard's Bluff. All of it."

Carla bent down and studied the property outlined in the deed. It was huge and spanned an area that was bordered by Old Pisgah Road on the east, the bay and various snaky inlets on the south, and swampland in the north and west. She saw Pixie's neighborhood outlined on the plat map, with its half dozen roads and handful of farmhouses. And there was Blanchard's Bait and Tackle. Out further she saw the Old Pisgah Church, but that was the last dwelling shown on the map. She had been told that Sookie lived much farther out. Carla was as far away from finding Pixie as before. "What about the other deed?" she asked.

Without glancing at it, the woman said, "Volume Twelve."

"How do you know that without looking at the deed?" Carla asked.

"Sookie Darbyville owned one other piece of property," she said. And on cue, without looking up from his work, her coworker said, "The Chez Marais estate."

"What did he say?" Carla asked, who had heard quite well.

"Chez Marais. Bull Clements's old place."

"But that's impossible," Carla burst out. "That property is held in trust." The woman shrugged and Carla went on. "The trust was supposed to give our family the use of Chez Marais indefinitely. Daddy would never have given up Chez Marais."

"Bull Clements was your daddy?" asked the woman.

"Yeh."

"He set up a trust?"

"Yeh. No, it was my mother, or maybe my grandmother." The woman raised her eyebrows under her glasses and Carla felt like an idiot. "I really don't know who set it up. I don't even live there, my stepmother does. Did Sookie really own the place? How long did she own it?"

"I don't know," said the woman.

"You don't?" Carla had assumed the woman knew everything.

"The dates will probably be on the deed. Let me see it." The woman turned the pages of the deed quickly, came to the correct place, and looked up. "According to this, the place was originally purchased by somebody named Rufus D'Arbanville."

"Who's Rufus D'Arbanville?" asked Carla helplessly.

"I don't know," said the woman.

"Well, then, when did he buy it?"

"Eighteen ninety," said the woman. "Looks like your daddy never owned it at all. And neither did your mama."

Carla watched apprehensively as Jake Munroe totaled up her bill on his pocket calculator. Maybe he should have just totaled the *car*. It had been a hot, sticky walk back to the garage with the late afternoon sun burning on the back of her neck. She was dripping wet and irritable.

"It don't idle perfectly smooth, but at least it'll start up okay. Best we could do without rebuilding."

"I'll have to pay you with plastic," she said finally, fishing in her purse for her MasterCard.

"That's okay, most people do. In fact, *you* usually do."

Carla crammed the bill into her purse and walked out to the car, blinking in the bright sunlight. She slid into the driver's seat.

"Goddamn!" She arched her body like a marlin trying to loosen a deep sea lure. Wouldn't you know damn Jake would leave the car parked out in the sun with all the windows rolled up. Sweat rolled down her arms as the upholstery seared her skin.

The Honda cranked with a soft purr and glided silently out of Jake's parking lot. Carla glanced in the rearview mirror and was relieved that no cloud of blue-gray smoke followed her down the road. She settled back in the driver's seat and headed for Chez Marais. She drove mechanically, the box of stuff on the seat beside her. Well, now she knew why Ronnie told Marietta she'd have to talk to her. She was still anxious to get to Blanchard's Bluff and see about Pixie, but the trip to City Hall had convinced her of two things. First, that even if she drove out to Blanchard's Bluff, she had no idea how to find Pixie; second, that she needed to talk to Marietta—now.

Carla had been on the only vacation of her life when her father had decided to get married again. She remembered her trip to the Tortugas and Jamaica vividly as one of the most liberating things she had ever done, but what stuck in her mind with even more clarity was her return to an engaged father. It was difficult not to accuse Marietta of gold digging, especially since the marriage had occurred so suddenly that Carla never even found out Marietta's last name. Yet such accusations would have been unfounded; Marietta had been in love with her father, a fact never as obvious before he died as after. She came from a socially prominent Panama City family and had met Bull Clements at a political function.

A charming woman in her early thirties at the time of her marriage, Marietta was seemingly created for the social whirl of parties and politics. Fairly attractive, well mannered, and gracious, she had made Bull Clements's last ten years lively and exciting. Her tall, willowy body wore clothes with a model's flair, strikingly set off by her red hair, which she usually wore vivid and set in ringlets like tiny springs that bounced halfway down her back. Marietta always seemed dressed for Paris, a place she often spoke of but had never been to.

The first two things Carla had noticed about Marietta were her clothes and her bright hair; the third was her face. It was a rough, sandblasted face, the result of a bad adolescent complexion. In the last few years, though, it had become reddened and coarsened by alcohol. The make-up she tried to mask it with only partially succeeded, making Carla think of plastic wood that was never quite the same color as the nail hole it was meant to camouflage.

Marietta had never been married before, and it was

fairly clear that she would never repeat the process. When Bull Clements died, Marietta began to withdraw from all her social organizations; had withdrawn, in fact, into the shell of Chez Marais. Her only pleasure these days was strong whisky, a fact Carla knew firsthand.

Carla guided the Honda between the rows of canopy live oaks bordering the gravel driveway to the estate. Marietta's Cadillac DeVille was parked outside the front entrance, at home beside the white pillars of the huge house. By contrast, Carla's Honda looked like a mongrel that had to beg at the door. Carla had lived with her stepmother in the house for over a year after Bull's death, until Marietta's alcoholic retreat threatened to engulf her as well. When Carla had found herself downing a glass of Black Label on the rocks instead of orange juice one bright Sunday morning, she knew it was time to make her escape. To do that, she'd sold the boats and bought her own house.

But the drinking wasn't the only thing that had made Carla want to leave. The truth was she just hadn't liked the old house any more. The nineteenth-century furniture Carla had sprawled over as a girl had been sold to make way for the plush modern junk that Marietta favored. A beautiful old magnolia tree had been removed so that Marietta could have an enclosed pool, and the main bathroom was so hideously modern that Carla had taken to using the old one next to one of the guest rooms. And her father had been worse. He had converted the beautiful old study into a place for cigar-smoking tête-à-têtes with political cronies and virtually destroyed the old servants' quarters where Sookie had once lived. Pretty much all that was left were a few things of her mother's, crammed into the attic—some photos in frames, a box of old Nancy Drew books that Carla had inherited, and a huge falling-apart clothes trunk…

…Yow! Carla yanked the Honda back to the road, narrowly missing someone's mailbox as the tires bumped against the curb. Her mother's trunk. The memory of it brought to mind a tiny bead painted with a scary face…not exactly the same as the ones on Sookie's necklace or the one worn by the scarf woman in the faded photograph, but close enough. Was it still there? There was only one way to find out.

Chapter Ten

Marietta stepped out of the shower and stood in front of the wall-length mirror on her side of the bathroom. Her pink marble counter was covered in expensive hair products, blow dryer, curling iron, makeup, and perfumes. Behind her on the opposite wall she could see Bull's side of the room with its black marble counter and sink, and all his toiletries regimentally lined up, ready for use. His black silk kimono that she'd given him a few years ago still hung, slightly worn, on the peg by the mirror. She stared and blinked, then let her breath out slowly and began to towel dry. Red curls dripped over her shoulder and down her back. She swept them up into a smaller towel and tucked in the edge so that it resembled a turban.

It was almost a year now and all Bull's stuff was right where he'd left it, as if she expected him to come barging into the bathroom in the middle of her bathing routine the way he'd done for nearly a decade. What would a psychologist say about that? That she should be trying to move on, that she should gather up all his personal things and give them to the Salvation Army or whoever? That she shouldn't make the bathroom a shrine to the departed? Marietta blinked again and took a deep breath. She needed a drink.

She tossed the oversized bath towel into a corner beside the tub and walked into the adjoining master bedroom, her damp feet making dark footprints in the velvet-soft ecru carpeting. Loosening the turban and giving her hair a final rubbing, she dropped the towel on the floor and shook her curls free. Standing naked, she smiled up at Bull, relaxed in his plaid shirt and chinos, posed on the deck by the pool but still very natural looking. It was her favorite portrait of him, and he hadn't objected when she'd wanted to hang it in their bedroom. There was a larger, more formal one of him downstairs, but it wasn't as good.

"Not too bad, for a woman my age, you think?" she said to the portrait, holding in her stomach. "Still a size 6," she said, pulling underwear out of a dresser drawer. "I can still fit into that dress you bought me for the Governor's Inaugural Ball." Not that it mattered anymore. She went quickly back to the bathroom, applied deodorant, blow-dried her hair, and massaged moisturizer into her face, hands, and feet. It was very important to *feel* well-dressed as well as look that way. She ignored several large bruises on her back, near the base of the spine, clearly visible in the mirror over the black marble counter. With a catch in her breath, she locked them out of her consciousness and hurried to finish getting dressed.

Marietta came back to the bedroom, opened her walk-in closet, and stared at the racks of clothing, feeling uninspired. It was hard to keep up appearances without Bull to please anymore, but she made herself do it. It was the only way she knew to hold back the terror of being alone in the world. Living in the house without Bull was lonely on good days and unbearable on bad ones. But in an odd way, the house itself was comforting because so much of it had Bull's stamp all over it—his dark wood-paneled study with its brass-studded leather chairs, the weights and exercise equipment in the Florida room that opened out onto the pool patio, the tennis court where he'd worked out twice a week in private sessions with a pro from the Tallahassee country club before his angina attack. These were home improvements he'd begun after becoming senator, and some of them—like the pool— he'd done especially to please her. And there were his cars. He had a collection of antique cars he'd restored—had them stabled in a garage remodeled from the old servants' quarters behind the mansion, like prize race horses. She supposed if money got tight she could sell one or two, but it would be hard to let them go.

Marietta dressed in new mauve Cardin separates,

stepped into strappy gold sandals with a slight heel that complimented her delicately manicured feet, and studied herself in the full-length mirror on the back of the bedroom door. The raw silk folds of the skirt whispered slightly as she twirled around, wishing Bull could appreciate the effect. The blouse hung lightly from her shoulders, her red hair a striking counterpoint. She went back into the bathroom a final time and applied her makeup. Finally, just before ten, she felt ready to face the world.

Downstairs in the spacious kitchen that had accommodated a chef and an assistant until shortly after Bull's death, Marietta made coffee, toasted an English muffin, spooned a couple of strawberries onto a plate, and was about to head out to the poolside table with her brunch when the phone rang.

"Marietta Clements," she answered, in her business voice.

"Ronald Wyche here. Hope I'm not disturbing you."

Marietta frowned. She knew Wyche as a political supporter of her husband, but she had never liked him much, despite his fake Southern gentility. He was good-looking in an odd, fashionable kind of way, and yes, he *had* tried to flatter her. But he had never been Bull's lawyer—even though Bull had asked him more than once. Something about a conflict of interest since he had been Bull's first wife's lawyer. She didn't understand it, but somehow she didn't think a call from the lawyer who'd worked for Miriam Clements could be a good thing.

"I trust you're well?" Wyche's voice was noncommittal.

"Well enough, Mr. Wyche," she said, with equal equanimity. "It's not often I get calls from prominent lawyers. Is there a problem?"

"That depends," he answered. "There's been a sudden change in circumstances regarding the trust that maintains the Chez Marais estate."

Marietta eyed the whisky cabinet. "What do you mean?"

"To put it simply, Chez Marais has a new owner. It seems that—"

"What the hell are you talking about?" Marietta interrupted as the implications of those few words sunk in. "What about the damn trust?"

"I'm not at liberty to discuss the trust with anyone, but I felt it was my duty to let you know that ownership of the estate has changed hands."

Marietta ran a hand through her hair. "How is that possible? No one's consulted me about this! I haven't agreed to put the house up for sale!"

"I don't think that's your choice to make," Wyche said evenly. "I'm just relaying information."

"But I don't understand!" Marietta struggled to keep from yelling into the phone.

"Why don't you meet with Carla and discuss the situation? I think she'll be able to tell you what you need to know."

"Carla? She told me months ago that she had no intention of living here. Don't tell me she's changed her mind?"

"I can't speak for her, but I think it would be a good idea if you contacted her. That's really all I can tell you."

All you're willing to tell me, you bastard, Marietta was thinking. "Then thank you for nothing!" She slammed the receiver down without waiting to hear whatever useless response he had to offer. Marietta collapsed onto a stool at the kitchen counter, her food forgotten. A new owner? After all that she'd— What the hell? Her heart was pounding so hard she could almost hear the blood thudding in her ears. She looked at the liquor cabinet again, but then decided she needed to be clear-headed and think this through.

Three hours later, Marietta was still sober, but reaching the end of her endurance. She'd gone through alternating bouts of anger and worry since calling that bitch Carla and getting hung up on, but now she was merely annoyed. It was clear that Carla wasn't going to call her back, so she'd have to figure out some other way to find out what was going on. This was not a time to uncap the bottle, not yet. She thought about calling Wyche's office back and demanding an explanation, but figured it would be a wasted effort. He obviously wasn't going to tell her anything. Bastard. But she was Senator Bull Clements' widow, dammit, and that had to count for something. She reached for the phone to dial Carla's number again when the bell to the front door chimed.

Looking out the kitchen window, she saw Carla's piece of junk Honda sitting in the driveway, probably leaking oil. She walked briskly to the door and yanked it open.

"I guess dropping by unannounced is less rude than hanging up on someone," she said. The snipe had its desired effect, as her stepdaughter's expression tightened.

"Sorry, I had things to do." Carla looked and smelled every inch the vagabond she was.

"So what's this talk about you selling the house?" asked Marietta. Might as well get right to the point. She left Carla in the doorway, entered the drawing room, and sat down on part of the large white sofa that dominated the central space. The sofa, as well as the beige shag carpet, the wall paneling, and the framed Audubon prints were all Marietta's additions and she loved entertaining polite company here. But Carla wasn't exactly that.

She watched as Carla sank deep into the cushions of a love seat that matched the sofa and crossed one grimy sandaled foot over the other. She resembled a destitute house painter more than anything else. "What the hell are you talking about, Marietta?" Carla asked, looking surprised. "You know I can't sell the house—it's part of the trust."

"Then what did that smarmy bastard Wyche—"

"Hold on, Marietta. If we're going to sit here and gossip about people's parentage, at least let me have something to drink first."

Marietta looked at her watch—a slender Rolex. "I've been on the wagon for a few days, if you're interested."

"I just meant Coke or tea."

Bull's wild-haired daughter shifted uncomfortably on the cushions. There was definitely something going on. "Two Diet Cokes." Marietta brushed out of the room and into the kitchen. Quickly, she opened the refrigerator door, extracted two Cokes, popped the tops, threw ice into two cut-glass tumblers, and wrapped the glasses in rice-paper cocktail napkins. When she returned to the drawing room, Carla had slipped off her sandals and was rubbing her bare feet into the thick shag. There was another cleaning bill right there.

Marietta handed one of the glasses to Carla and sat back down on the sofa. She sat up very straight and waited. "Spit it out," she said finally.

Carla, with a mouthful of Coke, looked alarmed.

"The news," Marietta said.

Carla swallowed. "Well," she began, "It's like I just told you. I don't own this house. Daddy never did either."

Determined not to put her emotions on display, Marietta got up and went to the window. Through the drawn lace curtains she could get a glimpse of the tree-lined driveway and vistas of mowed lawn. "All right," she said, her voice husky. She turned and faced Carla. "But I thought the trust was supposed to maintain the house for whoever was currently living in it."

"Right, the trust," Carla said. It unnerved Marietta the way the bitch wouldn't meet her eyes, but instead kept looking up at the full-length portrait on the wall of her father in his senatorial garb.

Marietta chewed the end of her finger. "Bull told me the trust was supposed to take care of the family. What the hell happened to the trust?"

"I don't know the terms of the trust," said Carla. "But I know who owns the house now."

Marietta was fuming. "Maybe you'd better make a short story long."

"Sit down, first," said Carla.

"Why, do you think I'm going to faint?"

"I don't like to talk up to people, and I don't feel like standing right now." Marietta sat down again. "Okay, here it is. This property and the house that's on it were bought and built by a man named Rufus D'Arbanville in 1890. When he died, he left everything to his daughter Sookie."

"Sookie?" Marietta said slowly. "I've heard that name somewhere before."

Carla nodded, sipping her Coke. "She died three days ago; you probably read about it in the *Tate's Tattler*."

"Are you kidding? I've never read that thing in my life. Maybe Carl mentioned her name to me once. Was she an old flame or something?"

Carla laughed out loud, a barking noise that made Marietta wince. "Sookie was in her eighties," she said.

Marietta forced herself to remain calm and spoke slowly, hoping what she'd just heard was some kind of misunderstanding. She felt the heat of her face glowing under the makeup. "So you're saying that some old woman owns this house?"

"Well, she doesn't own it now, because, like I said, she's dead." There was a look in Carla's eyes that Marietta couldn't read. She sat up straighter.

"There are a lot of things I don't understand," said Carla.

Marietta felt every frown line on her face sharpening. "Such as?"

"Sookie used to help take care of me after Mama died—at least she did until she had a falling out with Daddy. From some of the stories she and Mama told me, Sookie used to work here in the house for Mama's family long before I was born. After Mama died—I guess I was about twelve then—Daddy made her leave. He was really forceful about it and he never told me why. But he was actually kicking her out of her own house. It doesn't make any sense." She frowned over her glass at Marietta.

"So what am I doing here?" asked Marietta. "And what was Carl doing here? Or you?"

Carla shrugged and dug her toes into the shag. Marietta cringed. "The only thing I know for certain is that Daddy didn't have any legal ties with this place. He was sort of an interloper who married into the family."

"So how come your mother grew up here?"

Carla's expression clouded. "No idea, Marietta. It has something to do with the trust, which I can't get any information on. One of my mother's ancestors must've had some connection with Rufus—the guy that built this place— but that might have been over a hundred years ago."

Marietta's mind was in overdrive, all her assumptions about the comfortable life Bull and she had created crumbling away. "And what about now?" she asked. "You say the old lady died. Who owns Chez Marais now?"

"Pixie," said Carla simply.

"There's that name again," said Marietta. "Maybe you'll tell me who she is."

"A fourteen-year-old girl."

"A fourteen-year-old—"

"Sookie's great-niece. She's real cute. You'll like her when you get to know her."

Marietta glided up from the sofa. "I just went off the wagon," she said. "Join me?"

"Um, no, I've still got to find Pixie. Her daddy was killed last night in a fire."

"Jesus," rasped Marietta, clearing her throat again. In less than a minute she refilled her glass with the good stuff and went back to where Carla sat like a lump on the loveseat.

"Is there anything else you'd like to tell me, now that we're sharing," she said sweetly. The look Carla returned was somewhere between a glare and honest bewilderment.

"Well, there is something else," Carla replied.

"Sure, what other bombshell would you like to drop?" Marietta drew an engraved cigarette case out of her skirt pocket and lit up. She watched with satisfaction as Carla's eyes feasted on the curling smoke.

"I'm supposed to administer the estate for Pixie,"

Carla said. "Let me have one of those cigarettes, would you?"

Marietta got up, handed her the case and lighter, and sat stiffly on the edge of the couch. The two women stared at each other across the carpeted expanse of the drawing room. Marietta spoke first. "So," she said. "How do I figure in any of this?"

"I told you, I don't know. I will soon. I need to call Ronnie Wyche and see if I can get a copy of the trust." Carla took a lengthy drag on the cigarette. "I can't see Pixie wanting to live here, but I can't read her mind."

"What about you?" asked Marietta. Her stomach was a tight ball of pain, and she couldn't quite keep the bile out of her voice as well. "Do you plan on moving back here and opening up a boarding house with your little black friend?"

"Look, Marietta, don't get snippy with me," the woman shot back. "If I wanted to live here I wouldn't have bought my own place." Carla's eyes roved over the expensive, precisely chosen appointments of the room. "Ever since Daddy died, I've considered Chez Marais yours—even before that, when you started with all your modernizing. If there's one thing in this room that was here when I was a girl, I don't see it. If someone else owns the house now, it's not my fault and it's not your fault. We made assumptions about the trust and the house that maybe weren't true. Maybe we were both too busy feeling sorry for ourselves and should have paid more attention to the legal stuff. If you'll remember, I was crackerjacks for a few months there. But if you did have to move, it wouldn't kill you."

Marietta sank back into the sofa. Her eyes hardened as she watched her stepdaughter. "How would you know? You have no idea what I think or what I feel. Nobody does." Except you, she thought, looking up at Bull the Senator.

"Listen," Carla was saying, "no one has said you have to go anywhere. Just sit tight until you hear from me." Marietta nodded. Sitting tight was something she knew how to do quite well. "I'll find Pixie, get this trust thing straightened out, and get back to you, okay?" Carla continued.

Marietta nodded again. "All right. I don't have a lot of choices, do I?"

Carla stood up and wiggled her toes back into her worn leather sandals. "Oh, wait; I just remembered something else."

"For godsake, what now?" Marietta had just about reached the limit of her tolerance and couldn't wait to shut the door on her stepdaughter's backside.

"There used to be a trunk in the attic, my mom's stuff... Is it still there?"

"Who the hell knows, Carla; I haven't been up in that dusty mess."

Carla stubbed her cigarette out in a marble ashtray beside the loveseat. "Then, would you mind if I went up there and had a look?"

Marietta stood up as well. "Be my guest."

She walked past Carla and headed upstairs. Her stepdaughter followed close behind, her obnoxious sandals flapping loosely as they climbed the stairs. At the second floor landing, Marietta went to a small door that opened onto a narrow flight of stairs leading steeply up into darkness. She flipped a wall switch. "You first," she said, and stepped out of Carla's way.

Marietta hung back as Carla went up the steps, disappeared into the attic, and sneezed explosively. Marietta followed, pinching her own nostrils against the dust coating every surface and floating in the still air of the attic. A pale shaft of light came through one of the skylights, adding to the bright electric pool of white underneath the unshielded light bulb overhead near the stairwell entrance.

"Are you sure you want to root around up here?" she asked, careful not to brush against anything.

Carla was squatting down beside an ancient black trunk with a domed lid. Its brass fittings were green with age, and one hinge came loose as Carla pushed the lid up. She looked at Marietta. "It would help if I had a flashlight."

Marietta sighed loudly, but she wasn't really put out

by the request. It would give her a chance to refill her glass. She turned and went back down the narrow stairs, then down to the first floor. In the kitchen, she retrieved the big halogen flashlight Bull made sure they kept in a prominent place, ready at hand when the power was knocked out by thunderstorms, which wasn't that infrequent. She added more ice to her glass, filled it to the brim with whisky, and went back up to the attic. She was appalled to find Carla on her hands and knees in the dust, digging through the trunk, which mostly contained old clothes and stacks of books.

"Here you go," she said, offering the flashlight.

Carla took it and sneezed again. "Thanks, it's hard to see what's in the bottom."

"Are you looking for something in particular?" The ice clinked nicely as she tipped some of the golden fluid into her mouth. It bit going down, but then spread a warmth throughout her body that matched its color.

"Yeh, at least I think so, but I'm not finding it." Shining the light down into the trunk, Carla removed more old dresses, a quilt, and a large doll with a painted porcelain face; bisque hands and feet peeked out of its yellowed lace gown. Carla held it for a moment, and then put it carefully aside. Then she reached deep into the trunk and pulled out a small cedar box. "Found it!" she exclaimed and sneezed violently several times in a row. Then she worked the lid off the box and shone the light on its contents.

Marietta leaned in to see. "What is that?" She wrinkled her nose.

"It's something I remember from when I was little and played up here sometimes. I guess is belonged to my mother... I'm not really sure; maybe Sookie gave it to her."

Marietta took a closer look. The object was a rounded, gray stone or rock, carved to look like a face. A very nasty face. She reached out and took it from Carla's open hand. It was light. "Pumice," she said.

"What's that?"

"You know, volcanic rock. You can use it to sand

down rough skin on your heels." She gave it back to Carla with revulsion. "And you want this...why?" She drained her glass and took a step back toward the stairs.

"I saw something recently that reminded me of it, and I had to come look for it to be sure," Carla said. A slight rise in tone told her Carla wasn't being totally forthcoming.

"And what was it you saw?" she asked.

Carla stood up, brushing dust from her knees. She started putting everything back into the trunk, except for the cedar box, which she set aside. "I'm the one who found Sookie's body just after she died; I had to call the sheriff out there to investigate."

"*You*," Marietta began, then stopped. "That must have been just horrible. But what does that have to do with that... that thing inside the box?"

Carla picked up the box and headed for the stairs. "Sookie wore a necklace, a set of voodoo beads or whatever, that looked just like this," she said, holding up the box, "only smaller."

"You were raised by a voodoo devil. Nice," said Marietta, following her back downstairs.

Carla went straight for the door, but then stopped, her hand on the doorknob. Marietta waited, her fingers itching for another cigarette. Carla turned and looked at her.

"Aunt Sookie wasn't a devil."

"So she's your aunt, now, is she?"

"Everybody called her that..." Carla began, but Marietta cut her off.

"Not me. I have no idea who this Sookie person is, but it doesn't matter, does it, since you're telling me somebody else has inherited Chez Marais."

Carla's eyes softened. "Would it really be so bad if you had to leave this place?" she asked. "Don't you have friends anywhere, any things you like to do?"

"Butt out, Carla," she spat. If there was one thing she hated it was pity. She was the only one who knew what she'd gone through growing up, the almost superhuman desire she had needed to pull herself out of her family situation, the wiles and the determination she'd had to muster to keep what she had gained. Only she knew, and it was going to stay that way.

"You don't like me very much, do you?" Carla's question was more a statement than a query.

Marietta faced her. "I'd be lying if I said you were one of my favorite people. But I'm not going to shoot you just because you've come here bearing bad news." Carla seemed to be chewing that over, and still hesitated on the doorstep.

Finally, she said, "Look, how would you like to come out on the boat with me Sunday?"

"What, on the shrimp boat?" Marietta was incredulous.

"Yeh, get you out of the house, that kind of thing."

"If you're feeling sorry for me, forget it." Marietta studied the woman's hooded green eyes, looking for a hidden agenda. "I don't know the first thing about fishing," she continued.

"No problem, I can show you. Or you can just come along for the ride and watch me and Comer do all the work. What do you think?" She was smiling now.

Marietta swirled the melting ice around in her glass, thinking. It was a harebrained invitation, but maybe she ought to go. What harm could it do? At the worst she'd get dirty, or seasick, or sunburned. But it might also give her a chance to pump Carla for more information about this new development in their circumstances.

"I'll call you," Carla said, opening the door and hurrying down the steps to her little tin-can Japanese throwaway car. And before Marietta had a chance to refuse, she jumped in, cranked the car, and drove away. The door of the Honda had closed with a noise Marietta imagined a piece of scrap metal would make falling from a junkyard magnet.

Marietta chewed a piece of ice, watching the Honda make the turn out of the estate's shady drive and onto the paved road. Why on earth would Carla have asked her to go on a shrimping run? She couldn't get her brain around it any better than the idea of some adolescent black girl owning her beautiful house and its cherished treasures.

Marietta went back inside, heading for the kitchen. She'd decided to join Carla aboard the shrimper, although she didn't intend to have any fun.

Chapter Eleven

Carla was cursing herself steadily on the ten-minute drive back into town. Had she really invited Marietta to spend a whole goddam *day* with her on the boat? Shit on stilts; she must be getting soft in the head. If Marietta was so fucked up that she stayed in the house all day and had pretend tea parties with photographs of Bull Clements, that was her problem. Well, if she got belligerent or even too morose, Carla could always throw her overboard. That thought gave her some satisfaction as she turned left on Front Street, heading toward Crozier's Old Country Store. She would worry about Marietta later; right now she needed to find Pixie, and the denizens of the liar's bench might be able to help her. Approaching the familiar row of buildings, Carla slowed and coasted the remaining yards to the loafer's haven in front of the old store.

Those present were all hunched over boxes of Kentucky Fried Chicken and didn't look up until her sandals flapped against the porch slabs.

"Eating with the Kentucky Fried Colonel today, guys?" she smiled.

They all looked up and nodded in friendly recognition. "Tasty stuff," Hamp said, motioning her over with his leg-of-mutton arm, "but too expensive."

"Don't you go sayin nothin gainst the Colonel," said Billy Joe Lord. "He and I used to be drinkin buddies up in Lexington."

"When was you in Lexington?" asked Comer.

"During the war, when d'yah think?" retorted Billy Joe.

"Shee-it, it musta been the Civil War," said Clarence,

"and you never knew no colonel."

"If that's all you know, you should go on home and watch those mushroom-eating hippies dancin in your back forty. Me and the Colonel was so close I know ten of the eleven secret ingredients,"

The others yucked it up and Carla joined them. Billy Joe dropped a leg bone in the box and closed the lid. "Whatcha got in the seegar box, young lady? Givin up them sissy brand cigarettes?" They were all still laughing good-naturedly.

"No, I'm not into cigars. Let me show you what's in here." It occurred to her that these codgers might be old enough to know some of the nameless faces in the box.

The row of seats shifted down the bench a notch, making room for her. Normally, she would never have presumed to take a seat on the actual bench. But now both she and the old men ignored this tradition and watched as she dumped the contents of the box into her lap. The papers and stuff were all mixed together, but she spotted the oldest picture by its frayed edges. She picked it out and held it in her open palm. "Anybody know this guy?" she asked.

Balding heads and rheumy eyes leaned in around her.

"Hell, that might be old Tate hisself," asserted Clarence Revell, peering close at the photograph. "See that hair? You know why his hair turned white like that?" Without waiting for an answer, and obviously not expecting one, Clarence continued. "Got hisself lost in the swamps, way over beyond where they dug up those injun mounds. In them days, you couldn't get there by land—had to go in from the water side, along the coast. Tate's Hell was the thickest, most ferocious swamp that ever was, and it went on for miles. If I had a map, I'd show ya."

Carla really didn't need a story about Tate's Hell—a legend she had heard about so often that she knew it as well as the old men. The city of Tate's Hammock, in fact, was founded on the legend. Everybody had a Tate story and, though basically the same, all had wrinkles of difference. Clarence's immediate association of the photo with the legendary traveler made her want to hear him out. And if the photo really *was* Tate; well, not many people had a chance to turn a hundred-year-old legend into an actual historical event.

"Here, maybe you can improvise on this one," Carla said, unfolding Sookie's map. "It has some swamps on it." Carla was guessing that Pixie had retreated to her great-aunt's hidden home in the swamp, and if Clarence's tale had the detail she hoped, her chances of finding the place had just improved from zero to slim.

Flipping a gnawed chicken wing to one of the wharf dogs holding vigil in the shade nearby, Clarence wiped a withered hand on his pants and took the map. He scrutinized it silently, turning it in several directions. Then his tobacco-stained index finger traced a circular course around an area marked "Deep bogs and Marshlandes" on the map. "Awright, from the water, it woulda spread out like this. And old Tate, he—"

"Let me see that," cut in Billy Joe, pulling the map in Clarence's hand close to his nose. "That's the dadburned coast over by Blanchard's Bluff. See that little pear-shaped island just in front of that bay there, where it crooks in like a dogleg? And see, there's three little circles in a row with a loop at the end; them are the Dead Lakes."

"Dammit, Billy Joe, who's tellin this story, anyhow?" complained Clarence.

"Is that really an old map of Tate's Hammock?" asked Comer, elbowing in. Now the entire loafer's bench crowded around the map.

"This is probly Tate's Hammock right here," instructed Billy Joe, "and Tate's Hell'd be down here somewhere, past the dogleg. Can you imagine bein lost in that wild place, dying of thirst and your dogs long gone? Wahl, some of *us* mighta been able ta survive, but we's born here. Tate was a Frenchman who didn't hardly even know no English."

"Nobody even knows what he was doin around here," interjected Clarence, determined to finish the tale himself, "but they say that he struggled through pools ass deep in alligators and swarmin with snakes and skeeters. Wahl, after he'd been thrashin around through the ty-ty for a while, he grabbed what he thought was a injun necklace hangin on a branch, but it was really a coral snake. It didn't bite him, but old Tate dropped that snake like a tater that's been layin too long on the coals and lit out over the hill. He ran all the next day till he finally saw some smoke risin up above the trees, and he dragged hisself uphill to a clearing where it seemed to be comin from. He figured it was a damned big campfire, but when he got there, he saw it weren't no campfire—it was a column of smoke comin up out of a crack in the ground, and all around it was standin a town of giants."

"They weren't no giants," said Comer. "They was a lost tribe of the Creek injuns that everybody thought'd been drove off."

"And it was only a family of em," corrected Billy Joe. Clarence ignored him.

"These giant injuns was starin at him and pointin to his head and feelin all in his hair and Tate supposed that they'd never seen such fine wavy black hair as his was. But when they led him to a stream so he could get rid a some of his thirst, his reflection told him that all that fright he'd had while he was lost had done turned that long beautiful hair white as an albino hog bear. I reckon that shock was the one that sent him over the edge and he just collapsed there on the bank a that stream. It took months, but those giant injuns tended him back to health, and their youngest daughter fell in love with him—maybe because a that long white hair—so they give her to Tate and forced him to marry her.

"Wahl, this big old woman damn near wore him out, you know what I mean," he said, not looking at Carla. "And old Tate finally decided he would have to leave or die. So one dark night he snuck out of their hut and crawled off through the bushes. He wandered for days and nights, but was protected by a magical charm his wife had give him. Finally he come stumblin outta the bushes and scared the daylights outta some white men sittin on the beach. They had a fishin boat tied up in the bay. He tole em his story, but a course nobody believed him. They thought he was a ravin lunatic."

Clarence sat smiling, his tale told.

"So what happened to him?" Carla asked finally.

"Depends on who you talk to," answered Billy Joe. "Most people agree he hung around for a while and then just disappeared. Maybe he went back to that swamp gal."

"I also heard once that he died a short while after he come back and lies buried somewhere around here."

"You ever see his grave?' snorted Billy Joe.

"Hell, no, but..."

"And you ain't likely to, neither." There was a general chorus of chuckles, and knowing looks passed among the tale-tellers. The map fluttered in Clarence's greasy hand and nearly blew away. He smoothed it down over his knee.

"What's the name of this clearing marked here?" asked Comer, pointing to a roughly circular area on the map, corresponding, from what Billy Joe had said, to Blanchard's Bluff. "De... De-Arb..."

"D'Arbanville," read Carla. Sookie's family name. Was it the old name for Blanchard's Bluff? And if so, was it named for Sookie's people or was she named after the town?

"At least it don't say Tate's Hell," observed Clarence.

"Where did that map come from, Carla?" Hamp asked.

"Well," she hedged sheepishly, "I was sort of hoping you all would tell *me*. I mean, you *have* been around longer than I have." Various snorts and guffaws filled the air. "But I think," she continued, "from what you all have said about the lakes and loops and doglegs, that somebody who lived here years ago made it—maybe this guy in the picture. Maybe he was somebody Sookie worked for when she was younger."

"You mean like she used to work for your mama?" asked Hamp.

"Yeah, but..." Carla's words trailed off. "But that doesn't make any sense. Sookie didn't have to work for any body."

"Why not?" asked Comer.

"Because Sookie *owned* most of the property on this side of the map."

"Yah don't say," said Hamp.

"That old witch?" echoed Clarence.

"None of you knew that?" she asked.

They shook their wizened heads. "Don't rightly know why anybody'd *want* ta own all that swamp," said Clarence. "Less they was gonna build a zoo or somethin." He emitted a cackle at his own joke.

"What else you got there?" asked Hamp.

"Some more papers I want to ask about, but let me show you this first," she said, picking up the small cedar box she had retrieved from Marietta's. She opened it up and took out the large bead-face.

"Now that damn sure looks like somethin old Sookie would wear," said Comer.

"Yeah, but she never wore beads—just that old smelly leather bag," said Billy Joe.

"Well," retorted Comer," she probly put it on when she went to workin some mumbo jumbo on somebody."

Carla frowned and chewed her lower lip. "You think this is some kind of charm?" she asked, inspecting the bead more closely. It was primitive, yet carefully crafted, with bug eyes and pointed teeth.

"Hold that right there," said Hamp, getting up from the bench and hurrying into the store. The others shared puzzled looks, but Hamp was back before anyone could comment. Instead of taking his seat on the bench, he stood before them and held out a round stone almost identical to the one Carla was holding.

"What—"

"Where—"

"Who—"

"Shee-it!"

Carla, Comer, Billy Joe, and Clarence all spoke in

unison, but Carla managed to get in the first sentence: "Where did you get that?" she cried.

"Got it from Daddy Blue, years ago. He traded it to me for a couple of cans of beans and a package of cigarettes. Put it in my conversation piece case but it got covered up by that Confederate dollar bill I got in there."

"But where did Daddy Blue get it?" Carla asked, taking the bead from Hamp and feeling its rough texture.

"Donno."

"How long ago?" she persisted.

"Heck, I forget exactly, but it must've been right after Lizzy died."

"Lizzy," said Clarence. "That his wife?"

"Yep."

Carla was so stunned that she didn't know what to say. How many of the beads were there and what did they signify? With a start she realized that she hadn't even asked them what she had come to ask. "Listen, any of you guys seen Pixie Blue?"

Each of the men shook his head thoughtfully. "Nope," said Hamp. "Not today."

"Too bad about her daddy," said Clarence.

"Yeah. Nobody should have to die hot like that. There's enough time for that in hell."

"And I sold him the cigarettes and matches that done the deed when he was in yesterday."

"It's really a shame," said Carla, "but I'm worried about Pixie. Do any of you know where Sookie lived?"

"Just out in Blanchard's Bluff somewhere," said Billy Joe. "I never seen the house even when me and Pap was out huntin. There's supposed to be a dirt road or a path out that way now, but I ain't never seen it."

"I know how you can get there," said Comer unexpectedly. "I snuck up on her house once when I was fishin and got lost. Let me see that map again. Look—if you go by boat, you just cross this here channel, go down this fork, and keep to the middle. I remember a big limestone boulder and three old cypress trees in a row just up on the bank. But hell, you don't want to go out there."

"Hamp, can I see your pencil?" Carla asked. She took it and lightly made a small circle and three Xs near the spot where Comer's finger hovered.

Comer continued, "The house is right about there. Hell, the back window nearly hangs out over the water." He looked up at her and said, "Don't try it at low tide and stay to the middle of the stream. You think that's where Pixie is?"

"I don't know." She gathered up Aunt Sookie's artifacts and stood. "But I'm going to find out."

"You want me to go with ya?" yelled Comer at her retreating back.

"Not this time. Thanks anyway, though."

The Honda cranked with a soft purr and glided sway from Hamp's. Carla glanced in the rearview mirror—still no cloud of smoke following her down the road. At least something was going right.

At the dock she parked the car and hurried toward her boat, still carrying the cigar box filled with Sookie's papers and the bead from her mother's trunk. Then she stopped. The tide was out; she wouldn't be able to take her boat out to Sookie's tonight even if she wanted to.

Carla walked, more slowly now, past the marina and fish house, down to the seawall. She sat on the edge, hanging her feet over the side. Below her, hordes of translucent fiddler crabs scurried among the heaps of sand-crusted seaweed sculpted along the beach. She took the bead out of the box again and studied it at close range. Bulbous eyes glared out over the row of sharp teeth. The other ball-shaped carvings she had seen—on Sookie's necklace, in the photograph, and the one Hamp had gotten from Daddy Blue—may have been a little different, but there was no question that they came from the same source.

First the deaths, then the beads. Carla scoured her brains to make some sense of it all. If only she could get to Pixie, who was probably crazy with grief and needing help.

Then she remembered that Pixie had mentioned a neighbor—
Mae something, Mae Barnes—that she sometimes stayed
with when her daddy was drunk. Pixie had even pointed out
the woman's old, wood-framed house once when Carla was
driving Pixie home. Yes, she remembered now; the woman's
name had struck a chord because a woman named Mae
Barnes had made a fuss over her the day Sookie had taken
her to the old church. That must be where Pixie had gone. She
ran back to the car, settled into the driver's seat, and headed
for Blanchard's Bluff.

She probably should have gone there first instead of
getting tangled up with Marietta and the old men. After all,
what could be more logical than for Pixie to have called from
a neighbor's house? And the chances were, she was still there.
Thank god Pixie was adaptable. Losing both her aunt and her
father may have been traumatic, but she would survive.

When Carla reached the turnoff at Blanchard's Bluff,
she eased onto the dirt road and looked around to get her
bearings. Suddenly, the car thwacked into a pothole and
the shocks bottomed out. Carla's teeth came down hard on
her tongue. Shit! She winced and touched it with her finger.
Blood. She felt around in the glove compartment for a Kleenex
and dabbed it at the wound. A small dot spread out on the
white surface like red ink. It wasn't bad, but it hurt like hell.
A superstitious person would have called it an omen. Carla
wasn't superstitious, but she was stubborn as hell, and the
more obstacles that got in the way, the more determined she
became.

She turned left onto the smaller, deeply rutted dirt
road that ran through several blocks of mostly dilapidated
housing, including Daddy Blue's trailer. Her plan had been
to pass the trailer, which was the first up the bluff, and go
on down the curve to Mae Barnes' house. Instead, her foot
searched for the brake pedal as she neared the spot, and she
guided the car over the ruts with tense care. A gruesome
curiosity to see the place of death both drew her and repulsed
her. If there was anything left to salvage, she reasoned, Pixie

might need it. She could at least take a look.

Still dabbing at her mouth with the Kleenex, she craned her neck over the steering wheel for a glimpse of the driveway. The shoulders of the road rose sharply, and the dense trees threaded in and out of an old rail fence that crested the rise. The road cut through the hill like a sculptor's wedge. Where the fence ended, a steep driveway cobbled loosely with old brickbats, oyster shells, and tree roots led up into a weedy yard that had once contained Daddy Blue's Champion mobile home.

Carla shut off the engine and sat staring. She didn't really know what she had expected to find, but the effect was devastating. Almost all that was left were the metal beams that had once defined the edges of the structure. She stepped from the car and walked gingerly across the yard. A light breeze wafted across the ashes near her feet and filled her nostrils with the acrid smell of charred wood, cloth, and plastic. She reached the structure, holding her nose. The whole scene resembled more than anything else a giant's bonfire, with chunks of cauterized wood grouped like monstrous, smoldering coals. The metal kitchen table had buckled to its knees, its enameled surface crackled and crazed. A square woodstove stood intact except for a gaping crack that ran the full length of one side where the cast iron had heated and cooled too swiftly.

Carla wondered where the body had been found. On the remains of the bed? Her eyes dragged to a skeletal tangle of springs and coils. What a way to die. Carla shook her head to banish the images forming against her will.

She picked her way tentatively across the corner of what had been the living room. Footing was treacherous in the deep, slushy ash piles that obscured twisted metal siding and other debris. Turning a blackened lump over with her toe, she spotted the dull glint of metal. Jangled strings curled around the warped neck of a guitar. The box was gone entirely. Had Daddy Blue been musical? In what had once been another room, Carla spotted fragments of a girl's clothing—a melted tennis shoe, a wisp of charcoal-colored rag that might once have been a party dress. Nothing else was left to tell her anything about Pixie Blue—no schoolwork, no posters on the walls, no adolescent make-up kits. It was all gone. Suddenly Carla felt an overwhelming need to cry, to wash it all away. Her eyes stung. There was really nothing to salvage—get the hell away from there.

She backed up and stumbled into the twisted frame of a reclining chair in the living room, knocking it over and dislodging a swampy puff of ashes. Beneath the chair was what looked to be the remains of a Prince Albert tobacco can, spared the worst of the flames and the fire hoses. Some of the red paint was singed and flaking off, but that was all. Spellbound, she reached down and lifted the lid. If she had expected a hidden cache of twenty-dollar bills, or fetish beads with eyes and teeth, she was disappointed. The interior of the can held only a few scraps of tobacco, unburned because of the lack of oxygen in the tightly closed can.

Abruptly, she threw down the can with a clatter, dashed to her car, and cranked the engine. The car slithered back down the driveway rockslide and crunched to a stop in the dust at the bottom. Then she ground the gearshift into first and goosed the accelerator. The Honda responded with a gasp and leapt forward, spraying dirt and gravel in its wake.

She had visited the dead; now she would call on the living.

Chapter Twelve

Snip, snip. Mae Barnes worked down the row of bush beans, sweating in the heat and filling her basket. From time to time she straightened up, stretched her spine with a groan, then bent over again. The basket filled rapidly, and she moved on to the tangle of yellow crook-necked squash and sugar babies, a small variety of watermelon so sweet they melted on your tongue like cotton candy. Squash borers had done some damage, but she managed to find several good mature squash and melons. She snipped those loose and put them on top of the other vegetables. By the time her son Junius got off work, she'd have a pot of beans and squash simmering in bacon fat, ready to eat.

The large basket also contained a few other things from her garden: tomatoes, sweet banana peppers, and okra pods. Mae put the kitchen shears in her dress pocket and hefted up the basket. It was heavy, but she was a big woman; she'd carried heavier loads than this, many a time. Loads like stupid men who drank too much and couldn't get up their own front steps without help. This thought made her put down the basket again. Damn him, just damn him, she thought, wiping sweat and tears out of her eyes. It wasn't like her to shed tears over a man, especially one that mostly treated her bad…giving her a few nights of alcohol-fueled in-out and then next day acting like she was his hired help or something. He claimed she wasn't his type, but she'd never completely let go of the notion that he might come around, eventually, specially cause he needed a mama for his little girl. But now, with no warning, the damn sonofabitch had got himself killed.

From the garden, Mae studied the back of her house.

Like many houses in Blanchard's Bluff, Mae Barnes' home was a hybrid, each successive addition changing the style and often the level of the structure. The newest room had an abandoned air, its unfinished black tarpaper walls showing weathered holes and scraps flapping in the breeze. Hiram had promised to help Junius finish up that room and Mae had thought that maybe, just maybe, he might want to give up that tin can sweatbox of a trailer he lived in and move in with her, where there was plenty of room for him and Pixie, too. But now he was gone, and Pixie was who knew where. Mae wiped her face and hitched up the basket, heading for the back steps. Funny how things turned out, so different from what could have been. If that witch Sookie hadn't interfered way back then and got Hiram to marry that high-yellow queen Lizzy, he might have kept his interest in Mae, who was strong and sturdy and would have lasted him a lifetime. It wasn't fair, and she was not prepared to let go of the bitterness she'd nursed against the old—what had Hiram called her, an *ifa*?—all these years. Daddy Blue's revelation that Sookie'd been trying to lure Pixie into the *ifa* ways once Lizzy was lost to her made Mae's blood boil.

She stomped into the kitchen and set about cutting up onions and fatback bacon slices, to be seared in the pot till they were nearly scorched and then water and squash and beans added in to simmer for nearly an hour. Junius had told her the fire chief was convinced the death was an accident, caused by falling asleep in bed with a lighted cigarette. But Mae wasn't so sure. Just like Sookie, Daddy had enemies, although probably not the same enemies. Junius was a stock boy in Tate's Grocery and he heard every piece of scuttlebutt there was to hear. He told his mama most of it, so she felt sure there wouldn't be any investigation into Daddy's death, but she did wonder what was to be done about Pixie. A fourteen-year-old girl couldn't live on her own, but as far as Mae knew, there wasn't any next of kin for her to move in with. She'd offered to take her in, but then Pixie lit out, gone again.

Mae was enjoying the aroma starting to waft up

from the cast-iron pot when she suddenly stopped stirring and listened hard. She could hear a car engine, but it wasn't Junius—his battered truck was an entirely different set of noises. Mae put down her spoon and went into the living room. Looking through sheer curtains, she watched the little gray car come slowly up the dirt road that ran past her house. She assumed it would go on by, but no, it pulled up onto the dirt of her front yard and sat there idling, as if the person in it couldn't decide whether to get out. She stood without moving, watching through the curtains; she didn't like strangers, especially those who came to her house without warning. She couldn't see the person in the car clearly, but it looked like a woman. Frowning, she wondered what who this was—she didn't know anybody with a car like that.

She heard Henry barking from under the house, so she waited to see what the person in the car would do. Just beyond the front porch steps, she saw the family guard dog, a mongrel black and tan, emerge from the hole where he'd excavated his summer quarters under the concrete block foundation of the house. He gruff-gruffed and stood uncertainly in the front yard, out of kicking distance of whoever was in the car. Finally, the car door opened and a young white woman emerged. She looked sort of familiar, but Mae wasn't sure why.

"Hey fella, you're a good doggie, aren't you?" she heard the woman say to Henry, who was still keeping his distance. The woman made nice-doggie clucking noises and Henry rumbled deep in his throat. He wasn't bristling up, so Mae decided she didn't need to go rescue this intruder from an unpleasant scene.

The woman climbed the porch steps and negotiated her way over the missing boards of the uneven floor.

"Anybody home?" she called through the screened front door into the shadows of the living room where Mae stood like an obsidian statue. The sweet, pungent tang of onions and bacon fat filled the front room with an aroma that was hard to miss; Mae couldn't really pretend there was no one home. The woman called again.

"Ms. Barnes? Mae?" The guard mutt barked sharply in answer and marked one of the car's tires with a yellow stream.

Mae came to the door. "Henry!" she yelled at the dog. The woman on the porch took a step back. "You lookin for somebody?" Mae said, opening the front screen door and taking up the entire entrance with her solid female bulk.

"Oh, hi...uh, hello." The woman stammered around like she had no idea why she was there. Mae wondered that herself. "You're Mae, right?" the woman asked.

Mae nodded slightly.

"I don't know if you remember me... We met once years ago. My name's Carla Clements. I'm a friend of Pixie Blue. Pixie's mentioned you a lot. She told me that you take her in sometimes."

"She ain't here," Mae said, trying to place this Carla person who claimed to be associated with Pixie and her daddy. The last name was familiar too...wasn't there some fancy white family by that name living in a mansion somewhere on the other side of the town? Her brain was starting to pull in memories of black people in Blanchard's getting temporary work as waiters for parties held at that big white house not too many years ago. And then something clicked. She remembered seeing this tiny white woman at Sookie's funeral.

"Have you seen her, Mae?" the woman named Carla was asking. "I'm worried about her."

Mae continued to block the doorway. "Why? She in trouble?" Mae knew very well what type of troubles young Pixie was having—losing her daddy like that—but she wasn't about to give anything away to this semi-stranger who might be some kind of bad news, for all she could tell. Who might be a social worker come to put Pixie in some orphanage or something. "How do you know Pixie, anyway?" she asked.

"I...I've always known her. Her auntie was my nanny when I was growing up. I taught her to read, and sometimes she helps me out on my boat."

"What boat?"

"I run a shrimper."

"Funny she never mentioned you."

Mae saw from her flashing eyes that the woman was fixing to get huffy. "Whether it's funny or not, she called me early this morning. I couldn't get her to tell me where she was or I would have gone to get her. I thought she might have called from here."

"Wasn't from here," said Mae Barnes. "Ain't got a phone." She wondered why Pixie would be calling this white girl when Mae had offered to take her in after the volunteer firefighters were done putting the fire out and the remains had been discovered. Mae shivered—that was a death she didn't wish on anybody. Her eyes misted for a moment when she thought of Hiram.

Mae hesitated. "You ain't from the Social Services?"

"I told you—I'm her friend. I'm just worried about her."

"Okay, then. You can come in for a minute. I need to stir my dinner." She moved aside and waved Carla into a big chair with flower-print cushions while she moved to the stove and took up her spoon.

"Ms. Barnes...Mae." The woman named Carla hesitated, then said, "Did you see it? Did you see the flames?"

Mae wiped her hands on her dress and took a deep breath. "Sure, I saw it—heard it first, though. I thought maybe it was a loud wind roaring in the trees, but then we all smelled it. You want to know what it looked like? Like some kind of eruption. Flames in a sheet as tall as the trees. Wasn't nobody gonna live through that. Junius, my son, went out there to see what it was, then came running back and got in the truck so he could go to Blanchard's Pit Stop down the road and call the volunteers."

Carla Clements listened to this account with a horrified look on her face. "They tried to get him out?" she asked.

Mae shook her head. "By the time that water tanker

truck got here, there wasn't much left to rescue. They tried to put out the fire, but it wouldn't go, so finally they just let it burn." Mae took another deep breath. Yes, sweet Jesus, it was a bad way to go.

"I was hollerin and screamin, cause I thought the chile was in there too," she offered. "You could've poked a hole in me with a stick of butter when she showed up bout an hour later all wet and stringy-haired."

"Wet? Where do you think she'd been?"

"Don't know. But maybe it's a lucky thing she was gone last night."

Carla nodded. "Do you know what happened? I heard Mr. Blue fell asleep while smoking in bed."

Mae shifted her weight. "Could be. But maybe not."

"What do you mean? What else could it be?" The woman's face took on an expression Mae found interesting— concern tinged with a little bit of fear.

"It's true Daddy Blue smoked like a brick chimney and drank somethin awful, even with a youngun to raise, which I been helpin him do. But he got into it with some bar rats the last time I seen him. I waited outside after we was done talkin, thinkin I might get him to let me drive him home, no matter he say he don't need no ride. I seen them three try and jump him in the bar. Hiram he was too quick, though." Mae couldn't help herself and laughed deeply at the image still vibrant in her mind of Daddy Blue's fishing knife about to gut that foul-mouthed thug with the tight ass. That was the Daddy Blue she had invited into her creaking bed occasionally after Lizzy was gone—that dangerous man with the fast moves and no-nonsense way of dealin with shit like that.

"You think somebody came out here and killed him?" The little white woman's eyes were big as saucers. Mae shrugged.

"Well, this ain't the safest of neighborhoods, you might of noticed. Shit like that happens and nobody cares 'cept those like me who live here. Ain't nobody gonna look into it, I can bout guarantee you that much."

"I know," said Carla. "It's like that with Sookie Darbyville's death, too. I used to be close to her, and, well, I just felt obligated to try to make the sheriff find out who killed her."

"I ain't studying nothing bout that old witch," Mae said and crossed her arms over her ample bosom. "Good riddance, is all I got to say."

"Oh. Well, I didn't mean to offend," said Carla. "I'm just concerned about Pixie, who as far as I know doesn't have anyplace to go."

"She got me," said Mae, starting to feel irritated with this uppity person who had no cause to be out here interrogating her like the short arm of the law.

"Well, that's good to know." The woman stood up and walked back to the door, then turned around to face her again. "But I'm still worried about her. Do you think she could be at someone else's house around here?" Mae could hear a tone of frustration creeping into her voice. "I need to find her and I don't know where the hell else to look."

Mae studied her, then offered, "Maybe her losin Daddy was meant to be. Cut her loose from that cussin, drinkin old man. Ain't none of us knows what life has planned for us. But she ain't gonna come to no harm. Not Pixie Blue."

"How can you be so sure?"

"Maybe if you lived out here, you'd understand. Pixie's something special."

"She's special to me too, and I really need to talk to her. Thanks for your help. I'll just head back into town, but if she shows up, can you get word to me somehow?"

"Like I said, I ain't got no phone, but I 'spose I could ask her to call you from Blanchard's when she shows up."

"Thanks, I'd really appreciate it." The woman turned and stepped off the porch, got in her little car, and cranked the engine.

Mae followed her to the door, watching as Carla backed out of the yard, nearly decapitating Henry, who had tunneled into the cool dirt under her car tire, and sped down the rough dirt road in the direction she'd come from.

Mae pondered this strange encounter. That name, Carla Clements, was still bothering her. The name was attached to Sookie, as the woman had said, but there was more to it than that...something about the Pisgah Church. What was it? Something Sookie had done years ago? Mae was almost at the point of remembering a little girl all in white, being made much over by the congregation gathered around her, when she smelled the food, just on the edge of burning. Hurrying into the kitchen, she turned the gas flames way down and stirred the vegetables, relieved that nothing was charred. Burning was not something she wanted to think about. She hoped that wherever Hiram was now, saints bless his smoking, cussin, drinkin, adulterin soul, that he wasn't too hot.

Chapter Thirteen

Carla jolted awake from a dream in which her skin was on fire. She lay in a sweat, watching her bedroom curtains stir in the early morning breeze. Although she'd been bone tired by the time she'd gone to bed, thoughts of the burned-out hulk that had been Daddy Blue's trailer had kept her awake. She had gone over every word of her conversation with Mae Barnes, and had tried to make some sense of the *ifa* beads. What had Daddy Blue been doing with the bead he'd traded to Hamp? And what did it have to do with the nearly identical one she'd found in her mother's old trunk? How did both tie into Sookie and Pixie and the cigar box full of papers? Had the fire in Daddy Blue's trailer been an accident, or, as Mae Barnes had hinted, had it been set deliberately? There was a network of connections, even if she couldn't properly see it, but the knowledge that it existed kept her mind in turmoil late into the night.

She rolled onto her back and kicked off the sheet, staring up at the ceiling fan, rotating and creaking. She couldn't believe she'd made it this far into the summer without getting the broken bedroom window AC unit repaired, but there was just no money. She got up and made her way to the bathroom, turned on the tap in the sink, and let the cool water pool in her cupped hands. Immersing her face several times, she finally felt awake, the dream fading into thankful oblivion. Carla yawned and stretched, trying to get the blood moving—there was a boatload of shit to take care of today. In spite of Comer's grumbling complaints, she'd decided to spend the day on personal business instead of taking the boat out. She made a mental list of things that needed doing, the most important of which was to find Pixie and explain to her that she was now the owner of the house Carla had called home for years. There was also a check she had to write, and some investigating to do. This last task gave her a little rush of excitement. She wanted to see if she could locate any information about the D'Arbanville family and maybe even look into the Tate's Hell legend. She hadn't done any real research since dropping out of college and wondered if she could remember how to navigate the university library well enough to find what she was looking for.

She took the world's fastest shower, then pulled on her cutoffs and gave yesterday's shirt a sniff. Too ripe for another wearing. Tossing it into the bathroom clothes hamper, she pulled a fresh one from her T-shirt drawer and smoothed the Jamaican Princess logo over her chest. Then she brushed her hair a few licks, pulled it up into a tight ponytail, stepped into her sandals, and went to the kitchen in search of breakfast.

Quickly she got the coffee pot loaded and brewing. Popping a frozen waffle into the toaster, she sat down at the kitchen table, pulled her checkbook out of her purse, and began writing out a check to Buddy Love for $50, on account. All she could afford. On the bottom she wrote "For services rendered," then got up and put the check in an envelope and sealed it before it dawned on her that she had no idea what Buddy's address was. He'd said Killearn Lakes, but she didn't have a Tallahassee phone book. She stuffed the letter into her purse, leaving its undecided fate for later.

Almost ready to go, Carla took up her purse and keys, and then realized there'd been no cats roiling around her ankles, demanding breakfast. That was odd, especially when she saw their food bowl was empty.

"Mittens? Fangster?" She got no answer. Putting down her purse and keys, she stood listening. Too fucking strange. A quick search of the house revealed no cats playing hide and seek. Frowning, Carla unlocked the kitchen door that led out onto the screened-in back porch and cast a quick look around. Potted herbs on a shelf, piles of dirty laundry on the floor beside the washer. A clutch of clothes lay scrambled on the cushions of a sagging couch, although she didn't remember putting them there. She came out onto the porch for a closer look and her stomach turned to jelly—it was Pixie, dressed in what looked to be Aunt Sookie's old rags, stretched out like a jumble of broken sticks. All three cats sat crowded along the top of the couch like sentinels.

"Pixie!" Carla shook her gently by the shoulder.

Pixie blinked.

"Hey, girl! I've been looking for you all over the place. You scared me to death."

Pixie sat up, scattering cats.   "Mornin," she said, rubbing her eyes.

Carla stared, relieved and awkward. She wanted to comfort the girl, mother her if need be, but had no idea how to go about it. Weren't these things supposed to be instinctive? How were you supposed to tell someone who had just lost her entire family that everything was going to be all right? Especially when you had no idea how that could be true.

"You didn't need to spend the night out here on the porch," she told the girl. "Why didn't you wake me up?"

"Front door was locked," Pixie said simply. "Back door, too, so I came in here."

"You should have banged on my window."

Pixie shrugged and offered a small grin. "I had good company," she said, picking up Mittens. The other two cats had bolted for the kitchen.

"Well, whatever, I'm glad to see you. We have some things to talk over," Carla told her.

"Okay." Pixie got up and smoothed the folds of her thin cotton dress, its faded blue background the color of cornflowers overlaid with a tiny print of white daisies. Sleeveless and about as shapeless as it could be without being an actual gunny sack, it flapped just above Pixie's bare feet as she went past Carla into the kitchen. "You got any Pop Tarts?"

"No, and those things aren't a good breakfast for a growing kid."

"But I like em," said the girl.

"What's with the dress?" Carla asked, following her into the kitchen and pouring her a bowl of corn flakes and setting a carton of milk from the fridge beside it. "I thought you lived in shorts and T-shirts."

"The clothes I had on yesterday be too dirty," she said. "This dress was Auntie's—s'mine now. I like blue." Pixie put Mittens down and gave her a look. "All the rest got burned up."

Carla felt her face go beet-red. "Oh, right. Jeez, Pixie, I'm really sorry." There was an awkward pause. "That was stupid of me."

Pixie sat down at the table and stared into her cornflakes. "It's okay. I'm done cryin now. I got to deal with what I done."

"You haven't done anything," Carla told her. She poured herself another cup of coffee and sat down at the table.

"You don't know."

"Don't know what?" asked Carla.

Pixie looked at Carla with an unreadable expression on her dark face. Finally, she spoke. "I'm the one killed Daddy."

Carla was so startled that she dropped her coffee spoon. "Bullshit," she answered, wishing she were as sure as she sounded. "The fire was an accident."

"That part's true," Pixie said.

"Well, then. You don't have to blame yourself for any of it. I talked to Mae Barnes yesterday. She told me you weren't even there when the fire started."

Pixie implored Carla with her eyes—an adult expression in the girl's face Carla had never seen there before. "You don't understand," said Pixie. "I put the knife and fork in Sookie's hand."

"You did what?"

Pixie pressed her long fingers against the hollows of her temples. "Sookie told me I'm supposed to do for her now.

But I don't know if I did it right."

"Pixie, you're not making any sense. You're telling me you found the body?"

Pixie nodded. "I took a shortcut to the church right after you let me off, and I found her there. What I did, make somebody pay."

Carla sighed. "You shouldn't twist that crap of Aunt Sookie's into a way to blame yourself."

"Ain't crap," she said. "My mama was 'sposed to be Aunt Sookie's *ifa*-second, but she died. So now it's me."

"What the hell are you talking about, Pixie? What's an *ifa*-second and what did your mama have to do with anything?"

"Back in Africa days." Pixie said. "Sookie's people were Yoruba and an *ifa* is kind of like their doctor. Sookie's mama was an *ifa* and her mama's mama. Sookie was s'posed to pass all her conjure knowledge to *my* mama, but my mama died too soon. I'm the only one left. But I didn't get it all—I be too young and I don't know enough."

Carla had a dozen questions on the tip of her tongue, but finally just said, "Well, eat your breakfast and let's figure out where we go from here."

"I'ma go to the bathroom after this," said Pixie.

Carla looked and saw the trace of a smile. This was the Pixie she knew. Relieved, she gulped down the last of her coffee.

"I'm going into Tallahassee today," she said. "Come with me and we'll buy you some decent clothes."

"You ain't got any money, what you gonna buy em with?" Pixie was definitely smiling.

"I got plastic—we'll go to the mall and shop around. You have school starting up in less than a month, so you'll need supplies, too."

"Who says I'm goin back to school?"

"I do, especially if you're staying here with me. I'm not your mama or your auntie, but I'm going to make sure you get an education."

"Mm." Pixie appeared to be digesting that along with her corn flakes. Carla left her thinking and went back to her bedroom. Down on her hands and knees, she rooted around in the closet where the shoes were piled and pulled out a pair of high-top pink Reeboks, hardly worn. They'd been a little too large and a little too pink, and so had been worn once to a dance club in Tallahassee and then tossed to the back of the closet. But now, they were about to get a new lease on life.

"Try these on," she said, handing the shoes and a clean pair of socks to Pixie.

"Hey, cool!" The girl slipped them on and hopped around the room. "I like em."

"Perfect, they're yours. You ready?"

"In a minute." Pixie bounced all the way down the hall to the bathroom.

Carla waited by the front door, keys in hand. They still hadn't talked about the most pressing matter—namely, Chez Marais and the trust—but that could be done on the longish ride from Tate's Hammock to Tallahassee. At least Pixie was accounted for and in pretty good spirits.

When Pixie returned, Carla saw that she had unrolled her tight corn rows and shaken them out to form curly, cigar-shaped dreadlocks that reached out in all directions.

She suppressed a laugh. The hair, the granny dress, and the high-tops were an incongruous mix, but somehow the result was exactly Pixie.

Pixie ran out to the car in her new pink Reeboks and got in. Carla cranked the engine and headed out toward the highway, aiming north. After a few minutes, she popped a Peter Tosh cassette into the player. "Do you like reggae?" she asked the girl.

"Donno. Never heard much."

"What do you like?"

"Mostly blues," answered Pixie. "Daddy taught me to play some on his guitar. I could probly play reggae songs if I practiced. But Daddy's box was burned up in the fire."

Carla flashed on the sprung guitar strings and pieces

of charred wood she had seen in the trailer. "I didn't know Daddy could play guitar," she said.

"He did sometimes at parties, mostly when he was drunk. He taught me the chords and notes. I can sing Bessie Smith." She stopped and looked out the window. "But all my records and tapes got burned up too."

"We'll get some music in the big city, okay?"

Pixie nodded. "Cool," she answered, but this time her thoughts seemed somewhere else.

Down Second Street, up Cincinnati, and onto Front. Tallahassee was exactly one hundred miles north of Crozier's store. With the gas tank full, Carla settled into her seat, looking forward to the long drive. In the other seat, Pixie seemed reserved. She sat upright and looked straight ahead, no slouching or feet on the dashboard.

"I used to make the drive down this highway from Tallahassee back home every couple of weeks for the three years I was in college," Carla said.

"I remember," said Pixie.

"How could you?" asked Carla. "You were only, what, six?"

"And seven and eight." Pixie looked out the window as the last of Tate's Hammock's roadside shacks disappeared behind them. "We always knew when you were home."

"Who's we?" asked Carla.

"All of us. Me, Mama, Aunt Sookie, Daddy… We knew what kind of car you drove, what you got for Christmas. Sometimes you came down with your boyfriend, right? His name was Buddy."

"You're scaring the shit out of me, Pixie. What, was Sookie spying on me?"

"I guess. Her and some of the folks that cleaned house for your daddy."

"Why would she care about what I was doing?"

"Auntie always said you and me were special."

"Special how?"

Pixie shrugged. "Anyway, *you* told me bout Buddy

once. Showed me his picture in your bedroom."

"Ummm," voiced Carla, remembering. "I shouldn't have inflicted that on you."

"One of the times you came home with him—to Chez Marais, I mean—was the first time I ever fed the saint."

"Fed the saint? What's that?" asked Carla.

"Conjure," said Pixie. "Aunt Sookie wanted to do it, but she and your daddy didn't get on. So she gave me a mess of greens to take up to your house. As a gift. Then she gave me a picture of Saint Michael—you know, pretty long-haired white guy with big shiny wings and a flaming sword—and told me to put it near the back door. I put paradise seeds in a little bag behind it, too. Then I ran away."

"So that's what that picture was," Carla said. "I saw Daddy throw it in the trash. If I had seen the seeds I might have guessed it was some of Aunt Sookie's business. But what was it supposed to do?"

"Bring luck," said Pixie.

"Didn't work too good, did it?" said Carla. "Maybe if I'd graduated and got some boring teaching degree, Daddy and Marietta would have had something they could brag about to their friends at parties."

"It woulda worked if your daddy'd left it alone stead of throwin it away."

"You think?"

"Sure. What were you tryin to learn in college?"

Carla hesitated before answering. "I was a History major," she said finally.

"Like dates and stuff?" asked Pixie, wrinkling her nose.

Carla laughed. "Yeh, dates. No wonder I couldn't stick it out." The truth was, she couldn't stand sitting still at a desk for fifty minutes and had spent a lot of time twitching and staring out the classroom window. Still, she hadn't been a bad student—it was her breakup with Buddy that had sent her home with her tail between her legs.

Pixie turned her face back toward the window, her

face pensive again. Outside, pine and palmetto bushes grew randomly where the winds had carried their seeds to earth. Carla loved this part of the drive and found it calming, no matter what the season. In late summer, the ditches alongside the road were full of yellow and white flowers like black-eyed Susans and daisy flea-bane.

"Before we go to the mall, there's another stop I need to make. At the university library—that okay with you?" asked Carla.

"Sure. I'ma just hang out with you, I guess."

Carla drove for a few minutes in silence. The landscape was tedious now, with only a few shacks or trailers breaking the domain of the scrub pine. A string of cars, many of them pulling boats or with surfboards tied to the roof, filled the other lane, hurrying toward the coast.

Carla cleared her throat. It was now or never.

"Listen, Pix," she said finally. "I'm not sure how to explain this…your auntie left me a box of some important papers when she died. She left them to me because she named me as executor of her estate."

"What you gonna execute?" Pixie was looking at her sidelong.

"Well, I just make sure the terms of her will are carried out."

"Oh, okay."

"And the most important thing in the will is that all her worldly belongings are left to her next of kin, which is you."

Pixie looked out the window. "Mmm."

Carla shifted in her seat. "So, what that means is… well, I just found out that Sookie has been the legal owner of Chez Marais all this time, not to mention most of Blanchard's Bluff."

Pixie looked at her. "That's a lot of property."

"Right, and it's all yours now. And because you're a minor, the executor manages your inheritance for you until you turn eighteen." Carla waited, but Pixie had nothing to say. "I guess this is as much of a shock to you as it is to me, but I need to know, um, what do you want to do with the house and all that land?"

"I don't know. Guess maybe I can live in the house, huh?"

"With who? Do you have any relatives in Blanchard's Bluff?"

"Naw, not really. But I can live there by myself."

"You're too young to live by yourself. That house takes an enormous amount of upkeep."

Pixie turned and gave her a confused look. "Sookie house been there for years with no keepin up. Ain't no plummin to fix...don't no 'lectricity go out that far."

Carla realized her mistake. "No, I mean the big house, Chez Marais."

Pixie scrunched down in the seat. "Somebody already livin there."

"Well, yeh, somebody is," Carla said. "But it's your house. You can throw Marietta out any time you want."

"Can't I just live with you?" Pixie asked softly.

"Of course you can. I mean, I want you to, but the law might have another opinion about that. I don't want you to end up in a juvenile home or anything. When I see Buddy again, I'll...I mean, when I see Ronnie Wyche, my lawyer, I'll ask him for advice."

"You still see Buddy?" Pixie asked, shocked. "What about your Yancy-man?"

"Can we not talk about them? Why don't you tell me about *your* friends?"

"I don't got no boyfriends and don't want none, either. At least not from around here."

"And where *do* you want boyfriends from?"

"New York."

Carla snorted. "People are crazy in the north, you'd best stick with me," she said, keeping her eyes on the yellow stripes dividing the two-lane blacktop.

"Naw, I think your boyfriends be too old for me."

Pixie asked.

"Don't be funny," Carla said.

"I might decide to just run away to New York and get lost in all the people," said Pixie.

"I did that once," said Carla.

"Go to New York?"

"No, run away. I stole my daddy's boat and cruised off all by myself."

"No you did not!" Pixie laughed out loud, which Carla was glad to hear.

"I did so too."

"Why Auntie never told me?"

"Because *I* never told *her*," Carla replied smugly. "In fact, I never told *any*body."

"Why did you do it?" Pixie asked.

Carla stared at the road, remembering. "Payback. Only, I guess it doesn't count if the one doing the payback is the only one who knows about it."

"We talkin about high school now?"

"Graduation night," Carla said. "I didn't have anybody there to see me get my diploma."

"Where was your daddy?"

"Off somewhere. Some political thing. Something unavoidable."

"You musta been pissed, um hm."

"Big time." Carla frowned, remembering exactly how her temper had fueled that impulsive, reckless moment. Images filed away for years came back to her. She remembered being one of a handful of stragglers after the ceremony. Johnny Blanchard was one of them. So were his girlfriend Hazel and her twin sister Twyla Ann. And Stinky's cousin Claude. They'd milled around a bit, then Claude had invited them all to go behind the gym and get high. And they had, and evidently the pot made the others horny because pretty soon Johnny and Hazel were making out in the shadows of the goal posts and Claude had paired up with Twyla Ann. Carla had watched them with a kind of hazy curiosity until she decided to get the hell out and go to the Tortugas. It was as simple as that.

It took her most of the night to get everything ready, both on the boat and at home. Her father had left her a graduation card and a present—a Visa credit card. Told her to buy something nice. Well, a vacation was nice, wasn't it?

"Stupid, but yeh, that's what I did," she told Pixie. "Before Daddy got into politics, we used to do more things together. That's how I learned to fish, to shrimp, to drive a car. Shit on a stick, I could run his thirty-eight-foot Bertram a *hell* of a lot better than he could."

"Is that the boat you stole?" Pixie asked.

Carla nodded. "Yeah, his private fishing boat. By the time most the class of 1976 were getting over their graduation night hangovers, I was on board and cruising out of the marina with full tanks, a couple of spare ten-gallon cans for emergencies, every penny from my bank account, and a brand new Visa card in my pocket."

Of course, there had been other things, too, she remembered with an inward smile. A carton of cigarettes, a good supply of canned tuna and chocolate-chip cookies, a cooler of Cokes, *Treasure Island*, her daddy's 38 Special, a hot red bikini bathing suit, and several changes of clothes. She'd even palmed a couple of joints from Claude's stash the night before. She had been *set*.

"Weren't you scared?"

"A little, maybe, but mostly I just loved it. I loved the sun and the water and hell, I didn't really need the food—I could catch anything I needed—there was enough fishing gear on board to start a bait and tackle. And *tanned?* Girl, you think *you're* brown—you should have seen *me* after three weeks on deck."

Pixie giggled and tried to clean one of her fingernails with her teeth. "I'd be scared, bein all alone on a boat like that," she said. "Where did you go?"

"Well, first I cruised down the Gulf. That was pretty familiar territory," she began, and for the next half hour was regaling Pixie with her adventures on land and sea.

The first thing she had learned on the trip was that Florida was a hell of a lot longer than she had imagined, and had a lot of water traffic. She spent time on her CB radio (her handle, "Tiny-mite," embarrassed her now, but it had served her well then), both listening to people jawing or asking questions about the waterway she was passing over. From the CB she learned about the Everglades and the Ten Thousand Islands south of Tampa, and she'd anchored there for two days, making a few forays into the Glades to see the wildlife and hiking to the nearest small town for supplies. Then it was down to the Keys, where she just hung out for a couple of weeks, one boat among a myriad of others. But she soon realized that her money was not going to last forever, especially when she landed in places that didn't take credit cards. And gas for the boat was not cheap. From some other captains in the area she learned that in the Dry Tortugas, about an hour to the west of Key West, she could get work as a commercial fishing vessel. So she'd set up her poles, taken on a half dozen clients from Ohio, and with an old Conch named Alfred as guide and mate, had spent a few days out among the drift fishing boats.

At first, she'd had to pretend she was an experienced skipper, but after a week or so she felt she *was* one. And certainly she learned more about the Gulf Stream, the tides, the clouds, and the various kinds of sea life in a short time than she ever had in her life. But she was anxious to keep going, so after a while, she said goodbye to Alfred—whom she'd gotten to like for his gruff ways, thorough knowledge, and what she imagined was a secret desire to see her succeed—and was off again, this time to the Bahamas. She hooked up for two days with a couple of skin divers from West Palm Beach who showed her how to recognize coral heads from the ripples they made as water passed over them. These were the spots where lobsters were plentiful, and Carla learned to dive using a mask and snorkel, and to harvest foot-long lobsters with her bare hands.

She had been afraid that the constant running would test the limits of the *Miriam C.*'s capabilities, but its small, 300-horsepower twin diesel inboards were built for performance. She found that she could sell a few lobsters to a small outdoor market on Rum Cay, and it was there that she met Jaxon.

"Hold on a minute," said Pixie, who was now, Carla noted, hugely interested. "Who's Jaxon?"

"He was this gorgeous Jamaican man I met on the dock one day. Early twenties, deep brown skin, green eyes, and the most intoxicating accent I've ever heard."

"Dreads?" asked Pixie.

"No dreads, I'm afraid. He wore his hair pretty short, but he *did* have a tattoo of a swordfish on his right arm."

"Cool."

Carla remembered seeing him first on a small fishing vessel with several other young men, seemingly out for a good time and a little angling. One afternoon they had invited her aboard for a beer and she had accepted. A good time was had by all and she'd barely escaped with her honor intact. She hadn't remembered any of their names, but the next day she had run into one of them in the market when she arrived on the cay with a postcard for her father. He nodded to her and introduced himself as Jaxon Clagget, said he was a projectionist for a movie theater in Kingston, Jamaica, on a fishing vacation with two cousins, whose unseemly behavior he apologized for. She met him again the next day and even went to a bar with him, although she wasn't eighteen yet. They lay on a blanket on the beach, watching the sun go down, which led to some serious kissing and making out, but she ended up bunking by herself that night on the *Miriam C.* The next morning when she came up on deck, he was waiting for her on the dock. He was looking intently at her and her boat. "You goin, or you cahmin?" he had asked.

"Excuse me?" Carla had asked, as tongue-tied as she could be and still be alive.

"I like you boat. Maybe you give me a ride, eh?"

"If you like. Where to?" she'd said, teasing.

"Jamaica."

"Jam—I can't go to Jamaica. It's too far!" She was protesting, but in truth the idea of going to Jamaica was hitting her like a slug of strong caffeine.

"Not too far. Very nice trip, in fact. Dis vessel hondle it okay. I show you de sights and pay for your gosoline, too."

"You're stranded here," Carla guessed.

"In a monner of speakin. My cousins want to go up to Ondros Island and fool around. But I got to get bock to me job."

And suddenly, in the space of two minutes, there was no doubt that Carla would agree. And she did. And with Jaxon to guide her through the Windward Passage between Haiti and Cuba, they made the trip in three days. And during those quick three days, Jaxon shared with her his own particular knowledge of boating and fishing. They shared stories about their families, their likes and dislikes, and their plans for the future. And, after the second day, they shared more intimate things.

"So Buddy wasn't your first real boyfriend?" asked Pixie.

"Well," said Carla, blushing for the first time in recent memory, "I only knew Jaxon for a little over a week, but I guess you'd have to say he was my first."

"And what happened when you got to Jamaica?" Pixie's eyes were wide with the thrill of adventure, no matter that it was second-hand.

"Then I came home," Carla replied.

"Just like that? What about Jaxon?"

"Jaxon had his future and I had mine. We knew that from the first. Besides, Daddy would have the marines out looking for me if I missed my college registration. Jaxon and I wrote to each other a few times while I was going to FSU, then he told me he was getting married and I guess we just stopped."

"Do you ever wish you had stayed?" It was the most

obvious question the girl could have asked, yet it was also the one Carla had avoided facing for almost ten years. She answered it now.

"Every day," she said.

Chapter Fourteen

Because it was summer and a Saturday, Melanie Love didn't bother going around to the employees' parking lot; she found a space on Dogwood Way, right outside the five-story Strozier Library where she worked. Weekends at the library were slow, especially during summer term, but a few people were hanging around. Under the trees lining the walkway, a man smoking a pipe held two Afghans on leashes, their long, flaxen fur streaming in the humid breeze. On Landis Green, an open sward of grass and brown dirt that fronted the library plaza, a bare-chested man threw a Frisbee to a young woman in a halter top. Melanie dodged past them and brushed between the date palms flanking the library steps. Two black women sat on the steps beside the nearest tree, eating its round, slightly bitter orange fruit.

Inside, summer disappeared. In the chilled air, a student worker sat at a desk equipped with an anti-theft book detection device; two more were slouching without anything to do behind the long checkout desk. Melanie took a right; five steps later she had entered the Reference Department, which covered an area about the size of her living room, surrounded by dozens of shelves of books and almost as many rows of study tables. Behind the Reference Desk sat a sallow-faced young man of twenty—her student assistant—who was sweating even in the pleasantly cool temperature of the room. He looked up and ran a hand through already-mussed hair as Melanie placed her purse behind the desk.

"I...I'm sorry I had to call," he managed.

"It's okay," said Melanie, trying to make her voice more pleasant than she actually felt. "You shouldn't work if you're sick."

"I know you had that tennis match…" the young man managed.

"Easily postponed," she told him. "Now go home and get some rest."

The young man shoved his chair back and got up slowly, then shuffled unsteadily toward the door without another word—either very ill or having a bad trip, Melanie couldn't be sure which. As a precaution, she took a can of aerosol disinfectant and sprayed mist in an arc around her. Then she sprayed the desk and chair and wiped them off before sitting down. A message was taped to one of the shelves to her left and she took it down and opened it—a note to herself about a complicated reference question she had not had time to answer before leaving for the weekend. She thought about calling one of her other student assistants to see if they could come in, but decided against it. The tennis match—which she had been looking forward to!—had already been rescheduled for the next morning, and she could always use the extra money or extra time off. She glanced at her watch—a Movado Museum with black face, gold hands, and no numbers—and wrote down the time on her timecard.

The library was almost empty except for the student workers she had passed in Circulation. An elderly man from the English Department sat in his usual chair surrounded by books on Yeats. A young couple was studying together at one of the round tables at the very back of her department, and two other people—one black and one white—were standing by the card catalog whispering.

They were an odd couple. One was a black girl in her early teens wearing a colorful granny dress and new-looking pink Reebok trainers. The other woman was older, maybe her own age, and was wearing a faded T-shirt, ragged cutoffs, and sandals. Melanie looked at her face, then looked more closely. She had seen the face before, but never in person.

Melanie took a pen and the sheet of paper with the reference question to a part of the card catalog area next to where the two were standing. She absently extracted a drawer from the catalog, and placed it on the table in front of her. With easy experience she found the reference she was looking for and wrote down the call number on her paper. She slid the drawer back in the catalog and extracted another, peering curiously at the older of the two females as she worked. She even remembered the woman's name now: Carla, Carla Clements. She also knew that she was the daughter of a state senator who had died a while back, although she didn't look like one. Carla was a little shorter than she had imagined and her hair was thicker, pulled into a quick ponytail so that a few wisps fell down her neck. But it was her, all right. The eyes and cheekbones were unmistakable. She seemed undecided about something, pulling out drawers at random and jamming them back in again almost immediately. Melanie put back her own drawer and walked over. She smiled pleasantly and asked, "Can I help you?"

The woman, Carla, looked up, surprised. "With what?"

"With anything. I'm the reference librarian."

"Oh." Carla seemed nonplussed. "No. Yes." But before she could continue, her young companion approached, and after giving Melanie a suspicious stare, whispered something into the woman's ear that Melanie couldn't catch. The woman nodded and the girl went off in the direction of the rest room.

Melanie waited without a sign of impatience until the woman looked in her direction again. "What I mean is, I need to look up something but I don't really know where to find it."

"What is it you're looking for?"

"Genealogies," Carla replied.

"Good," said Melanie. "I like genealogies. What area?"

"Wakulla County."

No surprise there. "You've come to the right place. I've already done one genealogical search for Wakulla County."

The woman stared at her for a moment and finally asked, "Which family did you look up?"

"Barwicks," Melanie answered. "It's a big family—they actually have a family historian. I was able to help her locate some census data." As she spoke, she noticed that Carla Clements was openly studying her; glancing first at her shoes, her watch, her cream-colored georgette blouse, her light hair in its two braids set in soft ropes above each ear.

"My husband used to go to high school in Wakulla County," she smiled. Playtime was over.

"Your husb—"

"In fact, I think you know him. Buddy Love. You're Carla, aren't you?"

"Y—yeh. And you're, um, Minnie?"

"Melanie."

"Right. How do you know who *I* am?"

"Buddy showed me pictures."

"He did? Right. Well, I've moved on."

"I see."

Melanie let the silence settle between them. There was a time when she might have enjoyed hating this black-haired unkempt woman, but now she was merely curious.

She waited, and finally Carla cleared her throat and asked, "You mentioned census data. Do you think I could get a look at some of it?"

Melanie shrugged. "Sure, we have an extensive holding. There's a company that photocopies the census records of every county in the U.S. all the way back to 1800 or so. So far, they've only produced about three volumes that deal with Wakulla County; I think they're 1850 through 1890. If your family or whoever were part of the census in those years, they should be listed. Here, let me show you."

She led Buddy's ex-girlfriend across the carpeted room to a bank of high metal shelves crammed with huge green volumes. She opened one labeled 1890 and asked, "What name are you looking for?"

"D'Arbanville."

A voice from inside the stacks startled her. "That was my auntie's name." Melanie turned to see Carla's companion reappear like a sprite. "Well, almost," the girl added.

Melanie smiled despite the awkwardness of having just met her husband's ex. "That's a nice French name," she told the girl, paging through the book. "My father's family is French, too," she added incidentally.

"Cool," said the girl.

"Listen, um, Melanie," Carla began. "Pixie and I—this is Pixie, by the way—we're trying to solve a mystery."

"What kind of a mystery?" Melanie watched Carla's face go through a series of indecisions, then become resigned.

"Pixie's aunt was killed last week. Murdered, I think. Then her father died a couple of days later in a fire. The sheriff's office doesn't seem to care about either of them so we're, you know, trying to investigate for ourselves."

Melanie smiled openly. "Buddy told me you lived an exciting life, but I had no idea."

"Buddy told you that?"

"Buddy who?" asked Pixie. "Are you talking about the Buddy that Carla—"

"Hush, Pixie," said Carla.

Pixie clapped a hand over her own mouth, her eyes wide.

Melanie was about to panic, then relaxed as the girl let it slide. She knew that Buddy had been spending some time in Tate's Hammock recently, but she wasn't sure she wanted to know exactly what he was doing there. The appearance of his ex-girlfriend—the first person he had lived with—was a bit too coincidental. Yet Carla seemed to be both sincere and befuddled. Melanie had always had a problem disliking people, even people who deserved her suspicion, and it was as true now as ever. "Okay, I'm willing to help. But I need to know exactly what you're looking for."

"I don't...okay, Pixie's aunt's name was Sookie Darbyville, which is a corruption of D'Arbanville. She used to be my nanny and when she died, she left a box of papers for me and I've been trying to sort them out. There are references to some of her ancestors, and I'm trying to figure out when they lived and how they acquired a great deal of property in Wakulla County."

"And you think that might have something to do with the deaths?" It was a perfunctory question because she was thinking about something else. Melanie knew that names were often corrupted through time. The transformation of D'Arbanville to Darbyville had probably occurred over many decades of inaccurate spellings on census records and the like. But what an unusual family name for someone living in Tate's Hammock—especially an African-American family name. There might have been French slaveholders in north Florida—they'd certainly made their mark in Louisiana, which wasn't that far away. Melanie was curious now, and just might go to the trouble to do a little digging on her own, just for the fun of it.

"Come over here and sit down," she told Carla and Pixie. "We can spread out our books and see what we can find." Melanie led them to a round table by a window. Outside, she could see a hedge of Japanese honeysuckle covered in tiny fragrant flowers that perfumed the air near the parking lot entrance. Outside it was summer, but in here, institutional cool. She turned a couple of pages of the census book, then placed it in front of Carla, pointing to a column halfway down the page.

"Here, look. In 1890, there was one D'Arbanville in Wakulla County. Rufus. He was twenty-two years old, and he must have been a bachelor because there's no reference to any relatives living in the house." Carla and Pixie bent their heads over the book. "You can look up any name you want for any of the years that were published."

Pixie—after studying Melanie as thoroughly as Carla had earlier—had taken up the other two volumes of census records and was paging through them quickly. "Nothin," she said. "Not in 1850 or in 1870."

"So what does that mean?" asked Carla.

"Probably that he didn't come to Tate's Hammock until just before 1890," Melanie said. First a murder, then a mysterious landowner. She was definitely getting interested.

"Okay," said Carla. "I know that he bought the Chez Marais property in 1890, so I haven't learned anything new except that he was a young man then. But where did he get the money to buy the property and what happened to him?"

"What's Chez Marais?" asked Melanie.

"That's our family property," Carla responded. "At least I thought it was ours."

"So it was originally owned by this Rufus person?" asked Melanie.

"Yeh. And now it belongs to his descendents. Specifically, Pixie."

"You're a D'Arbanville?" she asked the girl.

"My mama was, but she died."

Melanie realized she was becoming completely sucked into this little drama unfolding in front of her. She studied the girl. Pixie could be an attractive teenager with the right clothes and her hair combed out of those horrible dreadlocks. Her teeth were almost perfect and her skin was smooth and immaculate. And she owned the property that Carla Clements had thought was hers. Curious indeed. "House in the swamp," she mused.

"What's that?" Carla asked.

"Chez Marais; it means house in the swamp," said Melanie.

"That's right, you majored in French," Carla said.

Melanie decided not to wonder how Carla knew that about her. She stood up. "Wait here," she told them. She went to the area in the stacks where books on Wakulla County were shelved. There were only a half dozen, so she gathered them up and took them back to the table. She found Carla and Pixie going through some of the other census books.

"Find anything?" she asked.

Carla shook her head. "We were trying some of the adjacent counties, but didn't see any D'Arbanvilles."

Melanie plunked the books down in front of Carla. "Here are the only other books the library has on Wakulla

County," Melanie told her. "These three are reminiscences of county residents. The others are just histories of North Florida. Who knows, maybe we can find something."

And for the next hour, Melanie sat between Carla and Pixie, poring over every mention of Wakulla County they could find. Most of the "reminiscences" were silly memoirs written by rich old dowagers who had rarely been off the plantation. Others were simple but factual accounts of North Florida life in the latter part of the nineteenth century. Although these were interesting, they didn't help Melanie understand who Rufus D'Arbanville was and how he was connected to Carla's family.

"What's Tate's Hell?" she asked. "I've seen a couple of references to it."

"Really?" Carla asked. "I always thought that Tate's Hell was just a myth the liar's bench guys liked to tell."

Melanie wondered what that was a reference to, but let it go. Instead, she browsed through the description in the book she was reading: a young man had gone into the swamp and become lost; when he finally staggered out, months or years later, his hair had turned from jet black to snow white. She looked for a reference to Tate's Hammock—the similarity in names suggested a connection—but she couldn't find one. She passed the book to Carla and opened another to the index. Under Wakulla County she found a subreference that interested her.

It was a report of a pillar of smoke being spotted in the area as early as 1840 and continuing until just before 1900, when it disappeared. Many explorers tried to reach what was referred to as "the Wakulla Volcano," but the thick jungle and heavy mud stopped the few explorers who tried before they could come closer than four or five miles.

She showed Carla the reference. "Here's something interesting," she said.

Melanie watched Carla's face change as she read the account. She looked up from the book and said with a puzzled expression. "It makes me think of Aunt Sookie," she said, "but I don't know why."

Intrigued, Melanie searched back through other books for mention of the volcano and, to her surprise, found several other references. Some speculated that it was a huge fire kept burning by an uncivilized tribe of Indians as part of an ancient religious rite. Others said that it was probably a vast peat bog set afire by lightning. Its exact location was variable as well, with reports placing it anywhere from south of Tallahassee to the forested swamps of nearby Franklin County. These, too, she passed on to Carla and Pixie and, although Carla read them with great interest, even taking notes, Melanie noticed that Pixie seemed to glance at them with little interest, even though it was her family they were researching.

"This is fantastic, Pixie!" Carla cried, then put her hand over her mouth. "Sorry," she whispered. "Pixie, I've found the connection!"

"Connection to what?"

"The connection between Tate's Hell and the Wakulla Volcano."

"You think there's a connection?" Melanie asked.

"It's something that I remember from an old man's story," Carla said. "about a huge, smoking crack in the earth."

"But what does that have to do with Rufus D'Arbanville?"

"Probably nothing," said Carla. "But it's a start. Pixie, I want to go back to Hamp's and ask him some questions." Melanie was about to ask who Hamp was when Carla stood up and held out her hand. "You're very efficient," she said.

"I try to be," Melanie said, shaking the hand that she imagined had once, or even recently, caressed her husband in hidden places.

"And, you know, nice."

"Thanks. I guess you're okay, too."

"Maybe we'll meet again. Discuss Wittgenstein or something," Carla said.

Melanie felt like she had been shocked by an eel. "How do you know about—" she began, then stopped.

"Never mind. I hope you find what you're looking for."

"You, too," replied Carla, as she and Pixie walked out the door, Pixie turning occasionally to get a few last glimpses of her.

Now what had Carla meant by that? Melanie didn't think she'd given any indication of dissatisfaction with her marriage. Or that she didn't have everything she wanted in life. Of course not, how could she? She had a new house, a good job, and a fine marriage. Didn't she?

It was odd that Carla knew about her being a French major, but that had been years ago, before she even thought about getting her graduate degree in Library Science. It's something that Buddy could have told Carla, when Melanie and Buddy were first dating. But her obsession with Wittgenstein and the language philosophers was more recent. In fact, she had begun his *Tractatus* only a few months ago.

Now—whether she wanted to or not—she knew why Buddy had been spending time in Tate's Hammock. As she put the Wakulla County books back on their proper shelves, the room began to feel very cold.

Chapter Fifteen

As soon as they were in the Honda, Pixie had burst out, "That was his *wife*?" opening her eyes wide in that way she had.

"Yeh, I guess so. What did you think of her?"

"She so clean!" Pixie said with emphasis. "I think she must shampoo her hair every day, maybe twice. Her nails, too, and they weren't fake, either."

"Do you think she was pretty?" Carla asked mischievously.

"Yeah…" Carla caught Pixie giving her a quick glance. "Well, sort of. You know, in a clean kind of way."

"And I'm just a dirty old hag," Carla said, only half joking. "An old has-been."

"Yeah, no, I mean, at least you don't wear the kind of shoes she had on."

Carla almost squealed as she guided the car away from the library and toward the Tallahassee Mall. "You noticed them, too?" she asked.

"Big, wide, black things with straps and little heels."

"Exactly," said Carla. "I haven't owned shoes like that since I used to read comic books."

"Huh?"

"They're Minnie Mouse shoes."

Pixie started giggling uncontrollably, which was good. Which meant that she was forgetting, at least for a while.

"I even asked her if her name was Minnie," laughed Carla.

"No you didn't!"

"Yes, I did."

As she pulled into the mall, Carla toyed with the idea of of seeing a movie, but doubted if Pixie could be quiet long enough for them—and the people around them—to enjoy it. But she knew something even better. "Let's go shopping," she said.

So they'd spent the next two hours just wandering around the mall, eating Chinese food and cinnamon buns, browsing through the shops and looking at merchandise that would probably never be on display in Tate's Hammock unless they got donated to a thrift store. Still, by the time they left, Carla knew she had come close to maxing out her only credit card. Most of the stuff she bought was for Pixie--clothes, shoes, toilet articles; it was amazing how much it cost to replace even the most basic items. But in Belk's she was glancing in a glass case when she saw a duplicate of the watch Minnie had been wearing: a Movado Museum watch with a black face, gold hands, and no numbers. It was so expensive that she'd probably have to declare bankrupcy, but at least she'd look good in court.

She'd spent the next morning engaged in a flurry of guilty housecleaning and an hour's worth of long-needed grocery shopping at the IGA. So it wasn't until after noon that whe parked in front of Crozier's Old Country Store, still excited about finding a possible connection between Tate's Hell and the Wakulla volcano—two stories old enough to have passed into local legend. But when she walked up the steps, it was with a couple of changes. Although she was wearing her usual jeans and halter top, her wrist was sporting her new watch. Another addition was Pixie herself, whom Carla had brought along for company. She didn't want to lose the tentative bond re-established the previous day, and Pixie seemed eager to hear some of the old stories.

When the old geezers saw her, they nodded their heads in her direction.

"Sorry bout yah daddy," Hamp Crozier said. "He was a good customer. Always paid cash for what he bought, unless he had somethin to trade. Never ran up no bills like some."

"He weren't the most friendliest feller I ever met," added Billy Joe, "but I wish he was with us here instead of where he is."

"Everybody that dies reminds old fogies like us that we have to go soon, too," explained Clarence Revell.

"I reckon," said Pixie softly. She stared down at her pink Reeboks.

Carla wondered if Pixie was starting to feel blue again, but the girl just seemed abashed by the attention. She sat down on the porch steps and began picking at her shoelaces.

"What are you doin up this early, Tiny-mite?" Comer joked.

"I want to find out about the volcano," she said, fishing around in her black pack and drawing out cigarettes and her library notes from the day before.

"What volcano?" two of the men queried together.

"The Wakulla volcano," she said, lighting a cigarette.

Billy Joe scratched his bald head and brought out his container of Kodiak and took out a pinch. "I dunno bout that," he said.

Carla looked at her notes. "I found a couple of references to a volcano when I was looking up other stuff yesterday in Tallahassee. The author of one of the books talks about standing on top of the hill near the capitol in 1860 and seeing the smoke of a volcano out in this direction. The only trouble was, nobody could ever get near it because of the swamp, which I guess was a lot bigger and thicker back then. I just wondered if any of you had heard a story that might mention a volcano."

Three heads shook slowly as Billy Joe, Comer, and Clarence sifted through their memories. Hamp sat with his lips pursed and a faraway look on his face. Carla tried to catch his eye, but when she did, he looked down without saying anything.

Carla tried another tack. "Listen," she said, looking at Clarence. "Remember that story you told us about Tate's Hell the other day?" When Clarence nodded, she continued. "You mentioned a crack in the earth with fire in it. I think that was the volcano."

"I thought volcanoes was like mountains with holes in the middle," said Clarence.

"Not always," said Carla. "They only get that way after they've erupted a few times."

"Well shee-it," said Comer. "If it was in Tate's Hell, no wonder nobody ever told no stories about it. Old Tate's the only one who ever went there and come back, and he didn't tell nobody nothin."

But Carla was looking curiously at Hamp, who finally tilted his head up and went into storytelling mode. "I recollect somethin that might be what you're after. It's a story my mama told me once, and I still remember every word she said."

"That's somethin real, then," said Billy Joe, sucking his teeth. "Hell, you'd forget your name if you hadn't got it wrote on a piece of paper in your back pocket." He looked pointedly at Carla. "He takes it out and looks at it from time to time, too," he added.

"I don't never forget how long your bill is," retorted Hamp. The two men glared at each other.

"What did your mother tell you, Hamp?" Carla asked.

Hamp turned back to Carla. "Why don't you and the other little gal pull that extra bench around here so's you can hear better. It's a pretty good story and it's about Pixie's great grandmother too. A little closer, that's right."

Carla sat down right across from Comer, while Pixie, a little reluctantly, joined her on the shallow bench across from Billy Joe and scrunched her knees up in front of her chin like a cricket.

"Now most everybody here's seen my mama; she

worked this store twelve hours every day up until the time
she got that stroke back in sixty-nine. She was a little tiny
woman, even littler than Carla, and she had a voice like a
mouse. Maybe that's the reason she didn't talk much, but
when she did talk, she usually had somethin to say.

"I remember hearin this story on a winter's night, and
a cold wind was blowing against the windows and seepin
in through some cracks that Daddy hadn't got around to
fixin. We was livin up above the store here then. I was a little
taddler, not much higher than a can a beans, and I wasn't
feelin too good. Been in bed sneezin and frettin and feelin just
about the way an oyster on ice must feel, when mama came
in with some stinky concoction in a mug. It was warm and
smelled like, oh, I dunno, somewhere between Vicks salve
and Mogen David."

"Blood purifier," said Pixie.

"Hmmm?" said Billy Joe.

"You mix wine, parched rice, and bay leaves with
some other stuff like pomegranate hulls depending on who's
sick."

"Well, you're a regular little root doctor, ain't ya?"
said Clarence Revell.

"I reckon," Pixie said shyly, and Carla knew the girl
was pleased. "Probly made you dizzy," she added.

"Yep, I was dizzy, but I was smilin," grinned Hamp.
"And my mama, seein I was feelin a mite better, sat down
with me on the bed and I asked her how come *she* never got
sick. So she put her arm around me and told me this story.

"'Hampton,' she said, 'Long before you was born,
when I was just a little girl myself, our family came down
from Louisiana. We was fishin folks but things wasn't workin
out for us there. We heared that things was better on the Florida coast, so we got our few little belongins together and put
em on a wagon. But our horse was old and the wagon wasn't
so hot neither and it took quite awhiles to even get to Florida.
And when we finally *did* cross the border, all kinds of bad
things started happenin. First my oldest brother ran away

from us in Tallahassee. When Daddy finally caught him up he'd already enlisted in the army. With him gone, the wagon kept breakin down and finally, bout twenty miles north of where we are now, the horse stepped in a hole and we had to shoot her.'"

Hamp stopped, glanced at Carla, and wiped his eyes. "You know," he said, "it's just like Mama is here right now tellin this story with me."

The three other Loafer's Bench storytellers were nodding their heads sympathetically, and Billy Joe leaned forward, elbows on his boney knees, and said, "This here's a new one for us, Hamp. What happened next?"

"Wahl," Hamp continued, "I remember that Mama had to dab at her eyes a bit, cause she loved that old horse. Then she looked back at me and said, 'Daddy had me walk up the road and wait, so I did. Sat down under a ole magnolia tree that had leaves big around as my head and so shiny I could almost see myself. Just as I heared the shot I felt somethin sharp in my leg. I thought that Daddy had maybe missed the horse and shot me instead, but when I looked down I saw that there was a snek fastened onto my leg. I didn't know what to do so I grabbed that snek by its rattles, pulled it offen my leg and swung it up against the trunk of that magnolia tree. I killed that snek dead, but it had already bit me and I was pretty sure I was gonna die too.

"'I called out for Daddy, but by the time he got back to me I was already dizzy and weak. Daddy seen a shack bout a mile back on the road and he carried me there fast as he could run.

"'There was a couple lived there, poor folks they was, but they got Daddy to lay me on their bed and the man took to takin off my shoe. I was sweatin bad now and so sick I thought I could almost see Jesus lookin down from the ceiling. I watched the man take out a pocket knife and put a match to it, but when he put the blade to my leg I passed out.

"'When I woke up, I wasn't in the house no more; I was in the swamp. It was a clearin with bout five huts made of wood and straw. All around me was twisted oaks and cypress crawlin with vines that looked like green sneks movin when the wind blew. The whole trees looked like they was movin closer and I heared creatures sloggin through the swamp. I tried to get up on my elbow to see, but I was tied down to a straw mat that was restin out in the open on some kind of wooden contraption built up offen the ground. I was warm and not from the sun neither. There was smoke seepin up all around me. I was beginnin to think I was dreamin that some cannibiles was fixin ta eat me, then I heard a voice. 'So you be awake, eh?'

"'I was plumb scared to death, but I looked around and there was the biggest woman I ever seen. She was a darky, but she was shore a strong and handsome woman. She wore clothes that hung on her like gunny sacks and they was all the colors of the rainbow. She had a bandana round her head and a bulb of garlic and a leather bag tied round her neck.

"'I tried to get up again but couldn't cause a the thongs round my arms and ankles. So I just craned my neck up and saw that my bed had been balanced out over a deep, narrow pit, and that pit was where the smoke was comin from. If I hadn't a been tied down I coulda fell right in. The big woman—'"

"It was Freeda!" Pixie interrupted Hamp's story-within-a-story in astonishment.

"That's sure who it was," responded Hamp. "And Freeda pulled on a rope contraption she had rigged up and hauled Mama's bed back from over that hole, untied her, and carried her into one of the huts. You all got to realize that by this time in Mama's story I was bout to conk out from that nasty concoction, but I forced myself to stay awake and listen cause, as I told ya, she didn't talk much more'n a cat, an hell, to a taddler of eight or so, this was a stupefyin fairy tale. She'd stop the story ever once in a while and look at me careful to see if I was asleep yet, but ever time she did, I managed to pop my eyes wide open, so she'd make me take another sip of the medicine and then start off on her story again.

"'Son,' she said, 'That big woman laid me light as a twig down on a grass bed she had in that hut of hers and she told me, 'Lil gal, you was bout gone. I had to put some roots on you I didn't even know I knew. Then I had to throw some in the volcano and pray to the spirit down there to bring yah back. You see, the volcano spirit don be likin sneks cause a all the trouble Ol Scratch got into when God cast the serpent out a Eden. But you been saved this time around. You rest a spell now, honey.'"

"An Mama said she went right to sleep again. When she woke up she was back in the white folk's shack. She figured they musta done everthing they could do for her, then sent for Freeda, who carried Mama alone into the swamp so she could work her roots better. It shore worked, too, cause after that, Mama was never sick a day in her life."

Hamp fell silent. It was obvious to Carla he was thinking about his mother and that short, intimate moment he had shared with her. The others must have felt this too, for they kept a respectful silence until Comer hawked and finally said, "Shoot, Hamp, why ain't yah never told that story before?"

"It's funny," replied Hamp. "Up until Carla started askin those questions bout that volcano, I never really believed that tale. Bein sick and drinkin medicine'll give you funny dreams. I thought I must've dreamed ever bit of that stuff Mama told me. Now I think maybe it was all true."

"So there really was a volcano of sorts," mused Carla aloud. "But what happened to it?"

"Shee-it, Carla," spoke up Clarence Revell. "That musta been close to a hundert years ago. When the damn paper company bought up the land out past Sookie's property, they drained off most of the swamp, cut down a spate of trees, and laid down roads. If there was a volcano around there, it's either drowned out or covered up."

"And you talk about smoke," added Billy Joe, serious for once. "Hell, I'm eighty-one years old and I ain't never seen any. Cept," he added with a twinkle, "the smoke comin out the back of your car."

"I got it fixed," said Carla, laughing. Then she turned to Comer. "I'm takin the boat out in a couple of hours. Are you up for it?"

"Hell, I been waitin for a week seems like."

Hamp spoke up. "Y'all better be careful. Madge heard on the TV that there's a storm buildin up somewhere in the Gulf."

"Hurricane season," nodded Billy Joe.

"Yeah, well," said Carla. "Seems like it's always hurricane season around here." She looked for Pixie, but the girl had wandered over to the car and was looking pensive. "We'll be careful," she said absently. "Look, I better get Pixie home. I'll meet you at the dock at about six."

"Okey dokey," said Comer.

Carla walked out to the car, then turned back and shouted, "And hey, Marietta's coming with us." Opening the door, she heard, "Oh, sheeeeee-iiiiiit," and smiled to herself.

When they were on the road, Carla glanced at Pixie and said, "Whatcha thinking?"

"Bout Freeda."

"What about Freeda?" she asked.

"That story the man told reminded me of stories Aunt Sookie used to tell me. She told em to me all the time, even though Daddy'd get mad."

"Why was that?" Carla asked.

"He was always fussin at her when he caught her teaching me remedies and stuff. And he thought all her stories about the volcano people were just superstition."

"What volcano people?" Carla cried.

"The folks who lived around the volcano."

"You mean I busted my buns to find out this stuff and you knew it all along?"

"Know about what?" Pixie asked.

"All the old history. The volcano, Tate's Hell, Rufus D'Arbanville."

"Sure," Pixie said simply.

"Why didn't you say anything when we were in the library?"

"Sookie told me they were secrets, but I thought you knew them too. You didn't?"

"Why did you think I was looking them up?" Carla asked with exasperation.

"I thought maybe you didn't believe, that you wanted to see them printed in books."

Carla could have kicked herself for ignoring the obvious. Pixie, with her family connections, probably knew more about Blanchard's Bluff than all the libraries in the country. She wheeled into her driveway and stopped the car. "You know, I've got a boatload of questions I need to ask you."

"Okay."

But just as Carla was unlocking the front door, she heard tires kicking up shells in the driveway behind her. She looked and saw a blue Corvette pulling to a stop. Not again.

"It's Fancy Yancy," said Pixie.

"Do tell."

Pixie smiled and fluffed the skirt of her dress.

Yancy was on the front step by the time Carla had the door open. "Hey," he said. "You said you'd call."

"I said I'd call you next month," Carla replied.

"Who's this?" Yancy asked. "Pixie?"

"Right." Carla held the door open for Pixie, but Pixie seemed contented standing in the doorway watching Yancy. "Pixie," she said, "go on in. Yancy, I'm still busy."

"You're always busy."

"I'm busy *sometimes*. Look, I've got a lot of things to do before tonight." She was blocking the door with her body and facing Yancy on the step. She saw Pixie watching curiously through the screen.

"What's tonight?" asked Yancy. "Got a date?"

"I'm working tonight."

"What, on the boat?"

"That's where I work." Cutting him short like that felt

good, but she couldn't help noticing that he was wearing a new brown suit—and not a leisure suit either. The blue tie didn't quite match but he still presented a good appearance. His shoes looked new, too. Must've spent more money than usual trying to make a good impression. In addition, he was obviously trying not to look hangdog, but without much success. Carla remembered the offhanded way she had treated him a few days before and felt a slight pang of guilt at having to do it again. But how was she going to get to the bottom of Aunt Sookie's murder if Yancy always kept interrupting her?

"Look," she said, more gently. "I'm sorry, but—"

"Did you really shoot a streetlight?" Pixie interrupted. The girl's nose practically pressed itself into the screen. Carla grimaced.

"What the hell...?" Yancy demanded.

"Jesus, Pixie, you have no tact," she told Pixie's nose. To Yancy, who didn't seem to know where to look, she said, "You might as well come on in." She opened the door and followed Yancy inside. "Yancy, sit down. Pixie, get us both a beer."

"What about Yancy?" Pixie asked.

"Both means me and him. You get a Coke."

Pixie disappeared into the kitchen with a pout and a snicker. When the beer had been brought and Pixie had folded her spindly legs under her skirt next to Carla on the couch, Carla gulped a third of her beer, lit a cigarette, and looked at Yancy, who was perched across from her on the edge of the overstuffed chair. Then she studied her new watch, saw that it was somewhere between 3:00 and 4:00. She sighed and said, "You have ten minutes. What do you want?"

"I want to know why you're going around telling everybody my secrets."

"In the first place, I'm not going around anywhere. In the second place, I'm not telling everybody. In the third place—"

"If I'm not sposed to know, I'll just forget it,"

interrupted Pixie.

"No," said Carla, putting her arm around the girl. "Pixie and I are family now and we don't have any secrets from each other."

"What do you mean?" asked Yancy.

"Pixie lives here now."

"Yeah?" Yancy looked suspiciously at Pixie, then at Carla. He cut his eyes back to Pixie and gave her an involuntary smile. "Did she really tell you about my run-in with the law?"

"She stopped before she got to the good part."

"There is no good part," Yancy said. "But that's right. Carla shooed me out of here before I could explain what happened."

"Wanna tell the rest now?" asked Pixie. It was tough to see Pixie's face from Carla's vantage point, but she could actually feel the girl's interest through her skin. A sudden realization hit her. Could Pixie have a crush on Yancy? The thought seemed preposterous, but when she chanced a look at Pixie's face she saw the same rapt expression she would expect to see if some pop music idol were across the room. She still thought the idea ridiculous, but decided to test it. She bent closer and whispered "Too old, huh?" and was rewarded with two blue saucer eyes and a brown hand pressed against her mouth.

Yancy put down his empty beer can and smiled uncertainly across the room. "What are you two up to over there?" he asked.

Carla pried Pixie's hand from her mouth. "I was, um, just telling Pixie how you haven't explained why you put your gun in my purse the other night."

"If I'm gonna tell this, I need another beer."

"Done." Carla started to get up but Pixie beat her to it. Carla shrugged and sat back.

When Pixie returned with two more beers (Carla noticed that hers was not full), Yancy drank a few large gulps from the can and began.

"When I got out of the army I took up hunting. With pistols, you know? I mean, using some high-powered rifle with a five-hundred-dollar scope on a squirrel or a coon wasn't sport, it was waste. Every few months, some of my Nam buddies would drive out to visit. We usually just hung out and drank beer, but sometimes they would go hunting with me. There's a huge national forest and a slew of bayous that run through Franklin and Wakulla counties, so we'd go out there and mess around with our pistols. Well, one day we heard some other guys in the woods. There were about half a dozen of them. They had guns, too, all kinds, but they weren't hunting. We sat back and smoked some reefer and watched them for a while without them knowing we were there. They were training."

Carla couldn't help herself. "Training for what?" she asked.

"We didn't know right off, but we could tell soldiers when we saw them, and these guys weren't, even though they were wearing what looked like standard issue gear. Not U.S. gear, though; more like gear I'd seen on soldiers in Africa or South America, but these guys were all American.

"We watched for fifteen minutes or so before we figured out they must be part of one of these outfits that charge guys money to teach em how to be tough."

"Survivalists," said Pixie.

"Right," said Yancy. "How'd you know that?"

"Seen em in the woods once not too far from Auntie's place."

"Here?" Carla burst out. "You mean we've got idiots..." Then she remembered that Yancy must be one of those idiots. He frowned at her.

"I'm not a survivalist," he said. "These were the kind of buttheads that try to get in shape to take over when the bomb drops and it's every white man for himself. But it didn't seem to be working, because most of em looked like that guy up at Blanchard's Bait and Tackle—kinda overworked and bloated, like they hadn't been out in the sun for six or seven years. The commander, or whatever he called himself, was different. He had a face like a beet and hair to match. He stood so straight he might have had a ramrod shoved up his ass—they kick his type out of the marines for being too gung ho. Hard as the toe of a boot and a little crazy in the head. Things got to be pretty clear when this guy hung life-size targets of black men from the branches of trees.

"There were three guys with me that day, and all four of us had been stationed together near the Ho Chi Minh trail around the Laotian border. I won't describe the things we went through for each other, but you can believe we were real tight. And of the four of us, I was the only white guy. You get the picture? So here we were watching these bozos shoot branches off trees ten feet away from their targets and get blown on their fat butts by the kick. And we watched for half an hour without anybody even seeing us. We were really pissed, you know, watching what these clowns were doing, but it was funny, too, because they were such terrible soldiers. If somebody ever does drop the Big One, these fools will probably end up shooting each *other*. We were trying to keep straight faces, but when we saw one guy break his bayonet in half trying to stick a target in the groin, we all started laughing our asses off. Especially since he nearly castrated himself.

"That did it. The commando-type in charge looked around and spotted us, so we stood up, thinking we'd just split and let these guys fool around in peace. But the commander starts yelling something about the revolution and tells his recruits to open fire.

"Now, we knew what it was like to be open fired on, so we hit the dirt. It was like being thrown right back in the jungle again. I was crawling toward the biggest tree I could find when I realized nobody had fired. We looked and saw that the recruits were either frozen stiff or looking around trying to find squirrels to shoot—as if there could be any in fifty miles after all the destruction they'd been causing with their R-4s. They were mean as hell with cardboard targets, but faced with live bodies, they kinda lost their charge."

"Lucky for you," breathed Carla. "But what did you do?"

"What did we do? Hell, we started laughing our asses off again. But this gung-ho guy got even redder in the face than he was already and pulls what looked to be a nine millimeter semiautomatic and points it in our direction. Then he yells at his troops. And seeing that he meant business, some of these jokers aimed at us too."

Yancy stopped, drank fully half a can of beer, and let out a breath.

"What happened then?" Pixie asked, wide-eyed. Carla leaned forward.

"Before the guy could pull the trigger, we each fired off a quick round. One shot knocked the nine millimeter out of his hand clean, one went *through* his hand, and one went through his knee. The fourth shot put a small hole in his forehead and took most of the back of his head off. Them boys laid their R-4s down right quick. Most of em had to because they were throwing up and they didn't want to filthy up those fancy shooters—they cost a lot of money."

Carla and Pixie were staring at Yancy spellbound, all sense of surroundings lost.

"We weren't looking for any trouble. Trouble just happened. We waited around for the police and went in and gave our statements. That's all of it. Well, all of it except one thing."

"What's that?" Carla asked.

"That commando guy we killed? It was Oskie Holt's cousin. Holt's been trying to get something on me ever since. I thought it was him in that squad car the night we went to Clem's. If Holt ever catches me carrying a pistol, he'll try to put the screws to me."

"Jesus," said Carla out loud. She remembered with embarrassment that she had accused Yancy of being racist and a criminal. Instead, he was sort of a hero. Attractive, too, in a dangerous sort of way, she realized as she saw him through what seemed a stranger's eyes—Pixie's eyes, maybe.

She also realized he was walking toward the door. "Where are you going?" she asked quickly.

"You're busy," he said.

"I know, but—"

"Maybe I'll call you next week," he said.

"Tomorrow," she said. "I'll be home tomorrow." But seeing what a noodle she had become, she added, "Probably."

"Then I'll probably call," he answered, his hand on the screen door. He was smiling faintly and his hangdog look was lost somewhere in a ty-ty thicket in the next county.

Still looking back at Carla and Pixie, he thrust open the screen door, which cracked against something hard on the doorstep. Something that said "Shit!"

Carla rushed to the door and saw what was indeed an oh-shit moment. Yancy Vause hovered on the step, one arm half outstretched, staring at Buddy Love, who stood glaring, holding one hand to his head and gripping a legal folder with the other.

"Sorry, man..." said Yancy, backpedaling. Carla knew that she had told him enough about her days with Buddy for Yancy to have a pretty good idea who this was. He had even seen Buddy's picture on her nightstand before she put it away in a drawer. Buddy, on the other hand, probably didn't know Yancy from Billy Joe Lord, but tended to be suspicious of everyone anyway. Warily, they faced each other, each looking the other over very slowly, from top to bottom. Their cars—Yancy's blue Corvette and Buddy's cream-colored BMW—faced each other in the driveway.

"What are you doing here?" asked Yancy finally. Evidently his abilities as a tactician were limited to the battlefield.

"I'm Carla's—" began Buddy indignantly, but Carla interrupted him.

"He's my lawyer," she finished.

Buddy glared at her, then at Yancy. "Who the hell are you?" he asked.

"I'm Carla's—"

"He's my automotive advisor," she broke in.

The two looked each other over again. Carla felt the instant antagonism and sense of combat between them. It was as if they were trying to determine which of them had the longest prick. Carla knew the answer but wasn't telling. In fact, they no longer seemed to know she was there. She felt like a stain on the steps.

Yancy Vause and Buddy Love might have stared at each other indefinitelyr had not Pixie stuck her head out the screen to see what was going on. The slight creak of the door startled all three participants. Yancy moved first. Forcing his eyes away from Buddy, he turned to Carla. "I'll call you tomorrow," he said. And, without looking back, he strolled to his Corvette and squealed out of the driveway.

"Classy guy," said Buddy, once the sound of Yancy's tires had faded down Second Street.

"Well, Mr. Love, I didn't expect to see you again." She hoped her voice sounded cold enough.

"You're Buddy?" Pixie struck Carla as a little too excited, and she gave the girl a quick shushing look, which had no effect at all.

"Right," he said, smiling at the girl's head, which was the only thing hanging out of the doorway. "And you're…?"

"Pixie Blue," she said.

"The heir to the D'Arbanville millions," he responded. "But who was that creep that just drove off?"

"That's Carla's—"

"That's none of your business," Carla said. "Pixie, please go inside and fetch my black bag. Mr. Love will only be staying long enough to get his check." Pixie's head disappeared back inside.

"What check?" he asked.

"For the legal work you did for me the other night. I appreciate it. I don't appreciate the other work you did."

"What the hell are you talking about? I thought we had fun the other night."

"People having fun don't split in the morning with

even saying 'bye, see ya. What, did you have a breakfast date with Minnie?"

"Who's Minnie?" Buddy asked, more puzzled than ever.

"Look, I don't know what I'm saying. Your wife is a dozen times the person you are. All you care about is a fast buck and a quick fuck."

A giggle from inside the house let Carla know that Pixie wasn't far away. "Pixie, give me my bag." Carla snatched it from the brown hand that popped through the door and quickly disappeared again. She took out the envelope with the check for fifty dollars and thrust it into Buddy's hand. He dropped it on the step and looked down at Carla, perturbed.

"I don't know what the fuck is going on around here or what my wife has to do with anything. I left here before you got up because I wanted to check out this business with Sookie Darbyville. I was trying to do you a goddamned favor. It took me a couple of days, but I managed to get her bank records and the records of the trust that has paid the bills for Chez Marais for the last fifty years. I probably should have left a note, but I didn't think it would take me more than an hour or two. I finally had to go to Tallahassee to type up some legal forms and I should have called you. I'm sorry, but I didn't think it was a matter for the U.N."

For about the millionth time over the past week, Carla felt chastened. Why could no one ever be as much of an asshole as she thought they were? And what made her think the worst of people in the first place? Because she thought the worst of herself, perhaps. She opened her mouth and managed to whisper, "You found a copy of the trust?"

"Yes, now are you going to tell me why I've suddenly got leprosy?"

"No, it's too confusing. Just come inside and try to forget it. I'll get us both a beer."

"I'll get them," volunteered Pixie, and she disappeared into the kitchen.

Buddy entered warily and sat down in the overstuffed

chair that Yancy had just vacated.

"How's your head?" Carla asked.

"It's okay."

"Good thing you weren't wearing your glasses."

"A good thing for him," said Buddy, frowning at the four empty beer cans.

"Don't be that way. It was an accident. What have you got in the folder?"

"A copy of the trust and a few other papers. By the way, what's Pixie doing here?"

"She's living with me now." With lowered voice and a finger to her lips, she added, "Her father was killed in a trailer fire the other night."

"That was him in the fire?" Buddy whispered. "Jesus, I saw the story in *The Tattler* but I didn't associate it with—"

Buddy broke off when Pixie entered the room with the beer. This time she had poured the cans into glasses. Carla suspected that the glasses held slightly less than a full can because she noticed a trace of foam on Pixie's upper lip. She reached up and wiped the fleck away.

"You're going to be a full-fledged drunk if you keep it up," she told the startled girl. "But don't go away. You need to listen to this, too." Pixie sat down beside her and reached for Carla's pack of Winstons. Carla was too fast for her and snatched them away.

"Emulate somebody else," she said, lighting one for herself.

"You all want to hear about this or not?" Buddy asked.

"Hear about what?" Pixie asked.

"The terms of the trust."

"I already know that," said Pixie.

"I doubt it," Buddy said, rather too smugly for Carla's taste. She also couldn't believe that every time she went to great lengths to cement a missing piece of Sookie's puzzle into place, Pixie had already finished the puzzle and framed it on the wall.

"Go ahead and tell him," she sighed.

"You talking about the trust for Chez Marais, right?" Pixie asked.

"Right."

"Okay. Sometime, probly about fifty or sixty years ago, Freeda decided that the house should take care of itself, so that nobody ever had to worry about paying no taxes or doing no repairs or selling it. So she put the house and the property in a trust. There's money in the trust too—I don't know how much, but I think that the interest is more than plenty to take care of it. Aunt Sookie was just like her mama; she didn't want to have to mess with all that money hassle neither, so she kept the trust going. I'll probly do the same."

Carla had a hundred questions and from the look on Buddy Love's face, he had more than that. But Carla got one of hers out first. "Why didn't Aunt Sookie live at Chez Marais instead of us?" she asked.

"It wasn't in the agreement," Pixie said.

"What agreement?" asked Buddy Love, his legal folder balanced uselessly on his lap.

"The one that Freeda and Tate made back in the eighteen seventies," began Pixie, little realizing that she was sending Carla over the edge of amazement and into despair of ever understanding anything at all.

The silence was so complete that Carla could hear the cat-clock's tail swishing. She looked idly at it, then more closely. Had Pixie actually said Tate? She stared at her Movado watch, wondering if maybe she had consumed too many cans of beer. Buddy was staring at the watch, too. He opened his mouth to speak, but Carla cut him off. "Shit, it's after five o'clock!" she cried. "Buddy, I have to go out on the boat—I promised Comer and Marietta both." Carla dashed into her bedroom, closed the door to a crack, and called through it as she took off her clothes and slipped into her cutoffs and other boat gear. "I'm sorry if I was cold to you earlier. You probably didn't deserve it, but I warned you there were too many things going on for me to keep completely sane." She threw on a "Clem's Clams" T-shirt like the one Stinky the Fish

Man usually wore and stepped into her deck shoes. She put her new watch in its case on the dressing table and hurried back into the living room. Buddy was just getting up. "Call me tomorrow," she said. Then she added, "Please."

When Buddy had closed the screen door after him, Carla asked Pixie, "Want to go, too? You can tell me about Freeda and Tate."

"No, it scares me."

"What scares you? Freeda and Tate?"

"The water."

"You can't swim?"

"I can swim. But I tried going out in a boat at night once. It was a full moon and I looked down in the water to see my reflection and it wasn't there."

"And that wouldn't have anything to do with the fact that you're the same color as the water at night, would it?"

"I don't care. I ain't goin out over no black water."

Carla was checking through her bag to make sure she had her cigarettes and some money. "If you don't want to go, make yourself at home. Help yourself to the kitchen. I'll be back around nine tomorrow morning."

"Can I have a beer?"

"When you're twenty."

"Can I have Yancy, then?" she asked, studying the carpet.

"When you're fifty," Carla answered, taking a second look at Pixie. "Listen," she remembered. "Aunt Sookie left me some papers and photographs in an old cigar box. It's on my bed. While I'm gone, look inside and see if you recognize any of the pictures."

"Okay."

"You can tell me about them when I come back. And," she added, "don't forget to tell me the story about Tate and Freeda."

"You don't know it?" Pixie asked.

"Don't act innocent with me, minx," Carla said. "I've been trying to solve this big mystery for a week now and you've known the answers all the time. Now I've gotta get over to Marietta's before she's too drunk to stand."

As the screen door banged shut behind her, Pixie's "What mystery?" followed her into the yard. Carla gnashed her teeth all the way to Chez Marais.

Chapter Sixteen

When Comer stepped out of the cabin, the wind was blowing hard enough to send an empty beer can clattering across the dock. The banners and riggings were snapping and boat hulls thunked against the pylons. Comer jammed his straw hat down tight, squinting into the wind toward the late afternoon sun. Like everyone else, 'cept maybe Carla, he'd been watching the weather these past few days with nervous attention. All the predictions coming out of the Hurricane Center in Miami said that storm building out there in the Gulf probably wouldn't make landfall anywhere within a hundred miles of Tate's Hammock even if it did come in toward the bay, so he wasn't really worried, but all the same, it paid to keep your eyes on the clouds. He watched them now, scudding low across the horizon. Not exactly squally weather, but not exactly smooth sailing either. Which might make this upcoming run real interesting—and messy, if Carla's guest had trouble finding her sea legs.

Comer saw them approaching a ways down the dock and frowned. Tiny-mite had on her usual fishing clothes, but the missus was decked out for a pleasure cruise, best he could tell. He didn't give that white outfit two minutes once they were underway. Dammit, this was a working vessel, not a party boat. He packed a wad of Red Man into his jaw and glowered at them. Stepping up to the rail, he called out, "Ahoy there, Captain, Miz Clements."

"Comer," Carla nodded and, all business, jumped from the dock into the boat with that black pack she always carried. Mrs. Clements stopped, looked at the boat, then at Comer.

"You must be Mr. Whitehead," she said.

"Yessum. Best shrimper in the county. Ceptin," he added, nodding toward Carla's retreating form, "the Captain, of course. Here, let me help yah." She accepted his hand of support and stepped gingerly from the dock onto the rocking deck.

"Captain, eh? I guess that means she really does know how to use all this…equipment."

Comer watched with stifled amusement as Marietta Clements, tall and glamorous in her white slacks and shirt with matching travel bag, took in the tangle of nets and lines of the rigging that wound upward like vines from the clutter of chains, ropes, buckets, floats, barrels, and mechanical equipment taking up a good half of the deck real estate. Her bumfoozled expression said it all.

"Yes ma'am, she does." Comer nodded genially, on his best behavior. He'd even put on a clean workshirt and jeans for the evening's run. He adjusted the ties on the brand new blue lifejacket he wore uncomfortably over his clothes.

Carla was giving him a good once-over with those green cat eyes. Hah! She wasn't gonna find nothing on him this time. She must have figured that out, because she shrugged and turned to her stepmother. "Of course I know how to run the boat."

Marietta's eyes were still going from one thing to another. "But there's just two of you," she said.

"Yeah, well," Carla answered. "Most shrimpers have a crew of three, but Comer and I have been doing okay so far with just us two. Come on and I'll show you around."

Comer followed the two women into the wheelhouse, an oval room above the deck. Constructed of oak varnished to a keen shine, it offered a panoramic view of the water ahead and on both sides of the trawler through a curving row of windows. A nautical map of the area was fixed to the wall directly over the galley, which included a small stove and refrigerator as well as storage cabinets.

"We generate our own power once we're under way." Carla said as she opened the refrigerator, which Comer had stocked with a fresh ham, cheese, some mayonnaise, mustard, onions, cold beer, and Coke. His fear that they might sink to the bottom of the sea at any given time had not abated, but at least they wouldn't starve before they got there.

"Bread and crackers in the cabinet, too," he offered as Carla stepped up to the steering wheel at the front of the cabin. She ran her hands along its smooth wooden arc and turned to the other woman, who hung back just inside the doorway. "We call this the navigation station," Carla told her. "I have the latest charts and instruments so we won't get lost during a storm or anything." Comer checked the sky again out one of the slanted windows. Stiff wind out of the south, low cloud ceiling above, sloppy gray water below. He tightened the ties on his life jacket.

"What's down here?" she asked, pointing to the below-deck area.

"Come see," Carla answered. "There are two bunks and a couple of extra cabinets to stash your stuff." Comer stood out of the way and watched as Carla descended the ladder with practiced ease. He decided to offer Bull's widow a hand as she angled herself awkwardly down the steps, clutching the steel handrail.

"I guess this takes getting used to," she said, smoothing her white slacks and stumbling against Carla as the boat swayed under their feet. Comer sat on his haunches at the top of the stairs, feeling kind of like a frog. The two women were crammed awkwardly into the tiny crew's quarters, Bull's missus stooped over because of her height. Marietta took cigarettes out of her travel bag, then placed it carefully in a cabinet adjoining the one where Carla had stashed her black pack.

"You all have time to sleep out here?" she asked.

"Sometimes," answered Carla. "You have to when you're out for several days at a time."

"It's so hot down here. How can you stand it?"

"Cools off at night," Comer piped up. "But when you've worked for ten or twelve hours at the nets, you don't give a flying—" Carla shot him a look and he blinked like an owl trapped in the daylight. He sucked on the wad snugged against his back teeth and tipped his hat toward the widow Clements. "I'll just go crank 'er up and cast off, if yah ladies don't mind. Nice havin yah aboard, Miz Clements," he lied. "Yah can have my bunk there if you need to take a nap, though it gets a mite loud down here. If'n the engine sounds like it's right next door, that's 'cause it is."

"Just get us underway, why don't you?" Carla snapped back up at him. She was testy as a hog bear with a prickly-pear spine in her paw.

Comer cast a seaman's eye at the racing clouds as he pulled the docking ropes loose and hopped back on deck. He figured it must be somewhere around six o'clock, which left about an hour or two of patchy light before sunset. The air smelled like rain. Nosirree, not gonna be a smooth ride this time out. Even though that almost-hurricane was way the hell out in the Gulf, the old hands he'd consulted on the dock were expecting bigger-than-usual swells out in the open water and maybe some heavy showers. Comer spat over the side. He and Carla had trawled in worse weather than this, so it didn't make no nevermind to him. He turned his full attention back to the *Miriam C.* and wondered if they could turn Marietta Clements into a third member of the crew. He cackled out loud at the thought of her takin on the header's job, assuming they caught enough shrimp to dehead.

Back in the wheelhouse, Comer piloted the shrimper away from the dock, and observed with an internal smirk that Carla was inspecting the hold. They both knew it was his job as mate to make sure it was well stocked with ice, but of course she had to look, anyway. The hold had eight large compartments, each with a basket that could be winched up and emptied of its catch in the morning at dockside, and he'd optimistically packed them all. He was on top of everything this trip; if the boat went to the bottom, weren't no slipups gonna be charged to his account. And this time he'd covered his bases if Carla got pissed enough to make him swim back to port. Hah!

The boat was chugging out into open water when both women joined him in the navigation cabin. Marietta lit a cigarette and blew smoke slowly from her mouth and nostrils. She was a classy dame, for sure. Bull did have an eye for the ladies, and some of 'em not as refined as this one, if he could believe half the stories he'd heard over the years. He wondered idly if Tiny-mite had heard them, too.

"Have a seat and relax. Enjoy the cruise," Carla told Marietta, indicating a built-in table with booth seats. Already the land was falling away behind them, and only a few small boats were visible plowing the sheltered waters of the bay.

"I'm surprised, it's, I don't know, comforting out here," Marietta said, staring out at the gray-blue water ahead of them. The setting sun was turning the underside of the clouds orange and deep salmon.

"I forgot to mention," Carla said. "Hope you don't get seasick…it's a little choppy today."

"No problem. I grew up in Panama City, remember? I've been out in charter boats before, but mostly just for parties."

Comer relaxed his grip on the wheel and leaned back in the captain's seat. That was one worry out of the way. "Whatcher think we could have a three-member crew this time?" he said to Carla.

She got up and to his surprise, gave him the slightest of winks. "I was thinking that very thing," she said, and smiled at Marietta. "I'll take the wheel while you show Marietta around the deck."

"Me?" he asked.

"And don't leave anything out," she told him. Comer opened his mouth to speak, but she didn't give him a chance. "And don't give me your usual…crap!"

Comer closed his mouth and surrendered the wheel to Carla.

Marietta tied her hair back with a scarf and said, "Lead the way, Mr. Whitehead."

Out on the flat deck, Comer looked around, wondering how to start. Best way was probably just the way he'd tell a kid how a spinning reel worked—describe the pieces and then explain how they worked. He led her toward the stern. "Those are the doors," he said, pointing to the two huge pieces of oak cased in steel molding. "See those two outriggers, the things that look like goal posts without the crossbar? Those get lowered until they make a V shape and dangle out over the water like big fishing poles on both sides. When that happens, the doors are lowered into the water."

"What do they do?" Marietta asked. She looked genuinely interested.

"They hold the net apart," Comer instructed, making a V with his palms.

"Oh."

"Yep. And see that tickler chain there between em?"

"Yes?"

"That slides along the bottom and stirs things up. It chases the shrimp out of the grass where they feed so they get catched up in the net. Then we winch up the net, empty it, and ice down whatever's eatable."

Comer spent the next fifteen minutes or so going over the rest of the operation with Marietta. He showed her the holds and told her what type of catch went in each basket, taught her how to operate the anchor winch and to unzip the net drawstring. He went on to explain what they might expect to catch and what to do with the shrimp, fish, and trash they brought up.

Marietta sat down on the spray-damp hold and lit a fresh cigarette. An offshore breeze freshened the air and she tilted her face into it and closed her eyes.

"Hope yah don't mind gettin yer clothes a tad dirty," Comer told her. He wondered if there would be a dirt print on her butt when she stood up.

"Dirty?" Marietta looked alarmed for a second, then shrugged. "I guess that's what cleaners are for," she said. Comer lit a cigarette of his own, shielding the match as wind whipped Marietta's ponytail in all directions. He was reassessing his opinion of Miz Clements and thinking that maybe she weren't so uppity as he'd expected. She might even be a good sport.

The boat was nearly out of sight of land now, and Carla had shifted course so that they were running roughly parallel to the coast. He was starting to wish he could have a nip out of his hidden bottle when Carla cut the motors and came out of the wheelhouse, looking like she had something on her mind. She sat down next to Marietta on the hold.

"So...are you going to tell me about the trust now?" Marietta asked. Comer had no idea what she was talking about, but he busied himself with the nets, making sure he stayed close enough to hear Carla's answer.

"What I know is this. Nobody's kicking you out tomorrow, so you don't need to look so uptight."

What the hell? Comer turned around and held his breath, the better to hear their voices.

"The trust was set up so that Chez Marais could be maintained without the people living in it having to worry about paying taxes and stuff. I'd always thought that my mother set it up, or maybe her parents."

"That was my understanding, too. Well, Carl and I never really discussed it in detail. He just referred to it as the family trust, which, of course meant the family he married into."

"Yeh, that makes sense. Turns out we were all wrong."

Comer sat down on the deck—just out of sight but within hearing range—and pretended to mend one of the nets.

"So I guess now you're going to explain to me how this Pixie person stands to inherit an estate she has no idea how to run?"

"I'll give it a shot." Carla's voice was edgy, defensive sounding, her reactions testier than usual this evening. And the missus seemed to be getting out of sorts pretty quick, too. Comer wondered what the hell Pixie had to do with anything. He and the other liar's bench regulars knew that Bull had married into money when he and Carla's mother got hitched, but it never occurred to him, or the others as far as he knew, that somebody else might own that big white house with the long driveway.

"It goes back a long way, back to Aunt Sookie's mother."

"Aunt... You mean the old root doctor?"

"Right."

There was a silence, and Comer chanced a peek. The two women were just looking at each other.

Carla cleared her throat and continued. "It seems that Freeda, Sookie's mom, somehow—this part I don't understand yet—had the means to set up the perpetual trust that maintains the estate. For all I know, the money to buy the land and build the house came from her, too."

"So how, exactly," Marietta said in tone of voice Comer couldn't peg, "did your mother's family end up living in a mansion belonging to some witch doctor from the swamps? Sounds like you've been reading too much Faulkner." Comer wondered who that was, some government buddy of Bull's, maybe?

"I don't know that yet."

"I mean, if Pixie's family owns the damn house, why aren't they living in it?" There was tightness in her voice.

"I don't know, Marietta. I just don't know, okay. That's at the top of my list of things to investigate. Buddy said he'd..." Carla's sentence trailed off, but Comer noticed that Marietta jumped on it like a grouper hittin a line.

"So now we have the ex-boyfriend involved?" Marietta asked. "The married one?"

Comer cackled silently.

"It's not like that. I just ran into him unexpectedly, and he offered to help me understand what an estate executor's supposed to do."

"So. What *are* you supposed to do? Decide who goes and who stays at Chez Marais?"

"Well, that's kind of up to Pixie, at this point."

"Back to her again." At the shift in Marietta's tone, Comer was almost tempted to join them and ask outright what they were talking about. Either that or sneak over and see if he could find that mist he had hidden without them noticing what he was up to.

"Yup."

Silence again, then the widow's voice. "You know, I'm going to turn forty this year."

"We all have to die sometime," agreed Carla. Comer shook with silent mirth. Score one for the captain.

"No, I'm serious. I'm nearly forty years old and I've never even been to Paris."

"Me neither," said Carla. Comer wondered what Paris had to do with the missus getting kicked out of the big house. And she didn't look no forty years old, leastways not from a distance.

"Bull and I had talked about traveling, retiring and seeing the world. It's…it's just not fair that all those plans got taken away from us."

"Yeah, nothing's fair. I lost a dad, remember? Not much to show for the years I had one, though."

"Well, you've been to college; you have this boat and obviously know how to use it. And unless looks are deceiving, you're an accomplished adulterer."

"None of those things are what they're cracked up to be," replied Carla. A guffaw slipped out of Comer's grizzled jaws, and Carla's head whipped around.

He jumped up, net in hand, and said, "Well, ladies, here we are. Time's a-wastin, if you take my meanin." He cast a glance toward the lowering clouds.

Carla doused her cigarette in a puddle and placed it in the plastic trash bag. "Then let's get this show on the road. You up for it?"

"Sure, I'm game," the widow Clements replied, getting to her feet and hanging tightly to the rail. "If you and the kind Mr. Whitehead will put up with a novice, I'll try not to get in your way. But I *would* like to help."

"We could use a header," Comer said at once, not daring to look at his employer.

"What's a header?"

"It's the mate who—nasty job."

"But somebody has to do it." Marietta started to laugh, and before Comer could grasp why this should be so funny, Carla had joined in. "I'll do it," gasped Marietta, catching her breath. "Just show me."

And for the next several hours, Comer and the captain did just that. She got a quick and dirty crash course in how to drop the outriggers, to separate the nets and look for torn places, to differentiate among the different types of colored lights on the *Miriam C.* and on the other boats they spotted. Luckily, there were almost no other boats, and their catch was just short of phenomenal. The nets came up full—bulging with fat shrimp instead of kelp slime or busted planks of rotten rowboats. The shrimps' glowing eyes filled the net with sparkling pinpoints of light that turned blue and winked out as the creatures died. There were fish, too, and Comer took turns with Carla identifying them for Marietta. He took particular care to show her how to separate the different types of shrimp on the culling board before they were iced away in the hold. To his surprise, Marietta insisted on putting her new knowledge to work. She picked shrimp, helped swab and squeegee the deck, and briefly steered the boat under Carla's watchful eye. She even learned how to tie off the full net and hoist it onto the deck, although her strength gave out after only one haul. Too much easy living. Still, Comer was mentally rewriting his opinion of Bull Clements' widow, and sincerely hoped she wouldn't be forced to give up her nice house and have to go take on a mate's job somewhere. Carla seemed pleased, and whatever bone the two women had been chewin over earlier was at least temporarily set aside.

Inside of an hour, Marietta was a mess. Her white outfit was an artist's canvas of brown and green stains. Her face, too, was undergoing a transformation. The spray and her whipping wet hair had stripped off layers of make-up, leaving a more hard-bitten look with rough skin and small close-set eyes. At the end of four hours, she was panting with exertion, shaking a pesky crab off her finger and into the Gulf, and begging Carla to let her take a cigarette break. Comer was more than ready himself.

Carla agreed, and once they had thrown the anchor out and secured the wheel, Comer decided to make his move.

"You ladies wash up and just rest for a bit," he said officiously, "and let me tend to supper." He searched Marietta's streaked and sweating face. "How you doin, Miz Clements?" he asked.

Marietta rubbed salt and mascara out of her eyes with her wrists and wiped them on her blouse. "I haven't enjoyed myself as much as this in years," she said. "No, I'm serious. I brought a fifth of Johnny Walker Black and a bottle of Chivas Regal in my case, but I haven't even thought about them."

Comer felt his heart skip a couple of beats. That there was some serious whiskey. He went to the fridge and pulled out the sandwich makings and three Cokes. For a fleeting moment he considered asking the missus if she'd like to doctor her Coke with a little "something," then thought better of it. Carla would blow a gasket. Instead, he whipped the sandwiches together and went out to the deck. The winds had calmed a bit, and the swells weren't so high. There was even a hint of moon and stars through the tattered remnants of storm scud. He offered Marietta the plate, then sat down on the deck, his back against the bulwark, and said, "I gotta tell ya, Bull used to be a damn good shrimper hisself before he got to be a senator, but I don't believe he caught on to the business near as quick as you, Miz Clements."

"Don't be silly," said Marietta. "I feel like an idiot slipping all over the deck. I've almost fallen over the side twice. Good thing you let me borrow your life jacket."

"Well, Bull, yah know, *did* fall over the side once. Lucky the motor wasn't runnin or he coulda got himself cut bad or killed. He was reachin over the side to try to free the net from a snag and leaned over too far. The boat lurched and left ole Bull treadin water." Comer cackled and popped the top of his Coke can.

"Fell into the net once, too," he said matter of factly. "Got caught in the catch."

Carla laughed out loud. "He didn't!"

"I wasn't with him, but I knew the man who was. Fella said he was showboatin, tryin to show how a-gile he was by climbin up in the riggin. Then he was crawlin over the cabin, checkin the paint job. We're talkin about the *Gargantua* now, not this little thing. Hell, there was more riggin on that vessel than there is in most boat supply yards. I suppose anybody coulda lost their footing and slid off the cabin like he did. Kinda lucky the net was where it was. Broke his fall."

"I like hearing stories about him," Carla said. "Makes me feel like a piece of him is still here."

"Me, too," the widow responded. There was an awkward moment of silence, then Comer cleared his throat and spit over the side. "Fer luck," he said, looking down at the dark water.

In fact, their good luck continued through another shift with the net in spite of a heavy shower that blew across them, soaking their clothes and rinsing the deck. In addition to the shrimp, they began pulling in striped bass, mullet, amberjack, and other fish, some of which would bring good prices in the supermarkets. The holds began to fill. Comer was about to offer his beat-up old yellow slicker to Marietta when she went below and came back in a weatherproof jacket sporting more snaps and zippered pockets than he'd ever seen on one piece of clothing. Carla must have warned her that she'd need something for warmth once they got into the wee hours. He was feeling a little chilled himself, now that the wind had picked up again. Carla had been on the radio, checking the weather reports, and they had been advised to head back into port. The storm was a full-fledged hurricane now and was expected to strengthen and pick up speed, but most of the forecasts had it taking a westerly track towards

Galveston. The worst they might expect around the Tate's Hammock coastline was some blustery weather and maybe a tornado watch along the squall line.

Marietta collapsed on top of a mess of hoppers, pushed herself over to the bulwark, and leaned back.

"I'm beat," she gasped. Comer's sixty-five-year-old bones were in complete agreement as he watched dawn struggling to get above the horizon, intermittently obscured by the growing cloudbank.

"This was the last load," Carla told Marietta. "Why don't you just rest there, and Comer and I'll cull."

Marietta struggled to her feet. "No, I'll get us some refreshments," she said.

Comer's hopes rose as he watched her disappear down the steel ladder.

When Marietta reappeared ten minutes later, she carried three Styrofoam cups and two bottles tucked under her arm. She took a seat on the hold cover, broke the seal on the bottle of Johnny Walker Black, and proceeded to pour. "Anybody want to join me?" she asked.

Comer joined her at the hold. "Maybe just to be sociable," he said, kicking stray fish and crabs from the last load out of his way. Marietta poured an ice-filled cup for Comer, which he took as if it were a gift from heaven. When the whiskey hit the back of his throat, he did indeed think he might have gone straight to the Pearly Gates. Marietta matched him gulp for gulp, but Carla appeared to just sip at her cup. Which was okay by him—somebody needed to be the designated driver to get them home, and he didn't intend for that person to be him.

"Who's ready for another round?" ask Marietta, filling her cup. Comer poked his arm out and watched with satisfaction as she filled it to the ice line. Classy dame that knows how to drink. He was liking the Widow Clements a whole lot more than when she'd first come aboard.

"You, too?" she asked, pointing the bottle toward Carla.

Carla quickly chugged the remainder in her cup and held it out. Comer noticed the captain's grin was a little lopsided. "Sure, why not?" Marietta emptied the last drops of Johnny Walker into Carla's cup.

They drank in silence for several minutes, watching the sun trying to come up. The seas were roughing up again, and wind came in bursts across the deck. At least they weren't getting rained on, which Comer read as an omen that they might get back to port alive. But as this thought came to him, he also discovered that his usual fear of drowning had taken flight and he now felt like the trawler was coasting serenely over the tops of the waves. Nice. He settled himself more comfortably on the hatch cover and closed his eyes, rolling the fiery amber liquid from the cup over his tongue.

"I've been meaning to ask you something." That was Marietta's voice. He cracked an eye open.

"Like what?" Comer noted that Carla's response was slurred and not quite as happy sounding as he was feeling right now. He opened his other eye a slit.

Miz Clements took another healthy gulp from her cup. Shee-it, now there's a woman who could pour it down. "About that hideous bead fetish thing you found up in the attic. What *was* that? And why were you looking for it in the first place?"

Comer remembered the bead face that Carla had showed them at Hamp's. "It's a conjure stone, don'tcha know?" he heard himself saying. "Come from them giants in Tate's Hell Swamp." He clamped his jaws shut and looked to see if Carla was about to bop him good for sharin something maybe she didn't want shared with the missus. But instead of threatening to pitch him overboard, she was just staring into her cup.

"It's a link to the past," she said solemnly, as if she were reading some voodoo omen of her own in the melting ice. Comer couldn't help but think of all the tales he'd heard Billy Joe Lord spout about what lurked in the deepest parts of the greater Tate's Hell swamp. Creatures weird enough to turn a man's hair white as snow. His skinny bones shivered inside his slicker.

"Whose past?" asked Marietta, half rising, half slipping to pour the rest of the bottle into their three cups.

"I wish I knew," said Carla morosely. Comer took a closer look; he'd never seen his employer in such a state. He'd seen her mad enough to chew an anchor chain and sassy enough to stand up to the bully sheriff that everybody tiptoed around like they was walkin on lobster eggs and hard-bitten enough to chase all the eligible men as far away as the next county, but he'd never seen her like this. She looked like she might dissolve into tears, and that scared him more than all those other moods put together.

Instead, she looked over the top of her cup at Marietta and said evenly, narrowing her eyes, "Something I been meaning to ask you, too." Comer's hackles went up. Was there a cat fight about to start hissin and spittin right there under his nose? Waste of a good drunk, he thought, sucking the last golden drops from his cup. Whiskey this divine was sposed to make you see the light, not curse the darkness, or whatever the hell that scripture was.

"Who's been punching you around? You got an abusive boyfriend?"

Marietta froze for a full ten seconds. Comer knew that to be true, because he was counting. Finally, she tossed back the rest of her cup and turned to face Carla.

"What on earth would give you such an idea?"

Carla chugged the rest of her whiskey and dropped her cup to the deck. It quickly blew over the side in the next gust of wind. "Those bruises on your bicep, for starters. Kinda finger-shaped, I'd say. Got any more where those came from?"

"You're a nosey little bitch, aren't you?" Marietta was glaring at Carla with a fury Comer could only begin to fathom. He got up unsteadily and moved himself out of the line of fire in case one or the other of them decided to mix it up. Come to think of it, he hadn't seen a good girl fight since that time Mae Barnes clocked some wharf rat's whore outside Clem's Clams. Now *there* was a woman who could pack a wallop, hah!

"I just think it would be a shame if you were sinking that low, letting some guy handle you like that after being married to my father, who treated you like royalty, that's all I'm saying."

Marietta stood unsteadily, staggering a few steps with the pitching of the boat. 'You...should just...shut up!" Comer saw her balled fists. Wheeooo, it wouldn't be long now. He backed further toward the wheelhouse door.

Carla continued to slouch against the deck rail, her hair whipping across her face. "Who is it? Anybody I know?"

Marietta swayed, her expression unreadable. "You couldn't possibly begin to understand—"

"So I was right! What does he do, tie you up and make you beg for it?"

"SHUT UP!" Marietta was screaming in fury, but Comer thought her eyes looked all watery.

"Bingo, again," said Carla. "Nothing like a li'l whiskey to bring up the truth."

"Yah know, I think this guy should go to jail, beating up on a fine woman like yerself," Comer offered, thinking maybe he should step in before things got really ugly.

"Yeh," said Carla, "report him to the sheriff."

To Comer's surprise, that one statement sucked all the temper out of the widow and she slid down with a thump to the deck. Her face was pale in the growing light. "I can't do that," she said.

Comer scratched at his neck hairs. "Hell, nobody likes to go lookin fer Big Jim on purpose, but he *is* the sheriff, ain't he?"

"I...I just can't." Crouched with her head hanging down, Marietta was a sodden, drunken mess.

Carla and Comer stared at her, and then Carla said softly, "Oh shit." She sat up straight, continuing to stare at the other woman. "It's him, isn't it?"

The silence that filled the space between them was dense as a pea-soup fog, Comer decided. He was about to respond, but clamped his jaw shut as Carla's voice cut through the rising whine of wind and sudden splash of rain on the deck. Those plops were big, and loud.

"But why? For what possible reason?"

"Damn it, Carla, he's the sheriff! He doesn't need a reason."

"The hell not!" They were close to shouting. "What the *fuck* does he think he's doing?"

But Marietta waved her question away. "No more. No more about him."

"But how could you…I mean, why *him*? You couldn't find anybody else?" Comer gulped. The look on the captain's face was truly scarifying.

This lady fight was slogging into territory Comer didn't want to hear about. "Maybe yah should just leave it lay where Jesus flang it!" Comer yelled at her and beat a retreat into the cabin. The image of the sheriff doing nasty things to that nice widow woman was more than his brain could accept. Time to thrag it back to port—he'd had all he wanted of this fishing trip.

The engine revved up and the boat surged forward. He peeked out the door, and saw that Marietta was chugging from the second bottle and then handing it to Carla, who clung to the railing, too drunk to stand up by herself. Comer wasn't in great shape either, but he could read a compass with very little effort. Tate's Hammock was thataway. Now that the boat was fully underway, he suddenly felt like spoutin…and getting a taste of the really pricey stuff before they swallowed it all.

"Ya daddy coulda drunk them two bottles by hisself," he shouted into the wind, "and back then whiskey was a lot stronger than hit is nowadays. But that's nothin. Sheee-it. Once, I saw him chug a bottle of tequila so strong it had a scorpion at the bottom stead of a worm."

"At least I haven't ever fallen in the net!" Carla shouted

back.

"Hell," replied Comer, "wasn't for me we'd probably drift into Africa."

"With you at the wheel, we won't *have* to drift," responded Carla above the engine's steady whine. "You'll steer us there."

He took another look out the door and saw the two women lying on the deck, side by side, staring up at the sky. The empty Chivas Regal bottle lay between them.

Comer was thinking he wouldn't mind a little lie-down himself, but if both ladies were going to pass out drunk on his deck, then by Jesus, he would get them home in one piece. The rush of the water against the sides of the boat, the pallid sun, the full hold, and the fine alcohol had put Comer into a very satisfied state of mind — that is, as long as he didn't think too much about the sheriff. He looked out the door and saw that Carla had turned over and lay face down on the deck, apparently not minding the small rivulets of water washing strands of seaweed and crab parts against her cheek. And even above the chugging of the engines, he could make out Marietta's heavy snoring.

Chapter Seventeen

When Carla opened her eyes to see Sheriff James Dickey staring down at her from the dock, she wondered if she were having a nightmare. Pale sunlight working its way through layered clouds sandpapered her eyes, and her brain felt like someone was using it for bait. Shit on fire, where was she?

She raised her head a few inches, but the effort was too much and she let it fall. Whoa! Pain pulsed between her ears. At least her forehead had thunked down on wood and not concrete: she must be on her boat.

Where was Marietta? With an effort, she opened her eyes again and crooked her head in the direction she had last seen Marietta's snoring figure. But the deck was empty. She twisted around to the other side but the movement almost made her throw up. And Marietta was gone. She squinted up at Dickey, who was chewing thoughtfully on a crooked cigar. He looked placid enough, but there was something about the man Carla didn't want to remember. She remembered anyway: Marietta. She shuddered inwardly, her revulsion hidden. He'd been with Marietta. Fuck it; it was her business, let her deal with it.

"What time is it?" she asked.

"Hmmm? Oh, round about ten or so."

"What are you doing here?"

"Looking for you."

"Well, you've been trying for weeks to catch me doing something stupid. Go ahead and gloat."

"What for?"

"Getting drunk and passing out on my own boat?"

"Maybe if I had your problems, I would too," he said.

He didn't look gleeful at all. In fact, he seemed dead serious. Carla pushed herself painfully to a sitting position. "What do you mean by that? Has something happened? Where's Marietta?"

"At Jody's with Comer. She told me I'd find you here."

"Oh." Carla got to her feet, brushing seaweed off her face and out of her hair. Her clothes were damp and she was certain she looked like hell—she sure felt that way. She looked around for her deck shoes. They were squelchy with water.

"Told me you got a pretty decent catch."

"Did we? Oh, yeh, but there were only a couple of boats out last night. It was rough out." Her head was still swimming. Looking the boat over as she slipped into her shoes she could tell that everything was swabbed out and shipshape except for the small grubby circle where she had fallen asleep. She peered into the hold, but the baskets had already been hauled out and the area cleaned. When had anybody had time to do all that? "Wait a minute, did you say *ten*?" She'd been asleep for over two hours.

"Ten, yeah."

"And you're here because…?"

"Some things I need to tell you."

"Did you find out who killed Aunt Sookie?"

"Hmm?" The sheriff looked slightly annoyed. "What difference does that make?"

"It makes a lot of difference."

"To who?"

"To me."

"You figure it out, then, you're so fuckin smart."

All of a sudden, Carla's hangover didn't matter any more and anger poured out of her like sweat. She stepped over the gunnel and onto the dock, where the sheriff was standing as still as a pylon. "Look," she said evenly, "I've been calling your office sixteen times a day and all I get is your flunky telling me that 'the sheriff isn't available.'"

"I'm available now."

"Then tell me what you've found out."

"That's not what I came to talk about."

Carla turned away. "Shit, I'm going to Jody's."

"You might not want anyone else to hear what I'm going to tell you."

Carla walked down the dock, the sound of the sheriff's boots clomping behind her. She sighed, stopped, and sat down on the steps of the processing plant. A couple of nearby posts held a sign so faded that only locals remembered its exact wording: "Tate's Fish Canning and Processing Barn." Stinky and a few other people were milling around outside, and she could hear the machinery and the bustle from within. "What, then?"

"It's about them boyfriends of yours."

"I don't have any boyfriends," she said.

Dickey leaned against one of the signposts and chewed thoughtfully. "Sometimes it gets hard to do your job when everybody thinks you're an ignoramus," he said.

"Okay, I'm sorry." Her head was aching too much to argue. "What happened?"

"I went to Clem's last night—not on business, but a little outing with my wife and boys. But after a half hour or so I hear a familiar voice and I look around and see Yancy Vause sitting at a corner table with a friend."

Carla looked up sharply, then eased her head down again. She wanted to know who Yancy might be dating, but she didn't want Dickey to notice. "After what he did last time he and I went to Clem's, what makes you think I care?"

"His 'friend' was a mister Buddy Love, esquire."

As Carla's mouth fell open, she suddenly had the conviction—as strong and as completely out of place as a shot of rum and vinegar in a juice bar—that dissimilation was the root of all evil. Why feign disinterest in things that obviously affected her deeply? Instead of hiding or disguising her emotions, why not just let them run free? For the last several weeks, her every guess had been totally wrong. Her character evaluations were nothing to write home about either. In fact, Dickey's cigar was probably a better judge of character than she was. In that strange instant, she resolved to do no more guessing. She would get the facts laid out before her and make appropriate responses. And if that meant openmouthed astonishment, so be it. But the expression on her face would have to do; she didn't know what to say.

Dickey watched her with amusement, then went on. "Now I wasn't having too bad a time up until then." he said. "The crawfish was hot and the ears of corn roasted to just the right crispiness. My kids weren't making racket for once, and my wife had been to the beauty parlor and was wearing the pearl earrings I gave her for our anniversary last month."

"You're not having a bad time now either, are you?" Carla asked through a stiff jaw.

"Nope," he replied.

Carla sat up straight and slicked her hair back. "All right," she said. "I'm interested."

Dickey brought a match from his shirt pocket, struck it on the post, and toyed with the idea of lighting his crook. He stared into the flame for a few seconds, then said, "The boys sat hunched over a couple of beers. They weren't talkin very loud but I still heard your name mentioned a couple of times." Dickey was watching the match burn down toward his well-manicured fingers.

"What did they say about me?" Carla asked. True to her new resolve, if she was curious, she was going to act like it. But in front of Dickey it was hard.

The sheriff flipped the match to the ground at Carla's feet. "I wanted to eat my dinner in peace, maybe go to the drive-in afterward, but those fellas started gettin a little too loud."

"So you went over to their table,"

"I was fixin to, but Yancy got up and came over to mine before I had a chance. Told me he and Buddy had something to tell me that would only take a minute. So I went back with him and sat down, but I was annoyed, you know, at having my dinner interrupted like that. But I went over and I heard them out. Any idea what they told me?"

"Of course not."

"So it's probably a surprise to you that each of em claims that you're his girlfriend. And they've decided to have a little contest."

Carla wiped the sweat out of her eyes and rubbed her temples. The air had that low-pressure, saturated feel to it, a pre-storm feel that all seamen, and sea-women, knew.

"What kind of a contest?"

"A tough guy contest."

"What?"

"The two of em are going out into Tate's Hell and try to bag a hog bear. Whoever shoots one first wins."

"Wins what?" Carla asked, but she thought she knew the answer. It didn't please her at all.

"Doesn't matter what," Dickey said. "It's the winning that counts."

"Those assholes," she said, half to herself.

"I suppose that pretty much describes them," Dickey said. He brought out another match and, with controlled menace, lit it against his badge and touched it to his cigar. "What we have is an upstanding lawyer traipsing out to a place that even God ain't been in centuries. Fella's got a wife, probably a little money tucked away. What happens if he gets lost out there in the swamp? Or drowns? Then we have Vause—a guy that's not...a guy that likes guns just a little too much for his own good. A Vietnam vet. What if he shoots Buddy-boy by mistake?"

"He couldn't, could he?" But she knew that the answer was yes, easily.

"Now neither of them is ever gonna be President, but they ain't the worst boys around neither."

"I know. Look, I want to say that whatever they do doesn't have anything to do with me, but it does. I don't want it to, but there it is. What do you want me to do?"

"Find em. Talk em out of it."

"When were they supposed to leave?"

"Sometime this morning, as soon as Buddy got back

with his rifle."

"You mean Buddy was going to take a gun too?"

Dickey blew smoke over Carla's head. "Can't shoot a hog bear with your finger."

Carla had a sudden thought. "Why didn't *you* stop them if you're so concerned about them?" she asked.

"Huntin's not against the law," Dickey said simply. He brushed lint from the stomach of his starched brown uniform and pulled his hat further down on his forehead.

"But, damn it, the last time Yancy went out in the woods with a gun—" Carla stopped abruptly; if she had been Pixie, she would have put a startled hand over her mouth.

The sheriff chewed on his cigar for a while, took off his hat and scratched his head. He stared at her for about five seconds before he answered. "You know about that, do you?"

"No," she backtracked. "I mean, I know about Oskie's cousin or uncle or whatever he was. He got killed, right?"

"What else do you know?" he asked sharply.

"I know that it was...I mean, Yancy told me it was self-defense."

Dickey seemed to relax but continued to stare at her with his steel-gray eyes. Finally he said, "Yeah, self defense. No doubt."

It was obvious to Carla that she had hit some kind of a nerve and she wanted to pinch it until she got a reaction. Dickey knew about Yancy's run-in with the survivalist group; that was to be expected. But he seemed to be worried about something. Worried that she might know more than the single fact of Oskie's cousin getting shot. But what more could there be? "There's something else, isn't there?" she asked.

Dickey blew a puff of smoke back towards the dock and gazed after it. A large shrimper was pulling into the choppy waters of the marina and several dock loafers sauntered past to meet it. "Nothin you need to worry about," he told her. "In fact, if I were you, I'd be worryin about those boyfriends of yours 'cuz that hurricane brewin in the Gulf is heading this way. Fast."

Carla stood up. "Shit!" she cried. She'd forgotten about the storm. Now those two assholes… "Okay, I'll do what I can. I'll go by Yancy's house or call or something. But what if I can't find them or they're already gone?"

"Then I'll send somebody out in three days to look for them."

"Three days?"

"Three days was the agreement. Yancy will be starting in the swamp from as far north as he can. Buddy'll enter from the southwest, down by Blanchard's boat ramp. Rules say they can't carry any food, but they shouldn't have any trouble shooting or catching something, as long as the hurricane stays away." The sheriff looked her up and down, rubbed his nose with the back of his hand, twitched his mouth, shook his head, and said, "You might think you've got a pretty nice ass, but no way I'd go out in that swamp for it."

A response was called for, but there were laws against what Carla would have liked to do. She simply turned on her heel and headed toward Jody's café, then looked back at the sheriff, who was still leaning against the post, fiddling with his cigar. "You're a prick," she yelled. "But thanks for the heads up." He waved her off and walked on down the pier toward the incoming boat.

Carla met Marietta coming out of Jody's. A light sprinkle was coming down, and Carla stood in the doorway feeling like a damp dog.

"Hey there," said Marietta. Her throaty voice was less raspy than usual, almost smooth, like a silky tumbler of Chivas Regal. "I was just coming out to look for you." After the night on the boat, Marietta's clothes were grimy and wrinkled. Her hair had been combed, but without shampoo or a conditioner it lay crinkled up on her head. She had it tied up in back with a rubber band. Her make-up had washed off as well, revealing the rough surface she usually tried so hard to conceal. But strangely, everything blended now. For the first time since she had known Marietta, she looked like a normal human being. Carla stared at this new Marietta, speechless.

Finally, Marietta spoke for her. "Want some breakfast?"

"Breakfast? No. I have to find somebody." She quickly repeated what the sheriff had said, avoiding the details of her own stake in it. Still, the way Marietta nodded told her that she wasn't fooling anyone. "So I need to drop by Yancy's," she finished.

"Don't forget you need to give me a ride home."

"Oh, right. Sorry."

Yancy lived in a duplex about a mile closer to town, but she preferred to look for him alone, so she made no offer to let Marietta tag along. After dropping Marietta off with a promise to stay in touch, Carla sped back, but Yancy's blue Corvette was not in his driveway. She went up to his door and knocked anyway, but after a few seconds got back in her car and headed toward town. She drove slowly past its three motels in the hope that Buddy might have decided to stay in Tate's Hammock overnight instead of going back to Tallahassee. He could probably borrow a gun from somebody, too. But his BMW was in none of the parking lots. Then it came to her that if Buddy were going to stay in town, he might be tempted to stay at her place. Pixie might even have let him in, so Carla wheeled around and headed home.

But her driveway was as empty as Yancy's, and her tires kicked up shells as she skidded to a stop. Inside the house, she shouted for Pixie, but Pixie was gone. She found no note so she supposed Buddy hadn't come by. Peeling off her reeking clothes and dropping them like clumps of seaweed across the carpet, Carla sat naked in front of the phone and started dialing numbers. She tried Yancy's number first, but hung up after ten rings. Then she called his uncle's car lot and found out that Yancy had taken a few days off to go hunting.

Too tired and wound up to think, she dialed information and got Buddy Love's number in Tallahassee. A woman answered on the third ring.

"Hello?"

"Hello, is, um, Mr. Love there?" Carla's heart squirmed and she took a deep long deep breath.

"No, he's out of town for a couple of days. This is Carla, isn't it? I recognize your voice."

"Um, no. When did he leave?"

"About dawn this morning. Are you expecting him?"

"Damn it, Minnie, I'm not expecting him. I'm just trying to find him! I...I'm a client."

"Minnie?"

"But it's nothing that can't wait. I'll give him a ring in a couple of days."

"All right, but—"

"Thanks." Carla hung up.

Well, she had done everything she could—except go out in the swamp herself and look for them—and that she wouldn't do, even it she knew where to go. Let them kill each other, or let the hurricane do it. She had a ponderous headache and was dog tired. Hoping she wouldn't dream, Carla got up, stumbled to her room, and fell into bed. She was asleep in seconds. It was a long, quiet sleep.

It was after six that evening when she woke up. The pounding between her temples was gone and if she had dreamed, she didn't remember. She took a long therapeutic shower and washed the sea scum out of her hair. Rejuvenated, she stepped out of the tub, wrapping a towel around herself.

"Pixie!" she called out. "Are you home?" There was no answer. Concerned, she padded barefoot into Pixie's room. The girl's few clothes were still in their places and her bed was unmade. Carla went into the kitchen and looked in the fridge. The remnants of a sandwich lay unwrapped on a plate. Pixie had eaten at least one meal while Carla had been gone. The cats had also been fed. Scrubbing her hair with the towel, Carla walked naked into her bedroom and sat down on the bed. The cigar box with Aunt Sookie's artifacts was on her night table with the lid open. Carla lay the towel across her lap and put the box on it. Idly, Carla sifted through the papers. Even with everything she had learned—from Buddy, from Hamp's story, and from the library—she still didn't know *enough.* Suddenly she realized something was wrong with the box. The three old photos were missing.

She bounced up from the bed and searched the house, including Pixie's closet and chest of drawers. Nothing. Pixie had taken the photos and disappeared, but why?

Carla threw on some clothes and sped back into town. Her Movado said seven as she pulled up to Crozier's store. Only Hamp was there, and he was inside, counting fishing lures. He looked up when he heard his screen door bang.

"Hamp, have you seen Pixie today?"

"No, can't say I have. Is she missing?"

"I'm afraid she's gone out to Sookie's again."

"That old place is probly as rickety as Billy Joe Lord by now," he observed. "Not the kind of place that little girl should be hangin out in in this kinda weather."

"I know. Thanks anyway." The screen door banged again behind her.

Carla now had one more thing to worry about. Not only were the two men who concerned her most in the world out in the swamp ready to blow each other's heads off, but the only other person she felt close to was probably headed there too. And completely unaware that there were two gung-ho machos hiding in the bushes with high-powered rifles who might mistake her for a young hog bear at night. And on top of everything, a hurricane! And in another hour it would be dark.

There was only one thing to do; she had to go after them. Pulling away from Hamp's store, she headed for the marina in a mood every bit as gray as the storm scud overhead.

Chapter Eighteen

Droplets of rain spattered on the prow of the small rented boat that Buddy Love guided toward the far bank of the river. Overhead, dark clouds flitted, bent, and swirled, as if they couldn't make up their minds which direction to go, or what shape to assume. Van Gogh had painted clouds like these; Buddy had once seen some of Van Gogh's paintings in a magazine someone had left in his office. The clouds—then and now—were terrifying, but Buddy tried to stay calm. He cut off the outboard and tilted it forward until the blades came out of the water, coasting the last ten feet to shore. He scrambled out of the boat onto what looked to be a thin deer trail, and pulled the boat halfway onto dry land, tying it securely to one of the thick ty-ty bushes that lined the shore. Their branches were grotesquely twisted and intertwined as if from decades-old storms and high water. Twenty feet ahead, one of the largest magnolia trees Buddy had ever seen loomed like a gigantic monster cloaked in gray and green, the wind rattling its great leaves. It would be a good natural landmark for when he returned.

Buddy reached into the bow and pulled out his Remington Mountain Rifle in its weatherproof case and a backpack containing some ammunition and other supplies he might need—first-aid kit, mosquito repellent, case knife, cigarettes, compass. He shouldered the pack and, rifle in hand, headed into deep woods.

Buddy had gone hunting a number of times over the past several years, ever since his job had given him the time and the money to afford it. But his trips had always been with colleagues or clients, and usually took place in safe hunting preserves in Alabama or Georgia. He had bagged a couple of white-tail deer, a rabbit, a squirrel, and a wild turkey, but had always given the meat to one of his friends—Melanie thought hunting was primitive. Well, it *was* primitive. And sometimes being primitive was liberating. Buddy loved the woods, but respected them. His outfit—from his hunting cap down to his walking boots—were not only waterproof, but bramble-proof. Probably snake-proof, too, although he was not anxious to have them tested.

He slogged through the bushes for half an hour, then stopped on a rise to consult his compass and map and to think about how life wasn't much more than a series of coincidences. If he hadn't had those signatures to pick up in Tate's Hammock, he would probably never have thought of visiting Carla again. If he hadn't spent the night with her, he wouldn't have had any reason to get an aerial map of the Tate's Hell area and Blanchard's Bluff to compare it with the old one in Carla's cigar box. If he hadn't stopped in Clem's Clams and seen that asshole Vause sitting at the bar like he owned the place, he wouldn't have challenged him to this contest. Or was it Vause that had challenged *him*?

"First one to find and kill a hog bear wins."

"Wins what?"

"Let's just say that the one who loses stays away from Carla."

"Fine."

"Great."

That's when the sheriff had chipped in his own two cents. "You boys ain't scared of bein out in the hurricane?"

"What hurricane?"

"The one fixin to coast into town...at least that's what I heard on the six o'clock news."

Buddy had seen Vause's eyes narrow, so he quickly said, "Fuck the hurricane!"

Vause had tried to brazen it out. "Who gives a shit about a hurricane?" he'd said, but Buddy knew that he was worried.

Buddy wasn't worried. In the ten years he lived in

Tate's Hammock, every hurricane that was predicted to slam dunk the town had swerved away like an air ball and missed completely. He didn't mind a little wind and rain. And if it really hit, well that was okay, too. It would be something to tell his hunting buddies when he saw them again.

The sheriff was a witness as they had outlined their plans. With the aerial map getting wet beer-mug stains on the table, they had fixed on their destination, Buddy coming in from one direction, Vause from the other. That would give them each a chance to hunt alone for several hours. After that, they would track together. Or, they might end up tracking each other. Buddy didn't know what Yancy's woodland skills were, but he *was* aware of the other man's military history. Not something he intended to ignore.

Buddy wondered what Carla would think if she knew he was out here—and that she was the prize? Probably shoot him for real with that wicked-looking .38 of hers, but he and Vause agreed that she would never know.

The rain was coming down thickly now and a cluster of leaves broke free from an oak and whipped past his face. Overhead, a starling separated from his flock struggled against the wind. Buddy tucked his map back in his pack, set his cap further down on his head, and continued his trek. The ty-ty was thinning out and almost before he knew it, he had stepped into a carpet of aquatic vegetation dotted here and there by patches of thigh-high grass. All around him were the dark ghosts of dead cypresses, some long, thin, and leafless, pointing accusingly at the revolving clouds. Some, the thicker and hardier ones, their trunks rippling with what looked like corded muscle, made Buddy think of bodybuilders posed in front of an audience, frozen in time. Most of the trees, however, were just stumps—most of them hollow—cut long ago for lumber mills. He was in one of the Dead Lakes—a trio of dry indentations like three dark ashtrays set in a roughly triangular pattern in the earth. The meeting place he and Vause had agreed on was the high ground in the center of this triangle, which was reputed to be thickly wooded. Buddy stepped behind one of the thickest of the cypress trunks to shield himself from the wind and rain. It was almost a perfect blind, giving him a clear view in every direction. If a hog bear—or deer or panther—happened by, he could take his time and get off a clean shot.

There was a thick log behind the trunk, and Buddy sat down and lit a cigarette from his pack. If the wind and rain got any worse there would be no way to keep the tobacco dry enough for more than a puff or two, no way his lighter would hold enough flame to light one. He took a water bottle from his pack and sipped slowly.

He kept that post for almost an hour, but except for a flock of ducks flying with the current, and a coyote that flashed through the ty-ty so quickly he was not even sure he'd seen it, there was no game. Making his way across the dry cypress lake toward the spot that Vause had marked with a greasy pencil on the map, Buddy stopped half a dozen times to rest, to sight for game, and to get out of the worst of the rain and wind, which were now strong and powerful enough to cause him concern. A hundred yards in front of him, at the edge of the dry lake, he saw a tall pine tree bend nearly parallel to the earth before its roots gave way, toppling it to the muddy ground—another corpus in a cemetery of dead trees.

He had almost reached the other side of the dead lake when a blast of wind blew him off his feet and propelled him headfirst into one of the seemingly hundreds of dead cypress logs around him. His head cracked against the hard wood, opening a cut above his right ear. When he touched his hair, his hand came away with blood. He was not so much hurt as surprised. His hunting outfit was flapping like clothes on a line and his skin felt like it was being tested in a wind tunnel. It looked like the only hurricane likely to hit the area in a decade was the one he had chosen to be out in. A blinding rain now pocked like b-bs against the bare skin of his arms and face as he searched wildly around for better cover. There: the largest cypress stump he had seen yet, lying like the hollow carcass of some long-extinct beast. It wasn't until he was halfway to the stump that he realized he was dizzy, he must've hit his head harder than he thought. In his haste to get under cover he twice tripped in the mud, his vision blurred. Throwing his rifle and backpack ahead of him, he crawled into the dark opening and breathed a sigh of relief. He was protected from both wind and rain, and unless the lake flooded somehow, he could wait out the worst of the storm. The trunk was completely hollow, blackened in a fire that might have raged before he had been born. And it was tapered. Where he entered, the opening was almost four feet wide; the other end was only half that but provided a lookout. In a few minutes he would get something from his pack to put on his wound, would get a pain reliever and maybe another sip of water. Right now, though, he would just rest for a while. Later, through the thin end of this telescopic cypress, he could watch out for any game stupid enough to be out in a fucking hurricane. Then he'd find Vause and…

When he awoke, it was nearly dark, but he didn't know if it was because of the storm or the time. He felt better, though. His dizziness had passed, and his head held only the shadow of an ache. The wind sounded even fiercer than before and through his lookout he could see high grasses swirling like they were being stirred in a boiling pot. Beyond, was a thickness of trees—oaks and more pines and another he identified as a cedar—all bending away from the high wind. But there was something else: a hulking shadow moving slowly between the trees. As he watched, the creature went down on all fours, still moving forward. It was a Florida brown bear, commonly called a hog bear by the locals. He quickly slid his rifle out of the case, checked to see that there was a round positioned in the chamber, and fired quickly through the narrow opening of the log. The sound reverberated in the hollow space, mixed with a human cry outside.

Shit! It wasn't a bear at all. He had just killed Yancy Vause. He crawled backwards from his hiding place, but before he could stand up, three shots rang out. A branch splintered ten feet away, either from one of the bullets or from the storm. Still crouching behind the great log holding his rifle and backpack, he called out over the howling wind, "Vause, it's me! Are you hurt? I didn't mean to shoot."

"Is that you, Love? Where are you?" Vause's voice came over the wind, now a good twenty yards from where he had been earlier. Relief flooded Buddy's mind. The man couldn't be hurt bad and still be able to move that quickly.

"Down in the lakebed. I'm coming over. Don't shoot!" he tried to yell loud enough to be heard through the storm.

"What!"

"I said don't shoot!"

Cautiously, Buddy shouldered his pack and made his way toward the place he had heard Vause's voice. He held his rifle in front of him, barrel pointed toward the ground. Nonthreatening. He realized that Vause could easily kill him and say it was an accident, but Buddy was almost numb with the thought that he might have had to tell the sheriff that very thing. And who would have believed him? Wow, Carla, it was quite a hurricane and, by the way, I accidentally killed your boyfriend. Hunching up against the wind, he made slow progress over the lip of the dry lake, through the swirling grass, and into the trees, where he felt immediate relief from pelting rain and surging wind.

"That's far enough!" The voice came from behind a large oak tree, followed by Vause himself, holding a pistol in his right hand. His left arm hung loosely at his side and Buddy saw that the shirtsleeve up near his shoulder was the color of blood drenched in water. Vause's hair looked like a seaweed; he blinked at Buddy with eels' eyes.

"Listen, I'm sorry," Buddy began. "All I saw was something moving, then you went down on all fours..."

"You thought I was a bear?" asked his rival incredulously. He raised the pistol toward Buddy's neck, then threw it furiously down into the wet carpet of leaves and balled up his fist. "You stupid fucking bastard!" The fist connected with his jaw; Buddy went down hard, and for the second time in only a few hours, he blacked out.

He awoke in a whirling darkness and groaned. Fuck, his head. He thought he might be blind except for the firefly he saw hovering nearby.

"You awake?" came a voice just behind the firefly, which Buddy realized slowly was the cherry-end of a cigarette. Buddy tried to rise, but the effort was so painful it made him nauseous. He groaned again—the side of his head felt like a tree had fallen on it.

"Sorry I popped you. I mean, I'm not sorry, but I didn't mean for you to crack your head open when you went down."

Buddy reached up toward the cut on his scalp and felt that a bandage had been wound around his head like a gauze headband. "I hit it…earlier," he managed. "The wind picked me up and threw me down." He seemed to be lying in the middle of a swath of high grass, surrounded by a triangle of fallen trees. Wind still shrieked above him, but there was very little rain. "Is the hurricane gone?" he asked. "Where are we?"

"It's let up a little for a while. I found this shelter about an hour ago. Three or four trees were ripped up and fell across each other. They made a little fort where we can rest."

"You carried me?" Buddy asked.

"Mmm. Dragged is more like."

The glow from Vause's cigarette told Buddy where the man sat, his back against the trunk of a tree that had probably—until a few hours ago—been standing for a hundred years or more. He sucked at the smoke, making the round point of light go red-hot, then fade, then glow, like a warning beacon. Buddy watched the red-hot tip suddenly rise up in an arc and disappear into the night as Vause flipped away the butt.

"That's the way forest fires are started," Buddy said, then started laughing and immediately stopped—the pain was blinding. Vause laughed as well. Buddy tried to raise himself to a sitting position, but it was still no go. "I think I may have a concussion," he admitted.

"And I have a bullet hole in my arm that you can shine a flashlight through," Vause answered. "I took some of the disinfectant from your first-aid kit. A few cigarettes, too."

"Yeah, okay, good. I really didn't mean to shoot you," Buddy said sincerely. "I was groggy from that first knock on the head. I guess I just wanted you to be a bear so that I could get back to civilization."

"Yeah, I know. Just try and take it easy. When you can walk, we can try to get out of here. How did you get this far anyway? I took a Ford pickup off the lot and drove it in as far as I could. Got stuck in a bog, though. I'll have to come back for it with a tow truck after I get back to town."

"I rented a little boat down at the docks from Claude Bateman. I pulled it out of the river and tied it up just to be safe."

"I sold Claude a 1977 Volkswagen once," Yancy said. "I think he still has it. It's good about the boat, though. It may be our only way out of here."

"So that's what you do when you're not traipsing around in the woods or annoying Carla?" Buddy asked, "Selling cars?"

"Annoying... Listen, man—" Yancy began, his voice angry, but then it shifted to resignation. "You're right," he said. "I'm a used car salesman and I *do* annoy Carla. I even got her arrested last week."

"Is that right?" Buddy was interested.

"Not much of a story, really. I got into some trouble a while back, and I'm not supposed to carry a gun, but I carry one anyway. I slipped it in Carla's purse when I saw a sheriff's car coming up on us."

"Carla probably took it in stride."

"Almost beat the shit out of me."

"That's the Carla we know and love," said Buddy.

Vause's voice came out of the darkness. "Sometimes I think that maybe I could have had a job like yours if I'd wanted to—don't know why I didn't make the effort. I would have liked to be Matlock or somebody. Perry Mason. A lot more exciting than hanging around a car lot twenty-four-seven."

Buddy closed his eyes. His headache was still blazing. "Would you get me some Advil out of my bag?" he said. He heard a rustle beside him, then his water bottle was thrust into one hand, two pills placed into the other. He felt an arm around his neck as Vause gently lifted his head. He popped the pills and drank a couple of sips of water, then nodded. Vause lowered him back into the grass.

"I can use some of those pills," Vause said.

"Help yourself."

The wind sounded like it was picking up some and Buddy saw lightning bloom faintly in the distance. He glimpsed Vause settling himself back down against his tree, cradling his bad arm. "I'm a divorce lawyer," Buddy said softly.

"What?"

"I'm a divorce lawyer. I sit in an office all day and talk to unhappy people. I help people break up their lives, and I take some of those lives for myself as my fee. I fill out papers all day, or rather, I have my assistant do it. I didn't tell Carla that. I'm sure she thinks I defend the innocent or help the needy. I make a lot of phone calls to other lawyers and we bill our clients for every minute we talk. My wife is a librarian from Boston who reads French philosophers at the breakfast table. In French." He stopped and took a breath. "I should have stayed with Carla—now *she* has an exciting life; she runs her own boat and her dad was a state senator."

Yancy interrupted. "Dates guys that put guns in her purse."

Buddy started to laugh, but caught himself before his skull could split open. "I guess I was pretty exciting, too, when we were dating. I was a varsity basketball player at FSU. Went into law so I could represent athletes or work for a professional organization like the Pacers or the Celtics."

"Why didn't you?"

"Chickened out, partly. And partly I wasn't smart enough." Buddy made an effort and sat up, moving his body just enough to enable him to lean back against a tree trunk. "When I finally passed the bar the only firm that would hire me worked mainly with divorce cases. After that I got married, got a nice house in a good neighborhood, got stuck."

"Yeah, me too," said Yancy. "I always thought I had enough excitement when I was in the army. Served a couple of hitches in Vietnam in swamps worse than this. But you know, today's the first time I ever got shot."

"You ever shoot anybody?" Buddy asked.

"Strange, that little girl asked me the same question. Pixie."

"You mean Carla's Pixie?"

"Yeah. She's got this weird way she looks at you that makes you want to tell her things."

"And did you?"

"I guess I did. I ended up telling her and Carla about me and a couple of my buddies shooting Oskie Holt's cousin in self defense."

"Hold on!" Buddy cried. "I know about that! You mean that was *you*? I go hunting sometimes with one of the lawyers who defended you. Told me those survivalist trainees or whatever they were had Jell-o in their heads where their brains should have been. Whatever happened to the rest of those guys?"

"One of them got to be sheriff." Buddy saw another match flare up as Yancy lit up again.

"You don't mean…?"

"Old liver-gums himself. But Jim's a lot different now. Back then he was trying to learn how to use his weapons. Just got in a little over his head."

"I don't remember his name coming up at the trial," Buddy said.

"Hah. When the shooting started, he ran for the trees. But I saw him, and he knows I saw him."

"And you didn't tell."

"Well, Oskie has pretty much dedicated his life to putting me in jail one way or another, and the judge told me I can't carry a gun, but at least Dickey owes me one."

"Carla hates his guts."

"Carla. Right. Fuck it, if it hadn't been for Carla, neither of us would be here right now feeding this damned place with our blood and...uh oh...here it comes again!" And before the words were even out of his mouth, a horizontal torrent of rain blew into their enclosure, accompanied by wind so fierce Buddy thought their tree-fort might be swept away like pick-up sticks. Leaves, whole branches full of leaves, uprooted ty-ty bushes swept over their heads like fast-forward images on a TV screen. Buddy could just make out Yancy's figure as he stood up to his full height, raised his good arm, and shook his fist at the sky.

"Yeehaa! It doesn't get any better than this!" he screamed.

And for some reason that he might never in his life understand, Buddy agreed.

Chapter Nineteen

Carla stood on the dock ready to cast off. Rain bands from the approaching storm had darkened the skies, blocking most of the sunset. Nobody was on the dock to see her heading off on this goddamned fool's errand because they'd battened down their boats, boarded up their windows, and headed indoors. She threw the ropes onto the deck and leaped after them.

It was rare for her to take the boat out alone; she only did it when she wanted to relax and be by herself. Now she wondered whether she'd ever be able to relax again. She turned the key and the engine purred to life. Easing the shrimper out of the harbor, she settled down at the wheel and taped Sookie's map to the paneling in front of her. The inlet and first set of landmarks she felt confident about. Beyond the dogleg of the river she expected some unpredictable sloughs and marshlands, but was counting on Comer's description of Sookie's house to guide her. It should be visible from the river if it really did hang out over the bank as he had said. The island would have to be her first reference point. The dogleg at the inlet crooked in just beyond it. There were a lot of smaller inlets and uncharted coves beyond the dogleg, and she hoped not to have to explore too many.

After twenty minutes of plowing along the coastline, Carla spotted the river's inlet and aimed for it. She slowed the engine to a moderate speed and entered the inland waterway. It stretched straight before her for several miles, a vast sheet of water between banks overgrown with ty-ty, cypress, and Florida creeper. Watching the water off her bow, she spotted a school of black bass feeding on the shrimp which she knew invaded the brackish areas nearest the sea.

Dead ahead of her lay the island, a rounded hammock of land, crowned with laurel oak and sparkleberry bushes. Above the oak she caught a flash of lightning, followed several seconds later by the pummeling of thunder in the distance. Shit on a raft. The last weather report she'd listened to still predicted that outer feeder bands of the hurricane would affect the coastline way west of Tate's Hammock, but still, that thunder sounded too close.

She navigated carefully past the island and down the center of the river, watchful for submerged logs or sandbars. From habit, she scanned the river's surface for nervous water, a sign of fish activity below. As the river's course began to meander, piles of logs jammed the inside of the bends, frosted occasionally with fine white sand spits. Carla's concentration sharpened. A long narrow spit carpeted at one end by emerald spikerush reached out toward the shrimper's hull. A brace of sanderlings skittered across the spikerush an instant before bursting into flight.

She thought of Aunt Sookie. Sookie knew every tree, plant, and thrusting fungus from the tidal pools to sawgrass prairie to upland forest for a hundred miles around, and although Carla had soaked up more natural lore from that old lady than she'd at first realized, she wished she had paid more attention when the chance had been there.

Carla lifted her head and searched the treetops at the killy-killy-killy of a kestrel soaring on the wind. Killy hawks, her daddy called them. *You sit real still, little girl, and they'll come snatch a grasshopper from off the back of your hand.* It seemed strange that in all their outings together, her father had never taken her in this direction. It had always been east, away from Blanchard's Bluff. Away from Aunt Sookie. Well, it was no secret that Bull Clements had something against Sookie, but Carla never fully understood what it was. She had hints, but it wasn't until she came home from her only Sunday at the Old Pisgah Church that Bull had done anything concrete. After that she had rarely seen Aunt Sookie, and to her discredit, she had never asked her father why he had sent the old woman away. She supposed now that it probably had something to do with the trust—Bull Clements had always been a proud southerner and probably couldn't deal with someone like Sookie being his landlord. But if that were the case, why didn't he just move out of Chez Marais when Carla's mother died?

Carla was wondering about this when she felt an unsettling shiver run through the floor of the shrimper. She had navigated past the dogleg and into the fork that Comer had marked on the map, but the fork seemed longer, thinner, and far more meandering than it looked on the map. And although she kept to the middle of the stream, the vessel had scraped bottom. She eased off on the throttle and coasted a moment, waiting for it to happen again. She stared hard at the water swirling away on either side of the bow, but it was getting too dim to see into its depths. And even darker because of the thick vegetation that grew up on both sides of the stream. Jeez, no wonder people never came out here. It was like floating into a thick, soupy shadow. She switched on the running lights and shone the high-powered spot ahead of her, which was some help, but not enough. With a little shiver of fear, she realized she was trying to do a very foolish thing in searching for Sookie's house. Although she was used to running the boat at night, this was not open water and the chances of getting grounded or worse were likely.

Carla peered at the banks on either side for a sight of the limestone boulder or three ancient cypress trees. No luck. The keel shimmied again and crunched. She killed the engine and waited. The vessel was still afloat, and rocked gently in the current. Reluctantly, she let the anchor drop and climbed up on the bow to decide what to do. She knew from Comer's annotation to her map that the house should be on the north or left-hand side of the river, but she couldn't tell how far she was from the remaining landmarks. Well, one thing was for sure; the boat was too big to go any farther. She knew that she should back out and turn around before she got completely stuck, but she was more worried about Pixie and Yancy and

Buddy than she was about being grounded. At the worst, she could always spend the night in the boat and leave on the next tide. Finding Pixie was her most important obligation, with her suitors a close second, and the only way to do that from here was on foot. She hoped she hadn't taken a wrong fork anywhere.

She studied the left bank. The sun was below the treeline, but there was still enough light to make out a marshy slough between her and the land. It looked pretty far across. With a sigh she pulled on her old tennis shoes and tied them tightly. She wrapped her pocket flashlight in a ziplock baggie and tied it to her belt. But she needed cigarettes too, and they were below. In fact, she needed a ciggie right now.

Sitting on her cot below deck, she stuck a Winston in her mouth and reached into the compartment for her matches. Then she saw the joint, crooked just slightly like an inviting finger. If there was ever a time she needed to get roasted, this was it. She put the cigarette back in its package and lit up the joint, sucking in the first blast of inhibition killer with deliberate abandon. She smoked the first half of it that way, digging the rocking of the boat and the shape of smoke swirls collecting over her head. Finally she felt ready to face hidden swamps, hog bears, and errant boyfriends—time to go. She carried the other half of the joint up on deck.

Well, well, the bank didn't look so far away after all. Maybe she could float across. She toked in another smoky breath and checked the sky. The clouds made it seem darker than it should be—no telling what time it was, and who cared anyway? She sealed her cigarettes, sulfur matches, and boat key in a baggie and stashed it in her pocket. The dope was hitting her quite strongly now, thank you, and when she stared down into the water, it stared back. Her stomach made a gurgling noise and she realized that she had eaten nothing since Comer's sandwiches of the night before. Her head was spinning: never get loaded on an empty stomach. She shook her head and toked the joint down to her fingertips, then flipped it into the river, which hissed at her.

She had to find Pixie, although she wasn't sure why. Shrugging, she simply slipped over the side and swam for shore. It was easy as shit; the water wasn't even cold, and after a dozen strokes her feet hit bottom. It was only when the water was at waist level that she thought about alligators. This was their home. It was also the home of water moccasins, leeches, and other swamp delights. She waded quickly toward a lush tangle of green snakes that looked like seagrass fronds, or was it the other way around? Hard to tell. She hoped that any critters would have been scared off by her engines but still found herself struggling more quickly through the strands of kelp at the river's margin. Suddenly she stepped in a hole and swallowed water as her head went under. Good thing she had tennis shoes on—no telling what she might step on besides mud slime and gator snouts.

Panting, her head spinning, Carla pushed her way into the tiny choked lagoon of cypress roots and ty-ty, when the smell hit her like a cloud of gnats. Years and years of composting vegetation, rotting fish, and layers of guano: an abandoned pelican rookery. She could make out a ring of old nests dotting the low-lying bushes. It was all coated with a thick crust of dampened guano that clung to her like library paste as she pushed the branches aside. The smell and taste of it clogged her sinuses and coated her tongue. Crawling on her hands and knees under the low-growing, tightly interlocked branches, at last she fell out into a clear pool of shallow water just offshore. She lay on her back in the water and let the waves wash away some of the mess. Would have been nice to just lie there awhile, but she thought of moccasins again and wearily got up, slogged to the bank, and pulled herself up into the shadows of the overhanging trees. Guessing that Sookie's cabin couldn't be too much further downriver, if she followed the riverbank as closely as possible she was bound to hit it, right? Right. She contemplated the darkening thicket ahead, and then saw something very unexpected, something that in her stoned state she'd failed to spot when she'd entered the water. Not far from where she'd crawled ashore, a small boat with an outboard motor was tied securely to a bush. It rested half in and half out of the water at the edge of a faint track leading into the underbrush.

At that instant, thunder boomed overhead like a mallet in her skull and she could smell rain on the air. Suddenly a shot echoed on the heels of the thunder, or was it really a shot? A tree branch cracking? Hard to tell when her senses were so revved. She listened for a few seconds and thought she heard a shout far in the distance.

"Hey!" she hollered. Her voice sounded monstrously loud, but no answer came back. Carla continued up the bank to firmer ground as cold raindrops splattered against her skin. Blackberry brambles tore at her ankles. Damn! She should have worn jeans—how could she have been so stupid? Instead of saving "the boys," as Dickey called them, she might end up needing to be rescued herself. A rustling noise moved across the treetops, and then the rain hit her in a blinding torrent. In despair she trudged farther up the track and flopped down under a towering magnolia to wait it out and try to get her head together. The trees were bending at funny angles, a sight both alarming and fascinating. Then they whipped around in the other direction as another gust hit them. She was doing something unthinkable, sitting under a tree with a hurricane blowing in…dangerous but, thanks to the dope, wildly exciting.

She glanced back down the bank at her boat. Its strings of running lights reminded her of a Christmas tree and illuminated the overhanging tree branches, the Spanish moss, and the rippling stream like a photograph seen through a frosty window. A window that Carla now wished she were looking out of instead of in through. Her T-shirt was soaked and she felt chilled, sitting out in the exact middle of nowhere, miles from home and probably a few more from Sookie's house, alone in the growing dark. Or maybe not, if that boat belonged to Buddy or Yancy. Wherever they were, she hoped they would realize what she was forced to go through just to make them see what maniacs they were. Not much chance of that.

But as she hunched in the muddy discarded leaves of the magnolia, rain cascading off her head like bird droppings, it occurred to her that this whole mess had intensified her longing to change things, to turn her pathetic life upside down. Fuck it, she'd find Pixie and get the hell out. Get up, she thought, get moving. The least she could do was try to find the limestone boulder and the three cypress trees. If she hugged the shore she shouldn't get lost. Eaten by bears maybe, but not lost. Yet still she sat in the stinging rain, soaked, stoned, and half afraid she'd never find her way out. She was scared, but the weed was doing something odd. It was making her horny. Where were Buddy and Yancy when she needed them? What she suddenly wanted most in the world was one of them, she didn't care which, to suddenly appear in front of her, naked like some pagan nature god, rampant and ready to perform. The eyelid movie that erupted in her brain at that notion was incredibly sensuous. She tilted her head to catch rainwater in her mouth and stood up, reaching her arms toward the howling wind and rain. Without thinking, she stripped off her T-shirt, unbuttoned her cutoffs and stepped out of them. Her panties and sneakers followed, and she walked just outside the magnolia's umbrage, letting the rain massage her entire body. Her fingers traveled from nipple to nipple, brushed down her belly, and then traveled further. Then she was aware of only the dark green of the woods with its earthy smells, the rain in her mouth, the rainbow lights of her boat, the spasm between her legs. For someone who should have been shivering with cold, she was white hot.

She screamed her release into the wind, pleased at the answering thunderclap, aware of herself as never before. Standing in the storm, naked and fearless, Carla resolved from that point onward that nothing was going to stop her from kicking her life up to full throttle. She sank back under the tree, savoring the little afterquakes that flickered across the inside of her thighs.

The downburst, too, was intense but short, and in

another minute the rain abated, although the wind still whipped the tops of the trees. Probably a lull between feeder bands, if the hurricane was indeed moving ashore. It was also nearly dark and Carla had lost all track of time. Shaking cascades of rainwater out of her hair, she reached out for her clothes when she realized with a shock that someone was standing behind a small oak not far away from her. The figure was hugging the tree with meaty-looking arms, shaking water from the leaves. Normal people didn't do such things and she was so scared that, for several seconds, she forgot how to speak, her earlier bravura fled on the wind. Finally she managed to breathe, "Who's there?" but the figure didn't answer. "How long have you been there?" she called out, louder. She remembered the flashlight, and took it from her belt as quietly as she could. Head spinning and adrenaline racing, she shone the light and revealed the imposing figure of a Florida brown bear. Carla switched off the light quickly and sat as if carved from granite.

The bear crooked its head around the tree and stared directly into her eyes. For eternal seconds it continued to hug the trunk in its paws, then it stepped away from the tree and ambled erect for a few steps. The only other bears Carla had seen had been in zoos, but she knew that this one didn't look full grown. But that wasn't cause for much relief as it still stood a good six inches taller than she was and must have outweighed her by a hundred pounds. Swaying, the young hog bear leaned its back against the tree and leisurely began to scratch back and forth. Carla listened, transfixed, as it grunted and whistled softly. In a moment it stopped, apparently resting, then began to scratch again. The sapling quivered with the rhythm of the rocking bear. Droplets of water showered down over its ears and snout. A part of Carla's mind watched in fascination; the rest was frozen with fear.

Abruptly the bear dropped to all fours and shuffled across the narrow clearing toward a rotting log directly in front of Carla and only yards from her outstretched foot. She longed to pull the foot in under her but dared not. The bruin snuffled the log with its wetly shining nose, eyes locked to hers again. It seemed to paw the log in slow motion, licking at insects uncovered by its two-inch claws.

Carla felt faint, the tension and suspense sending her blood in dizzying circles. The creature could toy with her almost as easily as it did with the log, drawing out the time before the kill, savoring it. She was barely breathing. A chunk of log broke free and rolled at her feet as the bear knocked apart another stratum of grub-laden wood. Carla watched and heard the bear crunching them in its jaws. It still held her with canny, knowing eyes. Finally the bear stood up to its full height, licked its lips, and gazed down at her. Then it dropped to all fours and ambled away into the swaying trees.

It was tame. It must have been. There was no other explanation. Unless Yancy had laced the reefer with opium and she was hallucinating. But what was a tame bear doing out in the swamp? Not quite as frightened as she had been, Carla stood up, batted the leaves and pine needles off her butt and struggled into her sopping clothes. She waited for several tense minutes, watching the spot where the bear had gone into the brush. Finally, she decided it wasn't coming back. But where was the path she was looking for? There was nothing but thick brush or forest in all directions. Wait. There: where the bear had gone in the trees she found the faint path again and began to follow it warily, flashlight in hand. Quickly it became a grassy track, worn by the hooves of deer and wild pigs. She saw their tracks, but the hog bear must've left the path and gone home to wherever hog bears live. She hoped so, anyway. Fifty yards ahead of her, she spotted the looming crag of a boulder. Up close it was head high, and its white limestone surface was pitted and channeled like coral. She assumed this was Comer's landmark, obscured from sight by the surrounding grove of trees.

The path was thinning into a tangle of sweet gum and elder, and she shone her flashlight into the growth in all directions, searching for Sookie's house. The trail had faded almost completely when she pushed through a last clump of bushes and brambles and abruptly stumbled into a rough clearing. Then she spotted the house, sitting on a bluff, which she assumed must be overlooking the river. She had found it! "Pixie!" she shouted, but the only answer was treetops creaking in the whipping wind.

Carla sloshed across the clearing and struggled up the steep stairs of the house to the front door landing. In front of her was a rusty screen door, patched in places with cloth sewn into the mesh. She stood there dizzy, panting, listening to her own heartbeat, and looking into the dimness of the house. Clinging to the landing, she became vividly aware that she was completely exhausted. Soaked to her skin, caked in pelican shit and swamp mud, incensed with sinsemilla and probably smelling like a bear, she was more tired than she had ever been in her life. She pushed the screen door gently and it grated inward on loose hinges.

Looking inside was like peering a hundred years into the past. Carla stood in the doorway while her eyes adjusted to the dim light. An oil lamp was lit and cast dancing shadows across the fireplace wall. A flicker of movement from an opposite doorway made Carla start, and Pixie stepped out of its shadowy hallway into the room. Her hair was sprinkled with water droplets, and her bare feet left damp footprints across the floor. She looked like a gypsy in a multicolored gingham dress that flowed down to her ankles and nearly engulfed her hands. A blue and white bandana was tied around her forehead and a leather bag hung around her neck. She was also wearing the bead necklace that Carla had seen on the floor of the Old Pisgah church the day that Sookie had died...

"Jesus, Pixie, you scared the shit out of me."

A smile opened and closed across the girl's dark features. "I see you made it," she said simply.

Carla stared at Pixie as if the girl were an apparition materializing out of the lamplight. In addition to the lamp, the room was lit cozily with fat tallow candles; a sweet smell of patchouli hung in the air. A huge wicker armchair with a high, rounded back stood against one wall, while the other side of the room was piled with puffy, overstuffed cushions of many colors. A small fire whispered in the fireplace and sent light flickering around the room.

Carla tried to shake the fog out of her head. Shivering, all she wanted to do was get dry, take off her grungy clothes, and lie down on those soft pillows. Dreamily, she pulled off her T-shirt, kicked off her tennis shoes, and dropped her cut-offs to the floor. She grabbed a folded quilt off an old sofa and wrapped it around her. "What's the fire for?" she asked. "Isn't it still summer?"

"It's to ward off the hurricane."

Carla stumbled toward the pillows, but stopped when she reached the fire. Her teeth were chattering. She edged as close to the red-orange tongues of warmth as she dared. "In that case, I don't think it's working"

"We'll see," Pixie answered.

Well, at least she knew why she hadn't been eaten by gators. All the animals had probably taped the windows of their nests, boarded up their caves, and got out their store of candles. "Why are you wet?" Carla asked, watching Pixie's eyes, shining in the firelight.

"I went looking for you."

"And how did you know I was coming out here?" asked Carla. "Your *ifa*-intuition kicking in? Ha ha."

"Saw your running lights out on the river," Pixie said simply.

Of course. Carla sneezed explosively and sank down in front of the fire, trying to shake off her feeling of other-worldliness. Must have been opium in the reefer. Damn Yancy.

"How the hell did you get out here by yourself," Carla went on, as much to herself as to Pixie, "and what are you doing wearing those clothes? That style went out about a hundred years ago."

Pixie continued to watch her solicitously.

"Where did you get Sookie's necklace?"

"Sheriff gave it to me when I went to his office."

Carla was slowly crawling toward the mound of pillows, keeping her eyes on Pixie. "What are you looking at me like that for?" Then Pixie was beside her, her hand on Carla's shivering forearm.

"I think you might be catchin a cold or something," she said. "I'ma get you settled and go make some of Auntie's tea. Get you feelin better in no time."

She fetched a pillow and placed it under Carla's head and pulled over several more and fluffed them up around her, forming a sort of low couch. Carla sank into them blissfully, and studied Pixie at close range.

Tight braids intertwined across Pixie's forehead like dark tentacles and stuck out behind her in longer strands that were themselves braided loosely. To Carla, the braids looked like snakelets writhing up from under the bandana. The rest of her hair was plastered across her skull with Vaseline.

"You know," rambled Carla thoughtfully, "I found this old pelican nesting place. Then a bear came up and scared me so bad I..."

"Shhh." Although Pixie still knelt beside her, Carla couldn't tell which direction her voice was coming from. She felt engulfed by the girl's dark presence. Pixie's eyes were bright blue marbles in the light from the hearth.

"Feelin better now?"

Carla scrunched further down into the cushions and pulled the quilt more tightly around her. "I could use that tea you were talking about. Just make sure it's strong enough to kill the taste of birdshit."

Pixie chuckled and stepped through the shadowy doorway where Carla had first spotted her.

Left alone, Carla studied the room more closely — worn sofas, the fireplace, antique three-sided cupboard in a corner, and everywhere piles of the huge goosedown cushions. The place was old and dingy, but in a comfortable, homey way. It felt good to be there, safe from the winds intensifying outside.

Carla adjusted her pillows and lay back, trying to stretch out her aching muscles. She was startled when her outstretched hands touched the base of a narrow freestanding set of stairs. They reached at a nearly vertical pitch into the darkness of the high pointed ceiling. She could see the rafters above.

"What's in the loft, Pixie?" she called.

Pixie came padding back into the living room, carrying a rolled-up piece of material. "Auntie's bedroom, mine now. Here, put this on." She handed Carla a long, somehow familiar-looking dress.

"What's this?"

"Old dress."

"What happened to my clothes?"

"Um, they be wet and you took em off."

"I did?"

Pixie walked away again and Carla listened to the sounds of crockery, pouring water, and the unmistakable iron clank of a wood stove door. Carla sat up and pulled on the dress. It was rough-dried and smelt of cloves.

"You don't have electricity out here, do you?"

"Nope," answered Pixie. "No running water neither. Got a well outside. A shithouse too, if you need to go. Auntie didn't need a lot of modern stuff," continued Pixie, coming back with a green and orange cup, a row of sunflowers decorating its sides. It looked hand-crafted and old. Steam billowed around the rim. "Don't burn your tongue on that," she warned.

Carla suspiciously accepted the cup. "Aren't you going to have some too?"

"Don't need any."

Carla put the cup to her lips and sipped. "Whew!" she managed. "What'd you put in that stuff? No, don't tell me, I'd probably throw up."

Pixie laughed softly and set about putting another log in the fire. She handled the tongs with practiced ease. Carla marveled at the self-sufficiency. Was this the Pixie she knew? Evidently not. She sipped at the cup again.

"That'll just warm you up and relax you good," said Pixie, nodding at the cup in Carla's hand. "Help you fight off a cold and make you sleep."

"Smells musty, like dead wood."

"Mushrooms."

Carla choked, spluttering. "Damn it, Pixie, are you trying to poison me?"

"Naw, honey caps ain't poison. Mix em with a little coneflower, comfrey, valerian root, chamomile, and lemongrass, just lightens your load."

"It's doing that, all right." In fact, Carla's tension and sense of unreality had been swept away, replaced by a languid numbness. She flopped back on the pillows, as dust motes billowed up like thousands of tiny kestrels. She closed her eyes. "You know every damn thing, don't you?" she mumbled, slipping toward sleep

"Mostly, I guess. 'Cept who killed Auntie."

"Don't worry about that," Carla said drowsily, feeling like she had just chugged a bottle of Nyquil. "I know who killed Sookie."

Chapter Twenty

I guess I know a lot of things—for a fourteen-year-old, I mean. I can name almost every plant in the woods—but the name I give em might be different from what a book says—and I can tell you what they do. I know whether they'd cure a boil if they're mashed up just right, whether they'll steep up into tea, or whether you can use them in a nice stew. I know some plants that'll make you well and some that'll make you itch. I wish I knew as much about people as I do about plants, but I think all people be different. Some people, like Aunt Sookie, are healers. Some others, like whoever strangled her, are killers. The rest of us are somewhere in between.

At first, I thought I knew who killed my auntie, but I wasn't real sure. When I ran into the old church that day and found her lyin in the bell tower, I saw bruises on her neck. There was something else there, too—a small cut, moon-shaped, but deep. It looked like somebody'd choked her. I know she wouldn't a wanted me to, but I cried and cried over that old woman. She was only my great aunt—my grandma's sister—but she felt like my mama and my teacher and my friend all in one. And I wanted to punish whoever'd done it. So I poked around in the church's old kitchen—it was almost falling down and thieves had grabbed most of the stuff that used to be there, but I found a plastic knife and an old bent fork not worth stealin and put em in one of Sookie's hands after I laid her out in the pulpit. Then I went outside and found the right-sized stick—I knew it was supposed to be a real cassava stick, but I didn't have time to run back here and get one. I put the stick in Sookie's other hand and ran away. It was a hex. It meant that whoever killed Auntie would die by violence.

It was only later that I thought about Daddy. He really didn't like Aunt Sookie, even though she gave him money sometimes to do odd jobs for her. He hated it that Auntie was teaching me to be the next *ifa*. He wanted me to finish school and maybe even go to college and not be hangin out here in the swamp all the time. He felt real bad that he was always drinkin up the money he was tryin to save for my college. One time I told him not to worry, that Sookie would pay for my college, that I could have a real job and be an *ifa* too, but that just made him drink harder, so I didn't mention it again.

But there are plenty other people who didn't like Auntie. Daddy tried to keep it a secret, but Mae Barnes always wanted to be my step-mama. She thought Sookie'd put a hex on her once before I was born, so's Daddy would marry Mama instead of her. That wasn't true, though—Daddy never liked Mae as much as Mama. If Carla's daddy Bull still be alive, I'da thought it was him. Nobody hated Sookie more than Bull. Carla never knew why, but I do. I can name more people in Blanchard's Bluff—a lot more—that thought Sookie'd done them some kinda harm, because when bad things happen to us, we want to believe that it's not our fault, that somebody else caused it to happen.

And that's why I thought Daddy killed Sookie. Because he died by violence so soon after I worked the hex with the knife and fork and the stick. And it was then that I remembered the mark I'd seen near the bruises on Sookie's neck. It was the kind of mark somebody's thumbnail might make if it was pressed down hard. My daddy had a long thumbnail on his right hand; he grew it on purpose so he could pick his guitar better.

So in one way, I was glad that Carla had gone to sleep (I musta made the tea too strong for her)—I didn't want to hear that I was right about Daddy. In another way, though, I wanted her to tell me that I was wrong, that maybe it was some hunters out in the woods, some of those survival people that had maybe found her by accident and decided to have some bad kinda fun with a frail old lady.

The storm outside was tearin through the bushes and causin bears and snakes to find places to hide, but Carla was sleepin like a baby. While I waited for her to wake up, I tidied up some, got more candles out of a cabinet, and found a few things I wanted to give her when she woke up. I put more wood on the fire, hopin to keep the storm from hittin the house. It done a good job so far, but the house was old—it shook like an old person with the heebee jeebies. Or the kind of shaking that happens when you cry real hard, knowing that the old woman who'd lived here for so long wouldn't be comin home any more.

I went into the kitchen and opened up a can of stew. I put it in a pan on the wood stove and added some greens and seasoning. The wind was rattling the door and I hoped that none of the windows would blow out. I felt sad; not for auntie or Daddy, because that was a different kind of sad. This kind of sad was because I was just now knowin that today was probly the last night I'd be spendin in this old house. That it was time to let the swamp and the woods take it back like the cemetery outside the old church had took back Sookie's body. I poured the stew into bowls and set them aside to cool, and when I went back into the living room, Carla was awake. That old dress of Freeda's was so big it made her look like a rag doll. She was smiling, so I figured she wasn't gonna be sick after all.

"You feel better?" I asked.

"Lots. I guess the hurricane hasn't passed yet."

"Naw. Few more hours yet, probly. I made us some stew." I saw her looking at me funny so I added, "Don't worry, it came from a can. I didn't put anything in it much."

I went into the kitchen and got the bowls of stew, and when I got back she was sitting in Auntie's wicker chair that had the big round back. It made Carla's head look like it had a halo around it. We ate a few bites, then I went back in the kitchen and got us both a cup of coffee I'd put on earlier. But then I couldn't wait any more. I had to ask. "You said you knew who killed Auntie."

"I did?"

"Um hum. Before you went to sleep."

She frowned and blinked. "I shouldn't have said anything before I was sure."

"You're not sure?"

"Close, but I need to prove it. If I'm wrong, I'll look like an idiot and get sued for character defamation or whatever. Don't worry, Pix, I'll tell you in a day or two. Can you wait that long?"

"I guess, but—"

"And in the meantime, before this storm blows this whole house to Jamaica, I want you to tell me about Freeda and Tate and all the other things you thought I already knew but don't."

"I was finta to tell you all that anyway." I stopped and waited, thinking.

"Well?"

"Well, I only know how to tell it like Auntie told it. She told it to me over and over and had me say it back just like she did. So the words I'ma say are exactly the words Freeda used a hundred years ago, so they might seem strange to you."

"You mean like an oral history? That's incredible, Pixie," she said. "I can't wait to hear it. I wish I had a tape recorder handy."

I eased down onto the pillows and closed my eyes. It was almost like I was looking for words written on the insides of my eyelids. I wasn't reading the words, though, I was remembering them. This is the story I told.

"Back in slavery time," I began, "Old Massa be gettin long in de toof, and all de folks round about say he gwinter die soon. Now de Massa, he treated his cullud folk wid respect, but he had im a son named Joshua who was mean as a snake in a lake. He allas be pickin fights wid de men and tryin to lift up de skirts ob de women. So when de Massa fell off his horse one day and broke his hip, a dozen or so ob de slaves started to thinkin dat dey best be somewheres else lessen Joshua come round de cullud quarters without Old Massa bein able to proteck his proppity."

I opened my eyes for a second and saw that Carla had closed hers, and was soaking up what I was saying. I was always able to see in my head what I was describing, and I hoped that Carla could see it too: I could see the plantation with its whitewashed house and veranda. I could smell the slave quarters with odors of sweat and bacon fat and mules. I could feel on my skin the roughness of the canvas shirts and flour sack dresses they all wore. Somehow, I was there watching at the same time I was sitting on my pillows with fairy tales comin out of my mouth.

"So dat night de moon was hid neath a passel of clouds, and de twelve set out through de woods. All dey carried with em was some biscuits, dried fish, an coffee. Dey all had knives and carried what clothes dey had in bundles.

"Dey was scairt, too, cause dey knew bout de panthers and gators and snakes and all de other varmints dat was out dere in dose woods. Still and all, dey druther have the varmints than Joshua. An dey had em a doctor, too—an *ifa* woman by de name ob Chloe, who knew roots and spells. She was bout to deliver a chile and her belly looked as full an hard as a ripe watermelon. But she had her amulets round her neck—de garlic sprigs an de necklace wid de objeck of great wonder which her mama had brought all de way from Africa."

I almost lost my place in the story when I heard the crack of wood splitting as a big limb peeled off from the trunk of an oak and crashed into the brush beside the house. Carla started up too, frightened for a minute, but relaxed again as I kept tellin the tale.

"Now it was hard goin—didn't but two of em have shoes—and it was cold. But dey had em a plan. Stead of goin nawth, like most ob de runaways did, Chloe took em south, towards de coast. De mens thought maybe dey could get em a boat and sail off to Mexico, or maybe Haiti. But Chloe had other ideas. She thought maybe dey could get to de Wakulla

Volcano dat nobody had ever been to, an live there secret-like. Whenever dey got onto a hill or high place, Chloe could see de smoke from dat volcano plain as she saw de clouds in de sky, an dat's de way dey headed.

"Now dey knowed dat people be missin em in ten-twelve hours, and dey also knowed dat Joshua had a set ob dogs dat could smell a tick at a hundred paces. So Chloe led em to a small stream and tole em to get in.

"'Lawdy, woman,' said one ob de mens, 'I ain't walkin in no cold water.'

"'Then you shonuff be walkin in heb'n come this time tomorra,' said Chloe.

"Now de rocks be hurtin dey feet somp'n fierce, but bye'm bye de cold water made em so numb that dey couldn't even feel de blackberry briars on dey ankles and legs, an so dey walked on. Dey kept to dat stream for six or seben hours, til dey found a path made by animals in de woods. One ob em killed a deer and dey made a small fiah and cooked it and got warmed up. Then dey went on. Dey walked for five days thout any sleep, then dey rested and walked for three days more. And each day dey used de smoke ob de volcano as dey nawth star."

The wind blew hard down the chimney and sent sparks out on to the hearth. Carla looked like she wanted to jump up from that chair and put them out, but I knew they wouldn't hurt nothin. She saw I was lookin at her and I could tell by her expression that she was seein her own movie of that band of slaves makin their way across the swamp and toward the smoke. She could feel how tired and hungry they must have been after two weeks of eating only a squirrel or wild turkey after that first deer, but they felt relief, too, because they didn't think they had to worry any more about Joshua and his dogs. That was what the story was sposed to do: make whoever heard it feel the scariness of the swamp creatures that slithered and snuck across their feet and hear the buzz of the insects that crowded around their faces day after day, and finally to feel the great happiness and freedom when, on the midnight of their sixteenth day, they pushed through the final thorny brambles and saw the clearing where the volcano was, with the smoke rising up like the steam over a hot bath. I picked up the story again.

"Dat volcano wasn't nothin but a crack in de groun, and all around it for mebbe fifty yards was a clear space where nothin growed. Roundabout de clear space was trees so thick dey was like walls. Like de walls of a great house.

"An dat next mawnin, dey trapped a wild pig an roasted it on a sharp stick over de fust real fiah dey had in more'n two weeks. An when dat pig was ate and dey was feelin fine and lazy, Chloe picked up some rocks she found round about dat smoky volcano. The rocks looked like de big face bead she had on her necklace dat she called de objeck of great wonder. An Chloe gathered all her people round her and she said—"

"Wait, Pixie, wait!" I opened my eyes again and saw that Carla had stood up and walked a couple of steps toward me. "What do you mean by a face bead?"

"I finta tell you," I said.

"Do you mean it was like those stones on that necklace you're wearing?"

"That's next in the story," I said.

"Okay, go ahead, but I'm going to have some questions later."

"Okay, then," I began. I closed my eyes again and continued Chloe's story. "Back when de worl was fust built, de water, de fiah, de land, an de air was all fightin to see which was de strongest. 'Ah is de stronges' say de air, 'cause Ah covers everything dat Ah see,' but de land say 'Naw, Ah is de most powerful cause Ah is de hardest.' But de water just laugh and say 'Put yo biggest mountain up gainst me an Ah'll grind it into lil tee-neency grains of sand.' De fiah, meanwhiles, isn't sayin nothin, but it's got mad a-hearin all dat lyin an boastin. Befo de others knowed what happened, it had boiled and a- bubbled de water into steam, melted de rocks, an covered de air wid black smoke. De others be scairt an went back off to dey own houses an never messed wid de fiah again. But just to make certain, de fiah left behin' a objeck dat would remind em of what it could do. De objeck is a rock dat's made of all de other elements together. It's hard lak a rock, but has holes in it where there's pieces of air, too. An if you throw de objeck in water, it floats lak a stick.

"Some cullud people in Africa saw de fiah from de volcano spit up some ob dese objecks so dey knew dat dis story is de troof. An dey took one of dese objecks and carved it and painted it into a face to protect em from de other elements. Dat was de objeck of great wonder dat Chloe's mama had brought with her from Africa and dat Chloe wore roun her neck.

"An when Chloe was done tellin de story, she held up de pebbles an threw em in a gourd dat was filled with water. De rocks floated. All twelve of de runaway slaves knew then dat dis was dere new home, an dey set to buildin shelters and gatherin wood.

"Dat night, Chloe had her chile, and she named it Freeda, an Freeda grew up knowin de same root doctorin dat her mother did. An Freeda set to carvin de pebbles Chloe had picked up into faces an she punched holes into em to make beads for a necklace. By de time Freeda was a teenager, de community by de volcano had growed. At fust, dey would sneak out of de swamp to see who else was livin roundabout, an sometimes dey would help nother slave to escape. An even though de smoke from de volcano was thick all de time, dat cypress an ty-ty swamp was so thick dat scasely a dog could pass, an for fifteen years nobody never came round lookin for it. Dey found a path to de water and learned to make a boat an in dat way found a little town called Gulf City only a few miles west. Then slavery was over an dey brought others to de volcano community. Dey was still not trustin de white person cause a what happened before. In fack, Freeda had never spoke to a white man til one stumbled out ob de surroundin swamp half dead with snake bite.

"Now Chloe be away vistin kinfolk up in Jaw-ja, an

Freeda, though she was only bout fifteen, took de man into her own house and applied de proper roots and medicines to his bite. She thought he was a good-lookin man, but eben though he had a young face, his hair had a-turned whiter den salt. She watched over him for three nights in a row an eben made a bed for dat man over de crevasse ob de volcano an threw in various medicines for a offering. An finally, dat man woke up.

"When he spoke, it was in de strangest words Freeda ever heard cause he was from a country called France, where they spoke funny. In fack, dere was only two she ever learned: Taittinger D'Arbanville. Dat was de man's name. Freeda couldn't make her mouth do right at fust, so she called him Tate."

"Pixie, stop again for a minute." Carla was sittin still in the wicker chair, her eyes were almost closed. The fire was still burnin in the fireplace, but lower now, and the wind was still causin leaves to crash into the windows like flapping moths. I stopped my story.

"Pixie," Carla said. "That's Tate. Of Tate's Hell."

"And Tate's Hammock," I told her.

"Then I was right. Tate's Hell and the Wakulla Volcano are in the same place."

"They *were*."

"Were?"

"I've seen the place where the volcano used to be. Aunt Sookie took me there a couple times. An underground stream broke through the limestone above it and covered it up. There's only a sinkhole there now."

"Well, what happened to Tate?"

"I was just finta tell you, but you made me lose my place."

"Can you tell me in your own words?"

"I guess. Anyway, it's the same story the old men told, cept that Tate really owned almost all that whole swampland. His daddy had been some big high-up in the French and Indian War and General Lafayette gave him the land as a present. Tate inherited the property and sailed over from France to check it out. Probly didn't mean to be in there more than a day or two, but that was before he got lost and wandered into that place where the volcano people were. But when Tate got better, he fell in love with Freeda. Steada couple days, he stayed there for a couple years and they had a son named Rufus."

"Rufus D'Arbanville!" Carla shouted. Then she jumped up from her chair and started pacing across the floor. "Rufus D'Arbanville was the man who built Chez Marais!" she cried.

"Yeah," I said. "And he be the dude in the picture in Aunt Sookie's box. The one where he went on vacation to the Flagler Hotel with his wife."

Carla walked to the window and looked out into the night and I got up and looked with her. Far down the river we could still see the strings of lights from her shrimper doing a dance in the wind. We could also hear the pounding of the river against the banks, and I was hopin that it didn't overflow and come callin.

"But in that picture..." she started. "If Rufus was Freeda's son, he would've been black."

"No more than you are," I told her.

"Say that again."

I reached out and smoothed Freeda's homespun dress over Carla's shoulders so that it wouldn't sag as much. "You heard me." And she looked like she had heard, all right, but maybe she wasn't sure what the words meant. She looked at me like she wanted me to explain it all, so I did. I smiled at her, because I was happy that she was finally going to know the secret we been keepin from her all her life. "Rufus was your great-grandpa," I told her. "You my cousin."

The wind outside was blowing the rain in circles. I never been in a real hurricane before, but Sookie had told me about the terrible damage they could do, especially to wooden houses like hers. I was pretty calm, though. I just had a feeling that this one last time, we would be safe. Carla looked like she wasn't so sure. She was looking out the window and watching the treetops bend over like people picking cotton. With Freeda's old clothes wrapped around her, she might have been a cotton picker herself. I went over and poked the fire, but didn't add any more logs. It was gettin hot inside and we couldn't open any windows or everything would get blown all over. I guess Carla was thinking about what I told her, because she didn't say nothin for a long time. I finally had to start, because I wasn't finished telling the stories; I knew I'd probly be telling her the stories for years.

"For about a hundred years, people in this house told that story exactly the way I just told you," I began. "Guess it was somethin Freeda made up. Sookie would tell it to her kin at fish fries or family reunions. She had me tell it a couple of times, too."

Carla came away from the window and sat back down on the pile of pillows. "Tell me about Rufus, then," she said softly.

"Someone else gotta do that," I said.

"But you told me—"

"I'ma let Miriam tell you."

"Mother?" The look on her face was like she thought I be losin my mind, so I explained.

"Before your mama's time, all the stories be by word of mouth, but when Miriam came along, she started writing it all down. Maybe that's because she was the first one here that had proper schoolin and knew how to write. She did it here in this house when she was bout my age."

"My mother was in this house?" Carla asked. She was starin at me with bugeyes.

"Sure. She spent a lot of her growin up years here."

"Why?"

"Sookie was teaching her all the old history—her and my mama Lizzy. They were kin and they were friends, too, but your mama was the oldest. She was afraid bout forgettin important things, so she wrote down some of the stories." I walked over and sat down beside Carla on the pillows.

"Here." I handed her a blue spiral notebook. On the front, Miriam's big, schoolgirl letters said, "Story Book, by Miriam C. Lawhorn."

Carla just looked at it for a minute, running her hands over the surface, feeling the letters her mother wrote there. I showed her where the part was about Tate and she started to read it out loud.

"Taittinger D'Arbanville and Freeda had a son born in 1871. His name was Rufus D'Arbanville, and he was as light as his father."

Carla looked at me. "This is it," she said. "This is about Tate." I nodded yes, and watched her as she read. She was sitting as straight as a cedar tree in winter. It wasn't her usual way of sitting, so it musta been the way she remembered her mother sitting. I saw tears running down her face like rain down the window panes. She wiped her eyes with the back of her sleeve, and handed me the book. "You're going to have to read it to me," she said. So I took the book and began. I never heard her mama's voice, but I did the best I could to make it sound right.

"Soon after Rufus was born, Tate left the swamp for good. The climate didn't agree with him and he had another family back in France. He remained in the nearby town only long enough to transfer a deed of property. For meritorious service beyond the call of duty, fourteen hundred and fifty acres of the land that once encompassed the vast swampland and volcano rift in the earth had been deeded to Count Jean Pierre D'Arbanville—Taittinger's father—by the Marquis de Lafayette in 1831. These were deeded over to Freeda and her son." Carla nodded to herself. I think she was starting to understand.

"Freeda's mother had been a slave, and although the war was over, Freeda knew how the civilized world treated black people. She also knew that no matter how white his skin, the son of a black woman and a white man would always be considered black. Therefore, the civilized world would never know who Rufus's mother was.

"Using money from Tate, Rufus D'Arbanville was sent away to the best boarding schools in the east, then educated in economics at Boston College. When he graduated, he returned to the town of his birth, but he was simply a well-dressed stranger to everyone in Gulf City except the volcano people."

If you read a story enough times, you can get so you see in your mind the way things musta looked back in the past. And what I was seeing was a handsome young man dressed in a clean suit—maybe linen—standing on the steps of a train and looking out at all the people ready to get on the train he was getting off. The other people weren't dressed as nice and they stared at him, while they be holding bags of flour or noisy chickens. I can see brown hair moving a little in the wind, blue eyes looking out in the crowd for the person he knew would be there to meet him.

"This young man immediately sold a portion of the wilderness tract to a timber farmer and purchased an estate of some twelve acres near the growing township of Gulf City. Upon the grounds he built the mansion known in his father's language as Chez Marais—The House in the Swamp.

"Believed by the white community to be one of their own, Rufus not only moved into Chez Marais, but moved most of his family in as well, although to the rest of the town, they were his servants. At the age of thirty-one he married Phoebe Crawford, a young white woman whose father was the wealthy lumber merchant who had bought part of Rufus's land. The marriage was blessed a year later by a daughter, Melissa, who was the image of her mother, though her eyes were as black as two coals.

"The D'Arbanvilles prospered and no one was surprised when they continued to support their large domestic staff, with Freeda as the housekeeper."

"But in 1905, something unexpected happened. Phoebe D'Arbanville was delivered of twin girls, christened Trixie and Sookie. These girls did not look like their mother at all, but had skins as black as the Africans who were their ancestors. The discovery of Negro blood in the D'Arbanville family would have meant their ruin, so the twins were quickly whisked away by Freeda to the swampland and a house Rufus had built on stilts near the Gulf inlet. Word was given out that the twins had been stillborn. Instead, their births were quietly recorded in Tallahassee, one hundred miles away from the nosey people of the town. So Trixie and Sookie lived with their grandma in the house on stilts. The white sister, Missy, continued to live in Chez Marais.

"Meanwhile, the volcano community—now called Blanchard's Bluff—had begun to spread out, with numerous houses and a church. And the larger town, called Gulf City, was renamed Tate's Hammock. More and more people were moving there to get in on the fishing and timber industries.

"In 1929, Missy was married in a June society wedding to a man who owned several fishing boats. His name was Ricky Lawhorn, and it was said that they were a very happy couple. Their only child was born a year later. Her name was Miriam Christine Lawhorn."

"Mother," whispered Carla.

"Miriam's daddy died in a boating accident when she was five, but her mother—helped by Aunt Sookie—brought her up to know both the new ways, and the old."

Carla looked up—she had been reading the book along with me. "Did Daddy ever know about, you know, the two sides of the family?" she asked.

"Sure. He hadta. It was in all your mother's legal papers."

"Why didn't he ever tell me?"

"Donno. He was shamed, I guess. Maybe he thought we'd go away."

Carla sat up straight on the pillows, her back against the wall. The wind was dyin down and it was almost like silence. "Maybe he thought it was a dream, I know I do. But let me get a few things straight. Rufus had three daughters, right?"

"Right. Missy, Trixie, and Sookie."

"And Missy was my grandmother. She died before I

278 HELL AND HIGH WATER

was born, but I've seen pictures of her. Trixie and Sookie were twins?"

"Umm hmm."

"And Trixie was your grandmother?"

"Yeah, but she died a long time ago, too."

"So Sookie was your great aunt."

"Yours, too," I said.

"Mine, too," Carla said. "Our grandmothers were sisters. I can't believe I never knew that. I mean, when we in the library the other day doing that research on the D'Arbanville family—that was *my* family. And I majored in *history* for god's sake. I'm such a dope."

"How you feelin?" I asked.

"A little lightheaded, but fine. Why?"

"Auntie say you might feel strange bout bein kin to black folk."

"About being kin..." Carla laughed. "Well, I might be if Idi Amin or somebody turned out to be my real father," she said. "But I like knowing I'm related to *you*. And you know my daddy was an only child. Five minutes ago I didn't think I had any real family left."

"There's a lot more stories in that notebook of your mama's," I said. "She made a family tree, too."

"Did she say anything about the trust?"

"Sure, but it ain't anything special. It's just an agreement that the white side of the family would get to live in Chez Marais, but the black side would always own it. Carla, there's a lot of money in the trust. Enough to buy a new boat, enough to send you back to college if you want to go. Enough so's I can go to medical school."

"You want to go to medical school? When did you decide that?"

"I sometimes get mad when people make fun of Auntie's remedies. They work, most of the time, and if I had real learning, I would know why. An I like helping people."

"That's great, Pix," she said. "Maybe I can—" But she didn't finish her sentence because just then we heard the scary sound of wood creaking and splitting. A tree was coming down somewhere out there in the dark. I felt Carla hold her breath, and I cupped my hands over the necklace. "Not on the house," I whispered to the wind.

But the wind, this time, didn't listen. There was more cracking and ripping sounds, then a noise like a bomb and it felt like somebody took the whole house up in a big plane and dropped it. I got thrown against the wall and then everything went dark.

Chapter Twenty-One

When the shaking stopped, Carla found herself bunched up against a wall in total darkness, buried under pillows, pictures from the walls, knickknacks, even the wicker chair. Luckily, they had been sitting on all those pillows or...Pixie! Carla called the girl's name, but there was no answer—just the howling of the wind, closer now, swirling around her—some of the windows must have blown out. Trying to push herself up, she realized the floor was pitched at a dizzying tilt. Feeling around in the darkness, she found Pixie's limp form under a heavy wooden table, two of its legs collapsed and two intact, creating a space underneath that may have saved Pixie's life. Carla pulled the girl gently away from the debris and arranged her as comfortably as she could on the pillows. The hurricane was too loud for Carla to hear breathing, but when she explored the girl's face with her fingers, she found a sizeable bump on Pixie's forehead.

"Owww!"

Thank goodness. "Pixie, are you okay? Can you move?"

"I...I guess." Carla felt Pixie's legs jerk, then her hands found Carla's. "Everything seems to be workin. What happened? Why is it so dark?"

"I think a tree fell on the kitchen and knocked the house lopsided. All the candles went out." Luckily the fireplace was at right angles to the tilt; the embers had shifted to the left, but hadn't escaped into the room.

"We need to get out of here." Pixie sounded frantic. "What if the house blows away with us in it?"

Carla was moving around in the house as best she could, holding herself up by clinging to the walls or doorways.

When she got to the kitchen she was hit by a flurry of wind and rain—the roof was gone in that part of the house, and something huge was in her way. She could make out the bulk of a tree taking up most of what used to be the kitchen. It had crushed down through the ceiling like a rolling pin on a house made of matchsticks.

"I, uh, I think we're safe," Carla said. "The tree that fell on the house is pinning it to the ground."

"We could try to make it to your boat—"

"My boat's probably either sunk or just a bunch of timbers strung out from here to the Gulf. Let's just wait it out here. Help me pile some of this stuff in front of the door to keep out the rain and we'll get into a dry corner and wait it out."

By piling up furniture around them and getting more pillows and blankets from Sookie's bedroom, they made a little nest and curled up in it together. They talked a little about their near escape from death, but mostly about what they were going to do when they got back to Tate's Hammock. Pixie mulled over her plans for school; Carla fantasized about the Tortugas. Both listened to the mesmerizing whine of the wind outside. Eventually, they slept.

When Carla woke up, her body was one tremendous ache. Her left arm was asleep where it had been folded under her. Groaning, she pulled herself to her feet and looked out the window. The storm was over, and morning sun straggled through remnants of clouds. The room around her was a total wreck. Tables were overturned, pictures curled up in broken frames, blankets and pillows a sodden mess. She looked for Pixie, but the girl had vanished.

"Pixie!" she called, but there was no answer. Where the hell had she gone? Carla spotted her T-shirt and cut-offs on the floor near the spent coals of the fireplace. Pulling off Freeda's old dress, she got into her own clothes. "Pixie, where are you?" Her voice felt like asphalt.

Carla jumped as Pixie spoke behind her. "Here I am." She whirled around and saw Pixie peering through the front door, although the room was so skewed Carla had to look up at an angle to see her.

"Damn! Do you always have to sneak up on me like that? Where have you been?"

"Just lookin around. I don't think you can get out this way. You'll have to go through the kitchen; the tree knocked the wall out."

"How's your head?" Carla asked.

"Lumpy, but I guess I'll live."

Carla gingerly made her way to the kitchen door. Pushing through the debris, she looked inside and gasped. The oak had fallen through the roof, taking out not only the kitchen rafters, but completely burying the wood stove Pixie had been cooking on. Crockery was everywhere and flour was caked in puddles. Carla stepped around the mess as carefully she could and clambered over the trunk of the fallen giant. Outside, she noticed that the kitchen must have been a later addition to the original house. If it hadn't had its own roof, the entire house might have collapsed on top of them.

Pixie appeared beside her. "Are you ready to leave?"

"What about all your stuff?" Carla asked.

"Sookie didn't have much. I got your mother's notebook and a few other things. We can come back for anything else later." She displayed a burlap bag, tied at the top.

Carla nodded. "I'm afraid to see what shape the boat's in."

"S'okay. I saw it. It ain't sunk...just a little high up on the bank."

"What do you mean? Is it beached?"

"Kind of on its side," said Pixie, tilting her head.

Shit on high! She'd never be able to get it righted by herself. Carla sighed deeply and jammed her hands into her pockets.

"Well, let's go look at it." Carla peered through the branches of the fallen tree. They loomed higher than her head. Her gaze followed the length of the bole where it stretched away from the house and down toward the riverbank. Past the tangle of uplifted roots and smaller trees she glimpsed a familiar shape.

"Is there any easy way to get down there?" she asked.

"Back out to the trail and then around to the sandbar," said Pixie. She led the way toward the clearing, stepping over fallen limbs and scattered brush. The ground was spongy and Carla squished after her through the trees and back to the grassy track.

"This used to be an old loggin road," said Pixie. "Auntie said all the pine trees got logged out during the war for railroad ties." Carla checked it out. Pixie was right, there were plenty of oaks, beeches, and magnolias, but few pines.

Pixie left the road and followed the downward slope of the land toward the river, then turned to the left, following the curve of the inlet. Ahead of them was a limestone boulder, its base submerged in water. Comer's landmark, she assumed. The storm surge had flooded the river well over its banks but was receding quickly. Sookie's house—what was left of it— was visible through the trees higher up on the bank.

"Pixie, how far does the water come up when it floods?"

"Every time it rains heavy it crawls up on the banks some. Auntie said it once came up all the way under the house."

So that's why Comer's landmarks weren't down near the water, Carla thought to herself. They were floodtime markers.

Just below the treeline rested the *Miriam C.* The prow had grounded facing the bank as if it were aimed directly at the house, and it listed slightly toward the starboard side. The rigging hung in tatters, with no sign of the strings of lights.

"Goddamn," whispered Carla. She sloshed out into the water for a better look.

"What you finta do?" asked Pixie from the bank.

"What?" Carla's mind had been elsewhere, assessing the probable damage.

"You gonna *push* it offa the bank?"

Carla glared at her for a minute, then said thoughtfully, "Maybe I'll do just that." She slogged back to the underbrush of the bank and headed up into the trees. "Come on and help me look for a big pole."

They scoured the wind-blasted woods below the house and finally Pixie yelled "Over here!" She slid down the bank, dragging the long and fairly straight trunk of a small sapling. Carla grabbed it and helped pull.

"Let's wedge it up under the bow there," she panted, "then use it as a fulcrum."

"Okay," said Pixie dubiously. "Whatever that is."

They pushed and maneuvered the pole under the boat, then pressed their weight against it. "Heave!" Carla ordered. The boat rocked and bounced in its berth. "Again!" she gasped. Carla's teeth ground together and her muscles trembled. The shrimper rocked, bounced, and lurched in the water, but not enough. The bow still stuck fast to the bottom.

"Shitfuck," Carla muttered under her breath.

"Nice mouth," said Pixie.

Carla pondered the situation, staring at the hull of the shrimper as if demanding it to come up with some solution. And, suddenly, it did.

"Winch," she said.

"Who?" asked Pixie.

"The winch on the stern. If I could hook a line from it to something, and the motor still works, it could pull the boat free."

"Over there on the other side," Pixie said, indicating an row of cypress and small water oaks relatively undamaged by the storm. Carla knew she could easily swim the distance, but did she have a line that long?

"It's worth a try. Bring your stuff on board and put it in the cabin." Carla waded out into the water and scrambled over the shrimper's gunnel and onto the deck. She reached for Pixie's bag, then helped the girl up over the side. The boat rocked and the deck angled steeply. Holding onto the cabin, she opened the deck locker and took out a coil of line. It took her several minutes to remove the anchor from the cable that was already on the winch, then attach the extra line to the cable. Then, with the free end tied to her waist, she jumped over the side. She swam with smooth, sure strokes to the other side of the engorged inlet, expecting at any second to be pulled back by the end of the cable, but in fact it was more than long enough. Near the bank, she found a suitable tree trunk, and wound the line around it several times, securing it with a hitch knot. The swim back to the boat was quicker.

As Pixie watched, she turned the switch to start the winch. It caught and began to turn the spool. It took a few seconds for the line to pull taut and Carla waited breathlessly to see if it would hold or snap. The deck shuddered as the line held, then the boat lurched and began to slide off the bank.

"All right!" called Pixie, who held both thumbs up. The *Miriam C.* bobbed like a huge cork in the murky water and clouds of silt billowed up around the keel. Carla was laughing gleefully. She sat on the stern by the winch and listened to it grind and strain as the boat inched steadily out into deeper water. Finally she cut the motor off and dove over the side to retrieve the line. Now if the trawler's engine wasn't dead she could get the hell out of the swamp. Maybe out of Tate's Hammock too, although she didn't know what she would do with Pixie. Back on deck, she coiled the line and stowed it back in its locker.

"Okay, Pixie, let's hit it!"

Carla waded into the ankle-deep water sloshing around the wheelhouse and got the key out of the ziplock bag she'd stowed in her pocket. "Okay, you sonofabitch," she whispered, sliding into the captain's seat and staring at the instrument panel, "Don't you dare let me down now." When she turned the key, the engine thragged, choked, and finally roared to life. Putting the boat in gear, Carla backed out into the channel. Feeling a jerk through the boat timbers, she realized one of her now-ragged nets was dragging, so she cut it loose.

She wondered if there was cola in the fridge. There was. It was warm, but who cared? She popped the top.

In deeper water now, she maneuvered the bow around so that it pointed toward the Gulf. Thanking Comer in her mind, she took her pack of cigarettes from the plastic bag and lit one. It was one of the most glorious drags of her life.

"Nice role model," came a voice at her elbow, and Carla turned around to see Pixie fingering a thin cord around her neck.

"You've got your herbs, let me have mine," Carla retorted. "What's that necklace? Is that—"

Pixie reached inside the collar of her granny dress and pulled out the carved necklace that had been Sookie's. "This is the necklace that Chloe carved out of those pebbles of volcano rock," she said. "Chloe and Freeda used it for special occasions. So did Sookie. But everyone born into the family got their own bead, too."

"I found a bead in my mother's trunk," Carla said, navigating carefully around storm debris. The shrimper's keel shuddered and bucked against unseen flotsam, but kept its course toward the inlet's mouth. .

"We were wonderin where it was. My mama had one, too, but Daddy took it and hid it."

"He traded it to Hamp Crozier for food," Carla said.

"No he didn't!"

"Yep. I can get it back for you if you want."

Pixie fingered the necklace thoughtfully. "You know," she said, "everything woulda been okay if I'da been a boy instead of a girl, because the teachings are passed down to women only. If I'da been a boy, Sookie woulda had to teach someone else."

"Who else is there?" Carla asked, her eyes straight ahead.

"You," said Pixie, stuffing the necklace back under her collar. "Shoulda been you anyway cause you're the oldest."

"*Me*? How do you figure that?"

"Pretty obvious. We're her only two grand-nieces and

there ain't any direct next of kin. She picked me."

"I guess I can understand why your father didn't want you to get sucked into this kind of thing."

"I guess I do, too. He was scairt of the powers and scairt of Auntie too. He was always tryin to stop me from seein her, but it didn't do no good. I liked comin here. Daddy didn't, though. He wouldn't come out to Sookie's house no way—thought he'd get bit by a snake. But he caught me comin in real late one night from bein with Auntie and he fussed at me for bout an hour. He went to see her and came back with some money and a new suit. Said we were movin to Tallahassee. That was the day before he died."

"Hopefully," Carla said, "you'll have some easier choices from now on."

"You, too," Pixie said.

"What're you thinking?" Carla asked.

"I mean you might find a way to choose between those two fancy men of yours."

"I don't want to choose," said Carla, frowning. "No choice to be made."

"Keepin em both?" Pixie was goading her again. "I don't get either of em? I thought kinfolks sposed to share."

"Those losers are yesterday's news, minx," said Carla. But her thoughts had leaped out into the storm where Buddy and Yancy must be holed up or slugging it out. Shit, it was bad enough in the house; what must it have been like for them out in the woods without any protection at all. Assuming, of course, that they had decided to go through with their idiotic contest.

"Today's news, you mean," Pixie said, and pointed over the starboard bow.

"What?" Carla looked in the direction Pixie was pointing, and there they were, Buddy and Yancy, sitting on a log twenty or so yards back from the shore. Carla slowed the engine to an idle and looked closer. They were sheltered by a giant magnolia tree that, except for a loss of half its leaves, seemed to have suffered no major damage from the hurricane. A campfire flickered sluggishly between them and they were laughing, making so much noise, in fact, that they hadn't heard the boat's engine. Carla studied them with mixed emotions. Yancy was wearing steel-toed boots and army fatigue trousers. He was bare-chested and had a thick bandage around his left bicep. His hair was a rat's nest that fell in his eyes and covered what looked like a bruise or a scrape on his temple. Buddy wasn't much better. His hunting outfit was in tatters and smeared black in front like he'd been in a fire. A piece of bloody gauze was tied around his head. Had they been beat up by the hurricane or had they buffeted each other?

But they had spotted her now and ran to the bank to get her attention.

"Carla!" she heard Buddy's voice wafting across the water. Yancy stuck out his thumb like a hitchhiker. Her hand went for the switch to kill the engine, but she hesitated. Indignation rose in her like the storm surge. She had expended a lot of emotional energy worrying over these two—in fact, had almost got herself killed—and here they were, relatively unharmed and hanging out together. On the bank, she spotted an outboard motor and two or three planks of what must have once been the small boat she'd spotted the day before.

Carla turned to Pixie as she cut the engine and drifted toward shore "I'll pick them up," she said, "but you'll have to talk to them. I'm all out of pleasantries."

Pixie only smiled, then walked forward to greet the two men, who were now hurrying down the slope, carrying their weapons. "What ya'll be huntin?" she shouted.

Chapter Twenty-Two

A gang of gulls skimmed the surface of the water, fighting over scraps from the fish processing plant. Carla watched them wheel and dive, some lighting on the pylons that held the *Blue Dancer* in place. From the dock, Carla studied the charter vessel for the umpteenth time, still astonished that she had made the decision to buy it. It was a forty-six-foot Bertram Convertible with twin Detroit Diesel engines. Its railing was as shiny as a new dime and the gelcoat finish so bright she almost had to put her sunglasses on to appreciate it.

She had sold the *Miriam C.* to get down-payment money. She would have sold her car, too, if anyone would have wanted it. Trouble was, the boat cost triple what even her house was worth. Well, that was up for sale, too.

A grizzled voice floated down to her from the boat's flying bridge, where Comer had insisted on climbing, probably just to show her how spry he was. "No sign of her yet, Captain," he shouted. The old sot was decked out (at her expense, natch) in blue trousers, white shirt, and brown deck shoes. The cost had been worth it; Comer looked fifty again, and obviously felt it. And she believed him when he told her that his drinking-on-duty days were over. Her own clothes were new, too. She had asked her stepmother, who had spent much of her early social life on yachts, to come out and let her know whether—in her expert opinion—the boat was worth buying. Right.

But Marietta was late.

Carla waved at Stinky the Fish Man, who was walking down the dock in her direction. When he got alongside, he took off his cap and wiped his forehead with it, then put it back on over his stringy hair. He looked at *Blue Dancer* appreciatively. "She's a beauty all right," he said. "Never thought you'd really do it, though."

"Shrimping's not what it used to be," she told him.

"You got that right," he said. "Seems like the catch is worse every year. Maybe you're gettin out at the right time."

"I just need to do something different, you know?" she said, knowing that he really didn't, couldn't know. Like Johnny Blanchard, like Sheriff Dickey, like Sookie and so many others in Blanchard's Bluff and Tate's Hammock who had maybe never even been out of the state. But Carla was ready; had been ready for years.

"I've heard that some people will pay hundreds of dollars a day to go out on a beauty like this," he said. "Some Japanese might even pay a thousand dollars a day."

"I'm not going to count my swordfish before they're in the hold." Carla smiled and squinted up at the sky. An old habit.

"With all those fish finders and depth gauges and radios and radars and whatnot that you've got in that cockpit, you'll do just fine."

"Well, if I don't make it as a charter captain, I'll just open up a radio shack," she said, still smiling.

Stinky smiled too, then went serious. "You going to be okay out there today?" he asked.

"Everything's covered," she said.

"Good luck then. I'll see you when you get back."

"Thanks, Stink."

When Stinky had sauntered back to the Barn, Carla stepped into the lower helm station where she'd left her smokes. Lighting a Winston, she slid into the captain's chair and settled back to wait. The salon fridge held plenty of food, and the diesel tanks were full. Her ship's clock showed fifteen minutes past ten in the morning on a still, sun-drenched, cloudless day.

It was time to get back to her life. She had installed Pixie in her extra bedroom—Ronnie Wyche had confirmed that Carla was now her legal guardian—and the girl seemed to be settling in. There would be no nosy visits by social workers. Buddy and Yancy seemed to have forgotten her; at least there had been no phone calls after she'd dropped them at the dock. Buddy swore he could drive to the hospital, so they'd eased Yancy into the passenger seat of Buddy's car and that was the last she'd seen of them. Just as well. They were part of her old life. Better to get on with what came next. There was only one thing that still needed closure—that's what this trip was for.

From above her in the flybridge, she heard Comer bellow, "Thar she blows!" and Carla heard running feet along the dock. She looked out and saw Marietta. She was dressed in old jeans, a dark T-shirt, and running shoes; the wide strap of a carry-on bag was slung over her shoulder. This wasn't the Marietta she was accustomed to seeing. Her stepmother's face wore no trace of makeup, and her mane of hair was tied back near the nape of her neck. She was huffing and puffing like she'd already gone through her first three packs of cigarettes. Her voice, when it came, was harsh and breathy.

"Shit, Carla," she said. "I've been looking all over for you. You don't mean to tell me *this* is the boat you're thinking about buying?"

"This is it."

"But it's bigger than the one Bull used to have!"

"That's the idea. Come on, let's shove off."

Comer had clambered down to the deck and was casting off the lines while Carla took his place on the flybridge and fired up the engines. Perched more than twenty feet above the waterline, she had the best view in the harbor, which enabled her to back out nice and slow. She and Comer had been out a couple of times already on practice runs and she had the process pretty much nailed down. Like Marietta said, it was bigger than the boat she had taken to the Bahamas when she was in her teens, but it wasn't all that much different to pilot. When she had the boat turned around, she set out for deep water. The engines were so quiet the gulls might have thought they were dead and floating on the tide.

When *Blue Dancer* was safely out from the harbor, Carla yelled down for Comer to take over from the cockpit while she climbed down to join him. Marietta had obviously been snooping into the staterooms and galley and salon, because she was walking toward them shaking her head.

Carla looked back toward the harbor. They were still in sight of shore and there were a couple of shrimpers not too far off the starboard bow. She touched a few dials on the console, glanced at a couple of screens, and turned to greet her stepmother.

"What are we stopping for?" asked Marietta, as she stepped into the cabin, still carrying her travel case. Carla gave the bag a second look. It seemed damned heavy to just have her windbreaker in it. Maybe she'd packed her entire liquor cabinet.

"'It's time for us to have a little talk,' said Carla. "Have a seat."

"Whoa, sounds heavy," said Marietta. Still, she parked herself on one of the spacious chairs built in to the back of the cockpit. Comer was already seated in another, his cap in his hand. But when Marietta saw him, she scowled and said, "What's he here for?" She looked at the first mate as if he was some kind of riff raff, even with his new togs.

"He's here because I want him here," Carla said. "Call him a witness."

Comer was staring at Marietta's wrists, where the too-obvious bruises made dark circles.

Marietta noticed his stare. "What're you looking at?" she snapped.

"Nothin ma'am," he answered.

Carla's first impression of Marietta had been right; she had changed. She seemed harder, more desperate. Nearer the edge. Bondage is a right bitch, she thought, tightening her mouth into a tight line.

Marietta cut her eyes back toward Carla. "So this trip isn't just so I can give you my 'valuable opinion' of this boat, right?"

"Yeah, I lied about that," said Carla. "But now that you're here, what do you think of her?"

"Well, Carla," Marietta began. "If you don't mind my asking, how can you possibly afford it? I mean, you can't even keep that ratty car of yours running."

"I'm going to trade for it," Carla said evenly.

"Trade? Trade what? This boat must cost a couple of hundred grand."

"I'm going to trade some of Daddy's antique cars."

"Cars?" Marietta looked like someone had snuck a bee down her T-shirt. She reached into her travel bag and pulled out a small silver case, extracted a cigarette, and lit it. "Carla, if I remember right—and I do—your daddy left those cars to me."

"That's why you're going to sell them to me for a dollar each. You can pay the transfer fee, too."

Marietta started to laugh, but it was kind of a nervous laugh, as if she thought that maybe there really was a bee somewhere down her shirt.

Carla glanced at Marietta's wrists again, then shrugged. "I'm not going to be greedy, Marietta. How many cars are back there in that garage? Half a dozen? And each one worth its weight in caviar. You can pick one—whichever one you want—and you can sign over the rest to me."

"Dream on," said Marietta. She opened her travel bag again and brought out a new bottle of Chivas Regal. She stripped off the cap. Comer watched every move with interest.

Carla gave her a hard stare. 'I don't allow booze on this ship," she said.

"Well now, that's just tough shit, isn't it?" Marietta said. Seeing that there weren't any glasses at hand, she took a swig out of the bottle—a hefty one. Comer looked like a hungry dog at a picnic, but didn't say anything. Marietta pointedly ignored him.

"Is this something about that trust again?" she asked

suddenly. "Well, it's about damn time. Do I have any money coming to me?"

"You're lucky to still have a roof over your head."

"Is that some kind of threat?" Marietta took a long gulp from her bottle.

"'It's not a *kind* of threat," said Carla. "It's a *real* threat."

"So you've brought me out here to tell me you're going to toss me out of Chez Marais? You and *Pixie* going to live it up with all that trust money?"

"Screw you, Marietta."

"Pixie," spat Marietta, shaking her head. "I still don't understand how someone like that has suddenly become the owner of my, of our, house. It doesn't seem right." She took another long swallow of whisky.

Sweat ran down Carla's chest. She had tried to keep her feelings in check, but now she could sense her face flushing. "I don't know what you mean by 'someone like that.' It's sudden, yeh, to you and me, maybe, but the line of inheritance is clear."

Marietta set down her bottle fall with a clunk. "Clear as mud. Your parents were white people. How did their maid end up with the deed to Chez Marais, for god sakes? I think they were swindled out of it somehow!"

Carla felt anger flame up her cheeks. "I'll tell you who was swindled, Marietta. Me. My father swindled me out of my own history. Never once did he tell me that Sookie was my aunt and that she owned Chez Marais. That Pixie was my cousin. He was too much of a big shot to want anyone to know that he married into mixed blood. Well, he fucked up good there. Fucked me up and fucked *you* up."

"What are you talking about?" Marietta asked. A scowl darkened her roughened features.

"A week ago I didn't think twice about the way you let him ruin Chez Marais by spending money on all that modern shit—or on those damn cars that he never drove— even though a lot of that money was probably my mother's. Hell, there's no probably about it. But she must have loved him and I respected him for that, but I can't believe that she wanted me kept in the dark about the rest of my family. That's why I'm taking it back."

"Taking what back?"

"The house, the cars, my life. There's just one problem."

"Yeah?" Marietta asked sarcastically. "Just one?"

"That dick Dickey. I don't like you, Marietta. In fact, I like you less today than I ever have before, and that's saying something. But Dickey is blackmailing you because you're a woman and because you're weak and I *really* don't like that. I can't let him get away with it."

"I don't know what the fuck you're talking about!" shouted Marietta.

"You may not be as stupid as you pretend, but I'm starting to wonder," Carla told her. "Maybe all murderers are stupid."

"So I'm a murderer now? You must be delusional."

Carla ground her teeth. "You've given yourself away half a dozen times. How do you know that Sookie used to be our maid?"

"I don't know. Bull must've told me."

"The other day you told me that you'd never heard of Sookie. You thought she was one of Daddy's old flames."

"You must have mentioned her when you were telling me about the trust."

"When we talked about the trust you made some crack about my 'little black friend.' But if you didn't know who Sookie was, you couldn't have known that Pixie was black."

"Really, Carla," Marietta said. "You've gotten yourself so confused that you're making things up."

Carla took a breath, then began again. "Pixie told me Sookie had a fingernail-shaped cut on her neck."

"Pixie again. I'm really getting sick of the way her name keeps popping up."

Carla had to stop herself from lunging at her

stepmother. "You have long fingernails, don't you?"

Marietta tucked her nails into her palms, then flashed them brazenly at Carla. "Lots of people have long nails," she said. "Some of us even manage to keep them clean."

Carla tried to remain calm, but it was tough. Marietta was almost flaunting the fact that she had killed Sookie. "So what was your motive? I'm guessing you somehow found out Sookie oversaw the trust that owned Chez Marais. If you killed her, she couldn't throw you out. All those clues were right there in front of me, but I would never have put them together if it hadn't been for those bruises."

"What I choose to do in the privacy of my own bedroom is none—"

"That's just it, Marietta, getting roughed up and handcuffed isn't something you choose. It's forced on you. You already admitted it's been Dickey knocking you around, and there's only one way that bastard could have gotten such a hold over you. He knows you killed her. Hell, he knew before I did. What, did you leave your fingerprints all over the church or something stupid like that?"

"I think we've talked all that needs to be talked." Marietta's voice was hard.

"We've just started," Carla replied. "How could you kill a defenseless old woman?" She stood up from her pilot's chair and stepped close to Marietta, looking her square in the face. "How did you do it? Plan it out, like I know you do with everything, or was it just a spur-of-the-moment inspiration?" Marietta's intake of breath was a hiss.

Carla was starting to shake with fury. "I loved that old woman! How could you—" Carla's breath was coming in shallow jerks, and she clenched her fists. "You could have worked something out with Sookie. There was no need to kill her!"

"She was going to kick me out!" Marietta yelled, standing up.

"I don't believe that."

"Then you're the stupid one. She sent some ratty-looking man in a hideous blue suit to my house with a letter. I thought at first he might be a homeless person looking for a donation or something, but all he did was deliver her note and drive away as fast as he could."

"Wait a minute, just stop!" Carla panted. She was starting to see the whole picture now. "That must've been Daddy Blue—"

"I don't give a shit who it was!"

"What did the note say?"

"I can't remember—something about meeting the new owner of Chez Marais at some church. To discuss my future, it said. I almost got lost trying to find the place and when I finally did find it, some dreadful old bag lady started cackling like a crow. She was going to take away my house and all the beautiful things Bull and I had put in it. Just like that. No reason given except we didn't belong there."

"That's still no reason to kill her," Carla said softly.

"It was an accident."

"Bullshit!" Carla stood her ground, staring up into Marietta's face. The woman was a few inches taller, but Carla was in better shape, maybe quicker on the draw. With those damaged wrists, she wasn't going to be punching anybody out.

"I told you, it was an accident. Sure, I might have grabbed her around the neck—I was excited and angry—but then we both fell and she hit her head." Marietta picked up the Chivas bottle and took a swallow.

"But instead of calling an ambulance or the sheriff, you dragged her body into the bell tower and assumed nobody would ever find her."

"I told you I was scared," said Marietta. "I didn't know what I was doing."

"How did Dickey find out?"

"Like you said, fingerprints. At least that's what he told me, but who knows. That bastard. I wish I could kill him, too. Swaggering sadist. Said he'd always wanted to do some things that he couldn't do with his wife. At first he just tied me up, twisted my nipples some, but the more pain, the more excited he got. And if I didn't play ball, he'd just suddenly remember where he put those fingerprints I'd left all over that church. If Bull were here, he'd—"

"Tell it to the fish, Marietta."

"Tell them yourself." Marietta reached into her travel bag and, before Carla could react, pulled out a shiny little Beretta pistol. Carla was caught off guard and stumbled backwards against the console.

"Hold it right there, Miz Clements," Comer said, moving faster than Carla would've expected and grabbing the woman's wrist. Marietta tried to fight off the old man but he wrestled the pistol out of her grasp and promptly threw it over the side. "I guess now ye'll—" he began, but Marietta had picked up the whiskey bottle from the seat and swung it in a vicious arc. There was a sickening crash as it connected with the side of Comer's head. The old man collapsed like a sack and lay, unmoving, amid the glass, blood, and expensive whisky.

"Comer!" Carla shouted. "Marietta, you fucking bitch! If you've killed Comer, I'll—"

Marietta rushed at her, brandishing the jagged end of the bottle. She thrust it toward Carla's face, but Carla ducked and scrambled out of the cabin and down to the deck.

Marietta was right behind her, but Carla knew the ship better. The pistol her father had given her was safely stored in her stateroom. If she could get there... But Marietta, in desperation, threw what was left of the bottle. That her aim was accurate was almost more of a shock to Carla than the fact that one of the jagged edges pierced the top of her shoulder before bouncing off the railing and into the Gulf. Carla stopped running and reached around to feel the wound. It was probably deep; already her new shirt was a-bloom with blood. But she had no time to worry about her shoulder as Marietta was already in her face, her crazed eyes glittering with purpose. Carla realized that this must have been one of the last things that Sookie saw on earth. Hands punched her in the face and chest, yanked viciously at her hair, but Carla grabbed Marietta's wrists, making her stepmother scream out in pain. She tried to kick but Carla was able to evade the worst of it. Then Marietta tried to bite, but Carla was ready for this. When Marietta's head was close enough, Carla lowered her own and butted her stepmother in the nose. There was another sickening crack. Marietta shrieked and staggered backwards, bringing her hands to her face. Backpedaling and off balance, she hit the rail. Carla watched in stunned surprise as Marietta's back arched and launched her body headfirst over the side. Her scream ended in a strangling gurgle.

Carla ran to the rail, gasping and sinking to her knees. She stared at the spot where Marietta's body had gone down. Seconds passed, and then the woman surfaced a few yards away, spluttering and thrashing around in the water. "Help me!" she screamed. "Throw me a line!" She began swimming frantically toward the boat, but her broken nose made it hard to breathe, and her strokes were just feeble splashings.

Carla didn't bother to answer; she just plucked a donut-shaped life preserver from the side and threw it in Marietta's general direction. Then she hurried back to the cockpit—trailing blood with every step—to see about Comer. To her relief, Comer was sitting up, feeling his head, and groaning.

"Carla," he moaned. "I mean, Cap'n. What happened? Did she get away? You're hurt! Let me—"

"You just rest for a minute, old timer," she told him. "Everything's all right."

Her shortwave radio was buzzing and she flipped the switch. "Tiny-mite here," she said. "Come on."

"Bitin' Billy here, Carla. Ya'll okay?" The man's voice was rough-sounding but concerned.

"A-okay," she said. "What's your 20, Billy?"

"Me and *The Tuna Tune*'re coming along your port side. There's someone in the water."

Carla looked out over the deck. The two shrimpers she'd seen earlier were traveling toward her at top speed.

"Close in, but don't pick her up yet," said Carla.

"Ten-four," said the voice.

"Shit on everything," Carla breathed, looking at the mess in her new cabin. It was dawning on her that Marietta must have suspected that Carla was prepared to throw her out of Chez Marais—she might have even suspected that Carla knew about her and Sookie—and come on board with the intention of killing her. She hadn't thought Marietta had it in her. But what did she expect to do then? Steal *Blue Dancer* and sail away to parts unknown or rely on her sadist boyfriend to manufacture some kind of alibi for her?

Carla walked slowly back out onto the deck and looked into the water where Marietta was still floundering and sobbing and grasping onto the donut for dear life. When she saw the two shrimpers approaching, she screamed out, "Help, murder! That bitch threw me overboard!"

Carla recognized Billy Blanchard—a distant cousin of Johnny's and someone she had been competing with for years. The other boat, *The Tuna Tune*, was captained by another old competitor, but it had always been a friendly rivalry and they had shared many beers together after two-day outings in the Gulf.

"Call the sheriff," Marietta screamed.

"Don't know that we can do that, Miz Clements," said Billy Blanchard. "Seein as how the two of you seem to be in cahoots."

"What are you talking about!" Marietta shouted.

Carla felt Comer come up behind her. He grasped the railing and looked down into the water. "You been set up, he he," he began, then groaned. He slid down on his skinny butt and folded over, holding his head in his hands.

Carla took over. "As soon as you came on board, I turned on the radio. Billy and Harvey and their crew heard everything you said."

"You're lying!"

"Nope," answered Billy. "She ain't. We heard you say you killed that old lady."

The other captain, whose name was Harvey and who was Clarence Revell's great nephew, chipped in. "And how you're into S&M with Dandy Jim. Don't know about Bitin' Billy, but I even recorded it all, haw haw."

"We need to get Comer to a hospital," Carla told the two other captains. "Me, too, I guess, but first we need to tell Marietta how it's gonna be."

Before she was hauled, dripping and cursing, out of the water, Marietta'd agreed to sign over enough cars from Bull's old fleet to pay for the *Blue Dancer* three times over. She'd also agreed, with the promise of no pursuit, to vanish into the night, as it were...as if she'd never intruded into Carla's life or tried to finish the decline of Chez Marais that Bull had started. If Dickey wanted to find her, Carla, Comer, Harvey, and Billy promised the trail wouldn't come from them.

Half an hour later, Carla piloted *Blue Dancer* back to Tate's Hammock. She could see an ambulance parked alongside the dock, EMTs waiting by the berth with Stinky. But Carla's mind was elsewhere.

How far to Belize? she wondered. Or even Cancun? *Cómo estás*, ya'll. Half her hair had been yanked out, her face felt bruised all over from Marietta's fists, her shoulder was still bleeding, but she couldn't help smiling. At this moment in time, she could go anywhere, be anyone. She felt lightheaded.

The first thing she was going to do after she got stitched up was get herself a tattoo of a swordfish. On her right arm.

About the Authors

P. V. LeForge lives on a horse farm in north Florida with his wife Sara Warner. In addition to writing, he does farm chores, plays music, and shoots target archery. Check out his other books, both in print and in e-book form from Smashwords and Amazon. Also see his website at www.blackbayfarm.com/pleforge/pvlindex.htm, and his blog at talltinker.blogspot.com

Anne Petty is author of four horror/dark-fantasy novels, three books of literary criticism, and many essays on writing, mythology, and J.R.R. Tolkien. Recent short fiction includes her award-winning story "Blade," and "The Veritas Experience," published in *The Best Horror, Fantasy & Science Fiction of 2009*. Anne is an active member of the Horror Writers Association, International Thriller Writers, and the Science Fiction & Fantasy Writers of America. She has a Ph.D. in English from Florida State University.

www.ingramcontent.com/pod-product-compliance
Lightning Source LLC
Chambersburg PA
CBHW061130200626
46817CB00016B/593